A trilogy of p...
stories of t...

O'CONNELLS
Dynasty

Conveniently Wed

Three compelling and satisfying novels by
bestselling and award-winning writer:

SANDRA MARTON

THE
O'CONNELLS
Dynasty

Conveniently Wed

SANDRA MARTON

All the characters in this book have no existence outside the imagination of the author, and have no relation whatsoever to anyone bearing the same name or names. They are not even distantly inspired by any individual known or unknown to the author, and all the incidents are pure invention.

Harlequin Mills & Boon Limited, Eton House,
18-24 Paradise Road, Richmond, Surrey TW9 1SR

THE O'CONNELLS DYNASTY: CONVENIENTLY WED
© Harlequin Enterprises II B.V./S.à.r.l. 2010

The Sheikh's Convenient Bride © Sandra Myles 2004
The One-Night Wife © Sandra Myles 2005
The Sicilian Marriage © Sandra Myles 2005

ISBN: 978 0 263 87706 9

012-0310

Harlequin Mills & Boon policy is to use papers that are natural, renewable and recyclable products and made from wood grown in sustainable forests. The logging and manufacturing processes conform to the legal environmental regulations of the country of origin.

Printed and bound in Spain
by Litografia Rosés S.A., Barcelona

THE SHEIKH'S
CONVENIENT BRIDE

SANDRA MARTON

Sandra Marton's popular O'Connell family saga
collected together into two special volumes.
Satisfaction & passion guaranteed!

February 2010

THE
O'CONNELLS
Dynasty

Business & Pleasure

March 2010

THE
O'CONNELLS
Dynasty

Conveniently Wed

Sandra Marton wrote her first novel while she was still in primary school. Her doting parents told her she'd be a writer someday and Sandra believed them. In school and college, she wrote dark poetry nobody but her boyfriend understood, though looking back, she suspects he was just being kind. As a wife and mother, she wrote murky short stories in what little spare time she could manage, but not even her boyfriend-turned-husband could pretend to understand those. Sandra tried her hand at other things, among them teaching and serving on the Board of Education in her home town, but the dream of becoming a writer was always in her heart.

At last, Sandra realised she wanted to write books about what all women hope to find: love with that one special man, love that's rich with fire and passion, love that lasts forever. She wrote a novel – her very first, and sold it to Mills & Boon. Since then, she's written more than seventy books, all of them featuring the sexy, gorgeous, larger-than-life heroes that have helped make Sandra a bestselling author. A four-time RITA® Award finalist, she's also received eight *Romantic Times* magazine awards and has been honoured with *Romantic Times* Career Achievement Award for Series Romance. Sandra lives with her very own sexy, gorgeous, larger-than-life hero in a sun-filled house on a quiet country lane in the northeastern United States.

Look out for Sandra Marton's latest exciting novel, *Blackwolf's Redemption* (May 2010), available from Mills & Boon® Modern™.

CHAPTER ONE

HE WAS a sheikh, the King of Suliyam, a small nation sitting on an incredible deposit of oil on the tip of the Bezerian Peninsula.

On top of that, he was tall, dark-haired, gray-eyed and gorgeous.

If you liked the type.

According to the tabloids and the TV celebrity-tell-all shows, most women did.

But Megan O'Connell wasn't most women. Besides, tall, dark, handsome and disgustingly rich didn't begin to make up for egotistical, self-centered, and arrogant.

Megan raised her coffee cup to her lips. Okay. Maybe that was superfluous. So what? Men like him were superfluous, too. What did the world need with penny-ante dictators who thought they were God's gift to the female sex? To everybody on the planet, when you came down to it?

She'd never exchanged a word with the man but she didn't have to, to know what he was like. Her boss—another egotistical jerk, though not a good-looking one—had transmitted the sheikh's message to her this morning and it had been clear as glass.

She was a female. That made her a second-class citizen in his eyes. He, of course, was male. As if that weren't enough, he was royalty.

Royalty. Megan's lip curled with contempt. What he was, was a chauvinist pig. How come she was the only one who seemed to notice? She'd been watching him charm the little group at the other end of the boardroom for almost an hour, tilting his head when one of them spoke as if he really gave a damn what that person was saying.

If only they knew what an SOB like him could do to someone.

She had to admit, he seemed good at what he did. Holding the attention of a bunch of self-important partners and managers of a prestigious financial firm wasn't easy but then, if you believed the Times, he was the leader of his nation's cautious steps into modernity and development.

If you believed the Times. It seemed more logical to believe the tabloids. According to them, he was a playboy. A heartbreaker on three continents.

That, Megan thought, was undoubtedly closer to the truth.

The only thing she was sure of was that he was Qasim al Daud al Rashid, King of Suliyam since his father's death and the Absolute Ruler of his People.

It was a title that would have gone over big a couple of generations ago. Too bad the sheikh didn't seem to care that such nonsense was a joke now…though it didn't seem a joke to what passed for the news media, or here in the Los Angeles offices of Tremont, Burnside and Macomb, Financial Advisors and Consultants.

Too bad she'd accepted the transfer from Boston, where nobody would have made this kind of fuss over a walking, talking anachronism.

"Oh, your highness," a woman said, the words accompanied by a sigh that carried the length of the room.

His Highness, indeed. That was the proper way to address the king, according to the belly-crawling sycophants in his entourage. Megan drank the last of her coffee. No way would she ever call him that. If she had the misfortune to speak with the man—which she surely wouldn't, after what had happened this morning—she'd sooner choke. His High and Mightiness was more like it. What else would you call a twenty-first century dictator leading a 16th century life? Someone who'd single-handedly set her career back five years?

The bastard.

To think she'd worked her tail off, researching and writing the proposal that had won him as a client. To think she'd spent days and evenings and weekends on the thing. To think she'd dreamed about what handling such a prestigious account would mean to her career, swallowed all those little hints that she'd be named a partner, believed they were soon to become reality.

Every bit of it had gone up in a puff of smoke this morning, when Simpson told her he was giving the Suliyam assignment to Frank Fisher instead of her.

Megan started to refill her cup, thought better of it—she was already flying on caffeine—and poured herself a Mimosa instead. The vintage Krug and fresh OJ were there because the sheikh supposedly liked an occasional Mimosa at brunch, thanks to the influence, some said, of the genes of his California-born mother.

He'd never know it but he was drinking them today, assuming he was drinking them, thanks to Megan's research. She'd learned about the Mimosas and ordered the champagne and the orange juice.

If only she'd ordered strychnine instead.

Damn, she had to stop thinking this way. She had to stop thinking, period, or she'd say something, do something that would cost her her job.

As if she already hadn't.

No. Why think like a defeatist? She wouldn't lose her job. She'd put in too much time and effort at Tremont, Burnside and Macomb to let that happen. She would not let the decision made by The King of All He Surveyed ruin her career. There'd be other big accounts, other career-changing clients.

Of course there would.

If only her worm of a boss hadn't waited until today to break the news.

She'd come in early, eight o'clock, to make sure she was ready for the meeting with the sheikh. She'd even checked with the caterer to make sure he'd be coming on time, bringing little sandwiches and pastries, the brand of coffee the sheikh was known to favor, the champagne and the juice. Fresh juice, she'd reminded the caterer, and vintage champagne.

By 8:10, she knew everything was ready. The caterer. The boardroom. The manager of this Los Angeles branch of Tremont, Burnside and Macomb, Jerry Simpson.

Quarter past eight, Jerry had stepped into her office, a smile on his pudgy face and a Starbucks' container in his outstretched hand.

"For you," he'd said.

She almost said *Thanks, but I've been drinking coffee for two hours straight...* But why turn down the friendly gesture? Jerry never came in early. He never brought her coffee. Mostly he never smiled. He never sat down beside her desk, either, the way he did as she took the container from him.

With the benefit of hindsight, Megan realized that warning bells should have gone off right there and then. Fool that she was, she'd simply figured Jerry was there early so they could get ready for the important meeting together.

"How was your weekend?" Jerry said.

She'd spent it on Nantucket Island at her brother's wedding, so it was easy to smile and say "Great," because it had been. He smiled back, said that was good to hear and didn't she look wonderful and oh, by the way, he was giving the Suliyam account to Frank Fisher.

Megan blinked. She told herself she'd misunderstood. How could he give her client to somebody else? Maybe she'd had too much champagne at Cullen's wedding, too little sleep, too many cups of coffee to try to get her brain in gear after the alarm went off this morning.

Simpson couldn't have said what she'd thought he'd said, so she gave a little laugh.

"For a minute there, Jerry, I thought you said—"

"I did," Simpson replied, and she looked beyond his smarmy smile and saw that he was telling the truth.

"But that's impossible," she said slowly, while she tried to make sense of what was happening. "Suliyam commissioned a study—"

"The sheikh commissioned it."

"Whatever. The point is—"

"It's an important detail, Megan." Simpson smoothed his hand over the pinstripes straining across his tiny potbelly. "His Highness speaks for his country."

"I don't see what that—"

"To all intents and purposes, he *is* Suliyam."

"The point is," Megan said impatiently, "I did all the work on this report. I did it because you said the king would be my client, if he signed on—"

"I never told you that. I simply asked you to prepare the proposal."

Megan narrowed her eyes. "It's standard practice in this firm that the person who works up the data for a client gets that client."

"You are not a partner, Megan."

"A formality, Jerry. You know that."

"His Highness wants someone with authority."

"Well, that's easily resolved. Make me a partner now instead of waiting until July."

"Megan." Simpson got to his feet, an unconvincing smile of sympathy curving his thin lips. "I'm truly sorry this has happened, but—"

"It hasn't happened. Not yet. All the partners have to do is vote me in and tell the sheikh I'm more than capable of—"

"You're a woman."

That had stopped her. "Excuse me?"

Simpson gave a deep sigh. "It's nothing personal. It's not you per se. It's only that—"

"That what?" She was still trying to sound civil. Not an easy thing when your wimp of a boss told you the job you'd been counting on, an assignment so sweet it had every other accountant in the office panting for it, wasn't going to be yours after all. "Come on, Jerry. What has my being a woman to do with anything?"

"Actually," her boss said, smoothly avoiding the question, "it's for the best. I need you to handle a new client. Rod Barry, the big Hollywood director."

"The Sheikh of Suliyam is the client I want." Megan rose from her chair and put her hands on her hips. "He's the client you promised me."

"Barry's a tough cookie. It'll take special skills to work with him. You're the only one I can count on to do the job. Do the great work I know you'll do and you're up for a partnership next year." Simpson stuck out his hand. "Congratulations."

If Megan had been born yesterday, maybe she'd have fallen for the whole routine, but twenty-eight years of living, a dual degree in economics and accounting, a master's degree in finance and a hard-won slip of paper that said she was a Certified Public Accountant meant she was neither innocent, stupid, nor easily bought off.

And then there was that little remark about her being female.

Her boss was trying to bribe her into accepting her fate. Why? The truth was, he had the authority to take this job away from her. Why would he be trying to buy her off? There had to be a reason.

"Back up a little," Megan said slowly. "You said I was a woman and that was a problem."

"I didn't say that. Not exactly. All I meant was—"

"Why is it a problem?"

Simpson folded his lips in so they all but disappeared. "Suliyam is a kingdom."

"I'm fully aware of that. There's a description of Suliyam's structure in my proposal."

"It has no constitution, no elected representatives—"

"Damn it, Jerry, that's what a kingdom is! I spent three months doing the research."

"Then you also know that its people live by traditions that might seem a bit, ah, old-fashioned to us."

"Would you please get to the point?"

Simpson's attempts to avoid the issue vanished. "You don't want to handle the new account, then the best I can do is assign you to Frank Fisher as his assistant. He'll go to Suliyam, you'll stay here and execute the orders he sends."

"No way am I going to play second fiddle to Fisher!"

"This discussion is over, Megan. You're off the account. The sheikh wants it that way, and that's the way it will be."

"The sheikh," Megan said coldly, "is an idiot."

Simpson had turned a deathly shade of white. He shot a look at her office door as if he expected to see the sheikh standing there with a sword in his hand.

"You see?" he hissed. "Aside from anything else, there's one reason you're not suitable for this assignment."

Dumb, Megan told herself, dumb, dumb, dumb!

"You know I'd never say such a thing to him."

"You'd never get the chance." Simpson stuck out his jaw. "Or didn't you notice, when you did your research, that women don't have the same privileges there as they do here? They have no status in the sheikh's world. Not as we understand it, anyway."

"What women have here," Megan said coldly, "aren't privileges, they're rights. As for the sheikh…he spends as much time in the west as he does in his own country. He deals with women ambassadors at the United Nation. You can't actually mean—"

"Our representative will have to work at his side. Deal with his people. Do you think, for one minute, those men agree to sit down with a woman, much less take criticism and suggestions from her?"

"What I think is that it's time they joined the twenty-first century."

"Getting them to do that isn't the function of Tremont, Burnside and Macomb."

"I also think," Megan said in a dangerously soft voice, "that *you'd* better join this century, too. I'm sure you've heard of anti-discrimination laws."

Simpson proved ready for that threat. "Anti-discrimination laws are valid only within the United States. There are place where even our female soldiers conform to local customs."

"What the military does has nothing to do with the sheikh's plan to raise capital to further develop Suliyam's resources," Megan snapped, though a lurch in her belly told her she'd just lost ground.

"It has everything to do with it."

"I doubt if a judge would agree."

Simpson slapped his hands on her desk and leaned toward her. "If you're threatening to sue us, Miss O'Connell, go right ahead. Our attorneys will make mincemeat out of your case. The laws of Suliyam take precedence over American law when our employees live and work there."

Was he right? Megan wasn't sure. For all she knew, Simpson might have already trotted the issue past the company's legal counsel.

"And, knowing the outcome, if you were still foolish enough to go ahead with a lawsuit," Simpson added with smug self-assurance, "what would you put on your résumé? That you sued your employers rather than follow their wishes? How many jobs do you think that would get you?"

Zero, but Megan wasn't going to admit that. "That's blackmail!"

"It's the truth. You'd be poison to any firm of financial advisors."

Her stomach took another dip. He was right. Legally, you couldn't pay a penalty for bringing an anti-discrimination lawsuit. Practically, things weren't quite that simple.

Simpson smiled slyly. "Besides, we never really had this conversation. I only stopped by to thank you for the fine work you did on that proposal and to tell you, sadly enough, that you don't have quite the experience you'd need to take on the job yourself. I'm sure you'll gain a world of experience staying here in the States and being Fisher's diligent assistant." Her boss rocked up on his toes, which elevated him to at least five foot five. "Nothing wrong with any of that, Miss O'Connell. Nothing at all."

Megan stared at him. He was a worm, but he was right. She probably didn't have grounds for suing the company. Even if she did, doing so would end her career.

She was stuck. Cornered, with no valid options.

The logical thing was to choke back her rage, pin a smile to her lips and thank Simpson for telling her she was going to become a partner and that she'd be thrilled to take on an important new client in the film business.

But she couldn't. She couldn't. She'd always believed in playing by the rules and Jerry Simpson was telling her the rules didn't mean a thing. He was beaming at her now, certain he had her beat.

He didn't.

"You're wrong," she said quietly. "Wrong about me, Jerry. I'm not going to let you and the Prince of Darkness shove me aside."

Simpson's smile tilted. "Don't be stupid, Megan. I just told you, you can't win a suit against us."

"Maybe not, but think of the publicity! It'll be bad for you—we both know what the senior partners think about negative publicity. And it'll be worse for the sheikh. Suliyam's floating on a sea of oil and minerals, but once investors hear his backward little country's up to its neck in a human rights lawsuit, I'll bet they'll gallop in the other direction."

Simpson wasn't smiling at all now. Good, Megan thought, and leaned in for the kill.

"You yank this job away from me," she said, "I'll see to it that Suliyam's dirty linen is hung out for the world to see." She stepped past her boss, then turned and faced him one last time. "Be sure and tell the exalted Pooh-Bah that, Mr. Simpson."

It had seemed the perfect exit line and she'd stalked away, realizing too late that she'd abandoned her own office, not Simpson's, but no way in hell would she have turned back.

As for her threat—she wouldn't take that back, either, even though it was meaningless. She knew it and she didn't doubt that Simpson knew it, too. He was an oily little worm but he wasn't stupid.

Her career meant everything to her. She'd devoted herself to it. She wasn't like her mother, who'd cheerfully handed her life over to a man so he could do with it as he chose. She wasn't like her sister, Fallon, whose beauty had been her ticket to independence. She wasn't like her sister, Bree, who seemed content to drift through life.

No, Megan had thought as she yanked open the ladies' room door, no, she'd taken a different path. Two degrees. Hard work. A steady climb to the top in a field as removed from the glittery world of chance in which she'd grown up as night was from day.

Was she really going to toss it all aside to make a feminist point?

She wasn't.

She wasn't going to sue anyone, or complain to anyone, or do much of anything except, when she got past her fury, swallow her pride and tell Jerry she'd thought things over and—and—

God, apologizing would hurt! But she'd do it. She'd do it. Nobody had ever said life was easy.

So Megan had stayed in the ladies' room until she figured the coast was clear. Then she'd started for her office, brewed a pot of coffee, dug out her secret stash of Godiva and spent the next hour mainlining caffeine while she thought up imaginative ways to rid the world of men.

A little before ten, the PA she shared with three other analysts popped her head in.

"He's here," she'd whispered.

No need to ask who. Only one visitor was expected this morning. Plus, Sally had that look teenage girls got in the presence of rock stars.

"I'm happy for you," Megan replied.

"Mr. Simpson says...he says he would like you to stay where you are."

"I would like Mr. Simpson in the path of a speeding train," Megan said pleasantly, "but we do not always get what we want."

"Megan," Sally said with urgency, "you're wired. All that coffee...and, oh wow, you put away half that box of chocolate. You know what happens when you have too much caffeine!"

She knew. She got edgy. She got irritable. She talked too much. A good thing she realized all that, or she'd show up in the boardroom despite what Simpson would like. Hell, she'd show up *because* of what he'd like.

Yes, it was a good thing she knew Sally was right. Staying put was a good idea.

"Tell Mr. Simpson I'll stay right here."

Sally gave her a worried look. "You okay?"

"Fine."

A lie. She hadn't been fine. More coffee, more chocolate, and she'd tried not to think about the fact that as she sat obediently in her cubbyhole of an office, Jerry Simpson and His Highness, the Sheikh of Smugness, were probably enjoying a good laugh at her expense.

And why, she'd thought, should she let that happen? She could show her face, just to prove she might be down but she wasn't defeated.

So she'd combed her hair, straightened her panty hose, smoothed down the skirt of her navy suit and headed for the boardroom.

By the time she'd finally strolled in, the formal handshakes and greetings were over. Jerry Simpson saw her and glowered but what could he do about it without making a scene? The sheikh hadn't even noticed, surrounded as he was by his adoring fans and his pathetic minions.

Megan had tossed Jerry a thousand-watt smile meant to let him suffer as he tried to figure out why she'd showed up. Then she'd headed for the buffet table, where she'd sipped more coffee before switching to Mimosas.

No caffeine there. Only little bubbles.

All she had to do was hang in long enough to make Simpson squirm. Once the sheikh and his henchmen departed, she could start the ugly business of crawling back into her boss's good graces, though she doubted he'd let her get that far anytime this decade.

Well, no rush. The sheikh wasn't going anywhere. Not yet. Everyone was having too much fun. She could hear Jerry's voice, and a deeper, huskier one she assumed was the sheikh's. She could hear occasional trills of girlish laughter, too, punctuated by loud male ha-ha-ha's.

Like, for instance, right now. A giggle, a ha-ha, a simpering, "That's so clever, Your Highness!"

Megan swung around and stared at Geraldine McBride. Geraldine, simpering? All two hundred tweedy pounds of her?

Megan snorted.

She didn't mean to. She just couldn't help it, not while she was envisioning the Pooh-Bah riding an Arabian stallion with Geraldine flung across the saddle in front of him.

She snorted again. Unfortunately the second snort erupted during a second's pause in the babble of voices. Heads turned in her direction. Jerry looked as if he wanted to kill her. The sheikh looked—

Mmm-mmm-mmm. He looked spectacular. You had to give him that. The tabloids were right. The man was gorgeous. They had his eye-color wrong, though. It wasn't gray. The color reminded her of charcoal. Or slate.

Or storm clouds. That's how cold those eyes were as they fixed on her.

There was no mistaking that expression. He didn't like her. Not in the slightest. Jerry must have told him she'd been a problem.

So be it.

I don't like you, either, she thought coolly, and couldn't resist raising her glass in mocking salute before she turned away.

Why care what the sheikh thought? Why care what Jerry thought? Why care what anybody thought? She had her own life to live, her own independence to enjoy—

"Miss O'Connell," a deep voice said.

Megan swung around. The sheikh was coming toward her, his walk slow, deliberate and masculine enough to make her heart bump up into her throat, which was silly. There was nothing to be afraid of, except losing her job, and that wouldn't happen if she used her head.

He reached her side. Oh, yes. He was definitely easy on the eyes. Tall, lean, the hint of a well-muscled body under that expensive suit.

D and D, she thought, and her heart gave another little bump. What she and Bree always joked about.

Dark and Dangerous.

He gave her what the people at the other end of the room would surely think was a smile. It wasn't. That look in his eyes was colder than ever, cold enough to make the hair rise on the nape of her neck. How could such a gorgeous man be such a mean son of a bitch?

Megan drew herself up. "Your Mightiness."

His eyes bored into hers again. Then he lifted his hand. That was all. No wave, no turning around, nothing but that upraised hand. It was enough. Someone said something— her boss, maybe, or one of the sheikh's henchmen—and people headed for the door.

Scant seconds later, the room was empty.

Megan smiled sweetly. "Must be nice, being emperor of the universe."

"It must be equally nice, not caring what people think of you."

"I beg your pardon?"

His gaze moved over her, from her hair to her toes and then back up again. "You're drunk."

"I am not."

"Put down that glass."

Megan's eyebrows. "What?"

"I said, put the glass down."

"You can't tell me what to do."

"Someone should have told you what to do a long time ago," he said grimly. "Then you'd know better than to try to threaten me."

"Threaten you? Are you insane? I most assuredly did not—"

"For the last time, Miss O'Connell, put the glass down."

Megan's jaw shot forward. "For the last time, oh mighty king, stop trying to order me ar—"

Her words ended in a startled yelp as Sheikh Qasim al Daud al Rashid, King of Suliyam and Absolute Ruler of his People, picked her up, tossed her over his shoulder and marched from the room.

CHAPTER TWO

CAZ hadn't intended to sling the O'Connell woman over his shoulder like a sack of grain.

He hadn't intended to deal with her at all. Oh, he wanted to, all right. Hell, yes, he wanted to. Simpson had told him how he'd given the woman a simple assignment, how she'd tried to make it seem as if he'd promised her something he hadn't...

And how she'd threatened to discredit him and Suliyam if she didn't get a job she wanted.

How dare she attempt to blackmail him?

He'd felt the rage churning inside him. His ancestors would have known how to deal with the woman.

Damn it, so did he.

Caz was the one who snorted now as he strode down the hall, past startled faces, the O'Connell woman beating her fists against his shoulders and yelling words a decent woman should not even think.

There was no need to go back to an earlier generation. Ninety percent of the men in Suliyam would know how to deal with her, and that was just the problem. After his hurried conversation with her boss, he'd known that if he let himself show his anger, he might as well put up a sign in Times Square that told the world he and his nation were still living in the dark ages.

So he'd decided to ignore her. There was no reason for

him to get involved. After all, Simpson said he'd made it clear to her that he was not going to give her the job.

"I took care of things, your highness," he'd said. "She's just one of those prickly feminists. You know the type."

Caz did, indeed. The western world was filled with them. They weren't soft-spoken or soft and welcoming, a safe harbor for a man who spent his days on the financial and political battlefields where empires were won and lost.

They were hard-edged and aggressive, unattractive and unfeminine.

He didn't enjoy their company. He certainly didn't understand them. Why would a woman want to behave like a man? But he'd learned not to underestimate their business skills, as long as they followed the rules.

If a woman wanted to play in a man's world, Caz expected her to play a man's game.

Threatening a lawsuit when none was warranted, pretending that things had been promised you when they hadn't, were things a woman would do.

Not a man.

Megan O'Connell slammed a fist between his shoulder blades. Caz grunted, stalked into Simpson's office and dumped her on a tweed-covered sofa. Then he stood back, folded his arms and glared at her.

She glared straight back. Didn't she have any sense of shame? Of guilt? Nobody glowered at him. Nobody! Didn't she realize who he was?

Of course she did. She just didn't care. He had to admire her courage.

He had to admire her looks, too. She didn't appear unfeminine, even in that shapeless blue suit. And she certainly wasn't unattractive, despite the blouse buttoned to the neck and the auburn hair tied back so tightly from her face that it made her sculpted cheekbones stand out like elegant arches. Her shoes were better suited to the legs of a soccer player than to ones that were so long, so artfully curved, so...

The woman sprang to her feet. "Who in hell do you think you are!"

"Sit down, Miss O'Connell."

"I will not sit down. I will not tolerate this kind of treatment." Eyes bright with anger, she started toward the door. "And I will not stay in this room with you for another—"

Caz kept his eyes on her as he reached back and slammed the door.

"I said, sit down."

"You have no authority here, mister! All I have to do is yell for help and—"

"And?" He smiled unpleasantly. "What will happen, Miss O'Connell? Do you really expect your boss to come running to your assistance after the threats you made?"

"What threats?" She folded her arms, lifted her chin and set one of those ugly shoes tapping with impatience. "I don't know what you're talking about.

Caz narrowed his eyes. Oh, yes. She was tough. She was also beautiful, but that didn't change a thing. She was prepared to ruin his plans for his country and his people for her own selfish purposes, and he would not tolerate it.

"Perhaps you'd like to tell me what threats I made."

"Don't waste my time, Miss O'Connell. The head of your office told me everything."

"Really." The foot-tapping increased in tempo. "And just what did he tell you?"

Caz's glower deepened. Simpson had told him more than enough to brand this woman as a schemer ready to lie and cheat and do whatever it took to get what she wanted, and what she wanted was the Suliyam account. She'd stop at nothing to get it, including threatening to file a lawsuit on the grounds that she was being discriminated against because of her sex.

"He explained what you said, your highness, that you cannot permit a woman to work alongside you."

Caz had never said any such thing. Not exactly. He'd simply explained that the status of women was an evolving issue in his country.

Simpson had assured him he understood. Obviously he hadn't. And now, Megan O'Connell was talking about hiring a lawyer.

Caz didn't give a damn about that. His attorneys would have the complaint dismissed without trouble. Suliyam's traditions were its own. No one could tell him or his people what to do or how to do it, not Megan O'Connell or all the lawyers and judges in the world.

Besides, the issue of her sex was secondary.

The woman was demanding a position for which she wasn't qualified. The man who'd actually created the proposal—someone named Fisher—was right for the job. His work had been excellent. It was the reason Caz had signed a contract with Tremont, Burnside and Macomb.

Megan O'Connell didn't have a legal leg to stand on. She knew it, too. Hadn't she admitted it to Simpson? You'd never win a lawsuit, Simpson said he'd told her, and she'd countered by saying she didn't care about winning.

Impugning Suliyam's name in the press and, worse still, in business and financial circles, would be enough for her.

Caz couldn't let that happen. Wouldn't let it happen. He'd spent the last five years readying his people for emergence from the past, but some among them would grasp any opportunity to end the progress he'd made. There were too many factions aligned against him. One whiff of scandal, one headline…

"Are you deaf, Sheikh Qasim? Or have you decided you made a mistake, conversing with a mere female?"

She was all but breathing fire now. Her face was flushed, her eyes were wide and dark; her hair was coming undone and tumbling around her face in wild curls. The suit and shoes were still ugly as sin but from the neck up, she looked like a woman who'd just risen from bed.

His bed.

The thought was unsettling. She was beautiful, yes, but her heart wasn't a woman's heart. She was intent on blackmail, and he was the target.

"It was your Mr. Simpson who made the mistake, Miss O'Connell, by letting things go too far."

Megan blinked. "What things?"

"It serves no purpose to pretend innocence." Caz folded his arms. "I told you, I know about your threats. Your Mr. Simpson—"

"He is not *my* anything!"

"He is your boss."

"He's a fool. So what?"

"He did what he could to keep the peace."

"Excuse me?"

"He was foolish to try. As soon as you began demanding undue credit for the little work you did, helping to draft that proposal—"

"Helping?" Megan gave a brittle laugh. "I *wrote* that proposal."

"No, you did not."

"Damn it!" Megan could almost feel the adrenaline racing through her veins. A couple of hours ago, she'd have voted Jerry Simpson Idiot of the Year. What a mistake that would have been. The barbarian barring the door was winner of the title, hands down. "You know what? I've had it." Resolutely she started toward the door again. "You get out of my way."

He bared his teeth in a smile. "Or?" he said pleasantly. "Or I'll go right through you."

He laughed. The son of a bitch laughed! Oh, how she wanted to slap that arrogant smirk from his all-too-perfect face.

Unfortunately, she could hardly blame him. Talk about empty threats! She could no more go through him than through a brick wall.

The Sheikh of the Endless Names was big. Six foot two, six foot three. He was as tall as any of her brothers and she'd never been able to go through them in a zillion touch football games. She'd hardly ever managed to go around them, except with a bit of subterfuge.

And then there were those shoulders wide enough to fill the doorway. The muscles that bulged even under his expensive suit. Except, they didn't bulge. They rippled.

Rippled? Megan did a mental blink. Who cared if his muscles undulated? The Prince of All He Surveyed was a male chauvinist jerk, and she'd be damned if she'd stand here and take his verbal abuse one more second.

"Perhaps it's the custom to detain women by force in your country," she said coldly.

That got a response! Red patches bloomed on his cheeks. The man didn't like hearing the truth. Good. She could use that to her advantage.

"Or maybe it's the only way you can get women to pay attention to you. You know, snatch them up, carry them off, lock them up—"

"You're trying my patience, Miss O'Connell."

"And you're trying mine."

"I promise you, I won't take much more."

"And I promise *you*—"

That was as far as she got. He reached for her, wrapped his hands around her arms and lifted her to her toes. His fingers pressed into her flesh and his eyes... Whoa, his eyes! Cold as that sea-ice again. He was angry. Enraged. Megan could see it, feel it, even smell his fury in the male musk coming off him.

She'd never seen or sensed such passion in a man before. *What would he be like in bed?*

The thought shocked her. She didn't think about men that way. Oh, she could joke with her sisters, sit in a bar sipping a glass of white wine and giggle with them over the buns on one guy, the biceps on the next, but she'd never looked at a man and actually wondered what it would be like to sleep with him.

That was exactly what she was doing now.

What if the sheikh turned all that rage into desire? If he were lying above her, holding her this same way, holding her so she couldn't turn away from him, so she didn't want to turn away from him, so she could feel the heat of his body against hers?

She felt her heart do a slow, unsteady roll.

"Let go," she said, and thanked whatever gods were watching that her voice didn't tremble.

He didn't. Not right away. He went on looking at her and her heart did that same little turn again because something changed in his eyes and she knew he was thinking the same thing, seeing her as she saw him, not here in this office but in a wide, soft bed, their bodies slick with sweat, their mouths fused.

Her pulse went crazy—but not as crazy as that thought.

"I said, let go!" she repeated, and twisted free of his hands.

A moment passed. She could hear the rasp of his breath.

Then his expression changed and it was as if nothing had happened.

"This isn't getting us anywhere," he said.

Megan nodded. "I agree."

"Fifty thousand dollars."

She blinked. "What?"

"Fifty thousand, Miss O'Connell. Surely that's ample payment for the time you'd like me to think you put in on this project."

She stared at him in disbelief. "Are you offering me a bribe?"

"I'm offering you payment for the job you claim to have done."

"My God, you are! You think you can buy my silence!"

His eyes darkened. "Let's not make a melodrama out of this. You've threatened to derail a project that's of great importance to me. I'm simply suggesting there's no need for you to do that." He smiled, and she wanted to wipe the smile off his face. "I don't carry a checkbook with me, of course—"

"Of course."

"But I will have a courier deliver a check to you here within—"

"No!"

"Ah. You'd rather we kept the transaction private." He reached in his breast pocket, took out a small leather notebook and a pen. "If you'll give me your home address—"

"I am not for sale, Sheikh Qasim!"

Caz looked up. The woman's face was white, except for two slashes of crimson across those elegant cheekbones. She was going to be more difficult to deal with than he'd anticipated.

"How much?" he said coldly.

"I just told you, I am not—"

"One hundred thousand."

"Are you deaf? I said—"

"I'm weary of this game, Miss O'Connell, and of your act. Name your price."

She laughed. Laughed! At him! And edged toward the door, still laughing, as if he were a lunatic howling at the moon.

"Goodbye, your Mightiness. It's been interest—"

She gasped as he grabbed her shoulders and swung her toward him.

"How dare you laugh at me?" he growled.

"Take your hands off me."

"You're a fool, Miss O'Connell. Did you really think you could threaten me and get away with it?"

Megan looked up into eyes filled with hostility. She knew that this was the moment to tell the sheikh that her threat, as he called it, had been made in the heat of the moment, that there'd be no lawsuit because Simpson, damn his soul, was right. The only thing she'd win, if she sued, was a reputation as a troublemaker, and that would mark the end of her corporate career.

That was the logical thing to do.

Logic, however, had nothing to do with what she felt at that moment.

The sheikh obviously thought he ruled the universe. Well, why wouldn't he? During her research, she'd learned that women were treated like dirt in his country. Well, she was a woman, but she didn't have to bow to this man. She was an American citizen, and she didn't have to take this nonsense.

"I asked you a question," he said. "Did you think—"

"What I think," Megan said, enunciating each word with precision, "is that you're a tyrant. You're so used to people treating you like a god, to *you* treating *them* as if they were your property—''

''Stop it! How dare you?''

''What you mean,'' she said, her voice trembling, ''is how dare a woman speak to you this way? Isn't that right, Sheikh Qasim? I'm a female. A worthless creature. And you are absolutely certain that women are only good for one thing.''

Caz could feel the anger rushing through him. Control, he told himself, control…but this woman needed a lesson.

''It's time somebody showed you what women really are,'' she said, and those few words pushed him over the edge.

''At least we agree on something,'' he answered, and before she could twist her head away, his mouth came down over hers.

His kiss was harsh. Dominating. He was a man intent on proving his strength and her weakness, his power to subdue her.

Megan fought back. Hard. When he tried to open her mouth with his, she sank her teeth into his bottom lip. He grunted, turned, pushed her back against the wall; she shoved against his chest, freed her hands, beat them against his shoulders…

And then, in a heartbeat, it all changed.

Later, she'd think back and remember the sudden stillness in the room, as if the universe was holding its breath. Now all she knew was the feel of his mouth as it softened on hers, the gentling of his hands as they slid up her shoulders, her throat, into her hair.

It was happening again. What she'd felt minutes ago, except now it was real. She was in his arms, her body pressed to his, and what was happening had everything to do with desire instead of anger, with wanting instead of hating.

She moaned, parted her lips to the feathery brush of his tongue, let him take possession of her mouth. Of her senses.

He said something in a language she didn't understand, but it didn't matter. She understood all the rest. What he wanted. What she wanted, and when he angled his mouth over hers, took the kiss deeper and deeper until she felt the earth spinning away, Megan raised her arms, wound them around his neck. He ran a hand down her spine, cupped her bottom, lifted her into him, into his heat, his hardness…

Someone knocked at the door. The sound was like a clap of thunder exploding within the confines of the quiet room.

Caz's hands fell away from her. He stepped back; her eyes flew open. Breathing hard, they stared at each other like partners who'd lost their footing in some intricate dance.

The knock at the door sounded again. A voice called out. It took Caz seemingly endless seconds to realize it was Hakim, calling his name.

"Sire? Sire, forgive me for disturbing you…"

Caz stared at the O'Connell woman. What in hell had just happened? A shared hallucination? An aberration? His gaze hardened. There were those among his people who would say she was not just a liar and a cheat but a sorceress. He knew better. She was only a woman. A seductive woman, and he'd played right into her hands.

Perhaps she thought she could sleep her way into the job she wanted, rather than blackmail her way into it. Or that she could use the last few minutes against him, either in a court of law or in ways that had the potential to be even more damaging.

He could almost see the headlines in the *Wall Street Journal*. Wouldn't his enemies love it if she denounced him to the press?

"Sire?"

She was still staring at him, her green eyes huge and seemingly clouded with confusion. If nothing else, she was an excellent actress.

Caz forced a smile to his lips. "Thank you for the taste of your wares, but you're wasting your time. I'm not interested."

"You arrogant son of a bitch!" Her face went white and she raised her hand, swung her fist at his jaw, but he slipped the punch with ease, caught her wrist and dragged her hard against him.

"Be careful," he said softly, "or before you know it, you'll be in water so deep it will be over your head."

"Don't you ever, *ever,* touch me again!"

A chilling smile angled across his mouth. "That's the first thing you've said that pleases me." He let go of her, took a breath to compose himself and opened the door. Hakim stood just outside, his expression as inscrutable as always.

"What is it, Hakim?"

"I am sorry to trouble you, my lord, but you told me to remind you of your luncheon appointment."

Caz nodded. He had not told Hakim any such thing, but his *aide de camp* had served first his father and now him. The man had a sixth sense about trouble, and the courage to act on his own initiative when he thought it necessary.

There were times it was an annoyance, but right now, Caz was glad he had.

"Yes. Thank you." He shot a glance at Megan O'Connell. She had turned away from him and was standing by the window, back straight, hands in the pockets of her mannish skirt, looking out at the street as if nothing had happened, but then, nothing had.

This had been a momentary slip in the fabric of time. Nothing more. It surely would never be repeated. Not only didn't she appeal to him; he would never see her again.

"A courier will deliver the item we discussed to your home this evening, Miss O'Connell."

The sheikh's voice was brisk and businesslike. Megan knotted her hands. Flying across the room and beating her fists against that arrogant face would serve no purpose. Besides, he'd never let it happen. He was too strong, far stronger than she. Hadn't he just proved it by overpowering her? Because that was what he'd done. Overpowered her. He'd forced that kiss on her, forced her to kiss him back...

"Are you going to give me your address? Or shall my aide get it from Simpson?"

She didn't answer. She didn't trust herself to speak. Let him send a check to her apartment. Let him send a dozen checks. She'd make the courier wait while she tore them into thousands of pieces and tell him precisely what he was to tell the sheikh to do with all those bits of paper.

At least she'd have the satisfaction of knowing his Mightiness would spend sleepless nights worrying that she'd sue. With luck, he'd have an ulcer by the time he finally realized she wouldn't.

"Miss O'Connell?"

Megan turned around. "Get out of my sight."

Caz stiffened. He heard Hakim make a sound that might have been a growl as he took a step forward.

"No," Caz said sharply, putting his hand on his aide's shoulder.

"But my lord..."

"She's American," Caz said, because that explained everything.

"Damned right I am," Megan said. "And you're a pig."

He forced a smile to his lips, as if she'd handed him a compliment.

"Goodbye, Miss O'Connell. You'll see my courier this evening." He moved toward her and was gratified to see the swift rush of panic in her eyes. "But for your sake," he said softly, so softly that he knew Hakim couldn't hear him, "you'd better pray that you never see me again."

The sheikh turned on his heel and strode from the room. His aide gave Megan one last, menacing look, then fell in after him.

Megan drew a shuddering breath and sank into a chair. The Prince of the Desert was gone. He was out of her life, forever.

And not a moment too soon.

CHAPTER THREE

MEGAN left work at six-thirty, almost an hour later than usual.

Since she'd expected to be quick-marched out of the building after her confrontation with the sheikh, leaving late wasn't too bad.

To her surprise, Simpson hadn't fired her. Either he'd believed her lawsuit threat or...

Or what?

She was glad she still had her job, but she couldn't figure out the reason.

Megan sighed as she stepped from the elevator.

Actually she couldn't figure out much of anything anymore, including why she'd never even imagined she could win a legal battle. Not that she regretted anything she'd said to either Simpson or Sheikh Qasim. It was just that nothing seemed quite as black and white as it had hours before.

Rain was beating against the glass lobby doors. Great. The weatherman had predicted overcast skies. How come those guys never got it right?

How come *she* hadn't? Megan asked herself as she turned up her collar and stepped into the street.

Threatening to sue had sounded good. Telling the sheikh what she thought of him had felt good. Great...except, all she'd really done was commit professional suicide. Odds were she'd be digging through the employment ads by next week.

A gust of wind blew the chill rain into her face. Too bad something like that hadn't happened hours earlier. She could have used an icy dousing around then.

Tremont, Burnside and Macomb was a prestigious firm. So what if her boss was an ass? That didn't change the facts. She'd behaved stupidly, first with her boss, then with her client...

Except, the sheikh wasn't her client, and that was probably a good thing because she never could have worked with him. How could you work with a man who was so obnoxious? So rude? So over-bearing and demanding and arrogant?

How could you work with a man who kissed you and turned your bones to jelly?

Megan reached the parking lot, unlocked her car and tossed her briefcase and purse on the passenger seat. She slid behind the wheel, started the engine and turned up the heat. She was drenched and her teeth were chattering.

There was no sense in lying to herself. Qasim had kissed her and she'd kissed him back. It had only been a kiss, but it had left her breathless. Who knew what might have happened if his aide hadn't interrupted them?

She swallowed hard and stared through the rain-streaked windshield. The other cars were blurs of color.

That was how she'd felt when they'd kissed. As if the world had disappeared and only the colors of it remained.

Damn it.

She gave herself a little shake, turned on the windshield wipers and headed into the street.

She'd absolutely made a mess of things, from start to finish. Too much caffeine. Okay, too much caffeine and too little common sense. She shouldn't have lost her temper and backed herself into a figurative corner.

And she shouldn't have been such an easy target for a

man who undoubtedly thought women were for only one thing.

The truth was that nothing would have happened if Hakim or Akim, whatever the Head Flunky's name was, hadn't shown up.

"Nothing at all," she muttered, and pulled out into traffic, which was even more horrible than usual. Well, why not? An extra hour spent creeping home on slick roads would be the perfect ending to a perfect day.

Her life was starting to feel like a soap opera.

She hit every red light between the parking lot and the freeway entrance ramp. Okay, she thought, drumming her fingers against the steering wheel. That gave her plenty of time to try and figure out why Simpson hadn't dumped her.

Could he really have fallen for the lawsuit thing?

No. The Worm was a rat and if that was a mixed metaphor, so be it. The point was, rats were miserable creatures but they weren't stupid. Her boss had seen through her threat.

He had to know that she wouldn't go to the media, either. Any action she took that would tarnish the company and the sheikh would tarnish her.

Goodbye, career. Goodbye, all these years spent climbing the corporate ladder.

Simpson had to know she'd calm down and come to her senses.

But the sheikh had no way of knowing it. He'd fall for anything she said. Obviously he had. That was the reason he'd made that loathsome offer to buy her off.

Had he gone to Simpson? Told her boss not to worry, that he had things under control? Was that why Simpson hadn't fired her, or even come near her for the balance of the day?

Maybe so.

Well, they were both in for a big surprise. Just let His Almightiness try and send her a check. Just let the Worm try to think she could be bought off. Just let...

"Stop," Megan said firmly. "Just stop." She was working herself up all over again, and for what? She'd already decided what to do with a check, if the sheikh sent one. As for Simpson... She wouldn't let him buy her off, either. To hell with the big Hollywood client. To hell with the partnership. She'd polish up her résumé, call up a headhunter, find herself a new job...

And lose the chance to make partner. Simpson saw it as a bribe but she deserved it. She was a hard worker. An excellent financial analyst. Was she really going to let Simpson and the insufferable Qasim of Suliyam make her lose everything she'd striven for?

She was not.

If she could just come up with the reason for Simpson's silence...

Her cell phone rang. Megan ignored it. She hated taking calls when she was driving, especially in heavy traffic made even worse by a steady rain. Whoever it was would call back. Or leave a message. Or—

Or be as persistent as an ant at a picnic. The phone rang again. And again. The fourth time, she kept her eyes on the wet road and dug the phone from her purse.

"This better be important," she said, "because I am knee-deep in rain and traffic and—"

"Megan?"

"Yes?" she said cautiously. It was a male voice, familiar, but she couldn't quite place it.

"Thank God," the voice said, and sighed with relief. "It's Frank."

"Who?"

"Frank Fisher. From the office."

"Frank?" Her mind buzzed with questions. Why was he calling her? And why did he sound so…panicked?

"Look, I hate to bother you, but—but, uh, I guess Mr. Simpson spoke to you about, uh, about things."

Mr. Simpson? Her eyes narrowed. "If you mean, did he tell me that you're stealing my work and claiming it as your own, yes. He spoke to me about, uh, things."

"Hey. I didn't steal anything. This wasn't my idea, it was Mr. Simpson's."

Oh, hell. Frank was right, it wasn't his fault. It would have been nice if he'd spoken up and told the Worm he wouldn't take credit for something that wasn't his, but Frank was spineless. Everyone in the office knew it. Intelligent, but spineless. Simpson had chosen him wisely.

"Forget it," she said wearily.

"I was hoping you'd say that."

A horn bleated behind her. She looked in the mirror, saw, through the water racing down the rear window, a small, low, obscenely expensive sports car. Typically L.A., and no doubt driven by a typically L.A. jerk who thought the car would make him look more important than he really was. She couldn't see the driver, thanks to the rain, but she didn't have to. She knew the type.

"Yeah, well, it's good of you to call, Frank. I mean, the apology doesn't change anything, but—"

"The apology?" Frank cleared his throat. "Uh, right, right. I'm glad you understand but actually—actually, I called to ask you something."

Megan frowned. "What?"

"Well," Frank said, and paused. "Well, see, I was reading through your—through my—through the proposal—"

Megan felt the blood start to drum in her ears. "Get to it, Frank. What do you want?"

"There are a couple of things here I don't quite follow…"

Frank began to babble. A couple of minutes later, it was clear there were lots of things he didn't follow. Like, for instance, the entire purpose of her suggestions for the investments the sheikh was seeking.

"He's rich, right?"

"Stinking rich," Megan agreed.

"And they've already got oil coming out of the faucets in Suminan, right?"

"Suliyam. Yes, the oil's pumping. But there's more to be found, and there are minerals in the mountains…"

And what was she doing, giving Frank a quick education based on her research? The man was an idiot. Why should she help him? Damn it, the jerk behind her was beeping his horn again.

"What?" she snarled, shooting an angry look in the mirror. Did Mr. Impatient expect her to fly over the cars ahead of her?

"I need answers, Megan. That's what."

"I wasn't talking to you, Frank."

"Yeah, but I need answers." Frank's voice cracked. "And soon. I'm meeting the sh—I'm meeting my client in less than an hour and, like I said, I just took a quick look at this proposal and—"

"And you're in over your head," Megan said sweetly, and hit the disconnect button so forcefully she thought she might have broken it.

The phone rang a second later. She ignored it. It rang again, and she grabbed the phone, shut it off and, for good measure, tossed it over her shoulder into the back seat.

This was why Simpson hadn't fired her.

He needed her. All that crap about her staying in L.A. to assist Fisher was just that. Crap. She was going to stay here and force-feed everything to her replacement. Frank would get the scepter. She'd get the shaft.

"Forget it," she snapped.

No way was she going to take that kind of treatment. What was with men, anyway? Three of them had tried to step on her today. Simpson. Fisher. And the sheikh.

"Don't forget the sheikh, Megan," she said out loud, but how could she possibly forget a man so despicable?

He'd kissed her. So what? It was a kiss. That was all, just a kiss. Okay, so he was good at it. Damned good, but why wouldn't he be when he'd been with a zillion women? That was what he did. Made love to women, ordered his flunkies around, and sat on his butt the rest of the time, counting his money, figuring out ways to make it grow.

What else would a rich, incredibly good-looking Prince of the Desert do with his life?

To think that such a man believed he could buy her...

The idiot behind her hit his horn again. This time, it was a long, long blast that seemed to go on forever.

Megan looked in the mirror.

"Go on," she snarled, "pass me if you can, you idiot!"

The horn blared again. Megan cursed, put down her window just enough so she could stick out her hand and make the universal sign of displeasure. She'd never done such a thing before in her life but oh, it felt good!

The driver behind her swung out, horn blasting in answer to her gesture. He cut in front of her, then put on the speed and zoomed away, in and out of the smallest possible breaks in traffic until he vanished from sight.

"Are you really in such an all-fired hurry to get to hell?" she yelled.

Then she put up her window, glared straight ahead and wished nothing but life's worst on the Worm, the Sheikh, Frank Fisher, and the idiot driving the Lamborghini.

* * *

California drivers were not only fools, they were foolhardy.

The mood he was in, Caz had half a mind to force the VW onto the shoulder of the freeway, yank open the driver's door and tell the cretin behind the wheel that making a crude gesture to a stranger wasn't a good idea.

Luckily for the cretin, he was in a hurry.

The traffic had been bumper to bumper. When it finally loosened up, he'd waited for the guy ahead to start moving. He hadn't. Or maybe she hadn't. Caz had pretty much generated a picture of who was behind the VW's wheel. A woman. Middle-aged, peering over the steering wheel with trepidation, nervous about the rain.

The finger-in-the-air thing had changed his mind.

No gray-haired Nervous Nellie would make such a gesture. She wouldn't yap on a cell phone while she was driving, either. At least, he thought he'd seen the driver holding a cell phone to her ear. It was hard to tell much of anything because of the rain, and who was it who'd said it never rained in Southern California?

Hell.

He had to calm down.

Driving fast would help. It always did. It was what he did at the end of virtually every meeting with his advisors back home, take one of his cars out on the straight black road that went from one end of Suliyam to the other.

From no place to nowhere, his mother used to say.

Caz always thought of her when he was in California. She'd left his father and come here, where she'd been born, when he was ten. She died when he was twelve, and he'd only spent summers with her for the intervening two years.

"Won't you come home with me, Mama?" he'd ask at the end of each summer. And she'd hug him tightly and say she'd come home soon...

But she never did.

He'd hated her for a little while, when he was thirteen or fourteen and Hakim let slip that she'd left his father and him because she'd despised living in Suliyam. He hadn't known that. His father had always told him his mother had gone back to her beloved California for a holiday, that she'd taken ill and had to stay there to get the proper medical care.

It turned out only part of that was true. She'd gotten sick and died in California, all right, but she hadn't gone for a holiday. She'd abandoned everything. Her husband, her adopted country…

Her son.

Caz frowned, saw an opening in the next lane and shot into it.

It had all happened more than twenty years ago. Water under the bridge, as the Americans said.

He had more important things to think about.

Caz sighed. He was wound up like a spring about tonight's dinner appointment. He had to relax. That woman was to blame for his bad mood. What an aggressive female! A feminist, to the core.

Was that the genie in the bottle he'd be setting loose, once he began implementing his plans back home? Maybe, and maybe he'd regret it, but you couldn't lead a nation into the twenty-first century without granting rights and privileges to all its citizens.

Even women.

Surely they wouldn't all turn out like…

No. He wasn't going to think about Megan O'Connell. He'd wasted too much time on her already. All in all, this day had been a mess.

First that abominable meeting this morning. He'd taken one look at the buffet table, the champagne, the people staring at him and he'd been tempted to turn and walk out. He hadn't, of course. He was his nation's emissary. Manners, protocol, were everything.

How come he'd forgotten that with the woman? He'd lost it with her and he knew it but, damn it, she'd deserved it. That temper. Those threats...

Those eyes, that mouth, the certainty that the body beneath the awful suit was meant for pleasure...

"Hell," Caz said, and stepped harder on the gas.

Business. That was what he had to concentrate on tonight.

It was what he'd wanted to concentrate on this morning, but Simpson had screwed it up. Instead of serious discussion with the man who'd written that excellent proposal, he'd had to endure an eternity of all those people fawning over him.

Bad enough his own countrymen insisted on treating him as if he were Elvis risen from the dead. That, at least, was understandable. It was tradition, the same tradition, unchanged for centuries, that would make implementing his plans a rough sell. His advisors would look aghast at his determination to create a modern infrastructure in Suliyam by opening it to foreign investors. He intended to commit much of his own vast fortune to the plan, as well.

His people would balk, protest, tell him such things could not be done.

It was tradition.

And it was tradition, too, that said he could not possibly bring a woman into Suliyam as his financial advisor.

He had explained all of that to Simpson from the first. He knew there were bright, well-educated women in the west. Hadn't his mother been one of them? But Suliyam wasn't ready for such things. He supposed it was one of the reasons his parents' marriage had fallen apart.

He hadn't told that to Simpson, of course, but he'd made

it clear he would not be able to work with anyone but a man.

"No problem, your worship," Simpson had said.

"I am not called by that title," Caz had told him pleasantly. "Please, just address me as Sheikh Qasim."

Hakim had given him a look that meant he didn't approve. Caz had ignored him. Hakim was devoted and loyal, but he believed in the old ways and those days were coming to an end.

"I will assign my best person to write this proposal, your majesty," Simpson had replied.

Caz put on his signal light and shot across three lanes of traffic to the exit ramp.

He'd given up correcting the little man. What did it matter how Simpson addressed him as long as he found the right man to get the job done?

He had. The proposal was everything Caz had hoped for and more. He'd searched hard for the right firm to handle the account, narrowed his choices to three and asked them to come up with written proposals for the best possible utilization of investment funds in Suliyam.

Three months later, each company had submitted a fine proposal. Still, making the final decision had been easy. The T S and M report stood head and shoulders above the others. Caz knew he'd found his man.

Simpson was an annoyance, but Frank Fisher, whose name was on the proposal, was brilliant. He was the right person for the job: logical, methodical, pragmatic.

All the things Megan O'Connell wasn't.

The woman was a creature of temper and temperament, all blistering heat one moment and bone-chilling ice the next. Their encounter proved, as if proof were necessary, that she could not possibly have written the document in question.

It took no great genius to figure out that Simpson was right about her.

She'd accept the money Caz had offered and be grateful for it. The thought of paying her off infuriated him, but sometimes the old saying was right. Better to placate the occasional jackal than to lose the entire flock.

Caz glanced at his watch. Almost seven. He was meeting Fisher for dinner. He hadn't intended to bother with such a meeting—Fisher was making the flight to Suliyam with him tomorrow, so there'd be plenty of time to talk—but Fisher hadn't been present this morning. He was tying up loose ends on another account, Simpson said.

No problem, Caz had answered.

But he'd reconsidered. He really did want to meet Fisher as soon as possible. There was always the faint chance they wouldn't hit it off. If Fisher were anything like Simpson, for instance. If Caz intimidated him simply by being there, they'd never be able to work together.

That was one thing about Megan O'Connell. She damned well hadn't been intimidated. She'd treated him as if he was a man, not a prince. She'd kissed him that way...

Enough.

He had to clear his mind for the meeting ahead. He'd set it up only a little while ago, on the phone with Simpson.

"I'd like to have dinner with Mr. Fisher this evening," he'd said.

Well, that might be difficult to arrange, Simpson had replied. It was late in the day. Fisher wasn't in the office. He might not be able to make a meeting called at the last moment.

"I'll expect him to meet me at seven," Caz had said, cutting through the excuses.

A more suspicious man might even think Simpson was trying to keep him from meeting Frank Fisher until it was too late, but that was ridiculous. Simpson would want Fisher to be on his toes for their first encounter. Meeting this way, after the man had put in a day's work, might not be the best time for him to shine.

Why else would Simpson sound nervous? Surely not because he didn't think Fisher couldn't handle questions on the fine points and subtle implications of the proposal he'd drafted.

The O'Connell woman wasn't capable of such complex work. Simpson had laughed at the very idea. Caz had come to that same conclusion on his own. She was a brash, fiery redhead whose talents lay in a very different direction than finance.

And he'd kissed her.

Her taste lingered on his lips, her scent in his nostrils. He could almost feel the softness of her breasts against his chest, the delicate tilt of her pelvis against him.

Damn it. He was turning hard, just thinking about that kiss.

Why? Why had he kissed her? He didn't like her. What man would like a woman who threatened his plans?

Sure, some men didn't have to like a woman to want to bed her, but he wasn't one of those men. The papers printed lies about him as a womanizer. He'd long ago given up protesting because the protests only added fuel to the fire.

The truth was, he never slept with a woman unless he found her interesting and intelligent.

Megan O'Connell was interesting and intelligent, but she was also a liar. He didn't want to sleep with her.

No, he didn't.

Caz muttered a word he'd learned not in Suliyam but in the American university he'd attended. The restaurant where he was to meet Fisher was just ahead. He'd been there before, always without his entourage. It was a small place with good food where nobody recognized him or bothered him.

That made it perfect for tonight. A pleasant meal with the man who'd written that excellent proposal... Yes. He was looking forward to it.

Caz pulled into the lot behind the restaurant, parked the Lamborghini and told himself, with relief, that there was no reason for him to think of Megan O'Connell ever again.

CHAPTER FOUR

MEGAN saw the red light on her answering machine blinking as she let herself into her apartment, but she ignored it.

She didn't want to hear another human voice, not tonight. All she wanted right now was to turn the long, awful day into a memory.

Like a snake shedding its suddenly constricting skin, she kicked off her sensible shoes, tossed her rain-soaked jacket on a chair, unzipped her soggy skirt and peeled off her silk blouse, her bra and pantyhose. She unpinned her hair, filled the tub, dumped in a handful of lemon-scented bath salts and sank into the warm, fragrant water.

Sheer bliss.

For the first time all day, she began to feel human.

Half an hour later, wearing old sweats that dated back to her university days and a pair of fuzzy slippers even older than the sweats, she padded into the kitchen and flicked on the light.

The answering machine was still blinking. According to the red dial on its face, four messages were waiting for her now. So what? She wasn't doing anything she didn't absolutely have to do tonight, and that included blow-drying and endlessly brushing her hair to make it straight.

Let it be a curly mop. Tomorrow was Saturday. She didn't have to worry about leaping out of bed at six and turning herself into Megan O'Connell, girl financial whiz. No need to dress-for-success or brace herself for another encounter with Jerry Simpson. What for? Her days of striving for success were over. Come Monday, she'd either be fired or get a big, fat, juicy new client.

All she could do was wait and see which way things went, though she had a feeling that hanging up on Frank a little while ago had kind of settled the issue.

Megan opened the fridge, took a slightly shriveled carrot stick from a plastic bag and bit down on it.

And it was all the sheikh's fault.

"The rat," she said, and tossed the half-eaten carrot into the trash.

Time to stop thinking about *el sheikh-o*. Time to dump him in the trash along with the carrot stick. Time to purge her mind of the miserable memories of the miserable day. Forget Simpson. Forget Frank Fisher. Forget Qasim the Horrible and the fact that she'd let him kiss her.

People under stress did weird things, and heaven knew she'd been under stress.

She'd concentrate on something positive. Something like dinner. An excellent idea. She was starved, and why wouldn't she be? Thanks to the sheikh, she'd skipped breakfast and lunch, spending the one getting ready for his visit and the other recovering from it...

And there he was, inside her head again.

Out with thoughts of the sheikh. In with thoughts about supper. Comfort food. That was what she wanted, something as homey and warming as the bath and the old sweat suit.

Megan opened the refrigerator again, her spirits sinking as she peered inside. Low-fat yogurt. Low-fat cottage cheese. Three little containers of low-fat pudding that was supposed to taste like the real thing and didn't.

Damn.

She didn't want anything sensible tonight. She wanted something like her mother's fantastic rice pudding, or a big bowl of macaroni and cheese, anything with enough built-in calories to soothe the soul in every delicious, decadent mouthful.

She sighed, shut the refrigerator door and leaned back against it. She didn't have macaroni in the pantry, and her mother was hundreds of miles away in Las Vegas, so there'd be no rice pudding tonight. A good thing, too, because how would she ever have explained to Ma that she needed it because she'd managed to let a man she despised turn her on?

Qasim hadn't just turned her on, he'd turned her inside out.

Damned if she'd let that ruin her weekend.

Forget the cottage cheese, the yogurt, the sheikh. A little Thai takeout place had opened around the corner a couple of weeks ago. They'd tucked menus in all the mail boxes and she'd put hers somewhere…

There it was, stuck to the fridge door with a magnet.

Megan read through the specials. Great. Coconut milk soup. Pad Thai with chicken. Sticky rice. It wasn't Ma's rice pudding or her own mac and cheese but it sounded wonderful. It probably *was* comfort food, if you were Thai.

She smiled for what felt like the first time in a century. Tonight, she'd claim honorary citizenship. Still smiling, she reached for the phone…

Someone rang the doorbell.

She looked up, frowning. Who'd drop over at this hour on such a wet, cold night?

The sheikh's courier, that was who. Her smile disappeared as she dropped the telephone. She'd told him what he could do with his money but that hadn't stopped him and now one of his rain-soaked flunkies, probably Hakim of the icy eyes, was at the door with one hundred thousand bucks in his pocket.

Pin money, to a man who owned a couple of dozen oil wells. A fortune to her, and he knew it.

He figured she'd leap at it like a dog jumping for a bone.

Bzzz bzzz bzzz.

The flunky was impatient. Megan's eyes narrowed. Right. So was she. How many times did a woman have to say "no?"

The almighty prince needed a lesson. What better than to see his check shredded into as many bits as there were raindrops pattering against the roof? Even a thick-skulled despot would get that message.

Bzzz bzzz bzzz bzzz.

Megan grabbed a pair of scissors from a pottery jug filled with kitchen tools and hurried to the door. Bristling with anger, she flung it open.

"Doing your master's bidding, are you, Mr. Hakim? Okay. It's time I showed you and him what he can do with—with—"

Her eyes widened. It wasn't Hakim on the tiny porch.

"Such a warm greeting," the sheikh said. His gaze fell to the scissors clutched in her hand. A wry smile tilted across his mouth. "Do your always greet your guests with shears in your hand?"

"What the hell are you doing here?"

"At the moment, I'm standing in the rain."

"You know what I mean. How did you get my address?"

"I'll be happy to answer your questions, Miss O'Connell, but not while I'm drowning."

She almost laughed at the sight of the man standing beneath the steady stream of water pouring from the sagging rain gutter. Her landlord had ignored her complaints about it.

Now, she was glad he had.

"Consider it a bonus for turning up unannounced," she

said sweetly. "What's the matter? Don't you trust your henchman with your money?"

"You're wrong about Hakim."

"And you're wrong in thinking I've changed my mind about taking your bribe."

Good. That sent a little shot of color into his face. "I haven't come here to offer you money, Miss O'Connell."

"And I'm not going to let you in. So, goodbye, your highness. Seems to me, that concludes our bus—"

"We have things to discuss."

"You're wrong. It's late, and you have nothing to say that would interest me."

"It is late, yes. As for what I might say that would change your mind…" Caz took a deep breath. "How about, 'I was wrong?'"

"Look, your highness… What did you say?"

Caz cleared his throat. A little while ago, he'd thought nothing could taste as bad as the bitterness of the food he'd eaten with Frank Fisher. He'd been wrong. Humble pie tasted a hell of a lot worse.

"Wrong about what?"

"I may have misjudged you." Wrong choice of words. He saw her reaction in her eyes. "All right," he said quickly, I *did* misjudge you. Now, do you think you could stand aside and let me step into your living room before I go down for the third time?"

He smiled, but he didn't mean it. Megan could see the banked anger in his eyes. What had happened? Why was he here?

There was only one way to find out. She stepped back and motioned him inside.

"You have five minutes."

"Thank you."

The "thank you" had all the sincerity of a cobra thanking a mouse for agreeing to dinner. What was going on here?

"Do you think you could put those scissors aside?"

"Why?" Megan smiled thinly. "Do they make you nervous?"

"Perhaps we can sit down, like civilized people."

"Me at your feet?"

"Miss O'Connell. I understand that you're angry—"

"Me?" Megan slammed the door, strode past Qasim and tossed the scissors on a table. "Don't be silly. What possible reason would I have for being angry?"

"I suppose I should have called first."

"Yes, you should. You'd have saved yourself a trip." She folded her arms. Her heart was beating as fast as a hummingbird's wings. Well, why wouldn't it? It surely had nothing to do with the way he looked, tall and incredibly handsome with drops of rain glittering like diamonds in his dark hair. "What's the problem, your highness? Why would you possibly think you'd misjudged me?" She smiled tightly. "Last I saw, you and your flunky had me all figured out."

"Hakim isn't anybody's flunky. He's an old and trusted friend."

"Friends don't click their heels and salute."

"Hakim does neither."

"A matter of opinion."

"A matter of fact." Caz ground his teeth together. Why was he letting her sidetrack him? Bad enough he'd had to beg to come in out of the rain, that he was going to have to plead for forgiveness. Did he have to take this woman's insults, too?

Yes, he thought glumly, he did. He was, as the Americans said, stuck between a rock and a hard place. Megan O'Connell had an attitude problem. Thanks to her employer's duplicity, he was going to have to get used to dealing with it.

Caz forced a smile to his lips.

"I haven't come to talk about Hakim."

"No?"

"No. As I said, I came to tell you I misjudged you."

Her eyes flashed. "Stop dancing around the subject, your highness. Say what you mean."

"I had dinner with Frank Fisher."

"And? What's the problem. Did Frank eat his peas with a spoon?"

He took a quick step forward. Megan's breath caught, but she stood her ground.

"I warn you," he said softly, "I'm not in a good mood."

"Good. Neither am I. I take it your meal didn't go well."

"It was fine, until I began discussing the proposal." Caz's eyes darkened. "Mr. Fisher tried to change the subject."

Megan folded her arms. "I'll bet he did."

"I was persistent, at which point he excused himself and went to the men's room." Caz smiled coldly. "He went to the men's room a number of times over the next few minutes."

"Ah. Well, maybe the food you'd eaten didn't agree with him."

"The conversation didn't agree with him. The last time he left the table, I followed him. He didn't go to the men's room, Miss O'Connell, he went to make a phone call. In fact, I'm sure he'd made several phone calls." He shot a pointed look at the blinking light on Megan's answering machine. "But the person he was trying to reach wasn't home...or wasn't interested in taking his calls."

"Why don't I save us both some time, Sheikh Qasim? You wanted to talk about the Suliyam proposal. Frank didn't. Maybe I should say he couldn't, because he doesn't know the first thing about it.''

''That's correct. And after some pointed questioning, he told me everything. That you'd written it, not he. That Simpson had promised you'd stay in the States and feed him whatever information he might need.''

''And that it wasn't going to happen, because I wouldn't play along.''

''Yes.''

''And when Frank came clean, you realized you had a problem. You've got a complex plan to deal with, and nobody who understands it.''

''That's an oversimplification but, yes, that's the bottom line.''

''Well, Frank's a quick study.'' Megan smiled coldly. ''It shouldn't take him more than, oh, two or three years to figure things out.''

''I'm sure you think that's amusing,'' Caz said, even more coldly, ''but I'm returning to my country tomorrow. There's no time for Fisher to figure things out—even if he could, which I doubt.''

''And you want me to save your bacon.''

Caz ground his teeth together. Thank God she'd said it, because he doubted if he could.

''Yes.''

Megan smiled. ''No.''

''What do you mean, no? Your company wrote this thing. We have a contract—''

''And you have Frank Fisher.'' She started past him, toward the door. ''Good night, Sheikh Qasim. I wish I could say I'm sorry to see you sweat, but—''

Caz caught hold of her and spun her toward him. ''All right,'' he said in a low voice, ''that's it. I've had enough.''

''And so have I.'' Megan's voice trembled with suppressed anger. "If you think I'm going to go along with you and Simpson, that I'm going to sit by a phone here in Los Angeles and feed information to Frank Fisher—"

"Fisher is out of the picture," Caz snapped.

"Try telling that to Jerry Simpson!"

"I already did. That's how I got your address."

"And I'm telling you again, you've wasted your time. I will not let Frank use my work, my ideas, my—"

"Damn it, woman, will you shut up and let me talk? I'm offering you the job!"

That did it. For the first time since he'd met her, Megan O'Connell was speechless. She just stared at him, eyes wide with shock, hair loose in a froth of autumn-colored curls, face scrubbed free of makeup.

He remembered what he'd tried to forget. That kiss. The taste. The feel of her in his arms, of her lips parted to his...

"The job?"

Caz cleared his throat. "The job you were supposed to have, as my financial consultant. Will you accept?"

Would she accept? Her career had just done a 180, and the man was asking if she'd accept!

"You'd still be working for Tremont, Burnside and Macomb at your regular salary arrangement, but I'd add a bonus."

"Really," she said, hoping she sounded casual.

Caz named a figure. Megan decided it was a good thing he was still holding her arm or she might have fainted with shock.

"Is that satisfactory, Miss O'Connell?"

It was wild, not satisfactory, but she wasn't going to let him off that easy.

"You offered more when you thought you could buy me off."

He nodded. "Very well. One hundred thousand dollars. Will that do?"

"It will," she said, as if that much money fell into her lap every day.

"Good." He hesitated. "There's just one problem."

"What problem?"

"The status of women in the traditional culture of my country."

"You mean, their status in your eyes."

"That isn't what I said."

"You are Suliyam, your highness. You made that clear this morning. All you have to do is wave your scepter and change their status."

"It isn't that simple, damn it! I—"

He what? He was a master at international diplomacy, but how could he explain the culture of his forefathers to a fiery American redhead? She'd never understand it, even if he had the time, and he didn't. He was expected home tomorrow.

"If you expect me to help you, you're going to have to accept the fact that I'm a woman."

Accept it? Caz narrowed his eyes. He was painfully aware of it, even more so now that he was standing close to her, inhaling a faint lemony fragrance that reminded him of the orchards at Khaliar in midsummer.

"I can accept it," he said carefully. "However, despite your view of me, Miss O'Connell, I can't change centuries of tradition in my country overnight."

"Then how can you offer me a job?"

She wasn't going to like this, and he knew it. "There's only one solution. I'll openly acknowledge you as my consultant in-house, at Tremont, Burnside and Macomb. In financial circles in general, if you wish." He cleared his throat. "But we'll adhere to Simpson's plan. Fisher will fly to Suliyam with me, you'll stay here and—"

"No."

"I'll double your bonus."

"I said no."

"Miss O'Connell—"

Megan folded her arms and began tapping her foot. Not a good sign, Caz thought uneasily. He remembered that from the morning.

"You really have a problem with that word," she said coldly. "Must be a cultural thing. Here, in the States, 'en oh' means—"

"I know what it means," Caz said, trying hard to sound reasonable, "but these are special circumstances."

"You're right. You want me to help you perpetuate a lie."

"How much clearer can I be? I'll have to take the proposal to my people. I'll need Fisher beside me."

"What good would Frank do if he had to do his running-to-the-bathroom routine each time someone asked a question?"

It was an excellent point, one Caz had been doing his best to ignore.

"No good at all," Megan said without waiting for him to answer. "Your choice, your highness. Me, or nobody."

It wasn't a choice. Caz knew that. He'd known it ever since he'd unmasked Fisher.

"Well? Do I go to Suliyam or don't I?"

"You drive a hard bargain," Caz said coldly.

"Is that a yes?"

"Assuming it is, you'll have to put up with some things you won't like."

Megan wanted to pump her fist in the air. Instead she smiled politely.

"I put up with today, didn't I?"

"For example, you can't walk beside me in public."

She wanted to laugh. Not walk beside him? "No problem," she said, pleased at the sincerity in her tone.

"You can't talk to me when we're with others. You'll direct your comments to Hakim, who will then repeat them to me."

"I can manage that." Another lie, but once she was in Suliyam, he'd see how wrong he was to think a man could keep a woman living in the ancient past.

He hesitated. "And there's one last thing..."

Megan lifted her eyebrows. "Yes?"

"But this one is strictly my problem, not yours."

"Well, what is it?"

Caz moved quickly, as he'd done in the morning. She knew what was going to happen, knew it in the sudden race of her heart as he clasped her shoulders and lifted her to her toes.

"I'll have to find a way to keep my hands off you," he said thickly, and crushed her mouth beneath his.

CHAPTER FIVE

HER mouth was warm as the sun and sweet as the flowers that grew in the gardens of his palace.

And welcoming.

So welcoming.

Caz felt as if he were sinking into the kiss.

There was no pretence this time. He saw her eyes widen in shock but the instant his lips brushed hers, she sighed, leaned into him and opened her mouth to his.

She wanted him as badly as he wanted her.

There was no way to pretend, not when he was holding her so close to him that he could hardly tell where his body ended and hers began. She was clinging to him, her arms wound around his neck, her breasts lush against his chest, her thighs hot against his.

The room, the world, everything but the woman in his arms, spun away. Caz whispered her name, slid his hands into the glorious mass of autumn curls that was her hair. He tilted her head back, exposed the long line of her throat to his kisses.

She moaned as he nipped her flesh with his teeth, then soothed the tiny wound with his tongue, and when he sought her mouth again she moved against him, a shift of her hips so that her pelvis thrust against his straining erection.

Caz groaned, slid his knee between hers and cupped her bottom. She made a wild little sound that sent a fierce surge of pleasure coursing through his blood.

He could have her now, and reality be damned.

"Please," she whispered against his mouth, "please…"

He put his hands under her sweatshirt and finally felt her naked skin against his questing palms. Felt the velvet-softness of her breasts, the delicate pearling of her nipples. He danced the tips of his fingers across that sweetly ruched flesh and she moaned.

There was a roaring in his ears. Now, it said, now…

But it was only the incessant ringing of the telephone.

They sprang part and stared at each other, her eyes wide with astonishment, his breathing ragged, and then his cell phone rang again and he swore viciously as he tore it from his pocket and put it to his ear.

"What?" he barked.

It was Hakim, calling about the orders Caz had given for their departure the next morning.

The words meant nothing. All he could think about was what had just happened, what would have happened if not for this call. He'd have made love to a woman he hardly knew, barely trusted…

He could read the same shocked realization in her face. It was drained of color except for two bright spots of crimson high on her cheeks and the soft pink of her mouth, swollen from the passion of his kisses. He wanted to say something reassuring, but what could a man say to a woman he'd almost ravished?

He liked women, liked the pleasures of mutual seduction. The teasing conversation. The brush of hands. The glances that said more than words, all of it leading to an inevitable culmination.

What he'd just shared with this woman wasn't that at all. They'd come together without any of the niceties of seduction. All that had mattered was the swift, hot rush of passion, the primitive need to taste, touch, possess.

He saw Megan's throat constrict as she swallowed. Then she turned her back to him and wrapped her arms around herself.

Was she trembling?

Hakim was still talking, droning on and on about the minuscule details of tomorrow's agenda. Reports to review, memos to dictate, all the things Caz had asked to be reminded of before the flight home but right now, he didn't give a damn for any of it.

All he could think about was what had happened. What *would* happen, if he went through with his plan to take Megan with him. She was a distraction he couldn't afford...but even now, with the scent of her still in his nostrils, he managed to summon enough reason to know he couldn't afford to leave her behind, either. Not if his plans for his country were to succeed.

There was only one solution, he thought, and interrupted his aide in midsentence.

"A change of plans, Hakim. Mr. Fox won't be going with us tomorrow. You will send a car for Miss O'Connell, instead."

"You are taking the woman with you, Sheikh Qasim?"

The tone in Hakim's voice made Caz narrow his eyes. "I am."

"But a woman..."

"You will pick her up at seven."

"My lord. Surely you do not intend to—"

"Hakim. Surely *you* do not intend to question me." Caz spoke harshly. It was deliberate. No one questioned his orders. That was more than tradition; it was the law. It would change someday—it had to, if Suliyam were to flourish in these new times—but his aide's reaction to learning that Megan would return with them was only a small taste of what lay ahead. It had to be stopped, and quickly. "I gave you an order. You will obey it."

A beat of silence. A clearing of the throat. Then, at last, acquiescence. "Yes, my lord."

"There are things you will do before morning," Caz said, and enumerated them.

"I will see to everything."

"I'm sure you—"

"Tell him not to bother."

Caz turned around. Megan glared at him, eyes hot with anger. So much for his thinking that what had happened had left her shaken. He glared right back at her.

"Be quiet," he hissed.

"I heard you telling your flunky to round up the things you think I'll need for this trip, and—"

Caz caught her wrist. "Silence!"

"You cannot talk to me that way! I'm not one of your servants. I don't take orders from—"

His hand closed over her mouth. Megan gasped, struggled, sank her teeth into his flesh. Caz winced at the pain but kept his voice steady as he spoke a few last words to Hakim before snapping the cell phone shut.

Then he let go of Megan.

A mistake, he thought grimly, as she came at him with both hands balled into fists. He caught her wrists again and tugged her hands behind her back.

"You insufferable son of a bitch!"

"I was in the middle of a conversation," he said coldly. "When I am, you are not to interrupt."

"You were in the middle of snapping out orders," she said, her face livid with fury, "and I'll interrupt whenever I please!"

"Not me," he said through his teeth. "Do you understand?"

"What I understand is that your boy doesn't have to bother rounding up those things you told him to buy."

Caz raised his eyebrows. "You won't need a portable computer?"

"No more than I'll need the printer and fax, or the files from my office. I'm not going with you."

"You are."

"No, I'm not. I'd sooner go to the jungle with Tarzan than to a—a backward pile of sand with someone like you."

Caz took a quick step toward her. "You are not to speak that way about my country or me."

"I'll speak any damned way I like, and if you grab me again, so help me, I'll scream!"

She would. He believed her. That was all he needed. It was another tabloid headline in the making.

"Listen to me, Megan. If you treat me with disrespect, you'll ruin what I'm trying to do."

"What's that? To be even more loathsome than you already are?"

"And you'll endanger yourself. My people will not tolerate such behavior toward me from anyone, especially a woman."

"Then it's a good thing I'll never meet your people."

Caz gritted his teeth. "We reached an agreement. You're going with me to Suliyam."

"In a pig's eye!"

"A most inelegant expression."

"I know others you'll like even less."

"My car will come for you at seven," he said, refusing to be side-tracked.

Her smile was deadly sweet. "You car will stand at the curb and turn to rust before I set foot inside it."

"We have an agreement," he said grimly.

"You already said that. To hell with your agreement!

Why any woman would be fool enough to do anything you say—"

"Is that who you are now? A woman?"

Megan cocked her head and looked at him through narrowed eyes. "What's that supposed to mean?"

"I just like to know who I'm dealing with, that's all. You've just said a woman would be a fool to do anything I say."

"She would be."

"A while ago, you made the point that you weren't a woman at all."

"Don't be ridiculous! I never said—"

"You claim to be a professional. A person whose only identity lies in those initials after her name. B.A. M.B.A. C.P.A."

"You left out C.F.P.," Megan said coldly. "Certified Financial Planner. And if you're trying to make a point, I can't figure out what it is."

"My point is that you take refuge in the identity that suits you at a given moment."

"You make me sound schizophrenic!"

"Do I?" Caz folded his arms. "When I met you this morning, you made a case for being judged by your ability, not your gender."

"Something you're incapable of, apparently."

"Are you suggesting what happened just now wasn't mutual?"

She felt herself turn color, but she kept her eyes on his. "I'm not going with you, Sheikh Qasim. That's final."

"You're making something out of nothing. What happened was a mistake."

"It certainly was. And it could never, ever, not in a million years, happen again."

"Another point of agreement. Which is why you're going with me tomorrow."

"I'd sooner—"

"Swing through the trees with Tarzan. Yes, I know, but then, you don't have a contract with Tarzan."

"I don't have one with you, either," Megan said, but even in her anger, she knew what he was getting at.

"You do. A verbal contract, enforceable in any court of law." He fleshed that I-Am-Brilliant smile that made her fingers itch to slap it from his face. "I'm sure you're aware of that, Miss O'Connell, considering your familiarity with what constitutes grounds for a lawsuit."

"You wouldn't sue." Megan flashed a smile that she hoped was the equal of his. "You wouldn't want the publicity."

"There's a difference between negative publicity and positive publicity. I'd get lots of excellent mileage out of my heartfelt attempts to hire a woman, only to find that woman unwilling to take on the responsibility of a difficult assignment."

"Your people wouldn't like to hear that you'd tried to hire a woman."

"My people will believe what I tell them, and I'll tell them that the press lies."

"I'd phone every newspaper, tell them what actually happened…"

"In that case, so would I. I don't think it would add much to your professional image if I described what went on in this room in intimate detail, do you?"

He smiled again. God, she hated that smile! It was so smug. How easily she could slap it from his face…but that wouldn't change the fact that he was right.

"I really, really despise you, Sheikh Qasim."

"A pity, Miss O'Connell. I was hoping you'd want to

head up my fan club.'' The tight smile vanished from his lips. ''Your boss has me backed into a corner, Megan. Like it or not, this job is yours by default.''

She glared at him. He glared back. He had her trapped, and he knew it.

''How long is this assignment going to last?''

Caz considered telling her the truth, then decided against it. She wouldn't want to hear that she might be expelled from Suliyam in a day, if things went badly, or that she might still be there months from now, if things went well.

''I don't know.'' That was the truth, more or less.

''A week.''

He shrugged his shoulders, as if he were considering the possibility.

''Two weeks is the longest I'll stay. Agreed?''

''Absolutely. Two weeks is the longest you wish to stay.'' That was the truth, too. Whose fault was it if she misinterpreted his answer? At least she wasn't fighting him anymore.

''Must I fly out tomorrow? That doesn't give me much time.''

''For what?'' Caz felt a knot form in his belly. ''If you think I'm going to delay my plans so you can say goodbye to a lover—''

''I have a family,'' Megan said coolly. ''I want to let them know where I'm going.''

''You can phone them from my plane,'' he said, and tried not to acknowledge the sense of relief he felt. Not that he cared about her personal life. She could have a dozen lovers, if she liked, so long as such commitments didn't impinge on her work for him.

''I suppose it would be foolish for me to think your Hakim can't buy computers and move files in the middle of the night.''

"You're right. It would be." Caz's smile was saccharine sweet. "There are some benefits to being a king." He shot back his cuff and checked his watch. "Any other questions?"

Megan almost laughed. She had more questions than she could count, beginning with why she'd ever wanted this assignment, but it was too late to ask them now.

"No, thank you," she said politely. "Not at the moment."

"One last thing. About the kinds of clothing you'll need to pack…"

"I'm a big girl, Sheikh Qasim. I don't need you to tell me what to do."

Caz had to admire her. She was beautiful, stubborn, defiant…and most definitely unimpressed by his titles or his wealth.

No wonder he found her desirable.

She was completely different from any of the women he'd been involved with. His lovers were invariably beautiful, invariably bright—despite what this American clearly thought of him, he'd always found unintelligent women dull.

But no woman ever disagreed with him, much less spoke to him with such boldness. No matter their nationality, they were always eager to please.

Not Megan O'Connell.

And, of course, that was the reason for the attraction. Knowing it didn't change things, but it would definitely make it easier to resist. Caz felt a weight lift from his shoulders.

"I was only going to point out that the desert can be as cool at night as it is hot during the day," he said pleasantly, "but let's not quarrel over it." He held out his hand. She looked at it for a long moment, then put her palm against his. Heat, almost enough to burn his palm, seemed to flash from that innocent contact point straight to his groin. He was sure she felt something, too, if only because of her quick intake of breath, but he forced a smile to his lips. "To a successful collaboration, Miss O'Connell."

"To one that ends quickly, Sheikh Qasim."

Her expression was defiant. He thought about pulling her into his arms again and changing that insolent look to a look of passion, but sanity prevailed.

"Good night, Megan."

"Good night, Qasim."

His brows lifted but he didn't say anything. Still, as he stepped into the damp night, he laughed softly to himself. She was, as the Americans would say, some piece of work. Calling him by his given name. No honorific, no title... It was, he supposed, her way of making sure he knew she wasn't impressed.

Caz turned up his collar, slipped behind the wheel of his Lamborghini and turned the ignition key.

These next weeks would be interesting, but they wouldn't last forever. Someday, they would meet on different terms, he as a man, she as a woman. When they did, he'd put an end to all this nonsense. He'd take her to bed and keep her there until she begged for mercy, until the both of them sated their hunger and grew weary of each other.

He pulled away from the curb, his headlights boring into the darkness of the California night.

Someday, he'd have all of Megan O'Connell he wanted.

But not yet.

CHAPTER SIX

WHAT did you pack for a trip to a place that was still a mystery to the world?

Megan phoned Briana. Her sister wasn't in, so she left a message on her voice mail.

Hi, Bree. I'm leaving for a place called Suliyam tomorrow early in the A.M. Details when I get back but boy, I wish you were there. Maybe you could help me figure out what to pack. Anyway, hope you're having fun. Talk to you in a week or two.

Sighing, she headed for the bedroom, flung open the door to the closet and stared inside. Bree had more stamps and visas on her passport than any of them except, maybe, Sean. But the odds were that not even Bree could have advise her on what was right for this trip.

Maybe she should have listened to Qasim when he'd tried to give her advice, but she'd been so furious with him by then that listening to anything he had to say was beyond her.

Don't cut off your nose to spite your face, her mother would have warned, just as she had years ago when Megan was fourteen and moaning over the fact that nobody had asked her to a school dance. Fallon, a stunner at sixteen with boys tripping over each other in efforts to please her, had volunteered one of them as an escort.

"Tommy says he'd love to take you, Meg," she'd said.

"He just wants to score points with you."

"Maybe," Fallon had said cheerfully. "But he's cute, he's nice, and you'll have fun."

"No, I won't. Tell him to forget about it."

Megan spent the night of the dance at home, looking sad and hoping for pity from her mother. Instead Mary had told her to stop sulking, followed by that no-nonsense advice about the folly of refusing something you really wanted, just to make a point.

Megan sighed and sank down on the edge of her bed.

Good counsel then. Great counsel now. Too bad she hadn't been ready to admit it an hour ago.

She knew a bit about Suliyam's culture, a lot about its finances and natural resources, thanks to her research, but that was it. What was the weather like, this time of year? What was its capital city like, and was that where they were going? What sort of hotel would she be in?

And what about that comment Qasim had made, that she wouldn't be able to speak to him when they met with his people? He'd sounded dead serious. Not that it mattered. She'd change that first thing. There'd been no sense in saying so because it would just have led to a quarrel and that was all they'd done since they met.

Well, no. They'd done more than that. They'd turned each other on with a touch.

That last kiss had been enough to turn her inside out. It didn't make sense. Qasim wasn't her type.

Megan rolled her eyes.

That was the understatement of the century. He was a king. A sheikh. A man tied to a past she could hardly imagine. Of course, he wasn't he wasn't her type.

Was that why they were so drawn to each other? Was it the old "opposites attract" thing? He was undoubtedly accustomed to women who didn't think for themselves; she dated men who treated women as equals. She'd never met a man who went through life taking what he wanted until today.

His attitude was infuriating. It was irritating.

It was incredibly exciting.

Soon, she'd be alone with him in a foreign land with none of the intrusions of the world to keep them from what they both wanted and yes, it was what she wanted, too. Qasim in her bed, his hands on her, his mouth…

Megan shot to her feet.

They wouldn't be alone, they'd be working. An employer and his employee. Better still, a financial advisor and her client. There'd be no time for the male-female thing. Why was she sitting around thinking about nonsense? She had to pack, and why was she giving a moment's thought to *what* to pack?

For all she knew, woman in Qasim's country wore potato sacks. So what? She wore suits, sensible heels, and panty hose. Why on earth would she change that? Why would she change anything about herself for this job or this man?

Megan took her suitcase from the shelf and began tossing garments into it.

She knew who she was.

Soon, so would the sheikh.

Three days later, sitting in her rooms in Qasim's palace, she wondered at the innocence of that assessment.

Who was she? A woman in a harem, that was who. All right. Not a harem. She was in the women's quarters, but it came to the same thing.

It turned out there was no hotel in Suliyam's capital city. Qasim had explained that as they'd been whisked from the airport to his palace.

She had to admit the palace was magnificent, gleaming under the hot sun like something out of a fairy tale. Her rooms were handsome: large, airy and elegant, with tiled floors and Moorish windows, and the view of a tranquil pond in a beautiful courtyard garden was to die for.

It was all perfect, except for the fact that she'd been relegated to the women's quarters.

"The what?" she'd said the first day, her voice rising in disbelief as Qasim led her along a series of corridors to a set of enormous double doors.

"The women's quarters, and keep your voice down. It's bad enough I'm permitting you to walk beside me where others can see us."

The arrogance of the remark had put a slow burn in her belly. And what "others" was he talking about? The bowing minions who'd greeted them on the front steps? The stony-faced guards who looked like leftovers from a bad late-night movie?

Megan had stopped in her tracks. "I don't give a damn about others, and I am not going to be relegated to purgatory just so you can maintain the status quo."

"You understood the rules when you came here."

"So did you. I'm your financial consultant, not a member of your harem."

He'd given a long-suffering sigh, as if her irritation were nothing more than he'd expected.

"I'm simply ensuring my people show you the necessary respect."

"And that means I have to live like Scheherazade? Next thing you'll tell me is that I'm going to have a eunuch around to make sure I behave!"

"Sorry," he'd said, so straight-faced that she'd almost believed him, "I fired the last eunuch a couple of months ago." His hand had closed on her elbow. "My grandfather was the last to keep a harem. Now, stop arguing and keep walking."

"You can't give me orders!"

His hand had tightened on her arm. "Use that tone to me again," he'd said in a low voice, "and you'll learn what purgatory really is."

"I already know. It's being here, with you."

"Is that supposed to upset me, Megan? It doesn't. I don't give a damn what you think of me or this place, just as long as you do your job." He'd opened the doors to the rooms that were now hers; a covey of giggling women had rushed forward to surround her. "Your servants," Qasim had said dryly, as if he knew being presented with servants would only add to her bad temper. While the ladies in question oohed and ahhed and touched her blue wool suit with exploratory hands, he'd bent forward and put his mouth to her ear so only she could hear him. "You want to know the truth, *kalila?* I think what angers you is that you know you'll be far away from me."

When pigs fly, she'd have told him, but the women had started trying to strip off her jacket and while she was fending them off, Qasim shut the doors and left her.

Now it was what she'd come to think of as Day Three of her Incarceration. She'd come all this distance to do her job, but she hadn't done a damned thing except pace her rooms and the garden outside.

And she'd had enough.

Megan shot to her feet, went out to the garden, opened the gate and marched down to the sea. The women rushed after her, crying out in distress. Apparently she wasn't supposed to leave her cage.

She ignored them.

At least she could breathe down here. Why had she tolerated such treatment? To come all this way only to be treated like a prisoner?

A sea bird called out overhead, but its cry offered no answers.

The situation was intolerable.

"Intolerable," Megan snapped.

She turned on her heel and retraced her steps back to the garden, to her rooms, to the double doors that she yanked open so she could march past the astonished guards while her women danced around her wringing their hands and wailing...

And stopped dead when she saw, just ahead, the Great Hall she remembered from the night of their arrival.

The Great Hall, and Qasim.

Qasim, and a woman.

A beautiful woman, even at a distance, petite and delicate with midnight-black hair that fell to her waist. Her gown was pale peach, so delicate it might have been spun from sunlight. She stood close to Qasim, bodies almost touching, her hands on his shoulders, her face turned up to his.

He's going to kiss her, Megan thought.

For the first time in her life, she understood what people meant when they said anguish could feel like a knife wound to the heart.

She must have made a sound because Qasim turned and saw her. She waited, unmoving. He would say something. Do something. Acknowledge her presence, come to her and explain that what she saw—what she thought she saw—was nothing.

Instead, he turned back to the woman, brought her hands to his mouth, put his arm around her waist and led her up a wide staircase. Led her to his bed. Where else would a man take a woman who looked at him with stars in her eyes?

Megan's servants surrounded her, scolding and tut-tutting and tugging at her hands. She let them lead her back to her rooms but when the doors closed behind her, she tore free of them, cursing Qasim and her own stupidity for being upset over something that should never have upset her, ranting in words that probably would have surprised her brothers.

The women watched her, wide-eyed, whispering among themselves and keeping their distance which, for some stupid reason, only increased her fury. Finally she snatched up a small porcelain vase and hurled it at the wall.

That got her audience moving.

"La, la," one said while another wagged her finger. It didn't take a genius to figure out that meant "no," but "no" wasn't going to work.

Qasim had ignored her here for three endless days, all so he could play games with another woman.

Enough. She'd come here to do a job. If she wasn't going to do it, she was going to go home.

Megan stormed to the doors and yanked them open. The guards looked at her as if she were the last person on earth they ever wanted to see again.

"I want to see the king. Damn it, don't look at me as if you're both deaf. Surely one of you understands what I'm saying. I want to see your precious sheikh. Qasim. Do you hear me? You are to take me to—"

"Good afternoon, Miss O'Connell."

The guards snapped to attention, then parted to reveal Hakim. Her serving women gasped and fell to the floor around her, doubled over like plump, silk-swathed hassocks.

"Stand up," Megan snapped, "you shouldn't kneel to any man!"

The women didn't move. They had no idea what she was saying but Hakim did. His eyes were cold as he clapped his hands and barked out a command that sent the women scuttling away.

"It is unwise to interfere in matters you don't comprehend, Miss O'Connell."

"Take me to your king."

"That is why I've come. His highness wishes to see you."

"It's a damned good thing he does."

"My lord does not like his women to use rough language."

"Then it's a good thing I'm not his woman. Where is he?"

"He waits for me to bring you to him."

God, the man was insufferable! Almost as arrogant as Qasim but then, Qasim probably wouldn't employ him otherwise. They started toward the Great Hall. Halfway there, Megan swept past the aide. Walking behind him, even if he were leading her somewhere, infuriated her.

She could hardly wait to confront Qasim. She'd tell the mighty Pooh-Bah what she thought of him, his harem, his servants and his country. Then she'd give him a choice. Put her to work or send her home. She'd be damned if she'd spend another day feeling useless while he did who knew what...

While he took a woman with long black hair to his bed.

They reached the Great Hall. Megan started toward the stairs. Hakim stepped in front of her.

"My lord waits for you outside."

"Your lord," Megan mimicked coldly.

Hakim's eyes flashed as she brushed past him. The guards at the huge entrance doors flung the doors wide. Megan stepped out into the sunlight, clattered down the steps...and stopped.

A Humvee stood in the curved driveway, engine purring, rear door open. Qasim stood next to it, Qasim dressed in white linen trousers and a white linen shirt with the sleeves rolled back, so beautiful, so desert-fierce with the sun beating down on his dark head that she felt her bones turn liquid.

A smile curved his lips as she started down the steps, and she remembered how those lips had felt against hers, how the hand he held out had felt against her breast the last time they'd been together.

"Megan," he said, and the truth shot through her quicksilver, the realization that part of her anger, all of it, lay in knowing that he hadn't come to her, come for her, and in knowing now that it was because he had someone else.

How could she have hidden that truth from herself? How could she want a man like him?

Her heart turned to stone. She'd never been a fool for a man and she'd be damned if she'd start now.

She took a breath, let it out and took another. Then, smiling, she went down the steps. When she reached him, she put her hand in his. He started to raise it to his lips but she remembered that scene a little while ago, the woman a breath from him, her hands against his mouth, and she pulled her hand down and gave him a vigorous handshake.

"Sheikh Qasim," she said politely. "It's good to see you. I'd started to think you'd changed your mind about working with me."

One dark eyebrow rose in a questioning arch. "Certainly not. In fact…" He motioned to the open door of the Hummer. "We're on our way to our first meeting this morning."

"I'm glad to hear it, but you might have done me the courtesy of telling me so in advance."

"My apologies," he said, climbing into the Hummer after her. He closed the door, tapped lightly on a glass partition that separated them from the driver and the vehicle shifted gears and started forward. "I've been busy."

"Yes. So I noticed."

He looked at her. "Sorry?"

"Nothing." She looked down at her skirt and smoothed it over her knees. "I want to talk about the rooms you've given me."

"Aren't they to your liking?"

"No, they're not. They're very handsome, but I resent being kept prisoner."

He'd looked uneasy a minute ago. Now, he sat back and laughed.

"The women's quarters are hardly a prison."

"They are to me. I came here to work. Instead I've spent my time doing nothing in an isolated part of the palace."

"I'm sorry about that, too. Some things came up that had to be dealt with."

"Yes. So I noticed."

She wanted to bite off her tongue, but it was too late.

"Am I missing something here, Megan?"

"Only that I'd like to get busy on our project."

"Of course. And since today seems to be my day for apologies, let me make one more. I should have explained why I put you in the women's quarters. It was for your own sake. I wanted to be sure my people understand our relationship. You're unmarried, you see, and a foreigner."

"And?"

"And, it's important we avoid any hint of impropriety."

"Ah. Then I take it that the woman I saw you with a little while ago is married as well as Suliyamese, or that you don't give a damn about any hints of impropriety where she's concerned."

Qasim looked surprised. Dear God, so was she! Had she really said something so stupid? His eyes darkened; they locked on hers and she felt a flood of heat rise in her face.

"I'm only asking as a matter of curiosity," she said stiffly. "You keep telling me about all these customs and traditions..."

"Alayna is one of us, yes."

One of us. Who was he kidding? The lady was more than that.

"But she isn't married."

"I see. In other words, it's all right for you to be seen with an unmarried woman as long as that woman isn't me?"

Qasim looked at her for an endless few seconds. Then he gave her a slow, sexy grin. "Are you jealous, *kalila?*"

"Certainly not. I told you, I'm just—"

"Curious." He sighed, as if a weight were on his shoulders, and his smile faded. "Alayna is my cousin."

His cousin. That gorgeous creature was his cousin. Why did she feel such a sense of relief? Qasim could have a dozen beautiful women around him, for all she cared.

"I would have introduced you, but Alayna has some personal problems just now. That was why she came to see me. To discuss them."

"You don't have to explain."

Qasim reached for her hand. She let him take it—it would have been ridiculous to try and tug it back—and tried to pretend she didn't feel the rush of heat his touch sent racing along her skin.

"I should not have neglected you these past days, Megan. It's just that I had many things to attend to."

Things like assuring Alayna that he would find a way to keep her from having to marry a man who had been chosen for her, that she could, instead, marry a man she loved. That, alone, had involved him for two days. And, after that, the careful plans he'd made for the first meeting he and Megan would attend had started coming apart.

It would be the most difficult of the meetings because it involved Ahmet, one of the most powerful traditionalists in Suliyam. Caz had arranged to meet with Ahmet and his men here, in the palace, to make no mention of Megan's presence beforehand.

But Ahmet had phoned yesterday to say he'd fallen ill and couldn't travel. Would Qasim bring the meeting to him, at his ancestral home deep in the mountains beyond the vast desert that stretched away from the sea?

"It would be a generous thing to do, my lord," Ahmet had said in a wheezing voice.

The wheeze struck Caz as overdone. He suspected the suggestion had less to do with illness and more to do with a power play, but going to Ahmet instead of demanding the man come to him was a gesture of respect that could help his cause.

The change in venue meant he'd had to tell Ahmet he was bringing a woman with him.

Ahmet had responded with outrage and disbelief. "How could such a thing be?" he'd said.

Caz had lied through his teeth. The woman was a clerk, he told him, sent by the company she worked for to keep their records organized. It was, he added, customary for western firms to employ females in positions too unimportant to be filled by men.

"Ah." Ahmet had chuckled. "Now I see. She is a meaningless creature."

"Absolutely," Qasim had answered, though he'd wanted to laugh. Megan O'Connell, meaningless? Wouldn't she love to hear that? She wouldn't; he wasn't stupid.

As for the traditions she'd encounter on this journey… Caz looked at her now, sitting beside him in the Hummer, dressed in that ridiculous wool suit and sensible pumps, and almost groaned.

If she thought the arrangements at his palace were restrictive, he could only guess at how she'd react to life in the territory ruled by Ahmet.

He felt a vague sense of unease, taking her on this trip, but if she behaved herself, things would go well. And he'd see to it she behaved herself, like it or not.

He wasn't looking forward to dealing with what came next. He'd always thought of himself as fearless. After all, death came to every man eventually. Why quake when a lion decides you look like dinner, which had happened to him on a photographic safari in South Africa? Why run when an assassin came at you out of the dark, as one had in the uncertain days after his father's death?

The trouble was, dealing with lions and assassins was easier than dealing with the temper of the woman beside him. So far, the only way he'd found to deal with her anger was to take her in his arms, and that was proving more dangerous than anything he'd ever done before.

"Are you going to tell me where we're going, or is it another of your deep, dark secrets?"

She had a half smile on her lips. Apparently she'd decided to forgive him. Too bad the smile wasn't going to last.

"We're driving to my helicopter."

"Your what?"

She was still smiling, but she was also looking at him as if he'd lost his mind. Maybe he had.

"It would take days to make the trip by land. It's only a couple of hours by air." He hesitated. "Megan. This place we're going to… You'll have to make some accommodations."

She gave a little sigh, but she wasn't angry. Not yet. "What now? Won't walking behind you be enough?"

"We're flying into an ancient city. Tradition—"

"Don't tell me." She flashed that smile again. "If you expect me to fold myself in half and bow—"

"That might not be a bad idea," he said. She shot him a look that made him laugh. "I'm joking. But…" His gaze drifted over her, then returned to her face. "You can't enter Ahmet's lands dressed like that."

The smile flickered. "Ahmet's a fashion maven?"

"You must wear what he thinks is appropriate for a woman as a sign of respect."

The smile died. Caz sighed; trouble lay directly ahead.

"And what would you like me to wear, Sheikh Qasim? Sackcloth and ashes?"

"The women of his village dress traditionally."

"There's that word again."

"Caftans, slit at the ankles," Caz said, refusing to be drawn into a battle. "Sandals."

"Shackles, too?"

"Did you never hear the saying, 'When in Rome…'"

"Roman women had more status than they do here."

"That's changing."

Megan folded her arms. "Not that I can see!"

A muscle knotted in Caz's jaw. "Must you fight me over everything?" His voice hardened. "You insisted you were the right person for this job. Are you?"

She swung toward him, ready to take him on, but the look on his face stopped her. Besides, he was right. Why wave a red flag in front of a bull? It just made her uneasy to give up her western suit for a caftan, and wasn't that silly? She'd still be the same woman…

She would, wouldn't she?

"Megan?"

Reluctantly she nodded. "Yes. All right. If I have to—"

"Good. I've told my driver to stop just before we reach the helipad. He'll set up a small tent. You can use it as a dressing room." Caz hesitated. "There's one other thing."

"Now what?"

"I've explained that you're a clerk."

Her eyes widened. She looked, he thought, as if he'd slapped her.

"Are you crazy? I am not going to let you pass me off as—"

She gasped as he reached out and caught her by the shoulders.

"What do you want them to think, damn it? In their world, there's only one reason a man would take a woman with him on such a trip."

"I have three degrees," she said, knowing how foolish she sounded, knowing, too, that she could not, would not let him relegate her to the role he'd clearly intended for her all along. "I will not—"

"You will do as you're told. Or—"

"Stop threatening me! You won't send me back home. You can't." Her eyes were bright with challenge. "You need me, Qasim, and you know it."

"You're right," he said through clenched teeth. "I need you here, but there's another solution." Heat slammed through his blood as he pulled her into his arms. "I'll simply let them think you belong to me."

His mouth claimed hers. She struggled, but only for the time it took him to nip her bottom lip and slide his tongue into her mouth. Then she made a little sound of surrender and arched against him, returning his kisses, crying out when he put his hand under her jacket, cupped her breast, felt the nipple rise and thrust against his palm.

He let her go so abruptly that she fell back in the seat. He had to; otherwise, he knew he'd have pushed up her skirt, freed himself, taken her, taken her, taken her...

She stared at him, her eyes bright with angry tears.

"I despise you," she whispered, and Caz decided that made a lot of sense because right now, he despised himself, too.

CHAPTER SEVEN

THE helicopter flew over a land that was as untamed as it was beautiful.

Undulating waves of golden sand. Vivid patches of dark green, guarding sapphire-blue pools of water. A vulture with black-tipped wings, soaring in lazy circles and once, most startling of all, a herd of horses galloped under the dark shadow of the 'copter as it passed over them.

Megan had questions about the land, the animals that lived on it, the village they were flying to, but there was no one to ask. Qasim sat across from her in icy removal, reading papers he'd taken from his briefcase as soon as they'd boarded.

She was on her own.

Well, that was fine with her. She had her own notes to read through, and any questions she had about where they were going would be answered soon enough. For a little while, she lost herself in facts and figures, but they began to blur and, finally, she closed her notebook and put it away.

She couldn't concentrate. She was nervous, though she'd sooner have died than admit it.

What would it be like, this place where the customs of an earlier time prevailed? Where she'd have to pretend to be a docile creature with no opinions or thoughts of her own?

She'd been assigned a role. Like it or not she was already playing it. She looked down at the dress she now wore.

Qasim hadn't mentioned it would be spun of cotton so fine it felt like silk or that it would have tiny pale blue flowers embroidered along the cuffs and hem. The skirt was slit to the knee on each side; the neckline was a sort of modified cowl, so that it could be drawn up as a hood against the chill that settled in the mountains at night.

Megan wiggled her feet, bare in the soft-as-butter thong sandals. You couldn't very well wear stockings with a strip of leather between your toes.

Standing in the little tent Qasim's driver had erected, wearing these new things, she'd felt a funny hollowness in the pit of her stomach. She'd looked back at the little pile of clothing she'd discarded, her suit and blouse, her panty hose and shoes.

Was this how a wild creature felt when it left the safety of its old skin behind?

What would Qasim think, when he saw her?

That she looked like an obedient female, she'd thought, and that had been enough to make her stop thinking like a silly girl and think like the woman she was.

"Am I suitably dressed, oh Lord of the World?" she'd said coolly, stepping out of the tent.

Qasim's gaze had darkened and moved slowly over her.

"You'll do," he'd finally replied, and there'd been a huskiness in his voice that had made her want to go to him, frame his face with her hands, bring his mouth to hers and ask him what he really thought, if he liked the way the thin cotton clung to her breasts, to her hips...

Megan picked up her notes and went back to work.

Ahmet's mountain village wasn't a village at all.

It was a medieval fortress.

Stepping out of the helicopter, staring at the horsemen who'd come racing out the gates brandishing steel-tipped

lances, Megan shivered as the men let out a bloodcur-
dling roar.

Qasim caught hold of her hand. She didn't even think of
trying to pull away. Instead, she laced her fingers through
his and moved closer, until she was almost leaning against
him.

"They're honoring me," he whispered. "Don't be
afraid."

The horsemen stopped a hundred yards away. Silver bells
adorned their horses' bridles and played softly as the animals tossed their heads. The riders gave an eerie, ululating
cry and spurred their mounts into a gallop. Qasim gave her
hand one last squeeze. Then he stepped away from her,
laughing as the riders surrounded him in a river of horses
and spears. A man rode forward, leading a stallion with a
coat like black silk. Qasim grabbed the horse's flowing
mane and leaped into the saddle.

Another wild cry, and the horsemen galloped toward the
gates of the city.

The wind tossed Megan's hair over her eyes. Her hand
shook as she brushed it back; she could feel her heart racing.
She felt as if she'd been sucked up by a tornado and tossed
back through time. She wanted to turn and run, but where
would she go without Qasim?

She saw a small group of women coming toward her,
materializing like ghosts from the blowing dust left by the
horses. Their faces were stern and set in lines of distrust as
they gathered around her. One, perhaps the eldest, reached
out, fingered Megan's auburn hair and said something that
made the rest laugh.

It was the kind of laugh that sent a chill down Megan's
spine. She jerked her head away, took a deep breath and
fixed the woman with a steady look.

"My name is Megan," she said, "and I am with Sheikh Qasim."

Those words, she sensed, would be her only protection.

Two days later, Megan felt as if she were going crazy.

She hated this place, hated everyone who lived in it, hated Qasim for bringing her to it...

Hated herself, for having let him lead her into a nightmare.

She spent her days at meetings, playing the part of an obedient slave, and spent her nights in this room, pacing like a caged animal. The room was enormous, easily the size of her entire apartment back home. The walls were tiled, the floors carpeted. She supposed you could describe her surroundings as beautiful.

But it was still a cage.

Compared to this, the harem in Qasim's palace had been heaven with its little garden, its reflecting pool, the soft breeze that blew in from the sea.

Here, she had only the four walls that enclosed her. At day's end, Hakim walked her to the door and left her to the ministrations of a pair of sullen women who brought her evening meal—a glob of unidentifiable something on a chipped plate that looked as if it had never been washed, a pitcher of liquid that tasted like warm beer, and a hunk of flat, tasteless bread. The women never responded to Megan's attempts at communication.

Hakim wasn't much better. When she complained at her treatment, he assured her that his master understood her situation, but when she demanded to see Qasim, he looked horrified and told her such a thing was out of the question.

Was Hakim telling her the truth? Did Qasim know what was happening? She had no idea. He acted as if she were invisible.

When she entered the meeting room the first day, just seeing him lifted her spirits.

"Qasim," she'd said softly, but he'd looked right through her. He'd warned her, told her what would be expected, but surely he could at least make eye contact? Didn't he want to know how she was being treated?

Hakim had pointed to a low stool behind his master. Megan had bristled. Sitting behind Qasim was one thing; sitting four inches off the floor with her knees tucked under her chin was another.

But the room had begun filling with men; she'd felt all those dark eyes on her and suddenly the stool behind Qasim had seemed like an eminently fine idea. She'd settled on it, struggled to find a way to get her long legs under her and her briefcase in her lap while she told herself the meeting and their time in this horrible place would not last more than a day.

Wrong.

It was two days later and they were still here.

Some things, at least, had changed for the better.

Qasim still ignored her. But the women who waited on her had taken to offering occasional smiles. She'd demanded Hakim arrange for her to get some air and last night, the women had produced lanterns and taken her for an hour's walk along cobblestone streets that twisted and turned and ended, abruptly, at the city wall.

Some of the changes were for the worse.

Ahmet had taken to looking at her. None of the other men did, not after that first time. They treated her as Qasim did, as if she were invisible.

Not Ahmet.

Qasim had said Ahmet was too ill to travel, but he didn't appear ill to Megan. He looked—there was no other word for it—evil. Evil, and fat, and filthy. And yes, he was always sneaking glances at her. She caught him a couple of times but mostly, she sensed him watching her. His eyes were like tiny black beetles. She could almost feel them crawling over her skin.

Like right now.

Megan shuddered. Concentrate on what you're doing, she told herself. Forget Ahmet, forget everything but the numbers and words on the papers in her lap, and Qasim's questions.

What a ridiculous procedure this was.

Qasim would address his comments to Hakim in his own tongue and then in English, probably so she'd have more time to find the information. Then she had to look at Hakim, give her answer to him so he could repeat it to Qasim.

It was a waste of time, and all done for no purpose she could see. Qasim had been worried her presence would offend the super-macho males of his country but how could she offend them when they ignored her?

Ignored her, except for Ahmet.

He was watching her again. She could feel it. She looked up and stared straight at him, something she knew was forbidden, but enough was enough.

Megan narrowed her eyes and gave him her best Don't-Mess-With-Me glare. It always worked with idiots who thought a woman alone in a restaurant was just aching to be hit on...but it didn't work now. Ahmet's beady little eyes assessed her with even greater interest. His tongue came out and licked slowly over his fleshy lips.

Her heart did a terrified two-step. She dragged her gaze from his and looked down, blindly, at the papers in her lap.

So much for staring him down. And so much for handling this on her own. Qasim might not want to talk to her, but she sure as hell wanted to talk to—

"Ouch!"

Megan swung around. Had someone kicked her? She rubbed her hip and glared at the man nearest to her. He glared back, spat a couple of guttural words and answered the question by kicking her again. It wasn't much of a kick, it was more a prod with the tip of his booted foot, but it was the final straw.

"What the hell do you think you're doing?" she said as she shot to her feet.

The room, normally humming with conversation, became completely silent. All eyes were on her now, even Qasim's.

"Sit down," he said quietly.

"I will not sit down! This—this pig just kicked me."

Qasim's eyes darkened. "I will deal with him later. For now, you must sit down."

"This is a horrible place." Megan's voice trembled as her anger gave way to the fear it disguised. "I want to leave. I want—"

"Sit!" Qasim roared.

She sank down on the stool, shaken and shaking. She sensed him glaring at her. Then he said something and everyone laughed.

She'd had never felt so alone in her life.

After a moment, Qasim cleared his throat. She heard the rustle of papers, the drone of his voice as the meeting continued, but she wasn't listening. Why had she ever agreed to his demands? He'd turned her into a woman she didn't know, brought her to a place where civilization didn't exist, abandoned her to the less-than-tender mercies of a gang of cutthroats...

"Miss O'Connell!"

She looked up. Hakim's face was like stone.

"My lord the Sheikh asked a question."

"I didn't... What question?"

"I will ask him to repeat it."

"Just tell me what it was."

"There is a procedure to follow," Hakim said coldly. "You will follow it."

He turned away from her to start the entire roundabout process again. Now she was supposed to sit patiently while Hakim posed a question to Qasim, wait again while Qasim replied in English, then in his own tongue. After that, she'd sit here docilely while Hakim repeated words she already understood. Then, only then, would she be permitted to speak.

To hell with that.

The English words were hardly out of Qasim's mouth when she replied to them.

For a second time, an awful silence filled the room. The men gave her startled, condemning glances.

Ahmet looked straight at her.

Megan had never had a man look at her that way, but the meaning was clear as glass. It sent a chill straight to the marrow of her bones.

She dragged her eyes from his and struggled to stay calm. All right. She'd made a mistake. Two of them, in one morning. She'd be more cautious from now on. When in Rome, Qasim had said, and he was right. Surely she could manage that for another couple of—

A hand closed on her wrist. She looked up, straight into Ahmet's ugly face. He grinned, revealing rotting teeth and revolting breath.

"May-gahn."

"Yes?" she said politely, and tried not to inhale.

Ahmet jerked her to her feet. "You come."

"No. No, thank you, Mr. Ahmet, but—"

"You come now."

"Really, I don't think—"

Qasim stood up. His lips drew back from his teeth in the

semblance of a smile and he said something to Ahmet. Ahmet smiled, too, even more coldly. His hand tightened around her wrist.

"Megan," Qasim said softly, his eyes locked to the other man's face, "don't do or say anything."

"But—"

"Damn it, woman, listen to me! Say nothing. Do nothing. Do you understand?"

"Yes, but—"

Ahmet curved his arm around her. His hand lay at her waist. He chuckled, his stinking breath hot against her face, his fingers kneading her flesh. Qasim said something, his tone harsh and commanding. Ahmet replied to it, and Qasim spoke again. Ahmet laughed. His fingers were still moving. Up. Up. Up...

Megan growled, spun toward him and plowed her fist into his gut.

The room exploded with action.

Wild cries. The clatter of overturned chairs. Shouts and yells, and hands clawing for her dress, her hair...

Qasim swept her into his arms.

"Qasim," Megan sobbed, "oh, Qasim..."

"Be quiet," he snarled, "or I'll have what's left of your body fed to the jackals!"

Then he tossed her over his shoulder, shouldered his way through the mob and strode out the door.

Hours went by.

Perhaps only minutes.

Megan only knew she was hoarse from saying she was sorry. Still, as Qasim paced by her again, she said it once more.

"I'm sorry, Qasim. I didn't mean—"

"Be quiet!"

She nodded and sank down on the edge of a chair. Whatever she'd started in the meeting room wasn't good. She could hear voices raised in anger outside the door to her room—a door Qasim had bolted. The women who served her sat huddled in a corner, their faces white. Hakim had scratched at the window a little while ago and Qasim had opened the shutters and let him in along with the helicopter pilot and the two guards who'd flown here with them.

Nobody said anything, but she could read rage in their eyes. She'd behaved stupidly and now they were all in danger.

"Qasim." She swallowed with difficulty. Her throat was so dry it felt parched. "He was going to—to touch my breast. I knew he was. And—"

"He was not going to touch your breast," Qasim snarled, swinging toward her. "It was an amusement for him. A test of wills between him and me. If you'd obeyed my orders—"

"That's easy for you to say. His slimy hands weren't on you!"

"If you'd obeyed my orders and hadn't drawn attention to yourself—"

"He's been staring at me for two days!"

Qasim felt a muscle knot in his jaw. Megan was right. He'd seen the son of a bitch watching her, but he'd told himself it was just an attempt to provoke him. Why would Ahmet, the most traditional of the tribal leaders, be interested in a foreigner?

He'd been the last to swear allegiance to Qasim after his father's death. Ever since, they'd played a game of wills.

How stupid he'd been, to think this was just another round.

"Why didn't you stop him when he put his arm around me?"

"What did you think I was doing?" Qasim said grimly. "You heard me talking to him. Didn't it occur to you I was telling him to take his hands off you?"

"You could have done more than tell him."

"It was a duel of wills." His mouth thinned. "He understood that if he touched you intimately, I'd have killed him."

"All that, in one little scene?" Megan snorted with contempt. "I think you have an overblown idea of your power, Sheikh Qasim."

"If I did," he said coldly, "Ahmet's men would have broken down that door twenty minutes ago. I'd be dead and what was left of you would be rotting in the desert."

The words rang with quiet conviction. Megan shuddered and wrapped her arms around herself.

"Then—then what do we do now?"

Qasim looked at her. She was pale, so pale that a tiny line of freckles he'd never noticed stood out clearly across the bridge of her nose. Her hair was a wild mass of curls framing her face. In the awful struggle in the meeting room, someone had half-torn off one of her sleeves, exposing the delicate curve of her arm.

Something seemed to expand inside his heart.

How beautiful she was. How brave. And how good she'd been, his Megan. He could only imagine what fortitude it had taken for her to play the part of a timid woman, sitting on that silly little stool, never speaking, never lifting her head, returning to this room in isolation each night and awakening each morning, knowing she had to pretend she was of no more importance than the walls.

He'd been proud of her...but he'd known it couldn't last.

And when she reacted to the pig who'd nudged her with his foot, he'd been torn between ordering her to behave and pulling her into his arms and kissing her.

You see? he'd longed to say, *this is what a woman should be like. Beautiful, and intelligent, and not afraid to speak her mind.*

He hadn't, of course. He had his nation to think of. He needed Ahmet's support for his plans. There was ore in these mountains and a small, painfully old-fashioned operation that mined it. He had plans already sketched out for a road, a small airport, a new smelter. None of it would destroy the vast, wild hills but would, instead, bring prosperity to a part of Suliyam that still lived with the poverty and diseases of ancient times.

And then Ahmet had touched her. Grabbed her wrist.

God, he'd wanted to kill him!

All that had stopped him was the cold realization that Ahmet's actions were part of a plan. The man wanted Megan, yes, but he wanted a confrontation with Qasim even more.

This was a test, then. Another grinding of will against will. He could not let Ahmet win, not with such high stakes. A fight here, where Ahmet ruled, and he'd die. Qasim had always known he might have to give his life for his country; he was prepared to do it, but not if it meant letting Ahmet and his followers impose their brand of cruel leadership on the rest of the kingdom...

Not if it meant letting him take Megan as a plaything.

So Qasim had forced himself to seem unruffled, even when Ahmet slid his meaty arm around Megan's waist.

Do not touch her, he'd said calmly. *It would not be wise.*

I think it would be, Ahmet had answered with a nasty smile.

It would not be, Qasim had told him. *I brought my people here in the spirit of friendship. Would you repudiate that friendship, Lord Ahmet? If so, you must also be prepared for the consequences.*

Check and mate, he'd thought, reading cold acquiescence in the man's face. One last dance of those meaty fingers, meant, Qasim knew, to save face...

And then Megan had taken matters into her own hands, and almost gotten both of them killed.

And he...hell, even as he'd figured he might have to fight his way out of the room, he'd felt his heart swell with pride at her courage.

How had this contrary female become so important to him in so short a time?

He turned toward her again. Her tear, like the tails of shooting stars, had left silvery streaks on her cheeks.

"Qasim?" she said in a whisper. "What do we do now?"

Qasim closed the distance between them in a few quick steps and gathered her gently into his arms. He heard Hakim's soft gasp, knew his men were staring, but he didn't give a damn.

For the first time since he'd ascended the throne, he was a man and not a king.

"Megan," he said softly, and when she lifted her face to his, he kissed her with all the tenderness in his heart. She sighed, leaned into his embrace and kissed him back.

"Stay here," he murmured, his lips an inch from hers. "Keep the door barred until I return."

"No! Qasim..."

He cupped her face and silenced her terrified protests with another kiss.

"I'll come back for you, *kalila*. I swear it."

She gave him a blurry smile. He brought her hands to his mouth and pressed kisses into the palms. Then he barked out a command to Hakim, to the pilot, to the two guards, unbarred the door and left the room.

CHAPTER EIGHT

DEAR God, what had she done?

Megan stood before one of the tall, narrow windows that looked over the mountains. Gray fog covered the barren plain, moving inexorably toward the walled city like a poisonous cloud.

Where are you, Qasim? Where are you?

Hours had gone by since the heavy wooden door had slammed behind him and still there was no word.

Time was moving as slowly as the fog. She felt helpless. Useless. The worst of it was that it was all her fault.

Qasim had warned her that working with him would be tough. *No problem,* she'd said, or words to that effect, and she'd glibly promised to follow all the demeaning rules of his country.

She'd been lying. To herself and to him.

What she'd really intended was to teach his people a thing or two about the proper role of women in civilized society.

Then they'd reached this awful place and she'd discovered that what he'd been trying to tell her was that parts of his kingdom had nothing to do with civilization as she knew it. And she'd done her best to keep her promise. She'd kept her mouth shut. She'd behaved.

If only she hadn't been forced to sit on that stool. If only Hakim hadn't acted like a self-important prig. If only Ahmet hadn't noticed her...

Damn it, why was she trying to come up with excuses?

Sure, those things had worked their way under her skin, but she'd been in the business world long enough to learn to roll with the punches. Her very first job with a prestigious firm, she'd traveled to Philadelphia with her boss. He'd stayed in an executive suite and arranged for her to have a connecting room.

"Makes things more convenient," he'd said, and she, innocent that she was, hadn't realized what that meant until she'd heard him rattling the doorknob in the middle of the night.

Meg? he'd called. *I have something here that will interest you.*

She'd lain frozen in silence, pretending she didn't hear him, and the next morning he'd acted as if nothing had happened and, damn it, so had she because she was afraid of losing her first really good job.

Lots of men still believed all it took was power to turn a woman into a conquest.

She could have dealt with the situation. She *should* have dealt with it, especially since Qasim had warned her.

What she couldn't deal with was the way Qasim had ignored her. Okay. Maybe he had no choice when they were with the others. She understood that. But that didn't explain why he hadn't found a minute to come to her room. Talk to her. Take her hand, as he had just before he'd ridden off with Ahmet's men. Tell her everything would be fine...

Megan closed her eyes.

Tell her he missed her. Wanted her. Longed for her, as she longed for him.

She turned from the window. She was thinking crazy thoughts, but didn't experts say that stress had weird effects on people? Hakim, for example, was standing like a statue in the same place he'd been when Qasim left.

She couldn't understand the aide's behavior. Why had he

let the man he called his master face whatever waited outside this door alone? Until now, Hakim had stayed at his heels like an obedient spaniel. Why had he abandoned him now?

Hakim swung toward her, eyes filled with hatred.

"I would never abandon my lord," he snarled, and Megan realized she'd spoken aloud.

"But you did. You let him face those barbarians all by himself!"

"The sheikh ordered me to stay here. I cannot disobey an order."

"Not even if it might save his life?"

"Obedience to him is not a matter of choice. You have no understanding of us, Miss O'Connell, or you would not question my actions."

"*You* have no understanding of what could be happening beyond that door, and damn your obedience!"

"Lord Qasim ordered me to watch over you." Hakim's mouth thinned. "I assure you, had I the power, I would not chose to do so."

"Oh, I'm sure of that. Why do you despise me, Hakim? I haven't done anything to you."

"You have bewitched the sheikh. He does not see it, but I do. You have clouded his thoughts."

"That's crazy!"

"He forgets that his duty is to Suliyam." Hakim came toward her, fists clenched at his sides. "Your witchcraft started when you wrote words in a document that made him want to change our way of life."

Megan threw out her hand, as if she were brushing aside a stinging insect. "You don't know what you're talking about. I made projections, estimated costs. Any changes for this—this godforsaken piece of earth come from Qasim, not me."

"And you show him disrespect. You refer to him by name, as if you were his equal."

"I *am* his equal," Megan snapped. "We don't scrape and bow to anyone in my world."

"That is the problem, Miss O'Connell. You think your world is the standard by which others must live, just as you think you know my lord. You do not! Soon, your witchcraft will wear off. You are only a female. In the end, his strength will be greater than any of your spells."

"I'm not going to listen to another—"

Hakim grabbed her arm. "You are a temporary diversion in the sheikh's life. Though he may bed you, I can promise that you'll never gain his heart."

"Touch me again," Megan said, grimacing as she twisted out of his grasp, "and I might just treat you to one of my so-called spells, you miserable old—"

A fist pounded against the door. Megan forgot Hakim, forgot everything when she heard Qasim's voice.

"Open up!"

Hakim started toward the door but she ran past him, slid the heavy bar free and flung the door wide.

"Qasim," she said happily, "Oh, thank God! I was afraid—"

"Nothing to be afraid of," Qasim said, and lurched sideways. "Nothing at…"

He fell toward her. Megan closed her arms around him but his weight was too much. The best she could manage was to slide slowly to the floor with him still in her arms.

"What did they do to you?" she whispered. "Qasim?"

"Caz," he said thickly, eyes closed and a loopy grin on his face. "You might as well call me…"

A snore rattled from his throat. Megan's eyebrows drew together. She bent over the man in her lap, sniffed…

"He's drunk," she said, looking up at Hakim in disbelief.

Hakim sighed. "That is good."

Good? It was good that Qasim had been drinking with his pals while she almost lost her mind imagining what had happened to him? That she'd been blaming herself for whatever awful fate had befallen him? That she'd been terrified she'd never see him again, never hear his voice, never feel his mouth on hers?

That such things had seemed to matter only made her angrier. She let Qasim's head down none-too-gently and shot to her feet.

"Be careful," Hakim snapped, rushing to ease a pillow under the sheikh's head.

"If this is good," Megan said grimly, "then you're right. I guess I really don't understand this country."

"It is not complicated."

"Oh, I think it is. Your sheikh goes off to be—to be drawn and quartered, and instead—"

"No one draws and quarters his enemies anymore," Hakim said, so seriously that she blinked. "Not even sheikh Ahmet." Hakim nodded toward the bed as he undid the top few buttons of Qasim's shirt. "Get that blanket."

She wanted to tell him to get it himself, but why play the role of sullen child? She was angry enough not to give a damn if Qasim froze to death, but she yanked the blanket from the bed and dropped it over him.

So much for thinking he'd been defending her or worried about her.

"There." Hakim waved his hand to the other men as he rose to his feet. "We will leave you now, Miss O'Connell."

"That's fine. Just don't think you can go without taking your sheikh with you."

"His highness will probably sleep for several hours. You may send for me when he awakens."

"Wait just a damned minute! You've got it wrong, pal.

You may call *me* when he awakens, and only so I can tell your fearless leader what I think of him.''

"Sheikh Qasim drank with Sheikh Ahmet."

Megan folded her arms and smiled with her teeth. "A brilliant deduction."

"That means they held a successful negotiation."

She looked down at Qasim. He'd rolled onto his side and was sleeping soundly as a baby.

"How? By drinking each other under the table?"

"They drank," Hakim said coldly, "because they solved their differences. That is how it was done in the old days. And, in the old days, to drink less than the man who was your enemy was to insult him."

"In other words, what we see here is an example of good manners."

Hakim nodded. "It is so."

"Good manners," Megan said again, and rolled her eyes. Would she ever make sense of any of this? Still, the threat to their safety was over. She could, she supposed, let Qasim sleep it off on the floor. It was only that she felt a knot of anger each time she looked at him. No matter what Hakim said, the negotiations couldn't have been very difficult, not if they ended in a party.

"Miss O'Connell? You will send for me when my lord awakens."

"With pleasure."

She took a chair to the window, carefully placed it so her back would face Qasim, and sat down. She heard the door shut; after a minute, despite what Hakim had said about successful negotiations, she went to it and slid the heavy bar into place.

Qasim was still sleeping. Caz. He'd told her to call him Caz.

She looked down at him again, at the thick, dark lashes

lying against his tanned skin. He looked peaceful, content, not at all concerned at how she'd worried…

At the anguish she'd suffered, imagining him hurt or dead.

Megan rose to her feet. She knelt next to Qasim, stroked his hair back from his forehead, and touched her hand to his cheek.

"I'm glad you're safe," she whispered. "Very, very glad."

Gently she brushed her lips over his.

Then she sat by the window, stared out at the fog-shrouded plain and wondered what was happening to her because something was, something she didn't understand, didn't want, had never wanted.

When darkness came, she lay her head back and drifted off to sleep.

Caz came awake all at once, heart pounding, fighting his way out of a nightmare that involved himself, Ahmet and a room choked with the stench of alcohol.

He blinked, forced his eyes open, and groaned. Bloody hell. He was lying on the floor. What…?

And then he remembered. Ahmet. His unbelievable demand. His response. The endless hours of finding a way out of a situation that could, in an instant, turn into disaster…and then the solution and the glass after glass of a clear liquid that had the smell of rotten potatoes and the kick of a mule.

His head felt as if it were going to explode. Slowly, carefully, he sat up and looked around him. A single oil lamp flickered on a low table. This room wasn't his. It was Megan's. Yes, he saw her now, asleep in a big chair near the window.

His heart turned over as he thought of what he had to tell

her. How would she deal with it? She was brave—he'd never known a woman with more courage. And she was intelligent. With luck, she'd understand what he'd done, why he'd done it, that he had no choice and neither did she. Yes, she'd say, of course, I'll do it if I must.

She might even lift her arms to him, whisper that it wasn't such an awful fate, that what they had to do might be— might be—

"Idiot," Caz mumbled, and tore his eyes from her.

Megan wouldn't tell him anything but what he deserved. She'd say he was an arrogant fool for having gotten her into this mess, but she'd agree to the terms he'd set.

It wasn't as if either of them had a choice.

He took a steadying breath and got to his feet. A red-hot lance of pain drove through his skull. There had to be a way to clear his head. He had to, before he told Megan that they—that he and she...

Black coffee. There was an earthenware pot of it on the table. It was cold and would probably taste like old socks, but he needed caffeine and to hell with the taste. Sugar, too. That would help. Caz filled a cup with viscous black liquid, added six misshapen lumps of raw sugar, stirred the resultant mess and slugged it down. He gagged on the last mouthful but a couple of deep breaths helped keep the stuff in his gut. Then he poured another cup and went through the whole process again.

Better. Much better. Damn, what he'd give for a shower.

His eyes fell on the pitcher and basin that stood on a small table in the far corner. One quick glance at Megan. Yes, she was still sleeping. Quickly Caz unbuttoned his shirt, unzipped his trousers, kicked off his leather boots, stripped down to his skin. He took a mouthful of the water—God, it was cold—and spat it into the basin. Then he gritted his teeth, raised the pitcher and dumped the contents over his head.

God!

His teeth banged together like castanets; he shuddered from his head straight down to his toes, but the coffee, sugar and icy water combined did the trick. He was stone cold sober and the pain in his head was almost—*almost*—bearable.

He dressed quickly, wishing he could put on stuff that didn't bear the lingering scent of the rotgut he'd had to swallow to convince Ahmet it wouldn't be wise to screw with him. Going toe to toe, matching him drink for drink, had been the only way to deal with the ugly son of a bitch.

Caz ran his hands through his wet hair, shoving it back from his face.

Okay. He was as ready as he'd ever be. It was time to wake Megan and explain the devil's bargain he'd made.

He made his way quietly across the carpeted floor, paused beside her chair and looked down at her. Her head was thrown back; her lashes lay against her cheek. Her pulse beat slowly and steadily in the hollow of her throat. He had kissed her there; he remembered the sweet taste of her flesh, the erotic whisper of her heartbeat against his lips.

Yes, she was beautiful and bright and courageous, but how had she gotten under his skin in so short a time? He'd known lots of women, had many lovers, been with a couple of them for months, but none had ever stirred his emotions this way. As often as he'd wanted to turn Megan over his knee and teach her some manners, he'd wanted to take her in his arms and make love to her.

And sometimes, sometimes it was enough just to know she was in the same room, that he could look over and see her face, enough to know she was part of his life...

A chill danced down his spine.

Amazing, what effect stress could have on a man, he thought, and hunched down beside the chair.

"Megan."

She didn't stir.

"Megan," he said briskly, "wake up."

Her lashes fluttered, the lids rose. She stared at him, her eyes dark and unseeing, and then a smile flickered across her mouth.

"Caz," she whispered, and he stopped trying to treat this as just another moment in his life, stopped trying to figure out what in hell was happening to him, whispered her name, bent his head to hers and kissed her.

Her mouth was sweet and soft, and when she sighed, he drew her breath in, let it mix with his. She moaned and he curved his arm around her, drew her close and deepened the kiss. A long time later, he drew back, looked into her eyes and brushed her sleep-tousled hair from her temple.

"Hello, *kalila*," he whispered.

"You're awake."

He laughed softly. "Yes."

She touched his hair. It was damp. "Were you outside? Is it raining?"

He took her hand, pressed it to his lips. "I took a shower. Well, I took what passes for a shower in this place. I'm afraid I used up all your water."

A picture flashed through her mind. Qasim, tall, proud, naked. "Here?"

"You were asleep."

"The last time I saw you, you were passed out on the floor."

His smile dimmed. "I'm sure I was."

"You were drunk."

"I know, *kalila*. I'm so sorry, but—"

"And you asked me to call you 'Caz.'"

"Did I?"

She nodded. "It is a nickname?"

"My roommate dubbed me 'Caz' my first semester at Yale, and it seemed a lot more American than Qasim, so from then on, that's what I called myself."

Megan traced the tip of her finger along his mouth. In the dark, with only the soft light of the oil lamp for illumination, with the silence of the mountains all around them, anything seemed right…and she'd wanted to touch her finger to his mouth for a long time, to follow those soft curves that could spark such excitement. She knew she should be angry at him for abandoning her and getting drunk, but right now she could only think how good it felt to be in his arms.

"Ah," she said softly, with the hint of a smile. "You didn't mind being a little bit American then."

"I never minded it. My mother was American." His smile tilted. "I liked her country far more than she liked mine."

"What happened to her?"

"She couldn't adapt to life in Suliyam and she went home."

"Without you?"

"Without me. Don't look so sad, *kalila*. Really, I had a happy childhood."

"Then why do you look so sad when you mention her?"

"Do I look sad?" Caz brought her hand to his mouth again. "It must be the light." He cleared his throat, and she knew he was going to change the topic. "We can talk about this another time, Megan. Right now…right now, we have another matter to discuss."

"Yes. We certainly do."

Her tone had changed. Well, he could hardly blame her for being angry, and he told her so.

"I don't blame you for being upset."

"Upset?" She pulled away from him and rose to her feet. "I wasn't upset," she lied. "I just think you could have found a way to let me know you weren't being murdered."

"I'm sorry, *kalila*. But there was no time."

"I imagined the most awful things, Caz. Terrible things."

"Sweetheart." Caz stood up and reached for her hand. "Forgive me for putting you through this."

His expression was contrite. She thought of her role in all this, and her anger faded as swiftly as it had taken hold.

"It's my fault," she said softly. "I made a mess of things."

"No!" Caz gathered her in his arms. "I should never have brought you to these mountains. I should have seen through Ahmet's lies. He wasn't ill, he only wanted me to bend to him. And, like a fool, I did." He paused. "But you're right. Awful things might have happened. They won't," he added quickly. "I promise."

Megan laid her hands on Caz's chest. She could feel the steady beat of his heart beneath her palms.

"I thought of what he might do to you." Her voice shook. "Caz, I thought—"

"Ahmet behaves like an animal when it suits him, but he's not a fool. He wouldn't harm me. He knows the other tribes would avenge my death and show him no mercy."

She laughed shakily. "And here I thought he was going to feed you to a pack of hungry wolves."

"You've seen too many bad movies, *kalila*," Caz said softly. "In fact, he went out of his way to be...gracious."

"There's a word I'd never use for him."

"You impressed him, Megan."

"I'll just bet," she said, with a little laugh. "He'd probably like to toss me off the top of a mountain."

"On the contrary. He finds you interesting."

"I'm sure there's a less polite word to describe it."

"He says he's never known a woman like you. And he's right."

Caz's eyes were like flame on her mouth. She felt her lips soften, her muscles turning liquid in sweet anticipation of his kiss, but he didn't kiss her. Instead he circled her wrists with his hands and drew back.

"We have a problem," he said quietly.

In an instant, the mood in the darkened room had changed. Megan stared at Caz and the expression on his face chilled her to the bone.

"A problem?"

"Ahmet wants…something."

"What?"

"He wants you."

"What?" She forced a laugh. This had to be a joke but Caz wasn't laughing. He wasn't even smiling. She could feel the color drain from her face. "What do you mean, he wants—"

"He wants to take you as his wife."

"Well, that's—that's…" Her stomach lurched. "You told him, of course, I'd never—that I would never, ever—"

She cried out as Caz clasped her shoulders and lifted her to her toes. "Listen to me, Megan. As he sees it, he's offered you a great honor." His voice softened. "Don't look like that, *kalila*. Do you think I would let this happen? He's not going to have you."

Megan slumped against him. "For a minute, I thought… But Hakim said things had gone well. He said that was why you'd had so much to drink. He said—"

"He probably said it was tradition. A word you've come to despise—and, in this instance, one I do, too." Caz shuddered. "I'd much rather celebrate with a handshake than with cups of horse piss." The muscle in his jaw tightened.

So did the grip of his hands on her. "But it was worth it. You see, I found the one reason Ahmet can't have you."

Megan smiled. "I'll bet it was creative."

"It was." He paused. "I told him that you couldn't very well marry him when you were already promised to me."

CHAPTER NINE

SILENCE. What was called a pregnant pause in bad novels, Megan thought wildly, but what could a woman say to a man after he'd just told her...after he'd said that she...that he...

Maybe she'd misunderstood.

"You told Ahmet," she said carefully, "that I couldn't marry him because—"

"—because you're going to marry me."

She waited for Caz to add something. When he didn't, she nodded as if what he'd told her made absolute sense.

"Oh."

"Is that all you have to say, *kalila?* Nothing but 'oh'?"

Caz sounded annoyed. Annoyed? At her? For saying "oh" after hearing him say—

The room shifted out of focus. Caz tightened his hold on her wrists.

"Megan?" His voice was sharp. "Are you all right?"

"Yes. Yes, I'm..." She cleared her throat. "Actually I'm surprised."

His smile was quick and wolfish. "I don't doubt it."

"That you'd have to come up with such a lie, I mean. You're the ruler of this kingdom. Ahmet is your subject. Surely you can simply tell him that what he wants is out of the question."

"I did."

"Well, then—"

"He laughed."

"I really don't follow this, Caz. You told him he couldn't—that he can't take me for his wife and he laughed?"

Caz let go of her. He dug his hands into his pockets and began pacing the room. He'd known this wouldn't be easy. How could a man explain ancient customs of the east to a woman of the twenty-first century west? Ahmet and his followers were the last of his people whose feet were firmly planted in the past. Moving them forward required a deft touch. His father had proven that; he'd tried to institute change through royal decree and it had only led to bloodshed.

Besides, a royal decree was impossible without the force to back it. Caz had deliberately come to these mountains without a show of arms. He'd meant it as a good faith gesture, but now his plan was about to backfire.

And bringing Megan with him had been another error. He'd figured it would present some problems. What he hadn't anticipated was that Megan would be a temptation to a man like Ahmet.

Now, Megan's fate was in his hands. Her fate, and the fate of this peace mission. One false step and Ahmet would surely decide to take what he wanted and the consequences be damned.

If that happened, Megan's future, and Suliyam's, might both be lost.

"Answer me, damn it," Megan demanded. "How can Ahmet even think he can get away with something like this? All you have to do is say 'no!'"

Caz turned to her. Her stance said she was ready to take on the world, shoulders back, chin up, eyes bright with defiance...and yet, he could see something beyond all that.

Fear.

What a fool he was, he thought angrily, and he crossed the room in a few quick strides and caught her in his arms.

"I *have* told him 'no,'" he said quietly. "And given him a reason why he must accept my decision." He tightened his hold on her, lifted her to her toes so she had no choice but to look into his eyes. "Telling him he can't have you wouldn't ensure your safety. The situation is complex but you have to trust me, *kalila*. Now that I've said you are to be my wife, you're safe."

"And I have nothing to say about it?"

"No," Caz said sharply. "Not unless you like the idea of having Ahmet as your husband."

"Don't be ridiculous! I'd never—"

"Then stop arguing, damn it! Why make such a fuss?"

Why, indeed? Megan thought. Caz had lied about their relationship. So what? Why this hollow feeling inside? Someday, this would make a great story. *And then there was the time I was in this little country in the middle of nowhere,* she'd say, *and the guy who ruled it had to pretend he wanted to make me his wife...*

"You're right," she said, forcing a smile to her lips. "What you did was creative. Heck, it's brilliant. Ahmet's a barbarian, but not even he would be foolish enough to try and steal his king's fiancée."

Part two, coming up, Caz thought grimly, and cleared his throat. "Unfortunately, he still might."

"But—but you just said..."

"It isn't enough."

"It isn't?" Megan shook her head. "You're losing me, Caz. Didn't you just tell me that I was safe? That now that Ahmet knows we're—that he knows, he has to accept defeat?"

"Being betrothed isn't the same as being wed."

Such formal words, so calmly spoken. He might have

been discussing the weather. Was she the only one who found the prospect of a phony engagement disturbing?

"Why not? He'll never know that we aren't really going to—"

"Of course he will," Caz said impatiently. "I know you think you've stepped into a time warp, but news travels here the same as it does in your world."

"Why are you putting words in my mouth? I don't think that. I'm sure not everyone's like Ahmet."

"Yeah." Caz nodded. "I'm sorry, *kalila*. I'm a little edgy."

"Well, so am I. It isn't every day I become engaged, especially to a sheikh."

Megan smiled, to make sure he understood she was joking, but he didn't return the smile. Instead his expression became grim.

"You might as well prepare yourself for another shock."

"What shock? Why are you looking at me like that?" Her heart seemed to turn over. "Caz? What is it?"

"Ahmet may be a brute, but he isn't stupid. Do you think he'd let you go just because I suddenly announced our engagement?" He moved closer to her, his eyes locked to hers. "He wants to give us a gift."

"What kind of—"

"A wedding," Caz said, his tone flat. "He offered to have our marriage take place here. Today."

"And you said…" Her voice was scratchy. She cleared her throat and began again. "And you said, 'thank you, but—'"

"And I said we would be delighted to have the ceremony here, in these magnificent mountains."

Megan stared at him in stunned disbelief, waiting for him to smile and say it was all a joke, but his steady gaze assured her that he'd meant every word.

"No!"

"You can't say 'no,' Megan. I thought I made that clear."

"I can say whatever I like, and my answer is—"

Caz caught her by the shoulders.

"I have not *asked* you to marry me," he said brusquely, "I've *told* you to marry me. There's a world of difference."

"You're insane! You can't tell me—"

"Yes," he said harshly, I can. I am the ruler of this country. My word is law."

There it was, the true nature of the Sheikh of Suliyam. He was a dictator and she, fool that she was, had done everything she could not to acknowledge that truth.

"Not in my world, it isn't. You can't force me to—"

She cried out as his hands bit into her flesh. "The world you know has no meaning here. Would you prefer to see the few men I brought with me slaughtered?" He lowered his head until his eyes burned into hers. "My men's lives are worth more to me than your foolish female pride."

"And me?" she said, in a papery whisper. "What am I worth to you?"

His mouth twisted. What he'd just told her was true enough, but it wasn't all of it. His men were prepared to give their lives for him, and he had been raised to willingly give his life for his people.

But when Ahmet leered at him and said he wanted Megan, he hadn't thought about his men first, or his people, or his responsibility to the throne.

He'd thought of Megan, lying beneath Ahmet's savage bulk. Of the barbarian's hands on her. Of her tears, her terror, and he'd come as close to insanity as a man could get without tumbling over the edge.

His hands had knotted into fists; his heart pounded. He'd looked into Ahmet's fat, ugly face and imagined it bloodied beyond repair, imagined the joy of beating him to his knees…

He'd reached deep inside himself, struggled to hold on to reason even as his vision reddened, and acknowledged that if he attacked the barbarian, he'd surely seal Megan's fate.

Could he tell her that? Tell her that he would gladly give his life for hers, if he thought it would save her? No. He couldn't. Such a thought was irrational and he couldn't afford to be irrational.

He was the king.

"You're very important to me," he said carefully. "I'm responsible for your welfare." She seemed to sag in his hands. What more did she want him to say? Caz searched for the words that would make this easier and finally found them. "Of course, the marriage won't be real."

Her head came up and she looked into his eyes. "It won't?"

"The ceremony will have meaning only in Suliyam, not in the States. I'll take care of nullifying it on my end. You won't have to do anything to set it aside."

"Oh. I didn't… I thought…"

"We'll return to the palace tomorrow, I'll put you on a plane and send you home." His voice, and his hands, gentled. "And then you can put what happened here out of your mind."

Put it out of her mind. She'd exchange wedding vows, then put them out of her mind?

"Megan? Do you see how simple this is?"

She looked at Caz again. His gray eyes were steady on hers. He looked like a man who'd just suggested an appropriate dinner menu instead of a marriage, calm and pleasant…except for a tiny flicker of muscle beating in his jaw.

"It isn't as if the ceremony will have any real meaning."

"No. I understand that now."

"All you'll have to do is play the part of obedient female a little longer." Caz's voice roughened. "Obedient, and eager."

"Excuse me?"

"Ahmet wondered why I hadn't married you already. It was an excellent question, and I answered by telling him I'd wanted to wait until I could plan an extravagant celebration but that being alone with you these past days had been difficult for me. For you, as well." Caz slid one hand up her throat; he could feel Megan's pulse drumming beneath his fingers. "A man doesn't sleep with the woman he intends to wed," he said huskily.

Megan nodded. It all made perfect sense. Her head told her so. Her heart was the part of her having a problem. She'd never really thought about marriage but surely if you did decided to say "I do," it was supposed to have some meaning.

Wasn't it?

Weren't you supposed to look at the man you were marrying and feel giddy with excitement? Weren't you supposed to want his kisses? Weren't you supposed to want to be with him all the time, to talk to him and yes, argue with him, and laugh with him...and feel everything she felt for Qasim?

The room tilted. Caz tightened his hold on her.

"*Kalila*. Don't be afraid. I won't let anything happen to you."

Something was happening already, but how could she tell him that?

"Besides," he added softly, "we have no choice."

His eyes darkened; his gaze fell to her mouth. Later, she would wonder who made the first move, she or he. Not that it mattered. His kiss consumed her, burned away what little remained of reason and replaced it with his taste, his scent, his strength.

Shaken, she stepped back.

"No choice at all," he said, and left her.

Time slowed to a tortoise's pace.

Caz didn't come back. She hadn't expected him to. Wasn't there some tradition about a bridegroom not seeing his bride on their wedding day?

And wasn't that a sad attempt at humor? Megan thought, as she paced back and forth. She wasn't a bride and Caz wasn't her groom. They were two people trapped in a nasty game of treachery, and the sooner they got things finished here, the better.

The one person she half expected to see was Hakim, coming to demand she not go through with the wedding...but why would he do that? Hakim would know, as she did, that the next few hours would be a farce.

In midmorning, her serving women showed up with platters of food and pitchers of fruit juice. Their sullen expressions were gone. Now, they approached her with their eyes cast down.

Megan waved the food and drink away. One mouthful of anything and her stomach would revolt. Farce or not, it wasn't every day she stood at an altar and said "I do."

The women sat down and watched her. They giggled and whispered to each other. They shot her little looks filled with meaning, poked each other in the ribs and giggled again. She'd gone to enough bridal showers to know what was going on.

"Trust me," she said, "it's not like that."

The youngest of them drew a deep breath. For courage, obviously, because a few seconds later, she spoke.

"The sheikh is very handsome."

Megan raised her eyebrows. "You speak English?"

"The sheikh is very handsome."

Megan hunched down in front of the girl. "Tell me, please, what will the wedding be like?"

"The sheikh is very—"

"Handsome," Megan said glumly, and rose to her feet.

So much for speaking English. So much for finding out what lay ahead. So much for anything, except pacing and pacing, and telling herself this would all be over in a little while.

This wasn't the way a bride was supposed to feel.

Not that she'd ever thought much about being a bride. Why would any woman want to give up her life?

That was what you had to do, even if the books said you didn't, even if her oh-so-independent big sister had taken the plunge. Fallon might have forgotten the great lesson of their childhood. She hadn't. She'd grown up watching their mother put aside her own needs for her husband's pleasure. Mary would settle into a new place, start turning a usually decrepit four walls into a home, make a few friends and then Pop would come home one night, filled with enthusiasm for some new get-rich-quick scheme, and announce that it was time to move on.

What men wanted always came first. That was just the way it was. Some women were okay with it, but she wasn't one of them.

Wasn't it a damned good thing this marriage would only be a sham?

She looked out the window, where trails of fog wound around the stunted scrub as they had last night.

Twenty-four hours, and nothing had changed.

Twenty-four hours, and everything had changed.

Real or not, nothing would be the same after tonight. She had the weirdest feeling, as if someone had popped the cork on a bottle of champagne and the bubbles were effervescing in her blood.

What if the wedding were real? There was no harm in imagining that. What if Caz had come to her and said, *Don't think. Don't ask questions. Don't ask for logic, because there isn't any. I only know that I want you more than life itself. Marry me, Megan. Stay with me forever.*

What would her answer have been?

No, of course.

That's what she'd have told him, wasn't it? Or would she have gone into his arms, forgotten what she knew of marriage, forgotten that she knew this man only a handful of days.

Would she have brought his mouth down to hers, whispered her answer against the warmth of his lips?

Her throat constricted. She swung around and stared at the silent women.

"I can't do this," she said. "I can't—"

The door swung open. Two more servants bustled into the room, hands and arms filled with silks and cashmeres and jewels.

Megan turned to the girl who'd spoken those half dozen words of English.

"Help me," she begged. "Please, get me out of here! I don't want to marry the sheikh. I can't—"

The women descended on her like wolves on a lamb. Megan shrieked, struck out in desperation, but there were eight of them and one of her. They stripped her of her clothes, dumped her in a wooden tub that appeared as if by magic, washed her body, her hair, dried and perfumed her.

"Stop it," she kept saying, "damn you, keep your hands off me!"

Maybe they thought it was a game. Maybe tradition said the bride was supposed to put up a fight. Nobody listened, nobody paid attention, nobody even spoke to her until she was dressed and hung with jewels.

Then the two eldest women dragged her in front of the full-length mirror that had appeared at the same time as the tub.

"Look," the youngest woman, the one who'd pretended not to speak English, said.

Megan looked. And stared at what she saw.

The glass was old. Some of the silver backing had worn off; in other places, her reflection seemed to shimmer like waves on the sea.

But the image was clear enough to make her catch her breath.

Looking back at her was a stranger, a seductive creature draped in jewels that were ancient and beautiful, her hair woven with flowers, her body draped in royal-blue silk.

Something old, she thought giddily, *something new, something borrowed, something blue.*

"You see?" the youngest of the women whispered.

Yes. Yes, she saw. They had changed her. Megan O'Connell was gone. In her place was—

"The sheikh's bride," the young woman whispered.

Less than an hour later, that was who she became.

The ceremony was long and probably beautiful.

If she'd been watching it in a travel film, that's how she'd have described it. An enormous room lit by candles. A pathway, strewn with rose petals. An altar. A canopy, at any rate, made of royal blue silk shot with gold.

And Caz, waiting for her. Caz, in a white silk shirt and black breeches with riding boots the color of the night. Caz, his face serious, his eyes locked to hers. Words spoken by Ahmet, who'd managed to look human for the occasion. Caz's husky responses, her choked "Yes" when he told her it was time to say the word. And then a roar went up from the throats of Ahmet's men, and Caz's arms went around her, and the roar grew louder as he crushed her mouth beneath his.

"You are my wife," he said softly, and she told herself it was all a game even as her arms went around his neck and she drew his head to hers for another deep, deep kiss.

Hands reached for her. Women's hands. Laughing, they dragged her away, surrounded her, tugged her along with them while the men did the same thing to Caz. The women brought her to another room, seated her on an intricately carved chair that stood on a high platform. The men seated Caz beside her. Music—the hot beat of drums, the haunting cry of a flute—filled the room.

The women danced. The men strutted. There were platters of food and endless glasses filled with a liquid that had no color.

"Don't even take a sip," Caz said, leaning toward her.

Megan looked at him. My husband, she thought. He's my husband. "Poison?" she whispered.

"Of a sort," he said solemnly. "It's what got me so polluted last night."

He grinned. She laughed. How strange, to hear such an American word in such a foreign setting. To hear the word on her husband's lips.

"Stand up, sweetheart."

"Why?"

"It's time for us to leave."

To leave. To be alone with this man who she'd just married. Her heart bumped again. "Won't that be rude? Ahmet might think—"

"Are you afraid to be alone with me?"

She was afraid of what she was feeling, but how could she tell him that?

"No, certainly not. I just—"

Caz rose to his feet and reached for her, lifting her from her chair and high into his arms. A roar went up from the crowd. She felt a rush of heat along her skin; she wound her arms around his neck and buried her face against his throat as he strode from the room.

"Hold tight, *kalila,*" he said softly, and she did, clinging to him, inhaling his scent until she was dizzy with it as he crossed the floor, climbed and climbed and climbed a staircase that she thought might be winding its way to heaven.

Hakim called out to them. "My lord! Lord Qasim!"

"Leave us," Caz growled.

"But my lord…"

Megan lifted her head. They had reached a narrow landing. Hakim stood halfway down the steep staircase. His eyes met hers and the hatred she saw in them made her catch her breath.

A massive wooden door loomed ahead. Caz shouldered it open, then kicked it shut behind him.

They were alone.

She knew it even before he slid her slowly down the length of his body and stood her on her feet. All she could hear was the beat of her heart and the snap of logs blazing on an enormous stone hearth.

Slowly she looked around her. They were in a silk-draped room lit by hundreds of white candles. The sole furnishing was a bed draped in sheer white linen and piled high with silk blankets and pillows.

"Megan."

Caz put his hand under her chin and lifted it. "It's all done now, sweetheart," he said softly. "Nobody's watching us. You can relax."

Relax? She almost laughed. Or cried. It was hard to know which was the better choice.

"Megan? Are you all right?"

"Fine," she said briskly. "I just... It's been a difficult day, you know?"

He knew. She'd begun the day an outcast, a modern-day Rapunzel locked away in the castle of a wicked magician, and ended it the wife of a sheikh.

His wife.

His pretend wife. He had to keep remembering that. The ceremony had been real enough, for Ahmet's people. Real enough for him, had he chosen to let it be so, but that didn't mean they were actually bound together in marriage.

The words they'd spoken weren't in his wife's language. The ceremony wasn't part of his wife's culture.

He wasn't the man his wife would have chosen for her husband.

And, damn it, she wasn't his wife.

How come he kept forgetting that?

Caz took a deep breath, then exhaled it slowly. Because he wanted her, that was how come. He'd wanted her from the first time he'd set eyes on her, sharp tongue, fiery temper and all. And now she was his.

How was a man supposed to remember he had no right to touch his bride on their wedding night? The moon was climbing the sky, casting its shy light through the window. The fire was as hot as his blood, the bed an invitation. He imagined what it would be like to undress her by the light of all those candles, watch as they cast shadows on her skin, as he exposed her to his eyes...

Hell.

Caz swung away. He was a man of discipline. A sheikh who had long ago learned to ignore his own needs when he had to. Surely, he could keep his hands off his wife for one night.

His wife, he thought again, and he knotted his hands, dug

them deep into his trouser pockets and walked to the far side of the room, deliberately putting as much distance as possible between himself and the woman he could not think of as his bride.

"All right," he said briskly. "I'll take some of those blankets and pillows and make myself a bed on the floor."

"You don't have to. I trust you. You can sleep..."

"No," he said sharply. "That wasn't part of our deal. I'll sleep on the floor. You sleep in the bed. And at first light, I'll take you away from here. All this will be over, Megan. We won't have to pretend this is the way we wanted things to be."

He almost told her more. That if he lay down in that bed with her, nothing would keep him from taking her.

But this was a charade. She wasn't his. She never could be.

So he tossed some pillows and blankets on the floor, went from candle to candle, snuffing out all but half a dozen nearest the bed so she wouldn't be trapped in the dark. Then he got beneath the blankets and turned his back to her.

"Get some sleep," he said gruffly. "You need it."

She didn't answer, but he hadn't expected her to. By now, she was probably terrified. The strange ceremony. The wild dancing. All of it must have struck her as barbaric.

Caz heard the whisper of silk, the creak of the mattress and shut his eyes to the images that danced through his head. His bride was in bed. He was on the floor. Damn Ahmet, anyway. Damn tradition, and custom, and the world itself.

What good was a kingdom when what a man wanted was—when the only thing he wanted was...

His wife.

CHAPTER TEN

HE HADN'T thought he could sleep but exhaustion reached up, dragged him down into the darkness.

Caz slept. He *must* have slept, because the next thing he knew, the few candles still lit were sputtering, moonlight filled the room...

And his wife stood by the window, weeping.

Caz was off the floor in a heartbeat. "Sweetheart?"

She kept her back to him, shook her head and fluttered her hands in that way women had of saying *Don't, stay away, I'm fine.* But he didn't believe it, not for a minute, and when he reached her, he took her gently by the shoulders and turned her to him.

"*Kalila.* What is it?"

Megan looked up. Moonlight striped Caz's face; she saw herself reflected in his pupils, a small, pathetic woman crying as if her heart might break, and for what reason? He'd done exactly as he'd promised. Saved her from Ahmet by marrying her, by pretending a wedding was what he'd wanted, by carrying her from the hall in the sight of hundreds of cheering barbarians and bringing her to this beautiful room...

To what should have been her wedding night.

The man she'd married was a man of his word. He'd done all he'd said he would...and her heart was breaking. Until this moment, she hadn't been brave enough to face the reason. Now, in that deepest time of night when truth is all that matters, she understood her despair.

She hadn't wanted Caz to bring her here and treat her honorably. She'd wanted him to lock the door, take her in his arms, tell her he was going to make her his wife.

"Megan."

His voice was ragged as their eyes met. Her heart began to race. Could he read her thoughts? What could be more humiliating than to have him realize that she wanted him?

"Megan," he said again, in a velvet whisper, and he lowered his mouth to hers and kissed her.

His kiss was soft; his touch gentle. He held her as if she were made of glass.

Still, she wept.

"Don't cry, *kalila*. I won't let anything hurt you."

He wouldn't, not if he lost his life defending her. She was safe now, but he knew what it had cost her. He'd put her through hell, brought her into the lair of a barbarian, forced her into marriage.

When you came down to it, how much difference was there between him and Ahmet?

But she'd accepted his kiss, even moved closer to him, her body pressed to his, taking comfort from his strength.

He rocked her against him, whispered words to soothe her in his own tongue.

She smelled of flowers, night and woman. Caz shut his eyes, buried his face in her hair, let her scent fill him.

His mouth twisted with irony.

His bride was clinging to him because he was the only familiar thing in her life, and he could only think how incredible it felt to hold her...

And how badly he wanted her.

So badly that he was going to give himself away, if he let her lean against him much longer.

Carefully he clasped her shoulders and tried to put some space between them. Megan shook her head and burrowed closer.

"It's okay," he murmured. "You're safe. I'll always keep you safe."

She sighed. He felt the flutter of her breath on his skin. Caz swallowed hard and reminded himself that this was all about offering comfort.

"Shall I get you a drink of water? Some coffee? I can slip downstairs…"

"Coffee's the last thing I need right now," she said with a little laugh. "Please, just—just stay with me."

Megan slipped her arms around his waist. Her cheek pressed against his chest. God, what was she doing to him? He had to think about something else. The night. Tomorrow's weather. Would it be okay? The helicopter…

"Caz?"

"What?"

"I'm sorry."

She was sorry? He held her away from him again, just enough so he could see her face. "For what?"

"Everything. I screwed up your meeting."

He smiled. "Livened it up, you mean."

"And I've put you at odds with Ahmet."

"I've always been at odds with Ahmet."

"Yes, but now… Is he angry? Because you and I are…because he thinks you and I are…"

"On the contrary." His smile tilted. "He's gained respect for me. I've got the girl he wanted."

That put an answering smile on her face.

"Better?" he said softly.

She nodded.

"No more tears, then." He plucked a silk scarf from the

back of a chair and gently blotted her eyes. "A woman shouldn't weep on her wedding night."

"Actually…" She gave a little laugh. "Actually that's the reason I was crying."

"I understand. When you agreed to come to Suliyam with me, you never imagined you'd end up being forced into marriage with a stranger."

"You're not a stranger," Megan said quickly. "In some ways, I feel as if I've known you all my life." She took a breath. "I was crying because I was thinking back a few weeks. One of my brothers just got married and the ceremony was, you know, filled with emotion."

"Ah. I understand. Our ceremony had to be an alien—"

She silenced him by putting her fingers lightly across his mouth. "You don't understand." Her voice softened. "It was a wonderful ceremony."

Caz's eyebrows rose. "Yeah?"

She smiled. A minute ago, he'd sounded like the exalted sheikh of Suliyam. Now, he sounded like a guy she might have met in the States.

"Yeah," she said gently. "The words that sounded so solemn, the bells, the dancers, and then, at the end, all those people sending up that wild cry…"

"They were happy for us."

"I know." Her smile dimmed. "And that's why I was crying, you know? I thought of how happy everyone was at my brother's wedding, and how happy they were at our— at the wedding today, and I felt, I don't know, guilty, maybe, because what happened wasn't real and…"

"You're a good and generous woman, Megan O'Connell."

"I'm a woman who's complicated your life."

Caz tilted her face up to his. "You've enriched it," he

said softly. "And you honored me enormously by becoming my bride."

"I am, aren't I?" Megan whispered. She could feel her blood humming. "Your bride, Caz. Your bride for this night."

They stared at each other. The sounds of the night, the sigh of the wind…everything faded away. There was nothing on the earth but this room. This moment.

"Caz?" Her voice flowed over him like liquid silver. "Do you want me?"

"Want you?" He made a sound that was half groan, half laugh. "*Kalila,* you're all I think about. You fill my mind, my soul, my heart."

"Then take me, Caz. Make me your wife tonight."

He looked down into her face and thought of a dozen reasons to kiss her and put her from him, to walk out of here and into the chill mountain night. He was a king. A man of honor.

But he'd never wanted a woman as he wanted her. And on this one night, he would be a man, not a king.

A man who would make love to his bride.

He gathered her into his arms and took her mouth with his. She moaned his name and wound her arms around his neck.

"I want to taste you, *kalila*. Every part of you."

Oh yes. It was what she wanted, too. All the arguing. The battle of words and will. Had it all been pretence to hide the truth? She sighed as Caz kissed her mouth, bent and nipped at her throat, brushed his lips over the straining silk that covered her breasts.

How could she have gone all these days without his touch? She'd wanted him from the beginning, wanted him, wanted him, wanted him…

"Turn your back to me," he whispered.

She did, and he pushed her hair aside and pressed his mouth to the nape of her neck. Her eyes closed; her head fell back as she felt his fingers at the tiny buttons that went from the top of her gown to her waist. He undid them one by one, turning it into an exquisite torment, pausing to kiss each bit of skin as he revealed it.

When he was done, she was trembling.

She began to turn toward him but he stopped her, slid the gown down her arms, lowered his mouth to the delicate juncture of shoulder and throat and pressed his lips there.

She moaned. Whispered his name. Reached back, took his hands, cupped them over her breasts.

Caz groaned as he felt the luscious weight of her breasts in his palms. Slowly he ran his fingers over her nipples, felt them bud and rise at his touch, heard her soft cry of pleasure. She leaned back against him, moved against him, and he slid his hand down to her belly, to the softness between her thighs, pressed her, hard, against his straining erection.

"Megan," he said, his voice low and rough. "Megan..."

She swung around in his arms and he slipped the gown from her shoulders, watching as it pooled at her feet. The gown had been Suliyam; what she wore beneath it was pure, unadulterated twenty-first century seductress, bra and panties of sheerest ivory lace.

"God," he whispered, "you're so beautiful."

Eyes locked to his face, she reached behind her. Undid the bra. Let it fall to her feet.

He felt every muscle in his body tighten with desire. Beautiful? No. The word wasn't enough. His bride was like a dream. Her face. Her eyes. Her mouth.

Her breasts.

They were small. High. The nipples were the deep pink of summer roses, already budding in anticipation of his kiss. A kiss he gave hungrily, bending to her, cupping her breasts, bringing them to his lips so he could lave the sweet, taut centers with his tongue and suck them deep into his mouth.

She sobbed out his name as he scooped her into his arms, carried her to the bed and laid her on it.

"Now," she whispered. Caz, please. I want you now."

She reached for him, ran her hands over his muscled shoulders, the soft hair on his chest, luxuriated in the race of his heart under her palms.

"Please," she begged, but when she touched his belt he caught her hands in one of his, raised them high above her head.

"Not yet," he said, and watched her face as he cupped his palm over the bit of lace between her thighs.

Her cry tore through the night, and when he slid his fingers under her panties and found the hot, passion-dampened flower of her womanhood, she exploded beneath him.

Megan sobbed his name; tears glittered in her eyes but now he knew they were tears of joy. They were for him, for what he made her feel, for what was happening to them both. The realization drove him higher than the mountains, the moon, the stars. He pulled down the scrap of lace, tore off his clothes and knelt between her thighs.

"Megan. Look at me."

Her eyes opened and filled with him.

"Who do you belong to?" His voice was a hoarse rasp; he barely recognized it as his own. "Who?" he demanded, and she lifted her arms to him.

"You," she whispered. "Only to you, Qasim."

He parted her thighs, touched the engorged tip of his penis to the soft portal that guarded the entrance to her body, her heart, her soul. She cried out and arched toward him, and Caz entered her.

God, oh God.

She was hot and wet and tight. So tight.

He gritted his teeth, forced himself to hold still. He didn't want to hurt her, he didn't want to hurt her, he didn't want to hurt her...

She sighed his name.

"Qasim. Qasim, my husband."

And he was lost.

Groaning, he thrust into her. Filled her. Slid his hands under her bottom and lifted her to him.

"Caz?" she said, her voice a breathless whisper. "Caz. I never knew..."

He drove forward until he was deep inside her. Drove again and again while she sobbed his name and rose to him. And when her body convulsed around him, when she screamed and bit his shoulder, Caz shuddered with a pleasure so intense he thought it might kill him.

But death would have been a small price to pay for what he felt as he fell over the edge of the universe with Megan, with his bride, in his arms.

The moon dipped behind the mountains and still they lay tangled in each other's arms, insulated from reality in their silk cocoon.

At last, Megan stirred. Caz gave her a long, tender kiss and rolled off her. She made a little sound of protest and he kissed her again as he drew her against him. She sighed, settled her head against his chest and laid her arm over his belly.

"I thought you were going to get up," she murmured.

"I'm not going anywhere."

"Um."

He smiled. "That's it?" he said, nuzzling a curl back from her throat and leaving a kiss in its place. "Just, 'um?'"

He felt her lips curve against his damp skin. "Were you hoping for applause, your highness?"

Caz laughed softly. "Well, if you're asking about wedding night traditions..."

Megan nipped at his shoulder. "Don't push your luck, my lord. You'll have to make do with 'um.'" She sighed, stroked her hand over his skin. "That was—"

"Wonderful."

"Yes."

"Amazing."

She smiled. "That, too."

Caz propped his head on his hand, stroked a tangle of soft curls from her face and his smile faded.

"Are you okay?"

"Yes."

"I mean—"

"I know what you mean. And I'm fine."

"You were so tight... I was afraid I'd hurt you."

"No." She caught the tip of his finger between her teeth as he stroked it over her mouth. "I just... I haven't been with anyone in a long time."

Why should that make him feel so happy? "Are the men in California blind?"

She laughed softly. "It's not them, it's me. I've been so focused on my career. You know. College. Grad school. Scrambling up the corporate ladder—"

"Difficult, I'd bet, when some men are busy sawing through the rungs." Megan's surprise showed on her face, and Caz tapped the tip of her nose with his finger. "Now who's being a chauvinist, *kalila?* Don't you think I know that it's tough being a woman in a man's world?"

"Do you, really? I thought—I mean, from the things you said that day in my office..."

"What I said was the truth. Most of my countrymen aren't prepared to see women as equals. Not the ones who live in—what do you call it? The sticks. Not them."

"And you want to change that."

"Yes. Absolutely. I *have* changed it, at least a little, in Suliyam City."

"But not in your palace."

"There, too."

"No way." Megan sat up and pulled the blankets to her chin. "You put me in the harem, remember? There's nothing equal about that."

"That was tradition."

"And that's a clever way of saying one thing and doing another."

"Hey." Caz grabbed her and tugged her down next to him. "Are we going to quarrel?"

Were they? She looked at him and the little sparks of anger that had come to life died away. How could she quarrel with this man now? She was in his arms again, looking up at him, seeing her reflection in his eyes…

And feeling an emotion so overwhelming it terrified her.

"No," she said, on a deep sigh. Smiling, she reached up and pushed his dark hair back from his forehead. "No, we're not going to quarrel."

Caz smiled. "Good. Because there's nothing to quarrel about, *kalila*. The tradition I referred to has to do with the king bringing an unmarried woman to live under his roof."

"Not good, huh?"

"Not good if that same king is about to set off on a tough selling job to a difficult audience."

Megan nodded. "Roads. Schools. Hospitals. All badly needed, and all requiring an infusion of capital."

"Foreign capital, and even the thought of foreign investors having a stake in Suliyam's resources makes some of the old tribal chieftains shudder."

"So, how will you manage?"

"I'll show them facts and figures. They're tough, but they're reasonable."

"Unlike Ahmet."

"Very unlike Ahmet." Caz smiled. "Amazing."

"What?"

"That in all the years I've dealt with financial advisors, accountants and auditors, I never once ended up in bed with one of them."

She laughed. "Not so amazing, considering your last financial wizard was a sixty-year-old man."

Caz tried to look horrified. "You checked up on me?"

"Of course," Megan said primly. "Would T, B and M take on a client without knowing something more about him than you can read in the gossip columns?"

"Damn those columns." Caz rolled onto his belly, bent over her and kissed her mouth. "Half what they print are lies and the other half are exaggerations."

"Ah."

"Ah, what?"

"Ah, no women beating down your doors?"

"No!" He chuckled. "Well, maybe a few."

"No big-spending, easy life?"

"I sowed some wild oats," he admitted.

"Because you could," she teased.

"Because I grew up hearing how I'd some day be king, and the job description didn't sound much like anything a man would want, given half a choice."

The humor had gone out of Caz's voice. He rolled on his back and folded his arms beneath his head.

"Hey," Megan said softly, scooting closer, folding her arms and resting them on his chest. "I was only joking."

"Yeah. I know." He looked at her and smiled. "Would you be shocked if I said being emperor of the universe isn't all it's cracked up to be?"

That was what she'd called him. The memory made her blush, especially now that she'd seen him in action among his people.

"I'd never be shocked at anything you said," she murmured, and brushed her lips against his.

Caz put his arms around her. "No?"

"No."

He cupped the back of her head, brought his mouth to her ear and whispered to her. She caught her breath and drew back.

"See?" he said huskily. "I did shock you, after all."

Megan smiled and gave a catlike stretch so that every inch of her body moved against his.

"On the contrary, my lord. You haven't shocked me. You've fascinated me. I just wonder...can two people really do that?"

Caz felt his body quicken. "Why don't we find out?" he whispered.

He rolled her beneath him. She wrapped her arms around his neck. And by the time they'd answered the question, the room was tinted with the rosy glow of dawn.

They fell asleep, still close in each other's arms, and were awakened by a knock on the door.

"My lord? It is I. Hakim."

Caz sat up and yawned. "What is it?" he called.

"You said you wished to awaken early. It is almost six."

"Six?" Megan whispered in disbelief.

"Hakim's a literalist," Caz whispered back, leaning over and kissing her.

She giggled. Giggled, she thought, and giggled again. Last night, she'd felt as if the world had come to an end and now...

Now, she was so happy it frightened her.

"My lord? I have brought coffee." The doorknob rattled and Megan dived under the blankets. "Shall I—"

"No!" Caz shot from the bed, searched for his trousers and settled for a silk coverlet he wrapped around his waist. "Leave it in the hall."

"But highness…"

"Leave it," Caz said sharply.

"As you wish, sir." Hakim paused. "I've told your pilot to be ready in an hour."

"Yes, yes." Caz glanced at the bed and opened the door just enough to take the tray. "Thank you, Hakim. That's all."

Hakim followed Caz's eyes. "I trust your plans are unchanged, Sheikh Qasim," he said coldly. "That we are, indeed, leaving this place this morning and not lingering for further…festivities."

"Watch yourself," Caz said sharply.

Hakim flushed. "I have only your interests at heart, lord."

Caz elbowed the door shut. "The hell you do," he muttered, and slammed the tray on a table near the bed. After a minute, he sighed and ran his hands through his hair. "Sweetheart? He's gone."

Megan sat up slowly. Her face was pink; the look in her eyes started his anger all over again.

"*Kalila,*" he said, and went to her. "I'm sorry."

She shook her head, pulled back as he tried to embrace her. But Caz was persistent, and the need to be close to him won. Sighing, she put her arms around him and rested her head against his chest.

"Hakim hates me."

"It's not you. It's what you represent. What he sees me doing. All the changes I've made, the changes I intend to make." He cupped Megan's shoulders and looked into her eyes. "He served my father."

"And now he serves you."

"That's just the problem, sweetheart. He wants me to be like my father, but I'm not." A muscle knotted in his jaw. "And I don't think he's ever forgiven me for the foreign blood that runs in my veins."

"Foreign…? Oh. Your mother."

"Yeah." A smile curved his lips. "You'd have liked her."

"But she left you."

"She left Suliyam."

"Why? If her husband was here, and her son—"

How did you explain to your American wife that your American mother couldn't handle the heat? The desert? The boundaries set by centuries of tradition?

A few words would have done it, but for some reason he couldn't quite comprehend, Caz didn't want to lay all those things out for Megan's inspection. And that, he knew, was foolish. Megan wasn't really his wife, not by the law of her land. He didn't have to worry about putting ideas in her head. She was going back to her own people, leaving Suliyam…

Leaving him.

The realization stabbed through his heart.

"Come here," he said gruffly, enfolding her in his arms. "Why should we waste time talking about other people?" He bent his head, brushed his mouth over hers. "For now, there's only you and me."

"But Hakim said—"

"Forget Hakim." Caz eased Megan down against the pillows. "Just think about me. About this." He touched his lips to hers, softly, then with growing passion. When he drew back, he knew he couldn't keep the promise he'd made to send her home. He wanted her here, in his arms, in his bed. He wanted to argue with her, laugh with her, share his days and nights with her for as long as fate would permit. "Megan." He took a deep breath. "I know I said I'd send you home as soon as we return to my palace, but…"

"But?"

"But I've been thinking," he said, hurrying the words, refusing to acknowledge the truth of what he felt spreading through his heart. "We still have work to do."

"Work." Her smile faltered. Why had she imagined he might talk about something else? "Yes, of course."

"It's been difficult for you, pretending to have no role in that work."

"Yes." She touched her hand to his cheek. "But I understand, Caz. It's just the way things are here."

"But that would all change, if I could introduce you as my wife."

Megan's heart fluttered. "What are you saying?"

"I know it's asking a great deal, *kalila*. But if you're willing to play the part a little longer…"

She stared into his face, thinking of all the reasons to say no, what he was asking her was out of the question, that it was impossible…

"*Kalila.*" His voice was low and rough with need. "Don't leave me. Not yet."

Their eyes met and held. Then Megan reached for him, brought his mouth down to hers and gave him her answer with her kiss.

CHAPTER ELEVEN

At NOON, their party left Ahmet's mountain stronghold.

They rode out, Caz on the same black stallion he'd ridden the day they'd arrived. Megan sat sidesaddle before him, secure in the circle of his arm. Ahmet and his men escorted them, whooping and cheering and waving their lances and rifles in the air.

"Tradition," Caz whispered in answer to Megan's inquiring look. "Ahmet honors us. I know it must seem bizarre, but—"

"It seems wonderful. It *is* wonderful." She turned to him and laughed. "The fortress, the horses, the riders...it's perfect."

Caz felt some of the tension drain out of him. All this was strange to his wife. Would she regret that she'd married a man from such an alien culture? It was only temporary, of course, but still, he wanted her to be happy and not judge his people and his country too harshly.

"Do you really like it?"

"Oh, yes! The colors, the sounds... It's magnificent." She laughed again and tilted her head up to his. "Even Ahmet."

Caz grinned. "I'll tell him you said so."

"Don't you dare!"

"What will you offer for my silence?"

Her smile was sweetly wicked. "What would you like?"

He bent his head to hers again and told her. Color flooded her face; heat suffused her body.

"You drive a hard bargain, my lord," she said softly, "but what can I do except agree?"

God, she was wonderful, this wife of his. Caz drew her back more closely against him.

"We have a deal," he said softly. They rode in silence for a few minutes. Then he cleared his throat. "I thought— I was concerned you might find all this...barbaric."

"I guess I might have, not too long ago," she said, with the kind of honesty he'd come to expect from her. "But now—"

"Now?"

"Now, I see things differently."

His lips grazed her temple. "Why, *kalila?*"

The answers were on the tip of her tongue. Because now she rode with a man who was no longer a stranger. Because she was wrapped in the arms of her husband. Because he, and all he represented, were part of her.

Because Qasim had become her life.

"Kalila." Caz spread his hand against her midriff, his thumb just under the rise of her breast. His voice was husky; his breath warmed her face. "Tell me what's changed since we first came here."

Megan turned her face to his. Tell him, she thought, oh, tell him...

A roar went up from the riders as they formed a circle around them. Caz muttered a curse and reined in the stallion. They'd reached the helicopter; Ahmet rode toward them, signaled for silence and began to speak.

Caz bent his head to Megan's, translating softly.

"Ahmet says his timing is lousy."

She laughed. This was far safer ground. "He does, huh?"

"No, but he should." His arms tightened around her.

"Actually, he says I am a lucky man to have won the heart of a woman more beautiful than the moon."

"Translation: He was outmaneuvered."

"Wonderful. The translator needs a translator."

"Am I right?"

"Of course you're right, but we don't have to tell him that. He also says that it's not too late to change my mind. He offers me a hundred horses for you."

"Is that good?"

"It's amazing," Caz said, with a quick smile. "A man can buy twenty excellent wives for one hundred horses. Don't poke your elbow in my ribs, *kalila*. It's the truth. Go on. Smile at our friend. Let him know that you're flattered."

Megan smiled brightly as Caz rattled off a reply.

"What did you tell him?"

"I said he did honor to us both and that it was a tempting offer should I ever—oof!"

"Tempting, indeed."

"Behave yourself, woman. A man doesn't get an offer of one hundred horses every day." Caz drew her more closely against him. "And I told him you were worth a thousand times a hundred horses, *kalila*. I'm a very lucky man."

Megan's heart thudded. She was lucky, too. Caz had changed her life. A week ago, she'd been working in an office, leading a quiet existence. Now, she was the wife of a man who fulfilled every fantasy she'd ever had and some she'd never dared imagine.

She'd almost been foolish enough to tell him so.

She had to remember that none of this was real. He'd made that clear and that was fine, wasn't it? That was exactly the way she wanted things... Wasn't it?

"*Kalila?* What's wrong?"

Everything. Everything was wrong...

"Sweetheart? What's the matter?"

"Nothing," Megan said brightly. "I'm just—I'm a little tired."

"Damn, but I'm a fool! Of course you're tired. I've given you a rough few days." Caz eased her to the ground, then dropped to his feet beside her and swept her into his arms. The crowd gave a throaty roar, but neither of them heard it. "Let's get out of here."

Hakim stepped forward, but the sheikh ignored his aide and carried Megan into the helicopter, settling her into a seat beside him. The 'copter blades began to whirr and the craft lifted, tilted forward and gathered speed until Ahmet and his men were black specks against the towering mountains.

Caz leaned close and put his mouth to Megan's ear. "We'll be home soon."

She nodded and closed her eyes, afraid he might read the truth glittering in them.

Home wasn't a palace by the sea. It wasn't a condo in L.A.

Home was right here, by the side of the man she loved.

Days before, when they'd first arrived at the palace, a handful of men had greeted them. Caz had left her in Hakim's care and driven off with the small delegation.

To a man, no one had acknowledged her presence.

It was all different now.

At least fifty men waited for them in the desert, a long line of Humvees purring behind them like big cats. The men bowed when Caz stepped onto the landing pad, but their dark eyes focused on Megan.

They know, she thought.

What had Caz told them? Had he explained he'd taken her as his wife to save her from Ahmet? Instinct told her they wouldn't understand such a gallant gesture.

But he'd surely told them his marriage was one of convenience?

Then, why were so many of their glances hostile?

Caz greeted them pleasantly. He drew her forward and spoke some more; she heard him use her name. The men looked at her again, then murmured among themselves. Finally, one stepped forward, bowed and began talking, clearly directing his remarks to her.

"He welcomes you," Caz said in a low voice.

Welcomes? She doubted it. She wanted to turn to Caz and burrow into his arms. Instead, she held her head high and smiled.

"Tell him I thank him for coming to greet me."

"He says you have only to ask for whatever you wish and he will scour the earth to find it."

"Tell him I thank him for that, too…and don't mention that I really think he'd like to dab me with honey and tie me to an anthill."

Caz's mouth twitched. "I like the dabbing you with honey part, but only if I can replace the ants with my mouth."

She felt her cheeks color. "Are you sure nobody here understands English?"

"I am positive, and what if they do?" He put his arm around her and drew her against his side. "A man may cherish his own wife."

"Tradition?"

"And one I don't intend to change. Come on, sweetheart. Tell Ari you're grateful for all his good wishes."

"Yes. Of course." She looked at the men, smiled at the one who'd spoken for them all and saw their wary expressions turn to pleasure when she delivered the message in their own language. Caz grinned at her as he led her toward the Humvees.

"You've picked up some of our language," he said. "I'm impressed...though nothing about you should surprise me any more."

"Caz? How did they know about—about us?"

"I sent word," he said as he handed her into the Hummer. "Some of these men are my advisors. It was important that they know of our marriage."

"They think we're really..."

She sounded shocked. Perhaps he should have told her he was going to inform his people that he had married her. Maybe then she wouldn't be staring at him with such a strange expression on her face.

What was she thinking? Moments ago, she'd seemed so happy. Now...

Now, she looked as if she had the weight of the world on her shoulders.

His belly knotted. Was she afraid she might be trapped in a place like this, with a man like him?

"Caz? They really think—"

"Yes." He told himself to smile. "That's not a problem, is it?"

A problem? She wanted to fling herself into his arms. Did this mean he didn't want to treat their marriage as a temporary arrangement? Had he fallen in love with her as she had with him? Did he want her to stay with him, live with him, bear his children and grow old with him?

"No," she said, "of course not. In fact—in fact..."

"In fact what?" he said, trying not to sound as if his life hinged on her answer.

Megan wanted to weep. His tone was polite. That was all. Polite, as if what they were discussing had no real meaning, as if this really were about nothing more important than what he'd told his men.

Caz had married her because he had to, and she couldn't

be fool enough to think that the one night she'd spent in his arms had made him fall in love with her.

"In fact," she said, "you handled it very well."

It? *It?* Their marriage, she meant, and its dissolution. Caz looked at his wife as the Hummer lurched forward. She turned her face to the window.

Apparently the view was more important than him or their marriage.

The warmth of the last minutes, of all the minutes that had slipped by since he'd made her his wife, drained from his heart. He was from one world. She was from another. What they'd shared in the mountains was a fantasy.

What he owed her now was reassurance.

"There's nothing to worry about," he said quietly.

"I'm not—"

"You are. And it's not necessary. We have an agreement. I intend to honor its terms. Why would I do otherwise?"

Why, indeed? Megan's eyes blurred with tears.

"Megan?" Caz touched her shoulder. "I promise you, I'll honor it."

She nodded. He would do what he'd said. He was a good man. An honorable man.

It wasn't his fault he hadn't fallen in love with her.

A week went by, filled with meetings with an endless stream of elders, advisors and chieftains. Of cautious give and take. Of protocol, even when there were times Caz wanted to slam his hand on the table and say, *Can't you see that we need to do these things if we're to survive as a nation?*

But he knew better. He hadn't done anything remotely like that. Instead, he'd listened to questions, provided answers, turned to the woman seated beside him time and time again and always, always, she was ready with a response, a circled paragraph, a list of figures to help him prove his point.

Thanks to Megan, the meetings he'd dreaded had gone well. They'd concluded weeks earlier than he'd expected, and he'd gained the approval he wanted for his proposals.

Even his people were impressed. They'd gone from raising their eyebrows at her presence to looking at her when she spoke. Today, one of his advisors had actually asked her a direct question.

He wondered if she had any idea what an enormous step forward that was, not only for her but also for women in his country. Late this afternoon, the most traditional of the elders had sidled up to him and murmured that perhaps, just perhaps, there was something to be said for educating females.

"Not too much," the old man had added hastily. "Only as much as is necessary for them to be as helpful as your wife, my lord Qasim. She is a gem among women."

Caz, strolling the beach, kicked a small white stone out of his way.

Coming home, he'd imagined what it would be like to show Megan the narrow streets of his city, the ancient bazaars, the hidden places he'd discovered as a boy.

He'd pictured her delight at the little shop that sold silks from China, the half-moon bay just up the coast where dolphins played in the shallows. He'd thought of what it would be like to spend their days exploring his world, their nights making love in the enormous bed that had belonged to five centuries of Suliyam's kings.

Caz bent down, scooped up a shell and tossed it into the sea.

Instead his wife and he were strangers. They were polite to each other. Pleasant. They conferred before the meetings and sometimes after them, but once the day was over, he went his way. She went hers.

And at night...

At night, he lay on the sofa in his sitting room, stared up at the ceiling and tried not to think about Megan lying alone in his bed.

She was only in that bed because he'd commanded it.

"I'll stay in the women's quarters," she'd said the day of their return to the palace.

"The king's wife does not sleep in the women's quarters," he'd said, silently cursing himself for sounding like a stiff-necked martinet. "It would generate talk, and it would not be—"

"Tradition," she'd said, with a taut smile.

Let her think that. The truth was, until his father's marriage to his mother, generations of wives had slept in the women's quarters. It had been the only workable system, back when a king had three, four, a dozen wives, but he'd be damned if he'd tell her that.

It was better than telling her he wanted to know she was in his bed, to be able to dream of her there, with her hair spread over his pillows, even if the image was torture.

How many times had he risen from the sofa, gone to the bedroom door, stood outside it with the blood roaring in his ears as he imagined opening that door, going to her, taking her in his arms and telling her...and telling her...

"Sire?"

Caz swung around. Hakim hurried toward him, huffing and puffing with the effort of walking through the white sand.

"What is it, Hakim? I'm not in the mood to be—"

"It is important, my lord. Your cousin wishes to see you."

"My cousin?"

"Alayna. She has been waiting to meet with you for days."

Hakim spoke the name with all the importance Caz knew it deserved, knew, too, that he had to deal with Alayna eventually. He owed her that...but not now.

"Later, Hakim."

"But Lord Qasim..."

"Later, I said. Tell my cousin that I will see her, but not today."

Hakim nodded stiffly. "Very well, sir. In that case, there is something else. A minor matter..."

"Get to it, man! I told you, I'm not in the mood to be bothered."

"It concerns the woman's departure."

"What woman? What departure?" Caz glowered at his aide. "What are you babbling about?"

"Sir, your pilot will not agree to the flight without your direct permission. I told him there was no need to trouble you, but he insists that—"

"What flight?"

"Miss O'Connell's flight, lord."

"Is this a riddle, Hakim? Her flight to where?"

"To the United States."

Hakim was looking at him as if he were slow-witted. Hell, one of them was.

"Why would Miss O'Connell think she's flying to the States?"

"Because her arrangement with you is at an end, sire."

"What?"

"Is it not so? The woman says—"

"You didn't think it necessary to speak with me?"

"I was only trying to save you the bother, lord. The woman—"

Caz took a step forward, his fists bunched at his sides.

"The woman," he said, his voice low and menacing, "is my wife. The Sheikha. You will refer to her by title. Is that clear?"

"But my lord…"

"Is it clear, damn you?"

He watched his aide's face whiten.

"Yes, lord. Of course. Forgive me, sir."

But Caz wasn't listening. He'd already started running toward the palace.

Megan had almost finished packing when the door burst open.

"What in hell are you doing?"

His voice roared through the room. He was angry, but she'd expected that. She'd expected him to confront her, too. Hakim had been happy to make the arrangements for her departure without involving Caz—the aide made no pretence of how eager he was to see her gone—but she'd suspected it wouldn't be possible.

Nothing happened in this antiquated corner of the world without the involvement of Sheikh Qasim, and she'd known he would not take kindly to letting her leave without some sort of confrontation.

All week, she'd sensed that his behavior—polite, formal, distant—masked a growing anger. And what in hell did *he* have to be angry about? She was the same woman she'd always been; Caz was the one who'd changed. One moment he'd been her passionate lover, the next he'd become…

There was no way to describe what he'd become. Cold, uncaring, disinterested. All that, and more.

And it hurt.

Still, she wasn't prepared for the rage flashing in his eyes. Well, she thought, taking a blouse from its hanger, that was fine.

She'd rather deal with his anger than with his disinterest. Better to go toe-to-toe with him than to lie in his bed, alone and unhappy, crying herself to sleep, and wasn't that a stupid thing to have done all these nights? What was there to cry about? She'd figured out, days ago, that she'd never really fallen in love with Caz. Pretty pathetic, when a modern woman had to feed herself a lie about love rather than admit all she'd wanted was to sleep with a man.

"Did you hear me? I said—"

"I heard you. What does it look like I'm doing?" Megan folded the blouse neatly. Damn, her hands were shaking. "I'm packing."

"The hell you are!"

She told herself to keep calm. He was trying to upset her, and she'd be damned if she'd let him succeed.

"Packing is generally the first step before a person leaves," she said calmly.

"Perhaps you've forgotten that you work for me."

"Perhaps *you've* forgotten that my job here is done."

"It's done when I say it is."

"It's done when the meetings end. Well, they ended."

"There's also the little matter of our marriage."

She looked up. His eyes were so narrow she could hardly see them and a muscle beat rapidly in his jaw. Dark and dangerous, indeed. How about dark, dangerous and insufferable? How kind of him to remind her of some of the things she hadn't liked about him when they met.

"There is no marriage, remember? Not a real one."

"Would you say that if we'd been married in Los Angeles?"

"We *weren't* married in Los Angeles, we were married in Suliyam, and you made it perfectly clear that—"

"Are you suggesting marriages here are not legal?"

"I'm simply reminding you of what you told me. This marriage isn't binding."

Caz folded his arms and glowered. She was right. That was what he'd told her. What was wrong with him? Why was he so damned angry?

And why did the statement about their marriage sound so different, coming from her?

Because he was the king, that was why. If anyone ended this union, it would be him.

He told her that, and when she barked a laugh, he felt the heat rise to his face.

"Just listen to yourself, Qasim. You are unbelievab—"

"I am your husband," he roared. "And in Suliyam, a wife may not leave her husband without permission."

"Is that what this is all about? You want me to grovel? Well, I won't. You told me I would be free to leave, that our vows had no meaning, that—"

Caz caught her by the shoulders and lifted her to her toes. "I said the marriage would have no meaning, that I would annul it, that you would have to do nothing once you were back in the States...but you're still in my country. Until I choose to set you free, you belong to me."

Damn it, he thought in disgust, was he really calling up one of the barbaric traditions he'd sought to destroy? From the way his wife was looking at him, he sure as hell was, but what was he supposed to do? Let a woman play him for a fool? Let a woman take the upper hand?

Let this woman, only this woman, steal his heart and walk out of his life?

Didn't she feel anything for him? She did. She had to. He remembered that long night she'd spent in his arms. How she'd sighed, moved, whispered his name, and suddenly nothing mattered but wiping away the deceit they'd woven and facing the truth.

"Megan," he said hoarsely, and when she looked into his eyes, he gathered her against him and kissed her.

She fought him. Struggled to tear her mouth from his. He didn't have the words to tell her what she meant to him, but he could show her. He could kiss her until she knew his hunger, until she responded as she had on their wedding night.

And then, when he'd almost lost hope, her mouth softened. Clung to his. She made a little sound that was as much despair as it was surrender. It almost broke his heart when he tasted the salt of her tears on her lips.

"*Kalila*. Don't cry."

She shook her head. "Caz. I beg you. Let me go."

"I don't want you to leave me."

"Yes, you do. Whatever was between us died when we came back here. That time in the mountains was an illusion."

"It was real," he said fiercely. She wouldn't look at him and he hunched down, cupped her face, forced her to meet his eyes. "I love you."

The words were true. He knew it as soon as he spoke them.

"I beg you, *kalila*. Don't leave me. Stay with me. Be my wife. Lie in my arms at night, stay by my side during the day. I love you, Megan. I love—"

Megan sobbed his name, brought his face down to hers and gave her husband the answer he sought in her kiss.

CHAPTER TWELVE

MEGAN awoke lying curled against her husband, her head on his chest, her hand spread over his heart.

Doves cooed to each other in the courtyard beneath the bedroom window; she could hear the sea beating gently against the crescent of white sand beach only a short distance away.

Caz, still asleep, lay on his back. With just a little effort, she could look up and see his firm chin, his softly stubbled jaw.

How she loved him! How she loved waking like this each morning, lying close to him, feeling the glorious weight of his arm wrapped around her

Two weeks ago, she'd probably have described the way he held her as possessive. Now, she thought of it as protective.

Amazing, how her perspective had changed in fourteen short days.

Sometimes, lying in his embrace, she wondered if other married people were this happy. It didn't seem possible. To begin each day with so much joy in your heart and end it thanking whatever gods might be listening for the miracle that had brought such love into your life?

Nobody else could feel this way. Nobody. Not even her brothers. Not even her sister. Keir and Cullen might look at their wives with their hearts shining in their eyes; Fallon's smile might turn soft and dreamy when Stefano entered the room, but could any of them really know such bliss?

Impossible.

Surely she was the only woman in the world who loved a man so deeply. Absolutely, she was the only one loved so deeply in return. Caz was—he was—

"Beautiful," Caz murmured in a voice husky with sleep.

Megan smiled as her husband rolled her onto her back. "Good morning," she said softly.

He smiled, too, and brushed his lips over hers. "Good morning, *kalila*. When was the last time I told you that I love you?"

"Well, let's see…" Megan linked her hands behind his neck. "Was it at dinner? Maybe it was when we came to bed. It might have been later than that, when we decided to go down to the beach to try to count the stars."

"Mmm." Caz nuzzled a tangle of auburn curls from her shoulder and nipped lightly at the tender flesh he'd exposed. "You forgot early this morning. I woke you at dawn, remember?"

Indeed, he had. Her skin still tingled at the memory. "Did you?" She batted her lashes. "I don't remember that, my Lord."

"You don't, huh?"

"No. You might have to remind—" She caught her breath as he kissed her breast, teased the nipple with tongue and teeth, then sucked it into his mouth. "Yes. Oh, yes, I remember you did that."

He slid down her body, kissing her belly, nuzzling apart her thighs, burying his face in the heat of her, the scent of her, the essence of this woman who had changed his life.

"Do you remember this, too?" he whispered, slipping his hands beneath her, lifting her to his mouth, opening her to him so he could taste her, feast on her, luxuriate in the soft moans that drove him crazy.

"Caz. Caz…"

"Tell me," he said thickly. "Say the words, *kalila*. I need to hear them."

"I love you," Megan whispered, "love you, love you, love…"

She cried out and he rose above her, sheathed himself in her, and when she cried out again, he fell with her into that heart-stopping moment in time when they were alone in the endless universe.

"Megan?"

"Mmm."

Caz propped himself on his elbow, smiled as he traced the tip of his finger down her nose, over her lips and down her chin.

"Come on, *kalila*. Stay awake. I have something important to discuss with you."

"What does that mean?"

"It means, I want you to pay attention."

"No." She rolled on her belly, pushed him back against the pillows and folded her arms on his chest. "Ka-lee-lah. What's it mean?"

"You don't know?"

"Uh uh. I've meant to ask you endless times."

"You've picked up so much of my language…" He grinned. "But then, I don't suppose any of the men we've met with address each other as 'sweetheart.'"

"Sweetheart?" He nodded; she smiled. "It has a lovely sound."

"I'm glad you approve."

Megan nipped his bottom lip. "Don't take that smart-alecky tone with me, Lord Qasim."

"Smart what?"

"You understand what I said. You're as American as I am."

"No, I'm not."

"You are."

He smiled. After a few seconds, he cleared his throat. "Megan? Do you miss America very much?"

"A little," she said, with the honesty he loved. "But I have you, and you mean more to me than anything else."

Caz pressed a kiss into her hair. "I promise, we'll go back for a visit very soon."

"And I'll introduce you to my family." Megan's smile faltered. "I'm not looking forward to that. Oh," she said quickly, "I didn't mean that the way it sounded. I only meant... They'll be hurt, that I didn't tell them we were getting married."

"Well, we'll explain that we didn't know about it until it happened—unless you don't want them to hear that part."

"That you married me to save me from the big, bad wolf?" She laughed. "Of course I want them to hear it. They'll love it. My brothers will take you straight into the O'Connell clan because you're so macho, and my sisters will ooh and ahh. It's not every modern-day woman finds her own knight in shining armor." Megan tucked a fingertip into a soft curl on his chest. "I guess what'll upset them is that they weren't part of our wedding. Well, I'll just point out that they couldn't have been."

"No," Caz said wryly, "not with Ahmet standing in for best man."

"And maid of honor." Megan giggled. "There's a thought. Ahmet, in a bridesmaid's gown. Can't you just see it?"

"What I can see," Caz said, getting up and scooping her

into his arms, "is you in white lace, me in a tux, your sisters—how many are there?"

"Two," she answered, puzzled, "but—"

"Two sisters in pink or yellow or whatever you like best, and those three brothers-in-law of mine in tuxes." He grinned as he carried her into the adjoining bathroom and set her on her feet next to the step-up marble tub. "If I have to wear a monkey suit, so do they."

"I'm sure they'll love you to pieces for your kindness, but what are you talking about?"

"Our wedding, *kalila*. What else would impel a sane man into wearing a tuxedo?"

"We've already had our wedding."

"Not a real one, sweetheart." Caz turned on the water and gathered her into his arms as it thundered into the enormous tub. "You deserve the kind of wedding girls dream of."

Megan leaned back in his arms. "What do you know of wedding dreams, Lord Qasim?"

"I know," Caz said with a lift of his eyebrows. "I'm at an age where I've been to enough weddings to know that it certainly isn't the grooms who want the tuxedos, the engraved invitations, the fiftieth microwave oven that you have to pretend is the first you've received."

"Just goes to show you've been going to the wrong parties. My relatives will know enough to give us a gift certificate for a day spent skydiving."

Caz raised his eyebrows. "Don't tell me. My wife skydives?"

"She does," Megan said primly. "And she's never found anything she enjoys more."

"She hasn't, huh?"

A smile curled across her lips. "Well," she said softly, "not until now." Caz kissed her and she leaned back in his arms and sighed. "You poor man. All those weddings, and I bet you never figured you'd go to one of your own."

Something changed in his expression. A shift of his smile, a darkening of his eyes...she wasn't sure what, but she knew she'd seen something.

"Caz? What's the matter?"

"Nothing."

"Tell me. You looked—"

"I looked like a man contemplating an incredible reality, sweetheart." He cupped her face, threaded his fingers into her hair. "I love you, with all my heart."

"That's good. It's very, very good because I love you, too."

"I want to make you my wife again, this time in a white wedding with your whole family present. Your mother. Your father."

"My stepfather." She kissed his mouth. "Amazing, isn't it, that there are still things we don't know about each other?"

"There's plenty of time to learn."

"Yes. There is. A lifetime." She smiled. "Where will we hold this wedding?"

"Here. In the palace. Unless you'd rather—"

"I love the idea. So will my sisters. And my sisters-in-law." A mischievous grin lit her face. "And my brothers, and my brother-in-law, and a bunch of fat, gorgeous babies. The O'Connells are a big clan, Sheikh Qasim, and growing."

"I hope so," Caz said, and spread his hand over her belly. "I want children, *kalila*. Little girls, with your beautiful eyes."

"Sons, with your wonderful smile." Her voice broke. "Caz, I'm so happy."

"Yes," he whispered, "yes, I know, *kalila*. I know."

He kissed her, kissed her again as he stepped into the huge marble tub with her in his arms, and soon the only sounds in the room were the soft splash of water, whispers and sighs.

Megan checked the time, tried to figure out the corresponding hour in New York, Boston, Sicily, Connecticut and Las Vegas, and gave up.

So what if she woke everybody? She was remiss as it was; she should have phoned home days ago to tell her family about Caz, but these new things—that she was bringing her husband home to meet them soon, that they'd all be attending a wedding in Suliyam—couldn't wait.

She called Bree first and reached her sister's voice mail.

"Aren't you ever home?" she demanded. "Honestly, Briana, how can I tell you my news if you're not there?"

Then she disconnected. It was a wicked thing to do, but Bree deserved it.

Keir and Cassie were next. *Hello,* Keir's voice said, *you've reached the O'Connells. We can't take your call right now...*

"For heaven's sake," Megan grumbled, and dialed again.

Fallon and Stefano weren't home, either. Their housekeeper answered, but since Megan's knowledge of Italian and the housekeeper's knowledge of English just about totaled zero, she didn't get much further than, "Just tell them Megan called."

Sean's cell phone didn't answer at all, and when she tried to reach Cullen and Marissa, all she got was static.

Megan hit the disconnect button and rolled her eyes. Great. She had the most wonderful news of her life and nobody to share it with.

Well, no. Her mother was probably reachable in Las Vegas, but she wanted to tell the others first. Ma would start making plans, and she preferred the plans she'd just made with Caz. Life would be simpler if she had the backing of Fallon and Briana.

And wasn't that silly?

Her mother would be thrilled for her. *Aren't you ever going to meet a man and fall in love, Megan?* Mary was always saying. She'd been saying it more often lately, at least once at each O'Connell wedding.

Megan smiled, picked up the phone...

"Miss O'Connell?"

It was Hakim. So much for ET calling home, Megan thought, and tossed the phone aside.

"Yes, Hakim. What is it?"

"Will you please come with me?"

He was supposed to address her as "my lady." She'd heard Caz tell him that. It was what everyone called her, even though she'd told her husband she'd be happy if they just called her Megan.

"'My lady' is traditional," he'd replied, and softened the starchy answer with a quick grin. "Trust me, sweetheart. If I told my people to address you by your first name, they'd die of shock."

So she was "my lady" to her husband's people, even to Hakim...except when Caz wasn't there. She hadn't made an issue of it. Her husband's aide had unresolved issues with all that had happened. He also made her uncomfortable as hell, but she hadn't told Caz that, either.

Hakim would come around.

"Come with you where?" she asked politely. "Has my husband sent for me?"

"Your husband is busy, Miss O'Connell. That is why I've come for you."

Megan nodded. Caz had some sort of meeting this afternoon. "Will you need me with you?" she'd asked, and he'd said no, not today.

"Tired of having me around already," she teased, and he'd caught her in his arms and gathered her close.

"Never," he'd told her, his eyes so serious, his tone so defiant, that she'd slipped her arms around him and kissed him.

Well, something must have changed, she thought as she followed Hakim down the wide hall that led to the formal meeting rooms of the palace. Perhaps she should have brought her briefcase. Her notes.

"Hakim. Wait a minute. Who's my husband meeting with? I'd like to go back to our rooms and get my papers."

Hakim made an abrupt right. They'd entered a narrow corridor, one she'd never seen before.

"Hakim? I said—"

The aide made another sharp right. A latticework door loomed ahead.

"You will not need your papers for this, Miss O'Connell."

His voice had dropped to a whisper that made the hair rise on the back of her neck.

"What is this?" she said sharply. "Where is my husband?"

"He is there, beyond that door."

Hakim pressed his back to the wall and motioned her past him. Megan stared at the cold eyes, the slash of a mouth. She didn't want to move...

Motion through the lattice caught her eye.

She saw her husband, standing in the center of a small room. A woman was with him.

Her heart filled with dread. *Don't look,* a voice inside her whispered. *Megan, don't look...*

Her feet moved forward, seemingly of their own volition.

She put her eye to the lattice, stared at the woman...and immediately recognized her. This was who she'd seen with Caz weeks ago, the stunning brunette who'd kissed him.

His cousin, Caz had said. She'd kissed him to thank him for not forcing her to marry a man she didn't love.

She wasn't kissing him now. Instead she was wrapped in his arms, her eyes closed, her face pressed to his chest. Caz...Caz's eyes were closed, too. His chin rested on the top of the woman's head.

A pulse began beating in Megan's temple. She swung around, brushed past Hakim and hurried down the hall.

"Miss O'Connell! Wait."

"I'm not going to spy on my husband."

Hakim caught up to her where the corridor made its turn. "You are my lord's wife. There are things you must know."

Megan spun toward him. "I *do* know! Do you think you can make me jealous? My husband told me of this woman. She is his cousin."

"Yes, that is correct."

"She was to marry a man she didn't love."

Hakim inclined his head. "That is correct, too."

"She loves another man. My husband arranged for her to be with that man."

"He did."

"And—and what we just saw..." Megan drew a shuddering breath. "What we saw was—it was just her, thanking my husband again."

"You are right, Miss O'Connell. It is all as you say."

"Then what is this all about? Why did you bring me here? Why did you want me to see this?"

"You are not one of us."

"Well, that's an amazing revelation!"

"You know nothing of our traditions."

"Oh, for God's sake—"

She started to turn away. Hakim caught her arm. It was, she knew, as close to a capital offense as one could come in Suliyam. She was not just a woman, she was the king's wife.

Her heart beat faster. She was alone in a place that looked as if no one even knew it existed, and the man with her had hated her from the minute he'd set eyes on her.

"Take your hands off me," she said sharply, "or my husband will hear of this."

"You have bewitched him, " Hakim said, his words thick with disdain.

"Did you hear me? Let go!"

"He thinks he loves you."

"He does love me. And I love him. Now, take your hand away."

"Love." Hakim spat out the word. "What does it mean?"

"Everything, but you wouldn't understand that."

"Love is a western fantasy. What we have believe in here is—"

"Tradition? As in, marrying off the sheikh's cousin to a man she doesn't love? The only thing that can come of such a tradition is the pain of a broken heart."

Hakim stepped toward her. Megan almost shrank back against the wall. She'd never seen such hatred in anyone's face.

"The woman is called Alayna. She was betrothed."

"Yes, to a man she didn't love. It's fascinating, but it has nothing to do with me."

"At first, when she came to my lord Qasim to beg his mercy, he denied her. He understood the meaning of tradition."

"But he's changed. Is that why you hate me, Hakim? Because you think I'm responsible for that?"

"When she came to him again, you had arrived in the palace." Hakim's mouth twisted. "Again, she pleaded for my lord's understanding. And that time, he said he would find a way to help her."

"Does it trouble you to know that your king has a heart?"

"Does it trouble you to know you are interfering in our way of life?"

"That's not true."

"You married Lord Qasim."

"I did. And I'm going to marry him again. Are you so blind that you can't understand the world is changing? Just because I'm a foreigner—"

"Our king is already betrothed!"

Megan stared at Hakim. "What?"

"To Alayna. They were pledged to each other at birth."

What had she said to Caz, just this morning? *There are things we don't know about each other...* And he'd smiled and said they had their whole lives to learn those things...

"A betrothal isn't a marriage," Megan said. Her voice shook, and she cleared her throat. "Obviously my husband changed his mind. He married me, not Alayna."

"He married you, and said he would divorce you. But he didn't. You ensnared him."

"I'm not listening to another moment of this non—"

"Alayna's people will not tolerate such an insult. They will not permit her to be disgraced."

"Don't you get it? Alayna didn't want to go through with this marriage. She won't be disgraced, she'll be thrilled! Her family will understand, once she explains it to them."

Hakim's face grew dark. "You are a fool, Miss O'Connell! Alayna will not be able to hold up her head. Her family will have to do something about what Lord Qasim has done, or she will never find another husband."

"Even if that's true, I'm not responsible for it. You said

yourself, my husband has already promised to help Alayna."

"Only after he met you. After you bewitched him, and then married him and refused to divorce him."

"Listen to me, old man. My husband doesn't want a divorce. He wants—"

"You. Yes. And to get you, he will bring dishonor to a foolish girl, to an important family, to an entire people."

"No. No, I don't believe you." Megan gave an unsteady laugh. "You make it sound as if I'm going to—to bring down the throne!"

"You well may," Hakim said grimly. "At the very least, you will make it impossible for Lord Qasim to implement the changes he's worked so hard to achieve."

"You're wrong," Megan said desperately. "I've been in all those meetings. My husband's ideas have been well-received."

"Your husband has had a difficult enough time convincing his people to follow his new ways. Now he stands to lose the respect of an entire faction. He's flaunted the centuries-old traditions that govern who he is to marry, who is to sit beside him as queen, who will provide him with heirs to the throne."

"Lies, all of it! Qasim's father married a foreigner, too."

"Only after his first wife died." Hakim leaned toward her so that she felt his hot breath on her face. "You have put the sheikh in great danger."

"Danger?" Megan felt her knees turn watery. "How—how can he be in danger?"

"We are a people of ancient traditions. The only way to assuage the stain of dishonor is with blood."

"No." She shook her head. "I don't believe that. Qasim has changed things here."

"Traditions are not changed as easily as plans for roads and hospitals."

"I'll speak with him. I'll ask him if—"

"What will you ask him? Or rather, what will he tell you? Do you think he'll let you know what he risks for you?" Hakim's eyes bored into hers. "You say you love the sheikh. Perhaps you do. Then I must ask... Do you love him enough to give him up, or will you wait until he loses his throne, his kingdom, his people...his life?"

Hours later, an eternity later, Megan lay beside Caz in their bed.

The night was silent and dark, heavy with moisture from a storm that was rolling in over the sea.

She knew what she had to do, and that she should have done it by now, but she'd wanted one more night, one more memory to warm her through the years that stretched ahead.

Caz had made love to her.

She had made love to him.

For the last time, her heart kept saying, for the last time.

Each kiss, each caress had been filled with the pain of what she knew would come next. And it was time to do it. Now, before she lost her courage.

But first—first, one last kiss...

Megan brushed her lips over her those of her sleeping husband. His mouth softened, clung to hers, and she almost let herself sink into the kiss.

But she didn't.

She slid from under his arm, rolled to the edge of the bed and reached for the robe she'd deliberately left within reach earlier in the evening. Once she had it on, sash firmly tied, she rose to her feet.

"Caz?"

Caz sighed and rolled on his belly.

"Caz, wake up. I want to talk to you."

"Mmm." He turned over and looked at her. A little smile tugged at the corner of his mouth. "What are you doing, *kalila?* Come back here," he said, holding out his hand. "It's the middle of the night."

"We have to talk."

"Can't you sleep?" His smile turned soft and sexy. "I'll bet I can think of a way to make you relax."

She looked at him. At his beloved face. Her legs were threatening to give way; she wanted to sit down before they did, but sitting near him would be the end of her resolve.

"I phoned my family, Caz. To tell them about us.

His eyes locked on hers. "And?"

"And—and…"

"And, they don't approve."

He saw the surprise on her face, but her family's concern was nothing less than he'd expected. If he had a daughter— and he would, someday, a perfect, beautiful image of his wife—if he had a daughter and she announced she'd married a man they'd never met, a man who was king of a country in the middle of nowhere, he wouldn't approve, either. Hell, he'd probably go crazy!

"No. They'd don't."

He sat up against the pillows, the silk blanket draping just below his navel. "Megan. Listen to me—"

"They—they raised a lot of valid issues."

"Valid issues?" he said, his voice suddenly soft as smoke.

"Yes. They asked me to think about what it would be like for me to live here instead of in America. To live here with—with someone so different from me."

"Who is 'they?'" His tone was flat. "Did you discuss Suliyam and me with your entire family?"

"No. Actually—actually, I only talked to Sean," she said,

plucking her brother's name out of the air. "But he gave me the same advice they'd all give me, I'm sure."

"And that advice was?"

"That I go home. Think things over."

Caz said nothing for a long minute. Then he threw off the blanket, reached for his trousers and pulled them on.

"Let's cut to the bottom line. You're going home, and you're not coming back. Am I right?"

Tears stung her eyes but she knew she mustn't let him see them.

"Megan? Am I right? Are you leaving me?"

No. Oh, no. How can I leave you, my love? How can I live without you...

"Yes," she said. "I am."

She hadn't known what to expect after she told him. Whatever it was, it hadn't been this. The stony face. The empty eyes. The terrible, awful stillness.

"I wish—I wish it could be different, but—"

"I don't."

She stiffened. "You don't?"

"No." He walked around the bed and she took an instinctive step back, but he went past her to the dressing room. "Actually it's a relief." His voice grew muffled; he came back into the bedroom tugging a black sweater over his head. "I let things get away from me when I suggested marriage. You're right. It wouldn't have worked. We have nothing in common, except in bed."

His words stung. Was he saving face, or was he telling her the truth? It didn't matter. This was the way things had to end. She'd known it, in her heart, from the minute he'd taken her to bed on their wedding night.

"I want you to know…" Her voice trembled and she began again. "I—I enjoyed our time together. It was—it was—"

"Yes," he said coldly. "It was."

Caz reached for the phone and pressed a button.

"Hakim? Have my plane readied. Yes, now. Miss O'Connell will be flying to the States. Have someone come for her." He hung up and turned back to Megan. "I really think it's best that you leave right away, Megan. I'm sure your brother would prefer to have you back among civilized people as soon as possible."

He started to the door. Megan took a step. "Caz? Caz, please. Don't—don't walk away from me. I want to—I want to—"

"What do you want?" He swung toward her, and now, at last, she could see the rage in his face. "A final roll between the sheets? Another reminder of what it's like to lie in the arms of a barbarian?"

"That's cruel! I never—"

"Perhaps my assurance that I won't try to claim our marriage is valid." He came toward her, his eyes the color of slate after a winter storm, and she stumbled back against the wall. "Believe me, I won't. Did I mention that our marriage could be dissolved, just like that?" He snapped his fingers an inch from her face. "It's one of the perks of being a man in my country. If a husband doesn't want his wife, all he has to do it tell her so." Caz's lips pulled back from his teeth. "I don't want you for my wife anymore, Megan O'Connell. I divorce you."

"You mean, all along, any time, you could have—"

"Anytime at all," he said smugly.

Why should that shock her? And yet, it did. The easily spoken words, the realization that she'd been little more than a toy, filled her with rage.

"Bastard," she hissed, and slammed her hand against his face.

He caught her wrist, twisted it hard enough so she gasped.

"Go back where you belong, Megan O'Connell. Where life is safe and sanitized, where nothing can touch you." He yanked her forward, crushed her mouth beneath his. She tasted him, tasted salt, tasted blood...

And then he was gone and she was alone, and the lifetime she'd lived in a few short weeks was little more than a dream.

CHAPTER THIRTEEN

BRIANA O'CONNELL leaned into her sister's refrigerator, surveyed the shelves and muttered an unladylike word under her breath.

"Honestly, Meg, there's nothing to eat in this thing!"

Megan, sitting on the living room sofa, hunched farther over the employment section of the Sunday Times and circled an ad with her pen.

"Unless you think cottage cheese is edible. Or yogurt."

Megan turned the page, circled another ad, then crossed it out.

"And what, pray tell, is this green thing? Yuck!"

Only one column of advertisements left and only one decent prospect so far. Just her luck, to be job-hunting when the economy was heading south.

"Megan," Bree said, slamming the fridge door closed, "I love you with all my heart, sweetie, but your taste in food leaves something to be desired. Do you hear me?"

"The entire city of Los Angeles hears you," Megan grumbled. "Order a pizza."

"Good idea." Bree yanked the takeout pizza menu from under the magnet that held it to the fridge and strolled into the living room. "How's this sound? An extra large with garlic, olives, onions, bacon, anchovies, sausage…"

Megan looked up. Bree grinned.

"Figured that would get your attention." Her voice softened. "Come on, sis. Put the paper away and let's go out for something to eat."

"I'm really not—"

"Hungry. Yes, I know." Bree plopped down on a chair opposite the sofa. "Well, who would be, considering the choice of yummy things in your refrigerator?"

"I haven't been paying much attention to what I buy lately. You want anchovies and bacon? Go ahead. Order it."

"Not even I'm that nuts." Briana sat back. She crossed her legs, bounced one foot up and down, then cleared her throat. "So, how's the big job hunt going? Anything good today?"

Megan sighed, tossed her pen aside and looked at Briana. "No."

"Nobody wants accountants in L.A.?"

"They want bookkeepers who think they're accountants, and accountants willing to be paid like bookkeepers."

"Which means?"

"Which means, I'm overqualified."

"How about trying a headhunter? Don't you need to go through a lot of mumbo-jumbo to find the really good listings?"

"I'm listed with somebody."

"Nothing, huh?"

"Nope." Megan stood up. "How about if I phone in the pizza order?"

"Fine. Just make sure you don't ask for bacon. Or anchovies. Or—"

"Sausage," Megan said, and grinned. "Don't worry. I'm not nuts, either."

Briana smiled back at her. Then she rose, too, unlocked the door for the pizza guy, and followed Megan into the kitchen.

"How about that economics degree of yours?" she said,

after Megan had phoned in their order. "Why not look for a job in that field?"

"I told you the reason."

"No, you didn't," Bree said, opening the fridge and taking out a container of orange juice.

"Yes, I did."

"You said the turkey at Tremont, Burnside and Macomb would never give you a decent reference."

"See? I did tell you."

"You said he wouldn't. You didn't said *why* he wouldn't." Bree opened the OJ and took a sniff. "I always thought you were good at your work."

"I am."

"But?"

"But…" Megan hesitated. "But, I sort of quit in the middle of an assignment."

"Whoa. Doesn't sound like you." Bree sniffed the juice again. "This stuff smells funky."

Megan rolled her eyes, grabbed the container and dumped the contents into the sink. "You should have told me you were coming, Bree. I'd have had time to shop."

"I didn't know I was coming, remember? I'd have to be psychic to know they were gonna ground all planes west of the Rockies because of bad weather in Colorado." Briana pushed out her bottom lip. "You want, I'll go to a hotel…"

"No!" Megan grabbed her sister and hugged her tight. "Of course I don't want that, Sis. I'm just—" She drew back. "I'm edgy, that's all."

"Yeah," Bree said wryly, "I noticed." She leaned back against the sink and folded her arms. "So, why'd you quit?"

"Huh? Oh. Oh, well, I—I just did."

"Try again."

"I, um, I wasn't getting along with the client. And, uh, and I decided it was in everyone's best interest if I just—"

"Remember when we were kids? And I sort of borrowed one of Fallon's skirts? And she'd told me a zillion times to stay out of her closet?"

"Bree. Whatever you're trying to say—"

"I burned a hole in it. Well, Donny Hucksacker burned a hole in it, trying to show how grown up he was by smoking a cigarette, except he dropped it and... Okay, okay, I'll get to the point. I was terrified of letting Fallon know what I'd done, and you took pity on me and said you'd take the blame, and you tried to but it didn't work because she took one look at your face and—"

"Oh, for heaven's sake! Where are you going with this?"

"I'm just pointing out that you are the world's worst liar. Whatever happened with you and that client was a lot more than not getting along."

Megan stared at her sister. "Aren't you supposed to phone the airline every hour?"

"I called them twenty minutes ago."

"Right. Well—well, I just remembered, I have an appointment with that headhunter."

"On Sunday?" Bree smiled sweetly. "I don't think so."

"Look here, Briana—"

"Look here, yourself, Megan Nicole O'Connell! When are you going to tell me what's going on, huh? A month ago, you left this cryptic message on my answering machine—"

"There was nothing cryptic about it."

"Oh, give me a break." Bree raised her eyebrows as well as her voice. "'Hi, this is Megan. I'm leaving for a place you never heard of and coming back who knows when, and, be still my heart, I'll be working with a guy who's absolutely D and D...'"

"I never said that!"

Briana flashed a triumphant smile. "You didn't have to.

You went to Suliyam, and your client was Sheikh Qasim Something-or-Other, and me oh my, if he isn't Dark and Dangerous, nobody is.''

Megan slapped her hands on her hips. ''How do you know all that?''

''It was in one of those business magazines, an article about him working with a consultant from T, B and M. And there was a picture of the guy and after I wiped the drool off my chin I said to myself, 'Self, big sister Megan is off in the wilds with a stud.''' Briana slapped her hands on her hips, too. ''And before you say, 'You? Reading a business magazine,' the answer is yes, me, reading a business magazine. I was at the dentist's and all the *Cosmo*s and *Elle*s were gone.''

''Now who's the liar?''

''Don't try and change the subject. Is he?''

Megan sighed. The right answer was, ''Is he what?'' But she'd only be delaying things. Her sister could be as persistent as a dog with a bone.

''Yes. He is. D and D to the core.''

''I knew it!''

''So what? Being dark and dangerous isn't everything.''

''Oh.''

The ''oh'' was filled with meaning. Megan refused to take the bait. Instead she yanked open a cupboard and took out two plates.

''Here. Make yourself useful. Set the table so that we can eat as soon as the pizza gets here.''

''Something happened,'' Bree said. ''Between you and the sheikh.''

''I told you what happened,'' Megan said, bustling around the kitchen as if it were the size of a skating rink instead of a closet. ''We didn't get along. For heaven's sake, are you just going to stand there? Take these napkins. Take extras. Take—''

''You and he had a thing going.''

Megan looked at her sister. ''Give it up,'' she said quietly.

''I'm right! You got it on with the sheikh!''

''Such an adult turn of phrase,'' Megan said coldly.

Bree batted her lashes. ''Was he good?''

''I am not going to discuss Caz with you.''

''Caz, huh?''

''You're wasting your time.''

''I am?''

''Yes. What happened in Suliyam happened. It didn't mean a thing. I've stopped thinking about it, and I'm not interested in talking about it.'' Megan's voice trembled and she glared at her sister. ''You hear me, Briana? I am not going to talk about this,'' she said, and burst into tears.

''Oh, baby!'' Briana hurried to her sister's side and wrapped an arm around her shoulders. ''Honey, I'm so sorry! I was just teasing, you know? I never expected...''

''No. Neither did—neither did—''

Megan buried her face in her hands and wept. She hadn't cried, not once since she'd left Caz. She'd been all business when she got home, picking up her mail from Mrs. Hansen across the way, going to work the next day, calmly telling The Worm that she'd be happy to bring someone else up to speed on the Suliyam assignment but that she was sorry, she'd have to sign off.

The Worm, as she'd anticipated, was overjoyed.

''In that case,'' he'd said, all but rubbing his hands, ''you're fired.''

She'd anticipated that, too.

The only thing she hadn't anticipated was the yawning emptiness in her heart, the questions that raced through her head like a cat chasing its own tail. Was it true? Had Caz been planning on putting her out of his life, or had he only said those terrible things because she'd wounded him? She told herself it didn't matter, that what counted was that she'd left him, left Suliyam, that he'd be safe...

But it did matter.

Hadn't he loved her at all? Hadn't she been the world to him, as he'd been to her, and the moon and the stars, all rolled into one until the end of time?

She could keep those thoughts at abeyance during the day. Interviews, networking, phoning old university classmates and the people she'd worked with over the years kept her busy.

It was the nights that were brutal.

She lay awake, remembering Caz with her body, her heart, her mind. The feel of him, in her arms. The taste of his skin. The way he'd sat beside her, holding her close as he talked about his plans for his people.

She dreamed of him, longed for him, ached for him. But she hadn't cried for him, until now. No tears. None, until someone who loved her asked a couple of simple questions, and then the tears she'd kept inside burst free.

Bree led her to the sofa, made soothing noises and patted her back, kept an arm clamped around her while Megan wept until there were no tears left. Then she wiped her eyes with one of the napkins she was still holding and blew her nose.

"I'm sorry," she said. "I don't know what happened just now."

Bree took her hand and patted it. "You okay?"

Megan nodded.

"You sure? Good." Bree's voice hardened. "Now tell me what that son of a bitch did to you."

"It isn't his fault. I—we—I thought I'd fallen in love

with him, and—'' She let out a gusty breath. "I *did* fall in love with him. And it was a mistake."

"Because he didn't love you?"

"It's not that simple. He married me, and—"

"He what?"

"He did it because he had to, to save me from… Oh, hell. It's a long story and it doesn't matter, because the marriage wasn't real. It was just for show. You know."

"No," Bree said, staring at Megan, "I do not know!"

"Don't look like that, Bree! I told you, it wasn't real. Or—or maybe it was, for a little while, until he dissolved it."

"This guy wasn't just D and D," Bree said coldly, "he's Dark, Dangerous and also Despicable."

"No. He's not. You don't know anything about him."

"I know that he talked you into marriage just so he could—"

"That's not the way he tells it."

Megan and Briana shot to their feet. "Sean?" Bree said.

Megan didn't say anything. How could she? It wasn't the sight of her brother standing in the open doorway that left her speechless, although seeing him suddenly appear was a shock.

What froze her into immobility was the man standing behind him.

It was Qasim. Qasim, looking, yes, dark and dangerous. And angry as hell.

"Qasim?" she whispered.

"Yes," he growled, and tried moving past Sean. Sean wouldn't let him.

"You're in my way, O'Connell," Caz said coldly.

"Damned right I am," Sean said, just as coldly. "And I will be, until my sister tell me to move."

"She won't have to. I'll move you myself."

"Come on." Sean swung around and put his fists up. "I'd love you to try."

"Listen, you thick-skulled baboon—"

"Stop it!" The men looked at Megan. She took a step forward. "Just stop it, both of you. Sean? Qasim? What are you doing here?"

"How come you don't keep your door locked?"

"Don't answer a question with a question, damn it! What are you doing here?"

Sean folded his arms. "This idiot turned up on my door-step yesterday. I was at my place in New York, and—"

"And," Caz said grimly, "I asked him some questions."

"I don't understand. What questions? What could you possibly want with my brother? How'd you even find him?"

Caz folded his arms, too. "I have ways."

"Bull," Sean said, rolling his eyes. "He has ways? He looked in the phone book, Meg. That's how he found me."

"But—but what for?" She looked at Caz. "Why did you go to see my brother?"

"I told you, I had questions." A muscle knotted in Caz's jaw. "And he couldn't answer them."

Megan shook her head. "I don't know what you're talking about."

"Yeah, you do." Caz glared at her. "I asked him what, exactly, he'd told you the night you phoned him."

"Oh." She felt color flood her face. "Well, I—I—I don't see what business that is of yours."

"You don't, huh? Well, let me spell it out for you, Megan. You said you left me because of what he told you." Caz's mouth thinned. "What he *supposedly* told you."

Megan swallowed dryly. "So?"

"So, why such an elaborate lie? All you had to do was tell me you wanted to end our marriage."

"Marriage?" Sean's voice snapped like a whip. "What

marriage? Listen, Qasim or Caz or whatever the hell your name is, you never said anything about—''

"What's the difference?'' Megan said, her eyes fixed on Caz's face. "Our marriage is over. You made sure of that. You divorced me, remember? You said—''

"Is everybody crazy? Bree, what's she talking about? Our Megan was married?''

"Your Megan *is* married,'' Caz growled.

"I'm not. You dissolved our marriage.''

"Not true.''

"But you said—''

"I lied.''

Megan blinked. "You lied?''

"Damned right.''

"Oh.'' She moistened her lips with the tip of her tongue. "Then—then just saying you divorced me didn't…''

Caz snorted.

"What's so funny?'' Megan said, slapping her hands on her hips and tapping her foot.

"I admit, Suliyam's not a lawyer's paradise but even in my country, divorce isn't that simple. There have to be witnesses to the declaration, papers signed…''

She stared at him. "So we're not…?''

"No. We're not. You're still my wife.''

"Is that why you came here? To tell me we're still married, and that you want a real divorce?''

"You know, *kalila*, for an intelligent woman, you can be awfully stupid.''

"Hey! That's my sister you're—''

"She's my wife,'' Caz said. He looked at Megan and his voice softened. "And you're going to remain my wife, because I won't let you leave me.''

"I already left you,'' Megan said, and told her heart to stop racing. So what if he wanted her back? So what if, by some miracle, he loved her? *She* loved *him,* far too much to let him risk his life, his throne, all he'd worked to achieve for his people. "And why did it take you four weeks to tell me this? Why did you go looking for my brother instead of me?"

"It took me that long because I let my pride get in the way. And I went looking for your brother because I thought he'd talked you into leaving me." Caz smiled a little. "I figured I had two choices, *kalila.* Either I'd change his mind—or I'd beat him into a pulp."

Sean started to speak but Caz ignored him.

"Do you remember that last time we made love?" His eyes darkened. "How we held each other afterward? How you kissed me?"

"Oh, man," Sean said unhappily, "I don't want to listen to this."

"Then don't," Bree said. She put an arm around Megan's shoulders and pressed a quick kiss to her cheek. "Sean and I are leaving."

"No," Sean said, "we are not. I told you, I'm not going anywhere until—"

"I love you, Megan," Caz said, his voice cutting across Sean's. "And you love me."

"I don't. I can't. Hakim said—"

"Hakim lied."

"No. He told me the truth." Tears rose in Megan's eyes and spilled down her cheeks. "They'll take revenge," she whispered. "Alayna's people."

"Nobody wants revenge, sweetheart. The old ways are gone. Hakim just couldn't accept that." Caz's mouth thinned. "When I told Alayna's father there'd be no marriage, he was relieved. He loves his daughter. He would have reneged on the agreement a long time ago, but he was afraid to defy me."

"Oh, Caz. Caz…"

Caz looked at Sean. "You need to get out of my way," he said politely. "Decking a brother-in-law I've only met eight hours ago isn't a good start, but so help me, I'll do it if you try to keep me from my wife a moment longer."

Sean opened his mouth, then shut it. He looked at Megan, whose eyes glittered with tears but whose smile spoke of such joy it made his heart ache.

"You'd better take good care of my sister, pal," he said gruffly, "or you're gonna have to deal with me and two other goons who love her as much as I'm starting to think you do."

Caz grinned and stuck out his hand. "Deal."

"Deal?" Megan said, trying to sound indignant. "You two make like—like a pair of Mr. Machos, then you shake hands and say you've got a deal, and nobody even thinks to ask me what I want?"

Caz moved past Sean and came slowly toward her. "I'm asking you now, wife. What is it you want?"

Megan looked into her husband's eyes. "You," she whispered. "Oh, Caz, I want you. Forever, with all my heart."

Sean jerked his head toward the door. Briana wiped her eyes and nodded. The door swung shut behind them, and Megan flew into her husband's arms.

Mary O'Connell Coyle wanted to make the wedding at the Desert Song Hotel, in Las Vegas.

"Ma," Megan said carefully, "Caz and I thought…"

"If that's what your mother really wants, that's fine, *kalila*," Caz said. He winked at her and pulled some photos from his pocket. "Mary? You want to take a look at these?"

Mary stared at the photos of his palace by the sea. Then she smiled and batted her lashes at her new son-in-law and said one of the best things about being female was that you could change your mind any time you wanted.

It was, of course, a wedding straight out of a fairy tale. The sea, beating softly against the shore. The palace, gleaming white against the perfect blue sky. The gold-tipped spires, the marble walls and silk carpets...

"Isn't it wonderful, Dan?" Mary whispered to her husband, just before he took his stepdaughter up the aisle. "My girls look like princesses."

They did, he agreed.

Briana and Fallon were both Megan's maids of honor. Matron of honor, in Fallon's case.

"Very pregnant matron of honor," her adoring husband said proudly.

Cassie and Marissa, Megan's sisters-in-law, were her bridesmaids. Cullen, Keir, Sean and Stefano were Qasim's groomsmen. After some initial verbal sparring designed to assure themselves he loved Megan enough to suit them, the entire male contingent of the clan had welcomed Caz with open arms.

Everything went smoothly. Even the O'Connell babies stopped squalling and watched Megan as she reached the altar on her stepfather's arm. He kissed her, gave her hand to Qasim, and the look on Qasim's face when he smiled at his bride made Mary weep.

She reached for Dan's hand when he sat down beside her.

"My baby's so beautiful," Mary whispered.

Dan smiled. "She is, indeed."

Another muffled sob. Dan reached into his pocket and took out a big white handkerchief. "Here you go, countess," he said, and his use of his wife's nickname set off another round of tears.

"I love you, Dan Coyle," Mary whispered, "and isn't it a perfect day?"

*   *   *

A perfect day, Sean thought, watching the festivities with a slightly jaded eye.

Well, sure. If you liked that kind of thing, it probably was, but why on earth would a man want to give up his freedom? Women were wonderful creatures, and it was a damned fine thing two of his sisters had found men who'd worship them, damned fine, too, that his brothers had found women they adored.

They were happy, the lot of them. He was happy for them.

But this brand of happiness wasn't for him.

Hell, he thought, running a finger inside the collar of his starched shirt, never him.

Give up the life he loved? The footloose, drop-everything-and-go freedom of it? Forego the thrill of the next toss of the dice, the next turn of the cards for the same four walls every night? A nine-to-five job?

Most of all, definitely most of all, give up the excitement of seeing a beautiful woman, the hot anticipation that came of catching her eye and knowing you'd be bedding her soon? That you'd enjoy her, and she'd enjoy you, until it began to get a little dull?

The chase was everything.

For him, anyway. And it would never change.

Sean turned his attention back to his sister. Megan was looking at Caz as if he were the center of her universe. He was looking at her the same way. Sean felt like a cultural anthropologist at a tribal ceremony, watching the natives go through a ritual he couldn't possibly comprehend.

The judge smiled at the bride and groom. "It is my pleasure," he said, "to pronounce you man and wife."

Everybody applauded, including Sean.

He was applauding his sister's happiness, of course.

And if he was also applauding his own independence, that was nobody's business but his own.

THE ONE-NIGHT WIFE

SANDRA MARTON

CHAPTER ONE

HE CAME INTO THE CASINO just before midnight, when the action was getting heavier.

Savannah had been watching for him, keeping her eyes on the arched entry that led from the white marble foyer to the high-stakes gaming room. She'd been afraid she might miss him.

What a foolish thought.

O'Connell was impossible to miss. He was, to put it bluntly, gorgeous.

"How will I recognize him?" she'd asked Alain.

He told her that O'Connell was tall, dark-haired and good-looking.

"There's an aura of money to him," he'd added. "You know what I mean, *chérie*. Sophistication." Smiling, he'd patted her cheek. "Trust me, Savannah. You'll know him right away."

But when she'd arrived an hour ago and stepped through the massive doors that led into the casino, she'd felt her heart sink.

Alain's description was meaningless. It fit half the men in the room.

The casino was situated on an island of pink sand and private estates in the Bahamas. Its membership was restricted to the wealthiest players in Europe, Asia and the Americas. All the men who frequented its tables were rich and urbane, and lots of them were handsome.

Savannah lifted her champagne flute to her lips and drank. Handsome didn't come close to describing Sean O'Connell.

How many men could raise the temperature just by standing still? This one could. She could almost feel the air begin to sizzle.

His arrival caused a stir. Covert glances directed at him from the men. Assessing ones from the women. Maybe not everybody would pick up signals that subtle, but catching nuances was Savannah's stock in trade.

Her success at card tables depended on it.

Tonight, so did the course of her life.

No. She didn't want to think about that. Years ago, when she was still fleecing tourists in New Orleans, she'd learned that the only way to win was to think of nothing but the cards. Empty her mind of everything but the spiel, the sucker and the speed of her hands.

Concentrate on the knowledge that she was the best.

The philosophy still worked. She'd gone from dealing three-card monte on street corners to playing baccarat and poker in elegant surroundings, but her approach to winning had not changed.

Concentrate. That was the key. Stay calm and be focused.

Tonight, that state of mind was taking longer to achieve.

Her hand trembled as she lifted her champagne flute to her mouth. The movement was nothing but a tic, a tremor of her little finger, but even that was too much. She wouldn't drink once she sat down at the poker table but if that tic should appear when she picked up her cards, O'Connell would notice. Like her, he'd have trained himself to read an opponent's body language.

His skills were legendary.

If you were a gambler, he was the man to beat.

If you were a woman, he was the man to bed.

Every woman in the room knew it. Too bad, Savannah

thought, and a little smile curved her mouth. Too bad, because on this hot Caribbean night, Sean O'Connell would belong only to her.

Again, she raised her glass. Her hand was steady this time. She took a little swallow of the chilled Cristal, just enough to cool her lips and throat, and went on watching him. There was little danger he'd see her: she'd chosen her spot carefully. From this alcove, she could observe without being observed.

She wanted the chance to look him over before she made her move.

Evidently, he was doing the same thing before choosing a table. He hadn't stirred; he was still standing in the arch between the foyer and the main room. It was, she thought with grudging admiration, a clever entrance. He'd stirred interest without doing a thing.

All those assessing glances from men stupidly eager to be his next victim. All those feline smiles from women eager for the same thing, though in a very different way.

Savannah the Gambler understood the men. When a player had a reputation like O'Connell's, you wanted to sit across the table from him and test yourself. Even if you lost, you could always drop word of the time you'd played him into casual conversation. *Oh,* you could say, *did I ever tell you about the time Sean O'Connell beat me with a pair of deuces even though I had jacks and sevens?*

That would get you attention.

But Savannah the Woman didn't understand those feminine smiles at all. She'd heard about O'Connell's reputation. How he went from one conquest to another. How he lost interest and walked away, leaving a trail of broken hearts behind him. Why set yourself up for that? Emotions were dangerous. They were impractical. Still, she had to admit that Sean O'Connell was eye candy.

He was six foot one, maybe two. He wore a black dinner jacket open over a black silk T-shirt and black trousers that emphasized his lean, muscular body. Dark-haired, as Alain had said. The color of midnight was more accurate.

Alain hadn't mentioned his eyes.

What color were they? Blue, she thought. She was too far away to be sure and, for an instant that passed as swiftly as a heartbeat, she let herself wonder what would happen if she crossed the marble floor, stopped right in front of him, looked into those eyes to see if they were the light blue of a tropical sea or the deeper blue of the mid-Pacific.

Savannah frowned and permitted herself another tiny sip of champagne.

She had a task to accomplish. The color of O'Connell's eyes didn't matter. What counted was what she knew of him, and how she would use that knowledge tonight.

He was considered one of the best gamblers in the world. Cool, unemotional, intelligent. He was also a man who couldn't resist a challenge, whether it was a card game or a beautiful woman.

That was why she was here tonight. Alain had sent her to lure O'Connell into a trap.

She'd never deliberately used her looks to entice a man into wanting to win her more than he wanted to win the game, to so bedazzle him that he'd forget the permutations and combinations, the immutable odds of the hand he held so that he'd lose.

It wasn't cheating. Not really. It was just a variation of the skill she'd developed back when she'd dealt three-card monte. Keep the sucker so fascinated by your patter and your fast-moving hands that he never noticed you'd palmed the queen and slipped in another king.

Tonight was different.

Tonight, she wanted the mark watching her, not her hands

or the cards. If the cards came the right way, she would win. If they didn't and she had to resort to showing a little more cleavage, so be it.

She'd do what she had to do.

The goal was to win. Win, completely. To defeat Sean O'Connell. Humiliate him with people watching. After she did that, she'd be free.

Free, Savannah thought, and felt her heart lift.

She could do it. She *had* to do it.

And she wanted to get started. All this waiting and watching was making her edgy. *Do something,* she thought. *Come on, O'Connell. Pick your table and let's start the dance.*

Well, she could always make the first move... No. Bad idea. He had to make it. She had to wait until he was ready.

He was still standing in the entryway. A waiter brought him a drink in a crystal glass. Bourbon, probably. Tennessee whiskey. It was all he drank, when he drank at all. Alain had given her that information, too. Her target was as American as she was, though he looked as if he'd been born into this sophisticated international setting.

He lifted the glass. Sipped at it as she had sipped at the champagne. He looked relaxed. Nerves? No. Not him. He was nerveless, or so they said, but surely his pulse was climbing as he came alive to the sights and sounds around him.

No one approached him. Alain had told her to expect that. They'd give him his space.

"People know not to push him," Alain had said. "He likes to think of himself as a lone wolf."

Wrong. O'Connell wasn't a wolf at all. He was a panther, dark and dangerous. Very dangerous, Savannah thought, and a frisson of excitement skipped through her blood.

She'd never seduced a panther until tonight. Even thinking about all that would entail, the danger of it, gave her a rush. It *would* be dangerous; even Alain had admitted that.

"But you can do it, *chérie,*" he'd told her. "Have I ever misled you?"

He hadn't, not since the day they'd met. Lately, though, his attitude toward her had changed. He looked at her differently, touched her hand differently...

No. She wouldn't think about that now. She had a task to perform and she'd do it.

She would play poker with Sean O'Connell and make the game a dance of seduction instead of a game of luck, skill and bluff. She'd see to it he lost every dollar he had. That he lost it publicly, so that his humiliation would be complete.

"I want Sean O'Connell to lose as he never imagined," Alain had said in a whisper that chilled her to the bone. "To lose everything, not just his money but his composure. His pride. His arrogance. You are to leave him with only the clothes on his back." He'd smiled then, a twist of the mouth that had made her throat constrict. "And I'll give you a bonus, darling. You can keep whatever you win. Won't that be nice?"

Yes. Oh, yes, it would, because once she had that money... Once she had it, she'd be free.

Until a little while ago, she hadn't let herself dwell on that for fear Alain would somehow read her mind. Now, it was all she could think about. She'd let Alain believe she was doing this for him, but she was doing it for herself.

Herself and Missy.

When this night ended, she'd have the money she needed to get away and to take care of her sister. They'd be free of Alain, of what she'd finally realized he was... Of what she feared he might want of her next.

If it took Sean O'Connell's humiliation, downfall and destruction to accomplish, so be it. She wouldn't, couldn't, concern herself about it. Why would she? O'Connell was a stranger.

He was also a thief.

He'd stolen a million dollars from Alain in a nonstop, three-day game of poker on Alain's yacht in the Mediterranean one year ago. She hadn't been there—it had been the first of the month and she'd been at the clinic in Geneva, visiting Missy—but Alain had filled her in on the details. How the game had started like any other, how he'd only realized O'Connell had cheated after the yacht docked at Cannes and O'Connell was gone.

Alain had spent an entire year plotting to get even.

The money wasn't the issue. What was a million dollars when you'd been born to billions? It was the principle of the thing, Alain said.

Savannah understood.

There were only three kinds of gamblers. The smart ones, the stupid ones and the cheats. The smart ones made the game exciting. Winning against someone as skilled as you was a dizzying high. The stupid ones could be fun, at first, but after a while there was no kick in taking their money.

The cheats were different. They were scum who made a mockery of talent. Cheat, get found out, and you got locked out of the casinos. Or got your hands broken, if you'd played with the wrong people.

Nobody called in the law.

Alain wanted to do something different. O'Connell had wounded him, but in a private setting. He would return the favor, but as publicly as possible. He'd finally come up with a scheme though he hadn't told her anything about his plan or the incident leading up to it until last week, right after she'd visited her sister.

He'd slipped his arm around her shoulders, told her what

had happened a year ago and what he wanted her to do. When she'd objected, he'd smiled that smile she'd never really noticed until a few months ago, the one that made her skin prickle.

"How's Missy?" he'd said softly. "Is she truly happy in that place, *chérie?* Is she making progress? Perhaps it's time for me to consider making some changes."

What had those words meant? Taken at face value they were benign, but something in his tone, his smile, his eyes gave a very different message. Savannah had stared at him, trying to figure out how to respond. After a few seconds, he'd laughed and pressed a kiss to her temple.

"It'll be fun for you, *chérie.* The coming-out party for your twenty-first birthday, so to speak."

What he meant was, she'd take O'Connell by surprise. She had yet to play in a casino; thus far, Alain had only let her sit in on private games.

She'd come to him at sixteen, straight off the streets of New Orleans where she'd kept herself and Missy alive scamming the tourists at games like three-card monte. She was good but her winnings were meager. You could only play for so long before the cops moved you on.

Alain had appeared one evening on the edge of the little crowd collected around her. He'd watched while she took some jerks who'd left their brains in their hotel rooms along with their baggage.

During a lull, he'd stepped in close.

"You're good, *chérie,*" he'd said with a little smile. He sounded French, but with a hint of New Orleans patois.

Savannah had looked him straight in the eye.

"The best," she'd said with the assurance of the streets.

Alain had smiled again and reached for her cards.

"Hey," she said, "leave those alone. They're mine."

He ignored her, moved the cards around, then stopped and looked at her. "Where's the queen?"

Savannah rolled her eyes and pointed. Alain grinned and moved the cards again. This time, his hands were a blur.

"Where is she now, *chérie?*"

Savannah gave him a piteous look and pointed again. Alain turned the card over.

No queen.

"Watch again," he said.

She watched again. And again. Five minutes later, she shook her head in amazement.

"How do you do that?"

He tossed down the cards and jerked his head toward the big black limo that had suddenly appeared at the curb.

"Come with me and I'll show you. You're good, *chérie,* but I'll teach you to use your mind as well as your hands. We can make a fortune together."

"Looks like you already got a fortune, mister."

That made Alain laugh. "I do, but there's always more. Besides, you intrigue me. You're dirty. Smelly."

"Hey!"

"But it's true, *chérie.* You look like an urchin and you sound like one, too, but there's a *je ne sais quoi* to you that intrigues me. You're a challenge. You'll be Eliza to my Professor Higgins."

"I don't know any Eliza or Professor Higgins," Savannah replied sourly.

"All you need to know is that I can change your life."

Did he take her for a fool? Four years in foster homes, one on the streets, and Savannah knew better than to get into a car with a stranger.

She also knew better than to let something good get away.

She'd looked at the limo, at the man, at his suit that undoubtedly cost more than she could hope to make in another five years of hustling. Then she looked at Missy, sitting placidly beside her on the pavement, humming a tune only she could hear.

Alain looked at Missy, too, as if he'd only just noticed her.

"Who is that?"

"My sister," Savannah replied, chin elevated, eyes glinting with defiance.

"What's wrong with her?"

"She's autistic."

"Meaning?"

"Meaning she can't talk."

"Can't or won't?"

It seemed a fine distinction no social worker had ever made.

"I don't know," Savannah admitted. "She just doesn't."

"There are doctors who can help her. *I* can help her. It's up to you."

Savannah had stared at him. Then she'd thought about the long, thin knife taped to the underside of her arm.

"You try anything funny," she'd said, her voice cold, her heart thumping with terror, "you'll regret it."

Alain had nodded and held out his hand. She'd ignored it, gently urged Missy to her feet and walked them both into a new life. Warm baths, clean clothes, nourishing food, a room all her own and a wonderful residential school for Missy.

And he had kept his word. He'd taught her everything he knew until she knew the odds of winning with any combination of cards in any game of poker, blackjack or *chemin de fer*.

He hadn't touched her, either.

Until recently.

Until he'd started looking at her through eyes that glittered, that lingered on her body like an unwelcome caress and made the hair rise on the back of her neck. Until he'd taken to pressing moist kisses into the palm of her hand and, worse still, calling her from her room in his chateau or her cabin on his yacht whenever he had visitors, showing her off to men whose eyes glittered as his did, who stroked their fingers over her cheekbones, her shoulders.

Which was why she'd agreed to take Sean O'Connell to the cleaners.

It was the best possible deal. Alain would get what he wanted. So would she. By the night's end, she'd have enough money to leave Alain and take care of Missy without his help. To run, if she had to—though surely she wouldn't have to run from Alain.

He'd let her go.

Of course he would.

Savannah raised the champagne flute to her lips. It was empty. Just as well. She never drank when she played. Tonight, though, she'd asked for the Cristal at the bar, felt the need of its effervescence in her blood.

Not anymore.

She put her empty glass on a table and smoothed down the shockingly short skirt of the red silk slip dress Alain had selected. It wasn't her style, but then the life she was living wasn't her style, either.

Savannah took a deep breath and emptied her mind of everything but the game. She shook back her long golden hair and stepped out of the shadows.

Ready or not, Sean O'Connell, here I come.

CHAPTER TWO

GOLDILOCKS was finally going to make her move.

Sean could sense it. Something in the way she lifted her glass to her mouth, in the way she suddenly seemed to draw herself up, gave her away. He wanted to applaud.

About time, babe, he felt like saying. *What took you so long?*

Of course, he didn't. Why give the game away now? He'd have bet a thousand bucks she had no idea he'd been watching her, no idea he was even aware of her.

He was.

He'd noticed her as soon as he'd entered the casino. Or not entered it, which, he supposed, was a better way of putting it. He'd learned, long ago, that it was better to take his time, scope a place out, get the feel of things instead of walking right into a situation. So he'd been taking his time, standing in the arched entry between the foyer and the high-stakes gaming room, sipping Jack Daniel's on the rocks as he watched.

Watched the tables. The players. The dealers. In a casino as in life, it paid to watch and wait.

That was when he'd noticed the blonde.

She was tall, with a great body and legs that went on forever. Her face might have inspired Botticelli and just the sight of that lion's mane of sun-streaked, silky-looking hair made him want to run his fingers through it.

Sean sipped his bourbon.

Oh, yeah. He'd noticed her, all right.

She was checking things out, too. At least, that was what he'd thought. After a while, he realized he had it wrong.

What she was checking out was him.

She was careful about it. Nothing clumsy or overt. She'd chosen her spot well. The lighting in the little alcove where she stood was dim, probably in deliberate contrast to the bright lights in the gaming area.

But Sean had long ago learned that the devil was in the details. The success of his game depended on it. He saw everything, and saw it without making people aware he was looking. One seemingly casual glance and he could figure out how Lady Luck was treating players just by taking in the expressions on their faces, or even the way they handled their cards.

Besides, a man would have to be blind not to have seen the blonde. She was spectacular.

And she was gearing up for something. Something that involved him. The only question was, what?

He'd thought about walking up to her, looking into those green eyes and saying, *Hello, sugar. Why are you watching me?*

It wasn't an opening line to use on a woman if she was about to come on to you, but instinct told him the blonde didn't have girl-meets-boy on her mind. No use pretending that wasn't unusual, Sean thought without a trace of ego. He was as lucky with women as he was with cards. That was just the way it was.

So, what was happening? Goldilocks was getting ready for something and it was making her nervous. He'd seen her hand tremble once or twice when she raised her champagne glass to her lips.

Curiosity had almost gotten the better of him when she began to move.

Sean narrowed his eyes as she stepped from the alcove and started toward him. Yes, the face was beautiful. Definitely Botticelli. But the body reminded him of a classical Greek sculpture. High, firm breasts. Slender waist. Those legs.

And a walk that made the most of all her assets.

Spine straight. Shoulders back. Arms swinging as she strutted toward him, crossing one long leg over the other so that she moved more like a tigress than a woman. It was a model's walk. He'd dated a German supermodel last year; Ursula had done The Walk for him in his living room, wearing nothing but a sultry pout and a lace teddy.

Goldilocks wasn't wearing a smile and her dress covered more than a teddy, though not much more. It was a scrap of crimson silk. He liked the way it clung to her breasts and hips. She had great hips, curved for the fit of a man's hands…

Hell.

He was getting hard just watching her.

Sean downed the last of his bourbon, told himself to concentrate on cold showers and on solving the puzzle of why the blonde had been observing him with such caution.

She was only a few feet away now. She hesitated. Then she lifted her chin, tossed back her hair, took a deep breath and smiled.

He felt the wattage straight down to his toes.

"Hi."

The tip of her tongue crept out, slicked across her bottom lip. Sean almost groaned but he managed a smile of his own.

"Hi yourself," he said. "I'd ask where you've been all my life, but you'd probably slug me for using such a trite line."

She laughed. And blushed. Another nice touch. He

couldn't recall the last time he'd seen a woman blush, but her smile still glittered.

"Not at all. Actually, I was wondering how to tell you I was here alone, and that I've been alone for too long."

Her voice was soft. A liquid purr. It reminded him of honey and warm Southern nights. He moved closer.

"Isn't it fortunate that I finally got here?" he said softly. "What's your name, sugar?"

"Savannah."

"Ah."

"Ah?"

"The name suits you. You have moonlight and magnolias in that sexy drawl. You're a Georgia girl."

Another rush of pink to her cheeks. Interesting, that she'd blush and still be so direct in coming on to him.

"Savannah what?"

She touched her tongue to her lips again. Did she know what that was doing to him? The tip of that pink tongue sweeping moistly across her rosebud mouth? He thought she did but when he looked into her eyes, he wasn't so sure. They were a clear green, but there seemed to be a darkness hidden in their depths.

"Just Savannah." She closed the little distance that remained between them. He could smell her scent, a seductively innocent blend of vanilla and woman. "No last names tonight. Is that okay?"

"It's fine." Sean cleared his throat. "I'm a sucker for a good mystery, Just-Savannah."

"Just...?" Her eyebrows rose. Then she smiled. "I like that. 'Just-Savannah.'"

"Good. That gives us two things in common. Honesty and anonymity. That's a fascinating combination, don't you think?"

"Yes. I do. What shall I call you?"

"Sean."

Something flickered in those incredible eyes. Relief? No. It couldn't have been that. Why would a simple exchange of names inspire relief?

"Just-Sean," she said, smiling.

"Just-Sean, and Just-Savannah. Two people without last names who meet and set out to discover what the rest of the night holds in store."

"I like that." She reached out and laid her hand lightly against his chest. "What game will you play tonight, Sean?"

He felt his body clench like a fist. "It depends on who I'm playing it with," he said hoarsely. "What did you have in mind?"

She laughed. Her teeth were small, even, very white against the golden tan of her skin.

"I'm not sure." Her eyes met his, then dropped away. "I'm new at this."

It was a great line, designed to set a man's hormones pumping. All of it was designed for that: the face, the body, the scrap of red silk and the sexy, let's-get-it-on banter...and yet, the only part of it he bought into was her being new at this. Somehow, that rang with truth.

The lady wasn't a pro.

Like moths to the proverbial flame, high-priced working girls were drawn to places where big money and big players congregated, but no matter how elegantly dressed and groomed they were, Sean could spot them at a hundred paces. Besides, a call girl would never get past the door of a private casino like L'Emeraude.

No, Savannah wasn't a pro. She had the looks and the lines, but her delivery was off. It was like listening to an actress who was still learning her part. And there were those moments he'd seen her hand tremble…as the one she'd put against his chest was doing now.

She was working at turning him on and she was succeeding, but she wasn't lying. She was, he was sure, a novice at this game. As flattering as it was to think she'd turned into a lust-crazed creature at the sight of him, he didn't buy it. There was the way she'd been watching him. Besides, he was too much of a realist to believe in bolts of lightning that struck with no warning.

Something else was going on here. He didn't know what, but he was damned well going to find out.

"Sean?"

He focused his gaze on the blonde's upturned face. The smile was still there but the pretty flush in her cheeks was back. Was she flustered? Embarrassed? Or was it part of the act?

"Sean. Have I been too… I mean, I'm sorry if—"

"Savannah." He smiled and covered her hand with his. Her skin was icy. Instinctively, he closed his fingers around hers. "A beautiful woman should never apologize for anything." Sean raised her hand to his mouth and pressed his lips to her knuckles. "Let's make a pact."

"A pact?"

"You won't say you're sorry again, and I'll buy you a glass of champagne. Okay?"

She took a long time before she answered. Then, just when he'd decided she was going to turn him down, she nodded.

"That would be lovely."

"Good." Sean's hand tightened on hers. "You have any thoughts on how to seal our agreement?"

Another rush of color swept into her face. "What do you mean?"

"It's simple. We have a contract." Sean lowered his

voice to a husky whisper. "Now we need some way to guarantee it." He looked at her slightly parted lips, then into her eyes. "You know. Sign in blood. Swear before witnesses. Cross your heart and hope to die." He flashed a quick smile. "Something to make it official."

He watched her face, saw the exact second she decided she'd had enough. Or maybe she'd decided to change tack. Try as he might, he couldn't tell which.

"You're making fun of me," she said.

"No, I'm not."

"You are. You think this is funny, and you're teasing me."

"Teasing. Not making fun. There's a world of difference."

"Let go of my hand, please."

"Why? I turn you on. You turn me on. That hasn't changed. Why walk away from it before we've discovered what comes next?"

He didn't know what he'd expected, though he'd gone out of his way to provoke a reaction. Would she blush some more? Lean into him and lift that luscious mouth to his? The combination of brashness and modesty was charming, even exciting, but it only made him more suspicious.

Whatever he might have anticipated, it wasn't the way she suddenly stood straighter, or the way her chin lifted.

"You're right," she said. "Why walk away now?"

Sean nodded. "That's better." It wasn't. She sounded as if she'd decided to go to the dentist after all. What in hell was happening? Acting on impulse, he reached out, put his hand under her chin and tilted her face up. "As for that contract," he said softly, "I know exactly how to seal the deal."

All of her was trembling now, not just the hand pressed to his chest. For a woman who'd tried to convince him of how eager she was to jump his bones, the lady was strangely nervous.

Sean smiled into her eyes, deliberately dropped his gaze to her mouth.

"No," she said quickly, the word a breathless whisper. "Please, don't—"

He hadn't intended to go through with it. The idea was to see how she'd react to the prospect of a kiss but when he saw her lips part, her eyes turn into the fresh green of a meadow after a spring rain, a shudder ran through his body. He wanted to kiss her. Kiss her, take her in his arms, carry her out of the noise and the light to a place where they'd be alone, where he could kiss her again and again until she trembled, yes, but trembled with need for him.

Sean stepped back, his pulse hammering, every muscle in his body tight as steel.

"Don't toast a deal with a bottle of champagne?" he said with forced lightness. "Now, that's definitely something no woman's ever asked of me before."

"Champ..." She caught her bottom lip between her teeth. He tried not to imagine it was his lip those perfect teeth were worrying. "Oh. I didn't... I mean, that would be nice."

"Besides, how could I let you go until I know why you stood in that alcove watching me for so long?"

Her face whitened. "I was not watching you."

"Telling fibs isn't nice, sugar. Sure you were. And now you're as nervous as a cat in a dog pound. Don't get me wrong, sweetheart. I like getting beautiful women flustered—but I like to know the reason for it. Somehow, I don't think your nerves have all that much to do with my masculine charms."

She looked up at him, conflicting emotions warring in her eyes. For a heartbeat, Sean felt as if she were on the verge of telling him something that would set him on a white charger like a knight ready to do battle with a dragon.

But she only smiled and angled her chin so she was gazing up at him through thick, honey-brown lashes.

"You're right about my watching you," she said softly, "but wrong in thinking it had nothing to do with your masculine charms." She smiled again, just enough to give those words the light touch they deserved. "I hoped you wouldn't notice."

"There's not a man in the room wouldn't notice you, if you were looking at him."

She laughed. It was a flirty, delicious sound. "That's very sweet."

"It's the truth."

Her hand was on his chest again, her fingers toying lightly with the lapel of his jacket. Her lips were slightly parted; she tilted her head back and now he could see the swift beat of her pulse in the hollow of her throat.

Sean almost groaned. He'd played games like this before but he'd never felt as if every muscle in his body was on full alert until now.

"I think it's time we got to know each other better, Just-Savannah."

"That sounds nice. What do you have in mind?"

Taking her to bed. That was what he had in mind, but he wasn't going to do that until he knew exactly what was going on here.

"The champagne I promised you, for starters." He linked his fingers through hers. "And some privacy."

"I'd like that."

Warning bells rang in his head. The words were right. So was the come-and-get-me smile, but the look in her eyes was wrong.

Maybe it was time to up the ante.

He turned her hand palm-up and lifted it to his mouth. He felt her stiffen as he pressed his lips to her flesh, felt her start to jerk her hand from his.

"Easy, sugar. I haven't taken a bite out of a woman in years. Not unless she wanted me to."

"I know. I just—I told you, this is all—"

"—new. Yeah, so you said." Sean's smile was deliberately lazy. "Unless, of course, there's more to the story than you're letting on."

"What more could there be, Mr. O'Connell? You're a very attractive man. I'm sure I'm not the first woman to show an interest in you."

The warning bells were going crazy. Mr. O'Connell? How could she know his name? He was Just-Sean. She was Just-Savannah. Definitely, there was more on her agenda. Should he call her on it? Should he play along?

He looked deep into the green eyes fixed to his. Hell. He was a gambler, wasn't he? What did he have to lose?

"Now, sugar," he said softly, "what kind of gentleman would I be if I answered that question?"

A slow, easy smile curved his mouth.

Seeing it, Savannah almost sagged with relief. For one awful minute, she'd been afraid she'd given everything away. She'd come awfully close, saying the wrong things, letting her nerves show, but then she'd turned the situation around by using her mistakes to convince Sean O'Connell she'd never come on to a man before.

That, at least, was the truth.

She couldn't afford any more screw-ups.

She'd thought this would be easy, but it wasn't. Using a deck of cards to scam a dumb mark on a dingy street corner was not the same as using your body, your smile, your words to scam an intelligent man in an elegant casino.

Besides, O'Connell was more than intelligent. He was

street-smart. She hadn't expected that. He kept looking at her as if she were a candy bar he wanted to unwrap, but always with a wariness that made her uneasy.

Not that it changed anything.

She was in too far to stop. Either she went forward or she failed. And failure wasn't an option.

He was still smiling, but was there something in his eyes that shouldn't be there? Time to come up with a clever move that would shut down his brain.

A squeeze of her fingers in his might do it. A sexy smile. A flick of her tongue across her bottom lip. He'd reacted to that before.

Yes. It was working. His eyes were darkening, focusing on her mouth.

"If you told me about those other women," she said huskily, "you'd be the kind of man I'd run from. I don't want you thinking about anyone but me tonight."

"There's no way I could," he said softly. Another light brush of his lips against her palm and then he tucked her hand into the crook of his arm. "Have you seen the terrace, Just-Savannah?"

"No." Her voice sounded thready. She cleared her throat. "No," she repeated, and smiled up at him, almost weak with relief. Things were back on track. "No, I haven't. I've never been here before."

"Then you're in for a treat." He began walking slowly through the casino. Because of the way he'd captured her hand, she was pressed close to his side, aware of the warm length of his body, aware of the muscles in his thigh as it shifted against hers. "Let's have a drink on the terrace and I'll show you the most beautiful sight in these islands." He glanced at her, angled his head down to hers and put his lips to her ear. "I take that back, sugar. The second most beautiful sight in these islands."

The warmth of his breath, the promise in his words sent a tingle of anticipation through her. For a moment, Savannah let herself imagine what it would be like if the story she'd spun were true. If she'd come here to gamble, noticed this tall, incredibly good-looking stranger, taken her courage in her hands and gone up to him with seduction, real seduction, in mind.

But she hadn't. She was here for a purpose.

Was O'Connell really as good a poker player as people claimed? Alain said he was.

Maybe. But she was better.

Tonight, that was all that mattered.

CHAPTER THREE

SEAN PAUSED just before they reached the terrace and signaled for a waiter, who hurried to his side.

"Sir?"

Sean drew Savannah a little closer. "What were you drinking, sugar? Cristal?"

She smiled. "Good guess."

"A bottle of Cristal Brut," Sean told the waiter. "Nineteen ninety. Will that be all right, Savannah?"

"It'll be lovely."

The waiter acknowledged the order with a discreet bow, and Sean opened the double glass doors that led onto the terrace.

"Here you are, sweetheart. The most beautiful night sky of the season, for the most beautiful woman in the Bahamas."

He put his hand lightly in the small of her back as they walked to the edge of the terrace. Her dress plunged in a deep vee to the base of her spine and her bare skin was as warm and silky as the tropical breeze drifting in from the sea.

"Oh," she said in a delicate whisper. "Oh, yes. It's perfect!"

"Perfect," he murmured, his eyes not on the softly illuminated pink sand beach or the star-shot black sky, but on her.

"It's so quiet."

"Yeah." A breeze lifted a strand of her golden hair and blew it across her lips. He caught it in his fingers and tucked it behind her ear, letting his touch linger. "Quiet, dark and private."

Did she stiffen under his caress? No, it was his imagination. He was sure of it when she looked at him, her lips upturned in a Mona Lisa smile.

"Quiet, dark and private," she said softly. "I like that."

He felt his body stir. "Me, too," he whispered, and bent his head to hers.

Her mouth was sweet and soft. One taste, and he knew it wouldn't be enough to satisfy the hunger building inside him. Sean swept his fingers into Savannah's hair and lifted her face to his.

He sensed this could be dangerous. She wanted something from him and he still didn't know what it was, but kissing her was irresistible. Even as he let himself sink into the kiss, he told himself it was okay, that playing along was the only way to find out what she was up to.

It was a great plan...except, he had miscalculated. He couldn't think, couldn't find out anything when deepening the kiss almost drove him to his knees.

God, her mouth! Soft. Honeyed. Hot. And the feel of her hair, sliding like silk over his fingers. The sigh of her breath as it mingled with his.

Sean forgot everything but the woman pressed against him.

"Savannah," he murmured, sliding his hands down her throat, her shoulders, lifting her to him, drawing her tightly into his arms.

She made a little sound. A whisper of surrender. Her lips softened. Parted. She was trembling, as if the world were shifting under her feet just as it was under his, and he gath-

ered her against his body until her softness cradled the swift
urgency of his erection.

She stirred in his arms, moved against him, and the blood
pounded through his veins. Groaning, he moved his hand
over her thigh, swept it under that sexy excuse of a skirt...

Just that quickly, she went crazy. Gasped against his
mouth. Writhed in his arms. Twisted against him.

Sean thought she'd gone over the edge with desire.
Thought it, right until she sank her teeth into his bottom lip.

"Goddammit," he yelped, and thrust her from him.

Stunned, tasting his own blood, he grabbed his handkerchief from his pocket and held it to his lip. The snowy-
white linen square came away smeared with crimson. He
stared at Savannah, his testosterone-fogged brain struggling
for sanity. Her eyes were wide and glittering, her face
drained of color, and he realized, with dawning amazement,
that she hadn't moaned in surrender but in desperation.

She hadn't been struggling to get closer but to get away.

"Oh God," she whispered. She took a step toward him,
hands raised in supplication. "I'm sorry."

"What the hell kind of game are you playing, lady?"

"No game. I didn't—I didn't mean to—to—"

Her hair was wild, the golden strands tumbling over her
breasts. Her mouth was pink and swollen from his. Even
now, knowing she was crazy, he couldn't help thinking how
beautiful she was—and how crazy *he'd* be, if he spent a
minute more in her company.

"Sean. I really am terribly sorry."

"Yeah. Me, too." He held the handkerchief to his lip
again. The wound was starting to throb. "It's been interesting," he said, brushing past her. "I just hope the next
guy you zero in on has better luck."

"Sean!" Her voice rose as she called after him. "Please.
If you'd just give me a minute..."

He kept walking, but he was tempted. The bite hadn't been passion but what? Anger? Fear? He didn't know and told himself he didn't care. He wasn't a social worker. Whatever this woman's problem was, he wasn't the solution.

But she'd felt so soft. So vulnerable. When he'd first kissed her, she'd responded. It wasn't until he'd put his hand under her skirt that she'd panicked, if that was what she'd done, and that didn't make a whole lot of sense, not when she'd been damned near asking him to screw her for the past hour.

"Mr. O'Connell! Please!"

He stopped and swung around. She was running toward him. Mr. O'Connell, huh? Sean narrowed his eyes. Two times now, she'd called him that. Pretty surprising, since they hadn't introduced themselves with last names.

So much for walking away.

Why had she pretended not to know who he was? Why act as if she wanted to sleep with him when she'd gone from soft sweetness to what sure as hell seemed to be terror at the touch of his hand?

She stopped a few feet away.

"Please," she said again, her voice a shaky whisper. "I didn't meant to—to—" She swallowed dryly. "Your lip is still bleeding."

"Yeah?" He forced a thin smile. "What a surprise."

She closed the distance between them, that elegant feline walk gone so that she wobbled a little on her sky-high, dome-baby heels.

"Let me fix it."

"Thanks, but you've done enough already."

She wasn't listening. Instead, she was burrowing inside her ridiculously small evening purse. What'd she expect to find? he thought grimly. A bottle of antiseptic and a cotton swab?

"Here. Just duck your head a little."

A froth of white lace. That was what she pulled from the purse. Sean glowered at her. She stared back. He could see her confidence returning, the glitter of defiance starting to replace the fear in her eyes.

"I'm not going to hurt you, Mr. O'Connell."

A muscle jerked in his jaw. "That's what they all say."

That brought a twitch to her lips. Sean told himself he was an idiot, and did as she'd asked.

Gently, she patted the handkerchief against the wound she'd inflicted, concentrating as if she were performing open-heart surgery. The pink tip of her tongue flicked out and danced along the seam of her mouth, and Sean felt his traitorous body snap to attention.

"There," she said briskly. "That should do—"

He hissed with pain as she pulled the hankie away. A bit of lace had clung to the congealing blood; yanking it free had started a tiny scarlet trickle oozing.

Savannah raised stricken eyes to his.

He'd gotten it right the first time. Her eyes really were as green as a spring meadow. And her mouth was pink. Like cotton candy. Maybe that wasn't very poetic, but he'd always loved the taste of cotton candy.

"I'm sorry," she said on a note of despair. "I know I keep saying that but—"

"You have to moisten it." His voice rumbled and he cleared his throat. "The handkerchief. If it's damp, it won't stick to the cut."

"Oh." She looked around. "You're right. Just give me a minute to find the ladies'—"

"Wet it with your tongue," he said. Hell. Now he sounded as if he'd run his words through a bed of gravel.

Her eyes rose to his again. "The hankie. You know. Just—just use your mouth to make it wet."

Her face turned the same color as her dress. Time stretched between them, taut as a wire.

"Sean," she said quietly, "I didn't— When you kissed me, I didn't expect—I didn't know—"

"Know what?" he said roughly, moving closer. He reached out, cupped her face.

"Sir?"

Sean swung around. The waiter stood a few feet away.

"Your champagne, sir. Shall I…?"

"Just—" Sean cleared his throat. "Just put it on that table. No, don't open it. I'll do it myself."

Saved by the proverbial bell, he thought as the waiter did as he'd asked. Kissing this woman again made about as much sense as raising the ante with a pair of threes in your hand.

He waited until they were alone again, taking the time to get himself back under control. Then he looked at Savannah.

"Champagne," he said briskly.

"For what?" She'd pulled herself together, too. Her voice was strong, her color normal.

"It's just what we need. For the cut on my lip."

"Oh. Oh, of course. Will you—"

"Sure."

Sean did the honors, twisting the wire muzzle from the neck of the bottle, then popping the cork. The wine sparkled with bubbles as he poured some on the hankie she held out.

"It'll probably sting," she said, and before he could reply, she moved in and dabbed the cut with the cold, wine-soaked lace.

An understatement, Savannah thought, as Sean O'Connell rocked back on his heels.

"Sorry," she said politely. The hell she was, she thought.

She'd made a damned fool of herself. Worse, she'd probably blown her chance at setting him up for the kill, but it was his fault.

Why did he have to ruin things by kissing her? If he hadn't, everything would still be fine. She hadn't meant for him to kiss her; she was supposed to be the one setting the boundaries for this little escapade, not him.

"Hey! Take it easy with that stuff."

"Sorry," she said again, and went right on cleaning the cut with as little delicacy as she could manage.

Some seductress she was. The mark made a move she hadn't anticipated, gave her one simple kiss, and...

Except, it hadn't been a simple kiss. It had been as complex as the night sky. She'd trembled under it. The texture of his mouth. The whisper of his breath. The silken glide of his tongue against hers.

And then—then, it had all changed. His hand on her thigh. The quick bloom of heat between her legs. The pressure of his hard, aroused male flesh, the message implicit in its power.

All at once, the terrace had become the yacht. She'd remembered the way Alain's friends had taken to looking at her and the way Alain talked to them right in front of her, his voice pitched so low she couldn't hear his words.

She didn't have to.

She had only to see their hot eyes, see the little smiles they exchanged, feel the way a beefy hand would brush against her breast, her thigh, always accidentally...

"Are you trying to fillet my lip or leave it steak *tartare?*"

Savannah blinked. O'Connell, arms folded over his chest, was eyeing her narrowly, his face expressionless.

"I, uh, I just wanted to make sure I disinfected the cut properly." She dropped her hand to her side, peered at his lip as if she knew what she was doing and flashed what she hoped was a brilliant smile. "It looks fine."

"Does it," he said coldly.

Oh, this wasn't any good! She'd had him right where she wanted him, and now she'd lost him. He was furious and she couldn't blame him.

Well, that would have to change if she was going to get anywhere tonight.

"Yes," she said, with a little smile. "I'm happy to tell you, you won't need stitches. No rabies shots, either."

He didn't smile back. All right. One more try.

"I suppose I owe you an apology," she said, looking at him from under her lashes.

Sean almost laughed. The cute smile. The tease. And, when those failed, the demure look coupled with an apology. All designed to tap into his masculine instincts. He was supposed to say "no, it's okay," because that was what a gentleman would do.

Unfortunately for Just-Savannah, he was no gentleman.

"No."

"No?"

"I don't want an apology."

She almost sighed with relief. He waited a beat.

"I want an explanation."

She blinked. Clearly, she hadn't expected that. Now she was mentally scrambling for a response.

"An explanation," she parroted. "And—and you're entitled to one. I, uh, I think it's just that you—you caught me by surprise."

"You've been coming on to me all evening."

"Well—well, I told you, you're an attractive—"

She gasped as he caught hold of her wrists.

"And yet, the first move I make, you react as if I dragged you into an alley."

"That's not—"

"Game's over, sweetheart."

"I have no idea what you're talking about."

"Nobody plays me for a fool." Sean held her tighter, applying just enough pressure to let her know he was taking charge. "I want answers."

"To what? Honestly, Mr. O'Connell…"

"Let's start with the 'Mr. O'Connell' routine. I was Just-Sean. You were Just-Savannah. How come it turns out you know my last name?"

Savannah swallowed past the lump in her throat. His face was like a thundercloud; his hands were locked around hers like manacles. *Missy,* she thought, *oh, Missy, I'm so sorry.*

"I told you," she said in a low voice. "I saw you and I found you very—"

"Forget that crap." His mouth thinned; he tugged on her wrists and she had no choice but to stumble forward until they were only a breath apart. "I knew something was up, but you were determined to keep trying the same con so I decided to go along. You've been scamming me, sugar, and I've had enough. You tell me what's going on or I'll drag you to the manager's office and see to it you're barred from ever entering this place again."

"You can't do that! I have as much right to be here as you do."

"Maybe you're a working girl."

"A working…" She began to tremble. "That's a lie."

"Is it? Once I describe your behavior, who's going to argue with me?"

"You can't do that!"

His grin was all teeth. "Try me."

Savannah opened her mouth, then shut it. For all she knew, he could do anything. He was known here. She wasn't. Everything was coming apart. She'd have to go back to Alain and tell him she'd failed, that his year of planning had led to nothing.

"Well? I'm waiting for that explanation. And I'll tell you right now, sugar, it damned well better be good."

Desperate, she searched for anything that might get her out of this mess. What could she possibly say that would change things? O'Connell was right. He wasn't about to believe she was interested in him, not after she'd almost bitten his face off when he touched her.

She wouldn't react that way if he did it again.

The realization shocked her. It was true, though. Now that she knew what to expect, if it happened again—which it wouldn't—but if it did, if she ever felt all that heat, saw the hunger in his eyes, she might just—she might just—

"Okay, that's it."

Sean started walking toward the door, dragging her with him. *Think,* she told herself desperately, *think, think!*

"All right," she gasped. "I'll tell you the truth."

He swung toward her, towering over her in the moonlight. He said nothing. Clearly, the next move was hers. Savannah took a steadying breath and played for time to work out a story. Something he would buy so she wouldn't have to return to Alain in failure and see that cool smile, hear him say, *Ah, chérie, that's too bad. I hate to think of your dear little sister in one of those state institutions.*

She took a steadying breath. "I owe you an apology, Mr. O'Connell."

"You already said that."

"Not for biting you. For—what did you call it? For scamming you."

It was a start. At least she'd caught his attention.

"I didn't mean to. Not exactly. I just—"

"You didn't mean to. Not exactly." Sean raised an eyebrow. "That's your explanation?"

"No! There's more."

"Damned right, there's more. Why don't you start by telling me why you pretended not to know who I was?"

How much of the truth could she tell, without giving everything away?

"I'm waiting."

"Yes. I know." She looked down at their hands, still joined, then up at his face. "It's true. I did know who you were. Well, I knew your name but then, everyone knows your name."

She fell silent. Sean let go of her wrists and tucked his hands into his pockets. He'd long ago learned the art of keeping quiet. Do it right and the other person felt compelled to babble.

"Everyone knows you're the world's best poker player."

He wasn't, though he was close to it. Still, he said nothing. She didn't, either, but he knew his silence was getting to her. She was chewing lightly on her lip. If she wasn't careful, she'd leave a little wound to match his.

A wound he could easily soothe with a flick of his tongue. *Damn, where had that thought come from?*

"And all this is leading where?" he said gruffly.

"To—to the reason I came over and spoke to you."

"Sugar," he said, smiling tightly, "you didn't speak to me, you hit on me. Understand, I've no objection to a beautiful woman showing her interest." His smile faded. "I just don't like being played for a sucker."

"I didn't—"

"Yeah, you did. Or you would have, if you could have gotten away with it." He pulled his hand from his pocket and checked his watch. "I have other things to do tonight. You have two minutes to answer my questions—or we can take that walk to the office."

Savannah knotted her fingers together. She was going to

do the very thing Alain had warned her against, but what other choice did she have?

"I play poker, too, Sean."

"How nice." His teeth showed in a chilly smile. "We're back to first names."

"Did you hear what I—"

"You said you play poker. What's that got to do with anything?"

She hesitated. What could she safely tell him? Surely not that the man he'd cheated out of a million dollars had sent her, or that she was going to wipe him out because she was as good a player as he'd ever met.

She certainly couldn't tell him the rest of it, that she'd planned to work him into such a sexual haze that by the time they sat down to play, he'd be so busy drooling over her that he wouldn't be able to concentrate on his cards.

But she could tell him part of it, fancy things up to appeal to his ego. She'd blown her cover as a *femme fatale*. Could she pass herself off as an overeager tourist?

"I'm American. Like you."

"Congratulations," Sean said dryly. "So what?"

"So, I'm on vacation. You know. Sun, sea, sand. Gambling. I really like to gamble, even though I'm new at it."

A muscle flickered in his jaw. "Go on."

"You're right about my name. I was born in Georgia but I live in Louisiana. That's where I learned to play cards. On a riverboat. You know, on the Mississippi? A date took me, the first time." She grinned, hoped it was disarming and that mixing lies and truth proved the ticket to success. "I picked up the game fast. I'm pretty good, if I must say so myself, but I've never played against serious competition. Against, say, a man like you."

Sean lifted an eyebrow. Was this the whole thing? Had she flirted with him just to convince him to take a seat at the same poker table? Anything was possible. Novices approached him all the time. In his own tight little world, he was a celebrity of sorts.

Except, he didn't buy it.

All this subterfuge, so he could beat her pretty tail off in a game of cards? So she could go home and say she'd played Sean O'Connell?

No way.

"I'd be thrilled if you'd let me sit at a table with you, Sean. I could go home and tell everyone—"

"Anybody can sit at any table. You must know that."

"Well—well, of course I know that. But I'm not that forward. I know you think I am, after all that's happened, but the truth is, I wouldn't have the courage to take a seat at a table you were at unless I cleared it with you first."

He still didn't buy it. She wouldn't have the courage? This woman who'd done everything but jump his bones?

"And that's it?"

Savannah nodded. "That's it."

He moved fast, closed the distance between them before she could even draw a breath. All at once, her back was to the wall and his hands were flattened against it on either side of her.

"You took a big risk, sugar," he said softly. "Coming on to me as hard as you did without knowing a damned thing about me except that I play cards. You got me going a few minutes ago. If your luck had gone bad, you might have gotten hurt."

He saw her throat constrict as she swallowed, but her eyes stayed right on his.

"I told you that I knew you were Sean O'Connell. And Sean O'Connell isn't known for hurting women."

"No." His gaze fell to her mouth. He looked up and smiled. "He's known for liking them, though."

"Sean. About what I've asked…"

"Why did you panic?"

"I didn't. I—"

Sean put one finger gently over her lips. "Yeah, you did. I kissed you, you kissed me back, and then you got scared." His finger slid across the fullness of her mouth. "How come? What frightened you?"

"Nothing frightened me."

She was lying. He could sense it. There was something going on he still didn't understand and, all at once, he wanted to.

"Savannah." Sean cupped her face. "What's the matter? Tell me what it is. Let me help you."

Her eyes glittered. Was it because of the moonlight, or were those tears?

"I don't know what you're talking about."

Sean smoothed back her hair. "Just as long as you're not afraid of me," he said gruffly, and kissed her.

She let it happen, let herself drown in the heat of his kiss. She told herself it was what she had to do but when he drew back, she had to grasp his shoulders for support.

"Tell me what you want," he said softly.

Savannah willed her heart to stop racing. Then she took a deep breath and said the only thing she could.

"I told you. I want to play cards. Then I can go home and tell everybody that I played against the great Sean O'Connell."

"And that's it? That's all you need from me?"

His eyes were steady on hers, his body strong under her hands. For one endless moment, she thought of telling him the truth. That she was here to destroy him. That she was in trouble and had no one to turn to for help but herself.

Then she remembered that he was a thief, and she forced a smile to her lips.

"That's it," she said lightly. "That's all I need."

CHAPTER FOUR

TWO HOURS LATER, Sean was sitting across from Savannah at a poker table in the high-stakes area of the casino and the warning bells in his head were clamoring like bells inside a firehouse.

The game was draw poker. She was still playing. He'd already folded, just as he'd done half a dozen times since they'd started. His fault, he knew. He'd played with lazy disinterest, underestimated the lady's skill.

And her skill was considerable.

The realization had caught him by surprise. Once it had, he'd played a couple of hands as he should have from the start. She'd folded. He'd won.

That had led to another realization. Goldilocks wasn't a good loser.

Oh, she said all the right things, the clever patter card-players used to defuse tension. She flashed that megawatt smile across the table straight at him. But her eyes didn't smile. They were dark with distress. What she'd said about simply wanting to play him wasn't true.

Just-Savannah needed to win. He decided to let her. There were all kinds of ways to up the ante.

And if she was new to the game, he was Mighty Mouse.

She played with the cool concentration of someone who'd had years to hone her talent. Her instincts were good, her judgment sharp, and by now he'd determined that the cute little things she did when she played, things he'd at first thought were unconscious habits, were deliberate shticks meant to distract him.

A little tug at a curl as it kissed the curve of her cheek. A brush of her tongue across her mouth. A winsome smile accompanied by a look from under the thick sweep of her gold-tipped lashes.

Most effective of all, a sigh that lifted her breasts.

The air-conditioned chill in the casino was cooperating. Each time her breasts rose, the nipples pressed like pearls against the red silk that covered them.

Forget about the odds, she all but purred. *Forget about the game. Just think about me. What I have to offer, you'll never get by winning this silly game of cards.*

It was hard not to do exactly that. The man in him wanted what she was selling with every beat of his heart. The gambler in him knew it was all a lie. And there it was again. The smile, just oozing with little-girl amazement that she was actually winning.

Bull.

Savannah wasn't a novice, she was an expert. Playing without using any of those distractions, she'd beat every man at the table on ability alone.

Every man but him.

She was good, but he was better. And once he knew what in hell was happening, he'd prove it to her.

Meanwhile, the action was fascinating to watch. Not just her moves but the moves of the rest of the players. Two—a German industrialist and a Texas oil billionaire—were good. The others—a prince from some godforsaken principality, a Spanish banker, a has-been American movie star and an Italian who had something to do with designing shoes—weren't. It didn't matter. The men were all happy to be losing.

Sean didn't think Savannah gave a damn. He'd have bet

everything he owned that she was putting on this little show solely for him.

Why? No way was it so she could go home and boast about having played against him. That story leaked like a sieve, especially because he could see past the smile, the cleavage, the performance art.

Under all that clever artifice, she was playing with a determination so grim it chilled him straight down to the marrow of his bones.

So he'd decided to lay back. Win a couple of hands, lose a couple. Fold early. Look as if he was as taken in as the others while he tried to figure out what was going on.

Right now, he and she were the only ones playing. The rest had all folded. She sighed. Her cleavage rose. She licked her lips. She twirled a curl of golden hair around her index finger. Then she looked at him and fluttered her lashes.

"I'll see your five," she said, "and raise you ten."

Sean smiled back at her. He didn't bother looking at his cards. He knew what he had and he was damned sure it beat what she was holding.

"Too rich for my blood," he said lazily, and dropped his cards on the green baize tabletop.

The German smiled. "The *fräulein* wins again."

Savannah gathered in the chips. "Beginner's luck," she said demurely, and smiled at him again.

It wasn't luck, beginner's or otherwise. The luck of the draw was a big part of winning but from what he'd observed, it had little to do with her success at this table.

The lady was good.

He watched as she picked up her cards, fanned them just enough to check the upper right-hand corners, then put them down again. It was a pro's trick. When your old man owned one of the biggest hotels and casinos in Vegas, you learned their tricks early.

Not that Sean had spent much time in the casino. State law prohibited minors from being in the gaming areas. More importantly, so did his mother.

One gambler in the family was enough for Mary Elizabeth O'Connell. She'd never complained about her husband's love of cards, dice, the wheel, whatever a man could lay a wager on, but she also made it clear she didn't want to see her children develop any such interests.

Still, Sean had been drawn to the life as surely as ocean waves are drawn to the shore.

He began gambling when he was in his teens. By his senior year in high school, he bet on anything and everything. Basketball. Football. Baseball. A friend's grades. His pals thought he was lucky. Sean knew better. It was more than luck. He had a feel for mathematics, especially for those parts of it that dealt in probability, combinations and permutations. Show him the grade spread for, say, Mrs. Keany's classes in Trig over the past five years, he could predict how the current grades would play out with startling accuracy.

It was fun.

Then he went away to college, discovered poker and fell in love with it. He loved everything about the game. The cool, smooth feel of a new deck of cards. The numbers that danced in his head as he figured out who was holding what. The kick of playing a hand he knew he couldn't lose or, conversely, playing a hand no sane man would hold on to and winning anyway because he was good and because, in the final analysis, even the risk of losing could give you an adrenaline rush.

By the time he graduated from Harvard with a degree in business, he had a small fortune stashed in the bank.

Sean handed his degree to Mary Elizabeth, kissed her on both cheeks and said he knew he was disappointing her but he wasn't going to need that degree for a while.

"Just don't disappoint yourself," she'd told him, her smile as gentle as her voice.

He never had.

After almost eight years playing in the best casinos and private games all around the world, he was one hell of a player. His bank account reflected that fact. He could risk thousands of dollars on each turn of the cards without blinking.

He didn't win all the time. That would have been impossible, but that was still part of what he loved about the game. The danger. The sense that you were standing on top of the world and only you could keep you there. It was part of the lure. Maybe it was all of it.

Maybe he just liked living on the edge.

He wasn't addicted to cards.

He was addicted to excitement.

And what was happening tonight, at *L'Emeraude de Caribe,* was as exciting as anything he'd experienced in a very long time.

A blonde with the face of a Madonna and the body of a courtesan was running a scam with him as the prospective patsy, and he was going to find out what she was up to or—

"O'Connell? You in or out?"

Sean looked up. The Texan grinned at him from around the dead cigar stub clamped in his teeth.

"I know the little lady's somethin' of a distraction," the Texan said in a stage whisper, "but you got to make a decision, boy."

"I'm in," Sean said, shoving a stack of chips to the center of the table.

Everyone was in, except for the prince. He dumped his

cards, folded his arms and never took his eyes from Savannah. She was, as the Texan had said, something of a distraction.

Soon, only he, Savannah and the German remained. The German folded. He had nothing. Sean had a pair of aces and two jacks. Could Savannah top that? He knew she couldn't. He raised her ten thousand. She saw it, smiled and raised another ten.

Should he meet it? Or should he let her think she'd outbluffed him, the way he'd done the last few hands?

Savannah began her little act. The tongue slicking across her mouth. The breasts straining against the red silk.

He wondered how she'd look stripped of that silk. Her breasts seemed rounded, small enough to cup in his hands. Were her nipples as pink as her lips? Or were they the color of apricots? They'd taste like honey, he was certain. Wildflower honey, and when he sucked them into his mouth, tugged at them with his teeth, her cry would fill the night...

"Mr. O'Connell?"

He blinked. Savannah was watching him intently, almost as if she knew what he was thinking.

"Are you in or out?"

He looked down at his cards again. The aces and the jacks looked back. What the hell, he thought.

"Out," he said, and dumped his cards on the table. He smiled at her. "You know, you're taking me to the cleaners, sugar."

It was true. He'd lost a lot of money. He wasn't sure how much. Seventy thousand. A hundred. More, maybe.

He waited for her to smile back at him. She didn't.

"You're not going to stop playing, are you? I mean—I mean, it's still early."

She sounded panicked. He'd had no intention of quitting. Now, he decided to pretend that he had.

"I don't know," he said lazily. "Heck, a man's a fool to keep playing when he's losing."

"Oh, come on." She smiled, but her lips barely moved. "One more hand."

Sean pretended to let her talk him into it. He watched her pick up the cards as the dealer skimmed them to her.

Her hands were trembling.

His cards were bad. Evidently, so were those of the others. Some fast mental calculations suggested Savannah's cards were excellent. The others dropped out. Sean raised the ante. Savannah folded before the words were fully out of his mouth.

"You won this time around," she said gaily, but he could hear the edge in her voice. And her hands were still shaking. "Aren't you glad you stayed in?"

Sean nodded and pulled the chips toward him. What she'd done didn't make sense. He was sure she'd had better than even odds on holding a winning hand. Had she folded only to make him want to stay in the game?

It was time to make a move. Change the momentum and see what happened.

"It's getting late," he said. He yawned, stretched, and pushed back his chair. "I think I've had it."

Savannah looked up. He could see her pulse beating in her throat.

"Had it? You mean you want to stop playing?"

"Enough is enough, don't you think?"

When she smiled, her lips damned near stuck to her teeth. "But you just won!"

"And about time, too," he said, and chuckled.

"Come on, O'Connell." The Texan flashed a good ol' boy grin. "You can't quit when the little lady's beatin' the pants off all of us. Pardon me, ma'am, for bein' crude, but that's exactly what you're doin'."

"And we love it," the German said, chortling. "Come, come, Mr. O'Connell. Surely you won't walk away when things are just getting interesting. I don't think I've ever heard of you losing with such consistency."

"True," the prince said, and nudged the man with a sharp elbow, "but then, I doubt if Mr. O'Connell's accustomed to playing with such a charming diversion at the table."

Everyone laughed politely. Not Savannah. The expression on her face was intense.

"Please. I'd be devastated if you left now." Her voice was unsteady, but the smile she gave him was sheer enticement.

Sean decided to let her think it had worked. "Tell you what. How about we take a break? Fifteen minutes. Get some air, whatever. That okay with the rest of you?"

It was okay with everyone except Savannah, who looked as if he'd just announced he was abandoning ship, but she responded with a bright smile.

"That's fine," she said, pushing back her chair, too. "No need to get up," she added, when the men half rose to their feet. "I'll just—I'll just go to the powder room."

Sean watched her walk away. They all did, and it annoyed him. Stupid, he knew. He had no rights to her, nor did he want any. Still, he didn't like the way the others looked at her.

"She is a beautiful woman," the Italian said.

The one-time movie star smiled. "That she is."

"You're a lucky SOB, O'Connell," the Texan said, shifting the unlit cigar in his mouth.

Sean grinned. "Lucky to lose so much money?"

"Lucky to have a woman like that interested in you." The prince leaned forward. "I'd be happy to lose twice what I have, if she'd do that little tongue trick with me in mind."

Sean's smile vanished. "I'll be back," he growled, and headed for the terrace.

The terrace was as empty as when he'd been out there with Savannah. Empty, quiet, and a good place to get some fresh air and reconsider the point of letting a woman he didn't know think she was getting the best of him.

He walked to the rail, leaned against it and stared blindly out over the sea. Maybe he was dead wrong about Savannah. He could be reading things into the way she was behaving. Wasn't it possible she'd told him the truth? That all she wanted was to play cards? Those feminine tricks could just be part of the action. She might have used them to advantage back on the riverboat, where she said she'd learned to gamble.

And even if she was lying about being new to gambling, about wanting to play him…what did that change? Not a thing, he thought, answering his own question. He was making a mystery out of something that was probably, at best, simply an interesting situation.

If she was up to anything at all, it might just be scamming him so she could take him, big-time.

So what if he could still remember the sweet taste of her mouth? If her eyes were deep enough to get lost in?

If her hands trembled, and sometimes he saw a fleeting expression on her lovely face that made him want to gather her into his arms and kiss her, hold her, tell her he'd protect her from whatever it was she feared—

"Lovely night, Mr. O'Connell, isn't it?"

Sean started. The prince, who'd come up alongside him, inclined his head in apology.

"Sorry. I didn't mean to take you by surprise."

"That's okay. I was just—just listening to the sound of the sea. I didn't hear you coming."

The prince leaned back against the rail as he reached into

the pocket of his tuxedo jacket and took out a slim gold cigarette case. He opened it and held it out to Sean, who shook his head.

"No, thanks."

"You don't smoke?" Sighing, the prince put the cigarette in his mouth, flicked the wheel of a small gold lighter and put a flame to the tip. "I've been trying to quit for years." He exhaled a plume of smoke and smiled. "My wife assures me it's a worse affliction than gambling."

Sean nodded. He wasn't in the mood for conversation.

"And I assure her that a man must have some vices, or there isn't much point in living." The prince inhaled again. "She's a stunning young woman."

"I'm sure she is." Sean made a show of checking the luminous dial on his watch. "Would you excuse me, Prince Artois? I want to make a stop in—"

"I wasn't referring to my wife—though she is, of course, a beautiful woman." The prince blew out a perfect smoke ring. "I was talking about our poker player. Savannah."

Something in the man's tone made the hair rise on the back of Sean's neck.

"Yes," he said carefully, "she is."

"You're fortunate she has such an interest in you."

"She's interested in winning," Sean said, just as carefully. "We all are."

"And yet, you are losing. I doubt if anyone has ever seen you lose this way before."

"It happens."

"Indeed." The prince turned to stare out over the sea, the burning tip of his cigarette a tiny beacon in the night. "What I find most amusing is that she's so good that the rest of us would surely lose against her even if she weren't such a distraction, but you—you shouldn't be losing at all. You're not easily diverted, or so I've heard."

"Diverted?"

"Come on, O'Connell. You and I both know the lady is doing her best to keep your attention off the game."

"Perhaps she's succeeding," Sean said, his eyes fixed to the prince's autocratic profile.

"Perhaps. Or perhaps you're letting her win, for your own reasons."

Sean straightened up. "I'll see you inside."

He began walking toward the lighted door, but the prince called after him.

"You know who she is, of course?"

A muscle knotted in Sean's jaw. He stopped, but didn't turn around.

"A woman named Savannah," he said, "from the American South."

"Savannah McRae," Artois said. "That's her full name."

Slowly, Sean turned and looked at him. "You know her?"

"We've never been introduced until tonight." He gave Sean a thin smile. "But I know who she is. And what."

Sean went toward him, his steps deliberate, his eyes never leaving Artois's face.

"Would you like to explain that?"

"She plays cards." Artois flicked the glowing cigarette butt over the railing. It flickered like a tiny shooting star as it arced toward the beach. "It's how she earns her keep."

Her keep. Not her living, which would no longer have surprised Sean, but her keep.

"Her keep?" he asked softly.

"Is this really unknown to you, Mr. O'Connell?"

The muscle in Sean's jaw leaped. "Get to it, Artois," he growled, "and stop screwing around."

The prince smiled. "She's Alain Beaumont's mistress."

HE DIDN'T BELIEVE IT.

Savannah, Beaumont's mistress? No. It was impossible.

Sean paced the terrace on the other side of the casino, far from the sound of the surf, the lights, the all-too-vividly remembered taunting smile Artois had shown him.

Beaumont was slime. His little cruelties to the maids who worked in the elegant houses on these islands and in Europe were whispered about; his perversions were the topic of quiet speculation among those who found him either fascinating or revolting.

Sean had met him at a casino in Monte Carlo. Just watching him fondle the backside of a waitress whose face blazed with shame, hearing his lewd jokes, listening to his boasts about his sexual prowess, had been enough to make him despise Beaumont.

Somehow, they'd ended up playing at the same baccarat table, the same roulette wheel, the same poker table, where Beaumont lost to Sean. Lost badly.

Beaumont's eyes had burned with fury but his voice had been unctuous as he invited Sean to give him the chance to win back his money. Sean had wanted only to see the last of him, but honor meant accepting the challenge.

"Deal the cards," Sean had snapped.

But Beaumont refused. He wanted Sean to play on his yacht, anchored in the harbor. And because Sean wanted nothing more than to see the man lose again, he'd agreed.

They'd taken Beaumont's tender to the yacht, just the two of them, and played through the night and the morning, Beaumont's line of oily chatter gradually giving way to tight-lipped rage as the pile of chips in front of Sean grew.

By noon the next day, he'd won a million dollars. Beaumont slammed his hand on the table, called Sean a cheat. Sean grabbed him by his lapels, hauled him to his feet, demanded an apology or he'd beat him to a pulp.

He'd almost hoped Beaumont wouldn't oblige. Beating him insensible held enormous appeal.

But Beaumont conceded, making up for not giving Sean the chance to beat him by wetting his trousers. Sean had laughed in scorn, scooped up his money and left. Once on shore, he walked into the first charity office he found and gave his winnings to a shocked and delighted little old lady seated behind a battered desk.

He had not seen Beaumont since.

Sean reached the end of the terrace and came to a dead stop.

Savannah, Beaumont's mistress? That greasy pig, taking her into his bed? His thick lips sucking at hers? His hands on her breasts, his thigh parting hers, his...

Sean balled his hands into fists, threw his head back and glared up at the stars as if they were to blame for what had happened. God knew, the fault was his own. He'd been fooled by Alain Beaumont. Now, he'd been fooled by Beaumont's mistress.

Obviously, Savannah was supposed to win back the million Beaumont had lost.

Sean narrowed his eyes.

Beaumont wanted to play? Sean would oblige him, only this time, he'd lose more than his money.

He took a steadying breath, thrust his hands into his hair and smoothed it down. Then he strolled back into the casino.

Savannah was in her alcove again. Her back was to him; she had one hand to her ear. She was talking to someone on a cell phone.

Another deep breath, this time to keep himself from giving the game away. He approached her quietly, from behind.

"I understand," she was saying, her voice low-pitched. "Alain, yes, you've told me that already..."

Alain. Alain. Sean felt his stomach roil, again saw Savannah in the pig's arms.

"I will. Of course, I will. I just wanted you to know that it might not go as we'd— Because he's clever, that's why. There are moments I think he's on to me, and..." Her shoulders bowed. Her head drooped. "No," she whispered. "Alain, please, just give me a little more time."

Sean stared at Savannah's dejected posture. Heard the desperation in her voice. For one wild minute, he saw that white horse again, saw himself in silver armor, galloping toward her.

"Yes, Alain. You know I do. Do you need me to say it? You mean—you mean everything to me."

Sean's gut knotted. He thought about going to her, spinning her around, slapping her face even though he'd never laid a finger on a woman in his life.

Instead, he swallowed past the bitter taste in his throat.

"Savannah?" he said casually.

She spun around, her face turning white when she saw him.

"There you are," he said, and forced his lips to curve in a smile. "Where've you been, sugar? We said fifteen minutes, remember?"

She stared at him blankly. "Sean?"

He mounted the two steps that led into the alcove. "Who are you talking to, sugar?" Still smiling, he held out his hand. "The folks back home, I bet. Are you telling them how you're playing and winning?"

Slowly, she took the tiny phone from her ear and looked at it as if she'd never seen it before. Then she hit the button to end the call, opened her evening purse and dropped the phone inside.

"Yes," she said. Her smile was shaky but he had to give

her credit for managing to smile at all. "That's exactly what I was doing. They're all green with envy."

"I bet." Sean waggled his hand. She took it, and he drew her into the curve of his body. "Well, come on, sweetheart. Let's see how well you do now that I've had some time to get myself together."

"Yes," she said. "Let's."

She laughed up into his face but he could feel a tremor run through her.

Hours later, he could actually see her shaking. He wasn't surprised. He'd played without mercy. The others had long ago folded. They were watching what was happening with the fascination of rabbits watching a weasel in their hutch.

Sean had won or intimidated them all. There were half a million dollars worth of chips piled in the middle of the table. He'd just added the hundred thousand that had brought the chips to that amount.

His cards were good. Savannah's were, too. He could tell by the way she ran her fingers over them.

Now she had two choices. Meet his bet and call, or fold.

He knew, with every instinct he possessed, she couldn't afford to fold. He also knew she didn't have any more money.

She had something else, though. And he was going to force her to risk it.

"Well?" He smiled at her. "What's it going to be, sugar?"

She looked at the chips, then at him. They'd gathered a crowd by now. Even high-stakes players had never seen a game quite like this.

"I don't—" She cleared her throat. "I don't have…" She looked around her, as if money might drop from the sky. "I'll give the casino a chit."

Sean's teeth showed in a hungry smile. "No chits here. Check, if you like, but those are the house rules."

"Then—then surely you'll take my personal note, Mr. O'Connell."

"My, oh my, just listen to that. We're back to the 'Mr. O'Connell' thing again." Sean leaned forward. "Sorry, Just-Savannah. I don't take personal notes."

"I told you, I don't have—"

"But you do," he said softly.

"I do?" Her gaze flickered to her wrist and the diamond watch linked around it. "My watch," she said breathlessly. "It's worth—"

"It's worth zero. What would I do with that watch?" Sean let his eyes slip over her, doing it slowly, from her face to her breasts and then back. She was pale and for one second, he felt sorry for her.

Then he remembered why she was here and who had sent her, who owned her, and his heart turned to ice.

"Make it something worth my while."

"I told you, I don't have—"

"Yeah," he said, and he could hear the anger, the hunger, damn it, in his voice. "One night."

"What?"

"I said, if you can't come up with the money, I'll take a night with you in its place."

The crowd stirred, a whisper of shock and delight rushing through it like the wind through a stand of trees.

"You mean—you mean—"

"I mean," Sean said coldly, "you win, the money's yours." He paused, drawing it out for all it was worth, trying not to listen to the blood thundering in his ears. "You lose, you come with me." She didn't answer. Anger and his hot, unwanted desire for her drove him on. "You sleep with me, babe. You got that, or you want me to be more direct?"

He could tell that she was holding her breath. Hell, the whole world was holding its breath.

He didn't know what he'd expected from her in response. Fury? Disbelief? She didn't show either. Nothing changed in her expression and when she spoke, it was slowly, with dignity.

"I understand."

It was Sean's turn to hold his breath. "And?"

"And," she said, "I'll see your cards."

She fanned her cards out. Some of the pink had come back to her face; when he didn't say anything, she even smiled. She had reason to smile. She'd been holding a straight flush. The three, four, five, six and seven of hearts were spots of bright color against the green baize.

"Your turn, Mr. O'Connell."

Sean pursed his lips. "You've got one fine hand there, sugar. An excellent hand. No wonder you were willing to make that bet."

The crowd sighed. So did Savannah. Her smile became real as she leaned across the table and began reaching for the chips.

Sean put his hand over hers. "Not so fast," he said softly.

Her eyes met his. Smiling, never looking away from her, he turned over his cards.

The crowd gasped. So did Savannah. Not Sean. He'd known how this would end. He had the ace, king, queen, jack and ten of spades. A royal flush.

Emotion flashed through him, so swift and fierce he knew he'd never felt anything even remotely like it before. He kicked back his chair, ignored the stack of chips and the crowd. He went around the table to Savannah and held out his hand.

An eternity passed. Then she stood up, ignored his outstretched hand and began walking. He moved alongside her, wrapped his arm tightly around her waist and led her into the night.

CHAPTER FIVE

SAVANNAH WANTED TO DIE.

People were staring, whispering behind their hands. Every eye was on her as Sean laced a hard, proprietorial arm around her waist and led her through the casino. The whispers that had started back at the poker table must have spread like wildfire.

Even in this place, where money and excess were as common as grains of sand on the beach, winning a woman on the turn of a card was big news.

She couldn't blame anyone but herself. What a fool she'd been! Sean had toyed with her, letting her win hand after hand. Had she ever been in control of the game, or had he only let her think she was?

She'd gambled for the highest stakes and lost. Lost her sister's future, her future...

Lost to a man in whose bed she would spend the night.

The realization sent a ribbon of terror whipping through her blood. Savannah stumbled and would have fallen if Sean hadn't had his arm around her. His grasp tightened, his hand spread even more possessively over her hip.

"What's the matter, sugar? You having trouble keeping up with me?"

His words were soft; he dipped his head toward hers and she knew those watching would think he was whispering something low and sexy into her ear. But she heard the hard edge in his voice and when she tilted her face up, she saw his eyes glittering like sea-ice.

"No," he said, his smile slow and cruel, "we both know that's not the problem. You can more than keep up. Fact is, you've been ahead of me from the start."

He'd gone from lust to rage in a heartbeat. Why? Did he know something? He couldn't. Alain had planned things so carefully.

Alain.

Her throat constricted as she imagined his reaction when he heard what had happened. Losing to Sean O'Connell hadn't been an option. Alain had made that clear. Right before the tender took her to shore, he'd cupped her chin and lifted her face until their eyes met. He'd smiled, almost the way he used to when he'd first taken her from New Orleans. For the first time in months, the light kiss he dropped on her mouth had not made her shudder.

"A kiss for good luck, *chérie.*"

"I'll do my best, Alain."

"*Oui.* I am certain you will." Another smile, but this one so cold it chilled her to the bone. "And if you need more than a good-luck kiss for a talisman, think of your dear sister as you play. That should cheer you on."

The warning had not been subtle. Remembering it, knowing how she'd failed, Savannah stumbled again.

Sean hauled her against his side. "You want me to pick you up and carry you out of here?"

He'd do it, too. It would add to her humiliation and he'd like that, though she didn't know why. And wasn't that funny? It was supposed to have gone the other way around. *She* was to have humiliated *him.*

Savannah reached deep inside herself and summoned up what remained of her pride. She'd be damned if she'd let him know the true depth of her despair.

"Don't push your luck, O'Connell," she snapped. "You won the bet. You didn't win the right to parade me around like a trophy."

"But that's what you are, sugar." A tight smile flashed across his face. "It's what you were meant to be. A prize I'd want so badly I'd think with my hormones instead of my head."

A cold hand seemed to close around her heart. Was that the explanation for his change in attitude? Was what she'd done so obvious?

"Surprised I figured it out?"

"I don't know what you're talking about."

"No. Of course you don't. You need an explanation, I'll give it to you when we get to my hotel room. For now, just keep moving."

That was all right with her. The sooner they left this place, the better. Anything to get away from the stares and smirks, the soft trills of laughter. The tragic part was that there was nothing funny in what was happening.

Alain's plan had failed. O'Connell hadn't been fooled by her brazen display of sexuality. It hadn't been her fault but Alain wouldn't see it that way. He'd lay the blame on her.

Yes, she'd changed things by telling Sean she wanted to play against him, but she hadn't had much choice. It hadn't bothered him. If anything, he'd seemed amused by her admission.

It had all gone so smoothly at first. She'd played as well as she ever had, better, really, because she knew how high the stakes were. And Alain's predictions had been correct. O'Connell was too busy watching her to pay attention to the game. She'd won and won and won—well, except for that time his interest seemed to be waning. She'd folded early and let him win.

Things had been going just fine… Until that break.

All the others at the table had wanted to take a breather.
She had to give in. What else could she have done? The
last thing she'd wanted was to call attention to herself.

But she hadn't wanted to give O'Connell time to think,
either. She'd thought of an easy solution. All she had to do
was ask him to go with her. Step out on the terrace for some
air. There, in the warm, sea-scented darkness, she could
have smiled up at him from under her lashes. Tossed back
her head when she laughed. Men liked looking at her when
she did that. She won because of her skill at poker
when she played for Alain, but that didn't mean she'd never
noticed the hot male eyes that took in her every motion.

And yet, she hadn't done it. Something about the idea of
being alone in the night with him again had made her feel…
What? Uncomfortable? Uneasy? Maybe it was because she
didn't like knowing she was cheating him, even though he
deserved it. Maybe it was because she wanted to win as
much on ability as she could.

Maybe it was because the thought of being alone in the
dark with Sean made her pulse quicken. Things could happen between a man and a woman on a warm tropical night.
He might reach for her. Draw her into his arms. Take her
mouth in a slow, drugging kiss.

It was hard enough, playing at seduction, promising
something she had no intention of delivering. She'd fled to
the ladies' lounge, let cold water run over her wrists, then
called Alain on her cell phone to tell him how well things
were going.

And jinxed herself.

She'd sensed a change in Sean as soon as he led her back
to the table. The Texan had started to say something but
Sean's sharp voice silenced him.

"Let's not waste time," he'd said. "Just play the game."

A couple of minutes later, she'd known it was all over.

Her adversary was playing with a single-minded intensity that was frightening, and exhibiting a level of skill and daring that made it clear he was out for blood.

He showed no mercy. A desire for something more than winning was fueling him.

Each time he looked at her, she saw rage in his eyes.

Smart players knew when to call it quits. Under normal circumstances she'd have bowed out but nothing about this night was normal. She *had* to win. So she'd kept playing. She won a couple of small pots, but she lost big each time it came down to only O'Connell and her until the others were simply spectators at what had become a blood sport.

Eventually, she'd stared disaster in the face. She was out of money. Every dollar Alain had given her was gone. No options left except going back to Alain and admitting failure. Then that terrible moment, Sean looking at her and in an impassive voice offering her a final, desperate chance...

"Get in the car."

Savannah looked up, startled. Somehow, they were out of the casino. A low-slung black sports car stood purring at the curb. A valet held the passenger door open.

The full reality of what awaited her was a dagger of ice straight to the heart. She was going to bed with a stranger. With a man who'd taken to looking at her as if she were something that had crawled out of a sewer.

Her steps faltered. "Wait a minute."

"Are you going to welsh on the bet, McRae?"

He'd called her by her name, but she'd never given it to him. *God, oh God, oh God!*

"Get in the car. If you walk away, I'll make sure there's not a casino in the world that will let you in the door."

She stared at him. His face was a mask of contained rage. Why? What did he know? Better still, what choice did she have? She could go with him or go to Alain.

Either way, she was lost.

Numb, Savannah did as he'd commanded. The valet shut the door. Sean got behind the wheel. "Fasten your seat belt."

She almost laughed. Who gave a damn what happened to her now? If the car went off a cliff and into the sea, what would it matter?

He muttered something, leaned over and reached for the ends of the belt. His hand brushed across her breasts. To her horror, she felt them lift, felt her nipples harden. He knew it, too. He stopped what he was doing and looked into her eyes and then, with slow insolence, at her breasts. He smiled when their eyes met again but this time, the smile didn't chill her to the bone.

It made her think.

Whatever O'Connell knew or thought he knew, he had no right to sit in judgment on her. He was a cheat and a thief. She wasn't either one.

As for losing… Yes. She had. But Alain wasn't an animal. She'd explain things to him. He wouldn't make good on his threats about Missy. No. He wouldn't do that to her. They'd sit down together, come up with a better plan to defeat Sean O'Connell.

In the meantime, she wouldn't let O'Connell see her fear. She'd do what she had to do, the way she used to on the New Orleans streets long ago.

She'd learned to block out the real world with a better world inside her head. Think of a million other things so she didn't have to think about her empty belly or her sister's soft weeping or the brush of a rat's tail as it ran across her legs while she and Missy slept huddled together in a doorway.

All those hard-earned skills would save her tonight. Sean O'Connell would claim his prize. He'd do what men did to women in bed. And she—she wouldn't be there. Not really. She'd be inside her own thoughts where there was no fear, no panic, no pain.

He'd won her body, but she'd never let him take her soul.

SEAN'S HOTEL was on the southern coast of Emeraude, far from the casinos and the glitter that drew the rich and famous of the world.

The hotel was a former plantation house restored to glory by the whim and wealth of a deposed European prince. One look at the elegant suites, the quiet beaches and coves, and Sean had known he'd never stay anywhere else when he was on this island. The place was a half-hour drive from the busy casinos and that had always seemed a fine thing. It gave him time to unwind as he headed home.

Tonight, he was sorry for the delay.

Damn it, he was angry. Angry? He choked back a laugh as he took his Porsche through the hairpin curves that wound along the coast. Hell, no. He wasn't angry. He was enraged. It had been all he could do to play out the game. To keep from reaching across the table, dragging Savannah from her chair, shaking her until her teeth rattled...

Kissing her until she begged him to stop.

He wouldn't have stopped. No way. She'd been set out as bait, and bait was expendable.

What kind of woman would use herself to break a man's bank account? What kind of woman would be Alain Beaumont's mistress? Sleep in his bed, turn her naked body into his arms, let him run his slimy hands over her soft flesh?

Sean gritted his teeth.

A woman who'd bet one night with a stranger against the stakes in a card game.

Headlights appeared in the darkness. The road was narrow, narrower still along this last stretch that led to his hotel.

Normally, he'd slow his speed, pull the car over toward the scrub palmetto and wild beach grasses that lined the verge. Not tonight. Instead, he stepped down harder on the gas. The horn of the oncoming vehicle blasted as Sean roared by. He mouthed an oath and drove faster.

Who gave a damn about safety tonight?

Not him. Jesus, not him! He'd been taken in by a woman with hair of gold and eyes of jade, a woman whose soft, pink mouth he'd imagined savoring the minute he'd first seen her. Her kiss had shaken him as no other woman's ever had.

And she was a pawn owned by a piece of scum like Beaumont.

But he'd come out the winner. He'd taken Beaumont's money once again. Now he'd take his woman as well. He'd use her every way a man could, until those big eyes glittered with tears of shame, until that sweet-looking mouth was swollen and her thighs trembled because he'd spread them so many times.

No way she'd be thinking about her pig of a lover by then.

The tires clawed for control as he made a sharp turn into the hotel's circular drive. The parking valet trotted up and opened Sean's door as he shut off the engine. The boy smiled and greeted him but Sean wasn't in the mood for pleasantries. He brushed by the kid and flung open Savannah's door before the doorman could get there.

"Get out."

The soft glow of the interior lights illuminated her face. She was as pale as death except for two red streaks along her cheeks. The valet threw him a surprised look. Sean didn't give a damn. All that mattered was getting his pound of flesh.

"Out," he said again, and bent toward her. She pulled

back, her face becoming even whiter as he reached toward her seat belt. She wasn't stupid, he thought grimly. She'd learned the limits of his patience and she didn't want him to touch her again.

Had the instant of awareness when he'd brushed his hand over her breast been part of the game, or had she actually responded to his touch? Sean narrowed his eyes. It had been an act, the same as everything else. Savannah McRae was Alain Beaumont's toy.

Tonight, she would be his.

He tossed the valet a bill, clasped Savannah's arm and hurried her up the wide marble steps to the lobby. Only one clerk was at the reception desk at this time of night. He smiled politely when he saw Sean but his eyebrows rose at the sight of Savannah. Women in too-short red dresses, wearing heels that made the most of their up-to-their-ears legs, weren't the standard here.

"Mr. O'Connell," the clerk said politely, his composure regained. "Good evening, sir."

"Edward." Sean looked at the man. "I'd ask you to have room service send up some champagne, but we won't need it. Will we, sugar?" He shot Savannah a smile he knew was all teeth. "Why waste a bottle of good wine when it's not necessary?"

Savannah paled. The clerk turned crimson. Good, Sean thought savagely. Two birds with one stone.

He tugged her toward the elevator. Once inside, he put his key in the lock that would take them up to the penthouse. She tried to pull away but he had a grip of steel.

"What's the matter, sugar? Not in the mood? I can't believe that. Not after the big come-on earlier."

She didn't answer. Damn it, why not? He wanted her to say something. To plead with him to forget their bet, or at least to ask him to treat her with courtesy.

The elevator doors opened; he hurried her straight through the sitting room and into a bedroom overlooking the sea.

Sean kicked the door closed and turned the lock. And that—the sound of the bolt clicking home—finally changed the expression on Savannah's beautiful face.

What he saw there was fear.

For a heartbeat, the fury inside him subsided. He wanted to go to her, take her in his arms, tell her he wouldn't hurt her, that he'd be gentle, make slow love to her until she was sobbing with pleasure...

"Unlock the door."

The words, almost whispered, brought him back to sanity. He'd almost forgotten how good she was at acting.

"Relax, sugar. I'm just seeing to it we aren't disturbed."

"We made a bet. I'm prepared to go through with it but—"

"But?" he said, cocking his head as if he really gave a damn what she said next.

"But..." She swallowed, caught her lip between her teeth. "But I won't—I won't do anything—anything—"

"Kinky?" He grinned, shrugged off his jacket and tossed it aside. "Oh, I think you will, Just-Savannah. In fact, I'm willing to bet on it."

He watched her breasts rise and fall as she took a deep breath, then exhaled. Color was returning to her face. If he hadn't known better, he'd have sworn she was willing herself to be strong, but that was crazy.

A woman who slept with Alain Beaumont would sleep with anybody, even a man who won her at a poker table.

"You'd lose that bet, O'Connell."

Sean shrugged his shoulders. "No problem, babe. You give me whatever you give your lover and we'll call it even."

"My lover?"

Oh, she was good! That look, the total innocence in her eyes, even the surprise in her voice... She was better than good. She was great.

Would she be that great in bed? Yes. Oh, yes, she would be. Sean could almost taste her mouth. Her nipples would be honey on his tongue, her belly would have the scent of vanilla when he kissed it. Her golden thighs would carry the clean, erotic scent of a woman aroused as he parted them to reveal the hidden essence of her.

God, he was hard as stone.

"Yeah," he said gruffly as he started toward her. "Your lover. Beaumont. Remember him?"

"I didn't—he isn't—"

Sean reached her. He looped one hand around her throat. She flinched but stood her ground. He could feel the hammer of her pulse beneath his fingers. Slowly, he ran his hand over her, lightly cupping her breast, then curving it over her hip.

"Stop lying. You didn't learn to play cards on a riverboat. Alain Beaumont taught you."

"I don't know what you're talking ab—"

She gasped as he put both arms around her and drew her up against him. He knew she could feel his erection. Hell, he'd never been this hard in his life.

"What else did Beaumont teach you, sugar?"

The idea of lying flashed through her mind. Sean could almost see her thought process.

"Come on," he growled. "Be honest just once tonight. Admit he's your lover, that he put you up to this, that you were supposed to take me down and walk away laughing."

She didn't answer. Sean cursed, pulled her to her toes and crushed her mouth beneath his. She gave a sob that pierced his heart before he remembered this was all a game. She was playing a part. Nothing more, nothing less.

"Admit it," he said roughly. "Beaumont put you on to me."

Tears glittered in her eyes. "You stole from him."

"I what?"

"Stole. Cheated him out of a million dollars. In a card game on his yacht."

"That's one terrific story, sugar."

"It's the truth!"

"Let me get this straight. I stole a million bucks from your lover and you decided to steal it back to get even?"

"I wasn't trying to steal your money. I was winning it in a poker game."

"You were winning only because you kept me so busy looking at you that I couldn't think straight."

"That's not true! I'm a good poker player."

"Right. You're so good that you lost your lover's stake and ended with nothing to put on the table but yourself." Sean took a step back. "And now it's time to deliver."

"Sean. Mr. O'Connell…" Savannah heard the sudden desperation in her voice. No. She'd promised she wouldn't let him see her fear or hear her beg… but Lord, how could she do this? Give herself to a man who despised her? Let him touch her, explore her, take the last of her innocence, the only innocence she'd been able to hang on to in her life?

He was leaning against the dresser, arms folded over his chest, feet crossed at the ankles, watching her with no expression at all on his face. He was a thief, yes, but he wasn't unkind. Another man might have laughed and dismissed her when she'd told him that lie about why she wanted to play against him.

He hadn't. He'd listened.

Maybe he'd listen now.

"Mr. O'Connell." Savannah moistened her lips. "There's—there's been a misunderstanding. I—I wasn't thinking straight when I agreed to—"

"Strip."

She blanched. "Please. If you'd just hear me out—"

"Are you going to pay me the money that you lost to me tonight?"

"I can't. But—but—"

But what? She owed him a small fortune. She didn't have the money to pay it. She never would. And Alain would never give it to her, either. It was bad enough she'd return to him in defeat. She couldn't return and ask him for money, too.

"Either pay me the money or start getting undressed. Take your time about it. I want to enjoy the show."

Sean waited, hardly breathing. What would she do next? Run for her life, probably. Make a dash for the door, fumble with the lock and, damn it, he'd let her get away. He wanted her, yes. Why lie to himself? He wanted her badly, but not this way.

He couldn't go through with this. Even if she was willing, he'd—he'd—

The slow movement of her arms as she reached behind her stopped his thinking. His heart hammered as she slid down the zipper of the sexy red dress. One strap drooped against her shoulder, then the other. Her head was down but she must have felt his eyes on her because she lifted her chin and looked at him.

What he saw on her face almost killed him.

Here I am, she was saying. *Do what you will. Take what you want. It doesn't matter. I won't feel anything you do to me.*

But she would. He'd make her feel. He'd make her know

it was his hands on her, not Beaumont, that she was in his bed, not anyone else's.

Eyes still on his, she began to ease off one of those incredible shoes. Sean cleared his throat.

"Leave them on," he said hoarsely. "Take off the dress and leave the rest."

She took a deep breath and the red silk slithered to the carpet. She was wearing a black lace bra that cupped her breasts as lovingly as a man's hands, a black lace thong that covered that part of her that was all female, thigh-high, sheer-as-a-whisper black stockings and those shoes.

She was the most beautiful woman he'd ever seen and, for tonight, she belonged to him. He'd make her forget everything else.

He walked toward her slowly. The tears trembling on her lashes might have gotten to him if he hadn't reminded himself that they were about as real as the rest of her act.

"Beaumont is a lucky man," he said. She didn't answer. Sean trailed a finger down her throat, skimmed the curve of her breasts. "You're a feast for the eyes, Savannah. Do you taste as good as you look?"

She was shaking. Hell, he thought coldly, she was incredibly good at this. He clasped her face, lifted it to him, intending to brand her with his kiss. Instead, he found himself brushing his lips over hers, gently, softly, groaning at the sweetness of her mouth.

Everything he'd been thinking fled his mind. He drew her close and kissed her, again and again, until she made a sound deep in her throat. Her hands came up, touched his chest, slid up to his shoulders. She was weeping silently now, her tears leaving glittering streaks down her silken cheeks.

It was the tears that did it.

The ice around Sean's heart melted. Savannah was afraid

of him. How could this be an act? She was terrified, but she
didn't have anything to fear. He wouldn't hurt her. He'd be
gentle, stroke her with slow hands, kiss her until she clung
to him with desire.

"Savannah," he whispered. "Don't cry. I won't hurt you.
Let me show you. Let me."

He kissed her again, still with tenderness even though he
wanted more, wanted her with a ferocity that shocked him.
He held back with a strength he'd never known he possessed. When her mouth began to soften and cling to his,
he nipped lightly at her bottom lip until she sighed. Then,
slowly, he eased the tip of his tongue into her mouth. She
made that little sound, the one she'd made before, and tried
to twist her face away but he wouldn't let her. He held her,
kissed her, whispered to her until she began to melt in his
arms.

She wanted him.

The knowledge hit him like a thunderbolt. She wanted
him.

Sean murmured her name and bent her back over his arm.
He buried his lips in the sweet softness of her throat, cupped
the high curve of her breast and caught her lace-covered
nipple between his teeth.

Savannah moaned his name.

And then sanity returned.

What in hell was he doing? Of course this was an act.
The woman in his arms was giving an Oscar-winning performance and he was letting himself get sucker-punched all
over again.

He let go of her, shoved her away. She stumbled; her
eyes flew open, and for one impossible second he let himself
believe that what he saw in their depths was confusion. But
she could make him see whatever she wanted. She had, from
the minute he'd laid eyes on her.

Sean snarled an oath as he snatched up her dress and flung it at her. She caught it and clutched it to her breasts.

"Get out!"

"But—but I thought—"

"Yeah. I know what you thought." His mouth twisted. "You thought wrong, sugar. I don't take another man's leavings." He took a step toward her, dug a handful of bills from his pocket and flung them at her feet. "Here's cab fare. Go back to Beaumont and tell him you still owe me. Tell him I'll come around one of these days to teach him a lesson he should have learned the last time we met."

He strode into the bathroom and slammed the door. When he opened it again, the bills still lay scattered on the carpet.

Savannah was gone.

CHAPTER SIX

WHAT DID A MAN DO to work off his anger when he couldn't get the woman who was the cause of it out of his head?

Sean paced like a caged lion. He took a shower so long and cold he risked frostbite. He grabbed the prior day's newspaper and flipped the pages without reading a word.

And yet, all he could do was think about Savannah and how she'd scammed him. He was a gambler, for God's sake. He'd seen people pull a thousand cons. Making it seem you were doing one thing while you were really planning another was at the heart of the game he played best.

But he'd never come up against a woman like this before.

What an ass he'd been. He'd known a lot of beautiful women in his life—too many, probably. He'd always been able to see past the lovely faces, the toned bodies, and figure out what they really wanted.

Not tonight. Savannah had pushed his buttons and gotten what she wanted.

And what had he been thinking, that he hadn't collected on their wager? Forget her tears. They'd been as phony as everything else about her. A bet was a bet. If he'd taken her to bed, he wouldn't be so damned angry now. The whole nasty episode would be behind him. He'd be done with that soft mouth. The silken skin. Those rounded breasts and endless legs. Done with her.

He flung the newspaper aside.

The hell he would.

If he'd had her once, he'd have wanted her again. All through the night, through the first flush of dawn. Once wouldn't have been enough, not for him, not for her.

Yes, the weeping, the trembling, had been part of the act. But maybe that little sob of passion, the way she'd melted against him, had been real. Maybe she'd really felt something when he touched her. Maybe...

Sean cursed in disgust. What pure, unadulterated bull. The lady hadn't felt a thing, except when she was winning. When he was *letting* her win. That was another reason he was so furious, not just at her but at himself. She'd played him for the worst kind of jerk, he'd let it happen, and she'd done it for Beaumont, the lying, cheating son of a bitch!

Okay. It was too late to change what had happened, but not too late to get even. Alain Beaumont would pay. So would Savannah. What was that old saying about revenge being a dish best served cold? Sean smiled with grim amusement. The time would come. He'd find a way. Until then, all he had to do was be patient.

Too bad patience wasn't in his nature.

He pulled on a pair of trunks, went down to the dark beach and plunged into the surf. He swam out beyond the breakers, swam out farther than any intelligent man would, but then he had no claim on intelligence, not after tonight. Under the cool gaze of the setting moon, he floated on his back in the warm sea until, finally, he felt the tension drain away.

When he returned to his suite, he fell into a deep, exhausted sleep.

THE RING OF HIS CELL PHONE jolted him awake.

Sean sat up and peered at his watch. It was four-fifteen. Nobody phoned with good news at this hour. Dozens of possibilities ran through his mind but when he heard his older brother say, "Kid, it's me," he knew that the news was the worst it could be.

"Is it Ma?" he asked hoarsely. "Another heart attack?"

"No," Keir said, but Sean's relief was short-lived. "A stroke."

The bed seemed to tilt. Sean swung his feet to the floor. "Is she—is she—"

"She's still with us, but I won't mince words. The doctors don't know how things are going to go."

The heart attack had almost killed their mother. If Keir was saying this was worse…

No. Sean wasn't going there. If Mary Elizabeth was alive, there was still hope.

"Where is she? Vegas? Same place as last time?"

"She's in New York. Mount Sinai Hospital, cardiac care ICU. She and Dan were on vacation when it happened."

"I'm on my way. I'll see you in…" Sean checked the time again and did some quick calculations. "Four hours."

"Right. Cull's here, and the girls, and—"

"Keir?"

"Yeah, kid?"

"Tell her I'm coming, okay? And that I love her."

"She doesn't…" Keir cleared his throat. "Sure. Sure, I'll tell her."

"Will she—do the doctors think—" Sean's voice broke.

"Just hurry," Keir said, and hung up the phone.

Sean sat still for a long moment. Then he punched in the number of a company that leased private jets. Forty minutes later, he was on his way to the States.

HOSPITALS ALL SMELLED the same. Not that Sean had been in many, but you remembered from one time to the next. Antiseptic. Disinfectant. Lots of both, as if they could cover up the stench of pain, despair and death.

Mary Elizabeth O'Connell-Coyle lay motionless on a bed in the cardiac care ICU. Sean's heart lurched when he saw her. His mother was a beautiful woman. Not now. Her normally ruddy face was white, her eyes were shut and her once-firm mouth was slack. Tubes ran from under the white cotton blanket that covered her to a stand holding bottles that dripped fluids into them. A tangle of thin wires led to a panel of blinking lights on a monitor.

He couldn't stop watching those lights. They marked his mother's continuing struggle to hang on to life.

He sat beside her, clutching her hand, talking to her in a soft voice, telling her how much he loved her, how he needed her, how they all needed her. Then he waited, hoped, prayed for a response. Anything. It didn't have to be much. A squeeze of her fingers. A flicker of the eyelid. He'd have settled for that.

The only things that changed were the nurses who came and went. They checked the tubes, straightened the linen, did things that didn't really mean a damn when what he wanted was someone to come in and announce they'd found a cure for her ailing heart, a magic potion that would make her young and whole again.

"Sean?"

He blinked back his tears and looked up at his brother, Cullen, who put a comforting hand on his shoulder.

"I know you just got here," Cull said, "but—"

"But everyone else wants to be with her, too." Sean nodded and got to his feet. "Sure. I understand."

Of course he understood. They were allowed into the cubicle for fifteen minutes each. Multiply those scant quarter hours by a husband and six children. Add two sons-in-law and the same number of daughters-in-law, and you could see that there just wasn't enough time.

There'd never be enough time.

His throat constricted as he leaned down and kissed his mother's pallid cheek. He and Cullen exchanged quick embraces. Then he went into the ICU waiting room and hugged the rest of the O'Connell clan before settling into an imitation leather armchair that looked as worn and weary as the room's occupants.

All they could do now was wait.

IN LATE AFTERNOON, his sisters went to the cafeteria and brought back sandwiches that might or might not have been edible. Nobody knew because nobody could manage more than a bite. Keir bought out all the candy bars in the vending machine; Cullen fed dollar bills into the maw of a contraption that promised coffee but oozed sludge. They all gulped it down, mostly because it gave them something to do. Nobody needed the caffeine. Though they hovered on the brink of exhaustion, sleep remained as elusive as good news.

Their stepfather told them he'd rented a large suite in a nearby hotel. "Get some rest," Dan urged. "What good will any of us be to Mary if we're out on our feet when she awakens?"

When, not if. They clung to the subtle message, nodded in agreement, but nobody left. After a while, Dan went back into the ICU to be with his wife. Sean watched his sisters, Megan and Fallon, lean against their husbands. He saw Keir put his arm around his wife and smile wearily when she laid her hand against his cheek, saw Cullen press a kiss to his wife's forehead as she whispered to him.

Only Sean and his kid sister, Briana, were alone.

Bree must have read his thoughts. She rose from her chair, crossed the room and sat next to him.

"Only you and me left," she said, with a little smile. "Everyone else got hitched."

Sean managed a smile in return. "Who'd a thunk it?"

Bree gave a deep sigh. "Guess it must be nice to have somebody at a time like this, though, don't you think?"

A face flashed through Sean's mind. A woman with cascading hair the colors of gold and caramel, and eyes as green as the sea. The image shook him and he pushed it away.

"We do have somebody," he said gruffly. "We have each other."

His sister took his hand and squeezed it. "Sean? You think Ma will be all right?"

"She'll be fine," he said with more conviction than he felt, and he put his arm around Briana and hugged her tight.

HOURS PASSED. Daylight faded and it was night again.

The men gathered in the hall for a whispered consultation. When they stepped into the waiting room, they all had the same determined look.

Sean nodded toward his two brothers-in-law. "Stefano and Qasim are going to the hotel," he told his sisters. "They're taking you ladies with them."

There was a blur of protest. The men held fast.

"No arguments," Cullen said firmly.

The women rose reluctantly. Sean turned to Dan.

"Come on," he said to his stepfather, and used Dan's own earlier words. "Ma's going to need you when she regains consciousness. You'll have to be here, one hundred percent."

Again, it was when, not if. They were all taking strength from that. Dan gave a reluctant nod. "I'll do it, but only so I can give your mother my opinion of the hotel. She always likes to know what the competition's doing."

It was a forlorn attempt at humor but they grabbed it like a lifeline, especially since it was a reminder of Mary Elizabeth's vitality as head of the Desert Song Hotel in Las Vegas. Keir, Cullen and Sean promised to phone if there was the slightest change and yes, of course, they'd take a breather themselves in a few hours.

When the others had gone, the brothers sat in silence for a while. Then Sean cleared his throat.

"How did it happen?"

Cullen and Keir shook their heads. "It just did," Cull said. "Dan and Ma were in Central Park. He says they were walking along, talking…"

"About what? Was she upset over something?"

"No, she wasn't upset. She was talking about you and Bree."

"About Briana and me?"

"Yeah. The usual thing. You know, how she'd be happy if Bree would find a guy to love, and if you'd get married and settle down."

"What do you mean, 'the usual thing'?" Sean frowned. "Ma never said—"

"Well," Cullen said uncomfortably, "she wouldn't. Not to you, but to us, you know, she says she worries about you guys, that you're alone."

"No," Sean said tightly. "I don't know. And if you're trying to tell me that's why she had—that I'm the reason for—"

"Settle down, little brother," Keir said quickly. "Nobody's even suggesting that. You asked what she was talking about. We're telling you."

Sean glared at his brothers. Then his face crumpled. "Right. I know that's not why this happened. It's only that—that it's hard to—to—"

"Yeah," Cullen said, "it is."

"What about the doctors?"

"They're doing everything they can."

"Did you call in a consultant? I know this guy's supposed to be top-notch, but—"

"He *is* top-notch," Cullen said quietly.

"We flew in Ma's own doctor," Keir added. "He agreed on her treatment."

Sean sprang to his feet. "Treatment? What treatment? She's lying in that bed. I don't call that treatment, I call that—"

"They gave her a drug. It's supposed to dissolve the clot that's causing the problem."

Problem? Sean almost laughed. That was a hell of a way to describe something that might kill their mother.

"Sean." Keir stood up and put an arm around his younger brother. "We're all going nuts here, but we have to wait. It's all we can do."

Sean's shoulders sagged. "You're right. It's just—"

He sat down. So did Keir. The three O'Connells were silent for a long time. Then Cullen mouthed an oath.

"I hate this place," he growled.

"Take a walk," Keir told him. "Get some air. Go around the block."

"No. No, I want to be here if—when…" Cullen fell silent, struggling for self-control. "Hey," he said, his tone as artificial as the flowers on a corner table, "did I tell you guys that Marissa and I drove down from Boston and took Ma and Dan to dinner the other night?"

He was, Sean knew, trying to change the subject, which was probably a damned fine idea. Okay. He'd do his part.

"Smart woman, our mother," he said briskly. "Won't catch her risking ptomaine by having a meal at Big Brother's la-ti-da restaurant in Connecticut."

Keir forced out a laugh. "Hey, kid. Just because you wouldn't know haute cuisine from hamburger doesn't mean the rest of the family has no taste. Ma and Dan came up for supper with us and stayed the night as soon as they hit the city.''

''Only because Marissa and I didn't get into town until the next day,'' Cullen said.

''Yeah,'' Sean added, ''and what's with that crack about my taste buds?''

''It wasn't a crack,'' Keir said. ''It was the truth. There we were, growing up with room service ready to provide anything from beef Wellington to lobster thermidor, and what did you ask for, night after night? A cheeseburger and fries.''

''Oh, not *every* night,'' Cullen said. ''Our little brother used to cleanse his palate with an occasional hot dog.''

''They were chili dogs,'' Sean said, ''and did you really just say 'cleanse his palate'?''

''What can I tell you? I've got a wife who decided she loves to cook. She gets these magazines, you know? And sometimes I leaf through them.''

Sean looked at Keir. ''Cullen's learned to read,'' he said solemnly.

''Miracles happen,'' Keir replied.

Miracles. Would one happen in this hospital tonight? The same thought hit them all and ended their forced attempt at levity. Sean tried to think of something to talk about but came up empty. Keir was the one who made the next try at conversation.

''So,'' he said, ''where were you when I phoned?''

Sean looked up. ''Emeraude Island. In the Bahamas.''

''Nice?''

''Yeah.''

More silence. Cullen cleared his throat. ''Marissa and I've been thinking of getting away for a long weekend. What's Emeraude like?''

"You know. Pink sand beaches. Blue water. Lush mountains."

"And casinos."

"A couple."

"How'd you do?"

Sean stretched out his legs and crossed them at the ankles. "Okay."

"Okay, he says." Cullen raised his eyebrows. "What'd you win this time? A trillion bucks?"

"No."

"My God," Keir said, "don't tell me. You lost!"

"I didn't say that."

"Well, that's how you made it sound." He smiled. "How much did you win, then?"

Sean gave a shrug. "A few hundred thousand."

"And that wasn't enough to make you happy?"

No, Sean thought in mild surprise, it wasn't.

"Kid? What's the matter?"

A muscle knotted in Sean's jaw. "I won something else."

"Ah. No, don't tell us. Let me guess. A car? A yacht?" Keir grinned at Cullen. "A French chateau?"

"A woman," Sean said flatly.

His brothers' jaws dropped. "A what?"

"You heard me. I won a—"

"Mr. O'Connell?"

The O'Connells sprang to their feet. Sean could feel his heart trying to pound its way out of his chest until he saw the smile on the face of the nurse who'd come into the room. They all let out a breath in one big whoosh.

"Your mother's regained consciousness, gentlemen." Her smile broadened. "And because she won't have it any other way, the doctor's agreed to let her visit with all of you at once."

MARY ELIZABETH WAS BACK.

Maybe not completely. After a week, she was still paler than anyone liked, still looking fragile. Her speech was a little slurred and there were times she had to search for words.

But her smile was the same as it had always been. Her sense of humor was intact. So was her determination to take charge, even from a hospital bed.

She insisted Dan had to fly home and oversee things at the Desert Song. She told Cullen and Marissa it was more important they be at home with their baby than here with her, and tried to shoo Keir and Cassie away with the same message. She gave marching orders to Fallon and Stefano, then to Megan and Qasim.

Yes, they all said, yes, of course, absolutely, they'd leave.

Nobody did.

In the end, the only people she didn't try to boss around were Briana and Sean. It was, she said, lovely having her youngest daughter nearby. And when she and Sean were alone, she told him it was better to know he was here than to imagine him wasting his time at a card table.

Sean knew his mother had never really approved of the way he lived but she'd never come out and said so before. He was surprised by her candor and she knew it.

"It's what a little glimpse of your own mortality does to you," she told him as he sat with her in the hospital's roof-top conservatory one afternoon. "A mother should speak bluntly to her favorite son."

Sean smiled. "I'll bet you say the same thing to Keir and Cullen."

"Of course," Mary said, smiling back at him. "You're all my favorites." Her smile dimmed. "But I worry about you the most. After all, you're my baby."

Sean raised his mother's hand to his mouth and kissed her knuckles. "I'm thirty years old," he said gently.

"Exactly."

"I'm almost disgustingly healthy."

"Good."

"And I'm happy."

"That's what you think."

"It's what I know, Ma. Trust me. I'm happy."

Mary shook her head. "You're a gambler."

"I like gambling. I'm not addicted to it," he said, smiling at his mother, "if that's what you mean. I can stop whenever I want."

"But you don't."

"Because I enjoy it. You should understand that. Pa was a gambler."

Mary nodded. "He was, indeed," she said quietly. "It was the one thing about him that broke my heart."

Sean stared at her. "I thought—"

"Oh, I loved your father, Sean. Loved him deeply." She sighed. "But I wish he'd loved me more than the cards."

"Ma, for heaven's sake, he worshiped you!"

"He did, yes, in his own way, but if I'd been enough for him, he'd have settled down. Made a real home for us. You remember how bad it was, the years before we stumbled on to the Desert Song." Mary clasped her youngest son's hand and looked deep into his eyes. "A man should find his happiness in a woman, not in the turn of a card."

"We're not all the same, Ma. What's good for Cull and Keir isn't necessarily right for me."

His mother sighed. After a minute, she squeezed his hand. "My birthday's the week after next."

"Your…"

"My birthday, yes. And don't look at me as if I've slipped 'round the bend, Sean O'Connell. I can change the subject without being daft, though I'm not really changing the subject. I'm just thinking how quickly life slips by."

"Ma—"

"Let me talk, Sean. Why shouldn't we admit the truth? I almost died."

"Yes." A hand seemed to close around his heart. "But you didn't," he said fiercely. "That's what counts."

"Lying in that bed, drifting in that place halfway between this world and the next, I kept thinking, 'It's too soon.'"

"Much too soon," Sean said gruffly.

"I don't want to leave this earth until all my children are happy."

"I *am* happy, Ma. You don't need to worry about it."

"You're alone, Sean."

"Times have changed. A person doesn't need to be married to be happy."

"A person needs to love and be loved. That hasn't changed. You have your father's itchy foot and his gift for the cards, but that can't make up for the love of a good woman."

Unbidden, a face swam into Sean's mind. Green eyes. A mane of golden hair. A soft mouth tasting like berries warmed by the sun. It was the face of a woman a man would burn to possess, but love? Never. Thinking of Savannah McRae and the word "good" at the same time was absurd.

Besides, his mother was wrong. A man didn't need love. He needed freedom. His father had loved his wife and children but Sean suspected he'd have been happier without them. In his heart, he was the same. It was the one bond he and his old man had shared.

"I know you think you're right, Ma," he said gently, "but I like my life as it is." He smiled. "You want to be a matchmaker, why not take on Briana?"

"Bree will find somebody," Mary said with conviction. "She just needs a little more time. But you…"

"I'll give it some serious thought," Sean said, trying to sound sincere even if he was lying through his teeth, but it was a white lie, and white lies didn't count. "Maybe, someday, when I meet the right woman."

Mary sighed. "I just hope I live long enough to see it happen."

"You'll be here for years and years."

"Nobody can see the future," his mother said softly.

What could he say to that? Sean swallowed hard, searched for a change of subject and finally found one.

"That birthday—"

"Ah, yes. Dan and I want to have a big party."

"Not too much, though. You need peace and quiet."

"What I need is to get back into life."

Sean smiled. "You sound as if you're back into it already. And what would you like as a special gift?"

"Just all my children and grandchildren gathered around me."

"Nothing more?" Sean grinned. "Come on, Ma. Tell me your heart's desire and I'll get it for you."

Mary's eyes met his. "You will?"

"Yes. Absolutely. What do you want, hmm? Emeralds from Colombia? Pearls from the South Seas?" He bent forward and kissed her temple. "Name it, Mrs. Coyle, and it'll be yours."

His mother gave him a long look. "Do you mean it?"

"Have I ever made a promise to you and broken it?"

"No. No, you haven't."

"Well, then, tell me what you want for your birthday and you'll have it. Cross my heart and hope to die."

Sean said the words as solemnly as if he were seven years old instead of thirty, and he smiled. But his mother didn't smile. Instead, she looked so deep into his eyes that he felt the hair rise on the nape of his neck.

"I want to see you married, Sean O'Connell," she said. And from the expression on her face, he knew she meant every word.

CHAPTER SEVEN

AMAZING, what a combination of medical science and determination could accomplish. Ten days after Mary O'Connell-Coyle's stroke, her doctors pronounced her well and sent her home.

Keir, Cullen and Sean accompanied Dan and their mother to the airport. They sat with her in the first-class lounge and asked if she wanted anything so many times that Mary finally threw up her hands and said if they didn't stop fussing over her, she was going to go and find a seat in the terminal.

"One seat," she warned, "with no empties nearby." She looked at her husband, who smiled, and smiled back at him. "All right. Two seats, then, but not another within miles."

The brothers looked at each other sheepishly. Then they hugged her and kissed her, waited until the plane that would take her to Vegas had safely lifted off, and headed, by unspoken consent, for a taxi and a quiet, very untrendy bar Keir knew in lower Manhattan.

"My arms hurt," Sean said solemnly. His brothers raised inquisitive eyebrows. "From doing all that lifting to get the plane in the air."

He grinned. His brothers laughed, and Keir raised his glass of ale. "To Ma."

The men touched glasses. They drank, then leaned back in the time-worn leather booth.

"So," Keir said, "I guess we can all head home. Me to

Connecticut, Cull to Boston." He looked at Sean. "You going back to that island?"

Sean felt a muscle knot in his jaw. "Yes."

"Can't get enough of the sea and sand?"

"I have unfinished business there."

"Must be important."

Getting even was always important, Sean thought coldly. "Yeah. It is."

Cullen grinned and nudged Keir with his elbow. "Something to do with that woman, I bet."

"What woman?" Sean said, much too quickly.

"Come on, bro. The babe you won in a game of cards." Keir reached for the bowl of peanuts. "You never did explain that."

"There's nothing to explain."

"There's nothing to explain, he says." Cullen dug out a handful of nuts, too, and started munching. "A man wins a night with a hooker, and he says—"

"Did I say she was a hooker?"

Sean's voice was glacial. Cullen and Keir exchanged glances. He could hardly blame them. What was he doing? Defending Savannah's honor? It would be easier to defend a Judas goat.

"Well, no. But I figured—"

"Forget it."

"Look, I didn't mean to imply you'd sleep with a call girl, but who else would—"

"Leave it alone."

"All I meant was, what kind of woman would—"

"I said, leave it alone, Cull."

Keir and Cullen looked at each other again. Sean sat stiff and silent, trying to figure out why he'd almost made an ass of himself defending a woman who was not much better than Cull's description of her.

He was returning to Emeraude to deal with Alain Beaumont. It had nothing to do with Savannah. With the way she came to him in his dreams so that he'd lived that same moment a thousand times, her suddenly trembling in his arms, returning his kiss, sighing against his mouth...

"So," he said briskly, "Ma really does seem fine."

His brothers nodded, both of them grateful for the change in conversation.

"Absolutely." Cullen grinned. "Did you hear her chew out the nurse who insisted she had to leave the hospital in a wheelchair?"

The brothers chuckled, then took long pulls at their mugs of ale. Keir circled the wet rim of his glass with the tip of his index finger.

"That birthday party is gonna be some kind of event."

"Nice of the girls to offer to plan it," Sean said.

Cullen gave a dramatic shudder. "Whatever you do, don't let 'em catch you calling them 'girls.' Besides, 'nice' has nothing to do with it. They just don't trust Dan or us to get it right." He motioned to the waitress for another round. "Either of you have any idea what you're going to give Ma as a gift?"

"Cassie thought maybe a cruise to Hawaii."

"Marissa's thinking along the same lines. She suggested a week in Paris."

"Not bad. Hawaii this winter, Paris come summer... Sean? Want to toss in a spring vacation?"

Sean shifted uneasily in his seat. "I've got a problem with that."

"What? With giving her a trip?"

"With what to give Ma. She won't want a trip. Not from me."

"How do you know that?"

Sean took a few peanuts from the bowl and rolled them in his hand. "Idiot that I am, I asked her what she wanted."

"And?"

"And she told me."

Cullen and Keir looked at each other. "Well?" Cullen said. "You gonna keep us in suspense?"

"She wants…" Sean hesitated. Even now, it sounded impossible. "She said she wants me to get married."

There were a few seconds of silence. Then Keir laughed. "Trust Mary Elizabeth to get straight to the point."

"It's what she wants."

"Sure it is, but she'll settle for a trip to… What?"

Sean took a deep breath, then let it out. "I promised."

His brothers stared at him. "You what?"

"Don't look at me that way! How was I to know she'd ask for something so crazy?"

"Right. And Ma won't expect you to keep a crazy promise. She'll understand."

"Exactly. It's like when you're joking around and somebody says, you know what I'd really like? And you say tell me what it is and I'll do it, but both of you know it's just…" Cullen's words drifted to silence. "You really promised?"

"I really promised." Sean looked up. "I'd do anything for Ma. But this…"

"Do you even *know* a woman you'd want to marry?" Keir asked, and sighed with resignation when Sean laughed. "Well, you could always hire an actress."

"Yeah," Sean said glumly. "Too bad Greta Garbo's dead."

The brothers all chuckled. After a while, the topic turned to the latest baseball trade and everybody but Sean forgot all about it.

MA WON'T EXPECT you to keep a crazy promise. She'll understand.

Sean turned off the reading lamp above his seat in Trans Carib's first-class cabin. That was the trouble. His mother *would* understand. She'd look at him and sigh, and give that little smile that meant he'd failed her again.

He'd always failed her.

Cullen won every athletic award in high school. Keir won every academic honor. They'd both finished college, gone to grad school and made places for themselves in the world.

What had he ever done besides cause trouble?

He'd been suspended more times than he wanted to remember in high school, mostly because he hated sitting in a classroom. He'd loved hockey and he'd been good at it. Great, maybe, until the day a puck damned near took his eye out because he'd been a smart-ass who wouldn't wear a helmet with a visor. Yeah, he'd finished college but he'd floated through, all the time just yearning for graduation so he could bum around the world with a backpack.

Sean frowned at his reflection in the window.

That was then. This was now. He'd made a fortune. The backpack had turned into handmade leather luggage, he stayed in five-star hotels instead of hostels, and if he didn't have a permanent base, it was because he preferred it that way. He'd changed. He'd found success. He was the luckiest O'Connell brother. The one with nothing holding him down, nobody holding him back...

He was the brother who had nobody.

The universe seemed to hold its breath. A chasm, dark and deep, yawned at Sean's feet.

"Mr. O'Connell?" The flight attendant smiled. "Your dinner, sir."

"I'm not..." Sean hesitated, forced a smile. "Great. Thank you."

The girl set down his tray, poured his wine. Alone again, Sean ignored the filet mignon and reached for the burgundy. His mother's brush with death must have affected him more than he'd realized. Funny, how easily a man's perspective could get skewed.

He had everything. He was living a life he loved. Sean raised his glass and saw his reflection. Not everybody could say that, he thought, and suddenly, the face he saw in the glass wasn't his.

Savannah looked back at him.

Was scamming strangers a life she loved? Coming on to men to ensure a win? Did having Alain Beaumont put his hands on her make her happy?

What was with him tonight? What did he care what made Savannah McRae happy? How come he couldn't get it through his head that the tears she'd shed, the way she'd melted in his arms, had all been part of the act?

Sean tilted the glass to his lips and drank. He was going to stop thinking about Savannah. She didn't mean a thing to him. And he was going to take his brothers' advice and tell his mother the truth.

Ma, he'd say, *I never should have made you a promise I can't possibly keep.*

But before he did that, he'd confront Beaumont and his mistress. They owed him, and he was damned well going to collect.

IVORY MOONLIGHT dappled the dark waters of the Caribbean where the *Lorelei* lay at anchor. The night was warm and still. Savannah, alone in her stateroom, was counting the minutes until Alain left to go ashore.

Only then would she feel safe.

A tremor raced through her. Despite the heat, she felt

chilled. She reached for a sweatshirt and pulled it on over her thin cotton T-shirt.

Ten days had passed since the night she'd ruined everything. Ten days, but it felt like an eternity. Alain alternated between rage and deadly silence. Of the two, she'd begun to think his silence was the worst.

He was planning something. She knew it. He had been, ever since...

She had to stop thinking about that terrible night, but how could she? Alain was going to do something to punish her for what had happened. Wondering what and when was killing her.

It had taken her a very long time to get back to the harbor that night. She'd left the hotel by a back door, walked down the hill, then along the road. At dawn, an old man with a donkey cart gave her a lift. He hadn't asked her any questions. Maybe women with tear-stained faces, limping along in evening wear, were standard issue here.

The tender had been waiting at the dock; for one wild minute, she'd imagined turning around and running away. Then she'd thought of Missy, and she'd stepped into the boat and let the crewman take her to the *Lorelei*.

Alain was waiting in the yacht's salon, his face white, his mouth twisted into a narrow line. One look, and she knew he'd already heard the story.

Not all of it, of course. Not what had happened in O'Connell's bedroom, how the realization of what came next had suddenly become real.

All Alain knew was that she'd lost. It was enough.

"Alain," she'd said quickly, "I'm sorry. I did everything I could and it almost worked, but—"

He grabbed her so hard that she'd borne the marks of his fingers on her arms for days. Grabbed her and shaken her like a rag doll.

"You stupid *putain!*"

Even now, she shuddered, remembering the venom in his voice.

"How could you do this to me?" he'd roared.

"I told you," she whispered, "I don't know what happened. He was losing. And then—and then—"

Alain slapped her, hard enough to whip her head back. "Do you know what you cost me tonight?"

"Yes. Yes, I know. Almost five hundred thou—"

"Almost half a million dollars. How will you pay it back?"

"I'll win it at cards. I promise."

"How? By playing with my money? Does that sound reasonable to you?"

"It's—it's the best I can—"

"Shut up!" His spittle flew into her face as he leaned toward her. "Did you think I was joking? About wanting you to make O'Connell look like a fool?"

"No. No, of course not. But—"

"You didn't make a fool of him. He made a fool of you!"

"Alain, you must believe me. I was winning. I don't know what happened, only that suddenly—"

"When did you tell him you know me?"

"I never—"

"Don't lie to me! You told him. And that's who you made a fool of, you brainless creature. Me. Me! O'Connell's probably still laughing."

"No. He didn't laugh. Not at you!"

"I told you not to lie to me." Alain flung her from him. "And I told you the price you'd pay," he snarled and reached for the phone.

Missy. He was going to take Missy out of her safe haven in Switzerland. Savannah threw herself between him and the desk.

"I beg you, don't take this out on my sister."

"You failed me, Savannah. Apparently, your sister's welfare doesn't mean as much to you as I thought."

"Alain." Her voice trembled. She'd swallowed hard, fought for composure. "I'll win back the money. Every cent. I swear it."

His smile was the epitome of cruelty. "And will you win back your virginity? That's all you ever had, you know. Your skill at cards and your hymen." He thrust his face inches from hers. "And now they're both gone."

She started to tell him he was wrong, that she hadn't slept with Sean, but she caught herself just in time. That might make him only more furious, knowing she'd reneged on her wager. In the small world in which they lived, it meant she and anyone closely associated with her would be known as welshers.

Alain cursed, grabbed her arm, hustled her out of the salon and into her stateroom, slamming the door after her. Savannah had stood in the darkened cabin, shaking and shaken.

What he'd said, the way he'd said it... He'd made her virginity sound like a prize in a lottery. She wasn't surprised he knew she was innocent; when he'd first taken her from New Orleans, he'd demanded she undergo a complete physical examination.

"I'm entitled to know if there's any danger you carry disease," he'd said, and she'd burned with embarrassment even though the doctor had been brisk and professional.

But what did he mean, that all she'd ever had was her skill at cards and her virginity?

You know, a sly voice had seemed to whisper. It had to do with the way he'd taken to looking at her lately. The way he'd started talking about her with his friends. The way they'd turn their eyes on her, smile, all but lick their lips.

Savannah had shuddered. No. She wasn't going to think like that. Alain was just angry. He'd get over it.

But he hadn't. For ten days now, she'd been waiting for something to happen. Thus far, Alain had done nothing. He hadn't arranged any card games on his yacht, or sent her to play on shore. And he'd made a point of assuring her that Missy was still in her school.

The cabin door suddenly swung open, cutting short Savannah's musings. She swung around, saw Alain—and, for a moment, felt a weight lift from her shoulders. He didn't look angry. He didn't look threatening at all. He was dressed in a tux and, most surprising, he was smiling.

Then she realized it was the kind of smile that made the cabin seem suddenly airless. Savannah forced herself not to react. Whatever happened next, she wasn't going to give him the pleasure of hearing her beg.

"Good evening, *chérie*."

"Alain."

"You have half an hour to dress."

"Excuse me?"

"Is there a problem with your hearing, Savannah? I said you have half an hour to dress. Wear something long. Slinky. No, on second thought, put on something elegant." A smile lifted the corners of his lips. "It always amazes me that people think they know what's in a book by the look of the cover."

She almost sagged with relief. She'd read him wrong. Everything was okay. Alain was going to take her to the casino, or perhaps to one of the island's mansions. She didn't care where he took her. What counted was that he was going to let her play for him again and win back the money she'd lost.

"Thank you, Alain. You won't regret it. Where are we going? I'll win a lot of money, more than I lost, and—"

"We're not going ashore." He shot back his cuff and checked his watch. "I'm expecting guests in a little while. Forty minutes, to be exact, but, of course, I want to see how you look before they arrive."

"Alain," she called as he swung away from her. "Wait." He looked at her, eyebrows raised, and she forced a smile. "Who am I going to play?"

"Play?" He chuckled. "I can't see that it will matter to you."

"You know that it does. You can tell me the weaknesses of the other players."

"Ah." He nodded solemnly and tucked his hands into his trouser pockets. "I'm afraid you misunderstood, *chérie*. You see, I've a plan that will enable you to repay me the money you lost."

"Yes. I realize that. And I promise, I'll play well. It shouldn't take too long."

"To win back the money?" He smiled, rocked back on his heels. "No, it probably won't. Now that I've had time to think things over, I'm willing to admit you're still worth something to me."

She nodded. Her mouth was dry with relief. She'd be playing again. Winning again. With all this time on her hands, she'd thought of a couple of ways she might be able to skim a little money. It would be dangerous, and it would take a very long time, but if she were careful, if she were lucky, she might be able to put together enough to see her through a few months of Missy's care while she found a job to support them both.

Just thinking about the future made it easy to smile.

"Thank you, Alain. You won't regret this. I lost to Sean O'Connell, but I'm still one of the best card—"

"I told you, that's not at issue. In fact, I don't want you to win."

She stared at him. "You don't? But if I don't win, how can I pay back what I owe you?"

"Darling girl, I'd expect more creativity from a street hustler! Why would you think there's only one way to repay your debt? You have other talents besides playing cards, Savannah. Many of my friends have noticed. And *I've* noticed that many of *them* lead dull lives. I've come up with a way to combine their appreciation of you with their desire to lead more interesting existences, *chérie*. Isn't that clever of me?"

A chill speared through her blood.

"Well," she said, forcing a little smile, "your friends always seem to enjoy playing poker here. The *Lorelei* is—"

"Most of them own yachts of their own," he said with a dismissive gesture. "Charming as *Lorelei* may be, she's nothing new to them."

"I don't—I don't—"

The sound of the tender's engine interrupted her words. Alain tut-tutted and checked his watch again.

"Our first guests. They're early but it's understandable. Who wouldn't be eager to play our new game?"

Savannah felt her legs giving out. She couldn't show weakness. Not now.

"I don't understand what you're suggesting, Alain."

"It's quite simple, *chérie*. I've devised an entertainment, something a bit unusual. It will be far more profitable than if you were simply to play against them and win."

Slowly, he reached out and ran his hand down her cheek. Savannah flinched. That won her an oily grin.

"Come on, darling, don't play dumb. The streets of New Orleans schooled you well, *non?* I'll provide the players. You'll provide the incentive. Why do you still look puzzled, Savannah? It's a simple plan. We're going to hold a poker elimination tournament. Several, to be precise, until the novelty fades. A timed game each weekday night, with the biggest winners to play against each other on Saturdays.'' He flashed another smile, bigger than the last. ''The stakes will be very, very high, *chérie*. High enough to be worthy of you.''

''Worthy of me?'' Savannah said in a small voice.

''Certainly.'' Alain grinned. ''Don't you see? The final winner wins you!''

Savannah felt the blood drain from her head. ''Are you crazy?''

''I admit, your value might be a bit greater if you were still, as we say, intact, but look at the amount O'Connell was willing to wager without even realizing you were a virgin.'' He chuckled. ''I suppose I should thank him, should I ever have the misfortune to see him again. After all, this is his idea, when you come down to it, and it's brilliant.''

She stared at him, struggling for words that wouldn't come. Her heart, her breath, seemed to have stopped.

''Alain,'' she said, trying to sound calm, ''this isn't funny.''

''It isn't meant to be.'' Alain tucked his hands in the pockets of his trousers and rocked back on his heels. ''Life can get so dull, *chérie*. I should think you'd applaud my efforts to brighten it.''

''I'm not a whore!''

His false smile vanished. ''You'll be whatever I tell you to be.''

''No. No!''

''After all I've done for you and that pathetic sister of yours, I finally asked one thing in return. 'Humiliate Sean O'Connell,' I said. And you didn't do it.''

''I tried. I'm sorry it went wrong, but—''

''There are no 'buts,' Savannah. Failure is failure. All

things considered, I think I'm going out of my way to be generous. After I deduct the money you owe me and expenses, there'll be a tidy sum left. It will be yours."

Bile rose in her throat. "I won't do it!"

Alain's false good humor vanished. He caught hold of Savannah's wrist. "Yes, you will."

"You're insane!"

"The lady's right, Beaumont," a deep, lazy voice said. "You always were a crazy son of a bitch."

Alain let go of Savannah and spun toward the door. Savannah caught her breath.

"Sean?" she whispered. "Oh God, Sean!"

Sean dragged his eyes from Beaumont long enough to look at Savannah. Her face was white; her eyes were enormous, but when she saw him they began to shine. Her mouth trembled, then lifted in a smile.

She made him feel as if he were mounted on that prancing white horse.

For one heart-stopping minute, he wanted to go to her, sweep her into his arms and tell her he'd protect her. Then he remembered what he'd overheard. It looked as if he'd walked in on a lovers' quarrel about money.

His gut knotted. He'd been a fool to let Savannah haunt his dreams and not to have taken her when he could. She wasn't even a call girl, as Cullen had implied. That was too high-class a term.

"O'Connell?" Alain's voice was strained. "How did you get on this boat?"

Sean turned his attention to Beaumont. "Why, you were kind enough to send your tender for me," he said softly. "I thought that was a mighty decent gesture."

"You lied your way onto this vessel!" Beaumont grabbed the intercom. "I'll have you thrown overboard. I'll have you—"

The words became a cry of pain as Sean caught his hand and bent it back. The intercom slid from Beaumont's grasp and he sank slowly to his knees.

"You're hurting me," he gasped.

"I want my money."

"What money? I don't know what—"

"Your lady friend played against me ten days ago. She lost."

"You just said, *she* played you. What has that to do with me?"

"Give me a break, Beaumont. She played for you."

Beads of sweat popped on Beaumont's forehead. "So what? She paid her debt."

"She didn't."

"What do you mean, she didn't? You won her for the night."

"Yeah, and I didn't collect."

Beaumont shot a look at Savannah. "What does he mean?"

"Nothing. Of course he collected, Alain. It's just—it's just that he wants more. Isn't that right, Mr. O'Connell?"

She turned away from Beaumont and stared at Sean. Her eyes, even her body language, implored him to go along with her lie. But why would he? He owed this woman nothing.

"Please," she mouthed silently.

"Yeah," Sean growled, mentally cursing himself for being a fool, "that's right. So I'm going to let you make up for it, Beaumont. I want a million bucks."

Beaumont turned whiter than he already was. "Why would I give you a million dollars?"

"Lots of reasons, starting with the fact that you wouldn't want me to spread the word that you're not only a liar, you're a man who sends a woman to seek a revenge he's too cowardly to attempt himself.'' Sean's smile had a savage edge. ''Then there's the little matter of the lies you've spread about me. I've heard the rumors. You said I cheated you last summer when the truth is that you couldn't admit you'd lost.''

''Alain?'' Savannah whispered. ''Is that true?''

''Your lover boy wouldn't know the truth if it bit him in the butt.'' Sean tightened his grip on Beaumont. ''A million bucks, and I'm out of here.''

''Even if I wanted to give you that much, I couldn't. Ahh! You're breaking my wrist, O'Connell. Let go!''

''Let him go. Please.''

Sean flashed a look at Savannah. She looked desperate. Was there a heart somewhere inside her, and if so, did she really feel something for this pig?

The possibility made Sean's jaw clench. What in hell did it matter to him? Savannah McRae could have the hots for King Kong for all he gave a damn. Still, he was tired of listening to Beaumont whimper. Abruptly, he let go of the man's pudgy hand.

''Get up.''

Beaumont dragged himself to his feet as if he were dying and cupped his hand against his chest.

''You're almost as good an actor as your lady friend.''

''I think you broke a bone.''

''No such luck. Come on, Beaumont. I know your safe is in the salon. Take me to it, get me what you owe me and I'm gone.''

''I don't have that much money here. If you wait until Monday…''

Sean laughed. Beaumont swallowed hard.

''My marker is good everywhere.''

''Maybe, but not with me. I want cash.''

Braver now that Sean had let him get to his feet, Beaumont's mouth thinned. "I could charge you with theft."

"No, you couldn't." Sean jerked his chin at Savannah. "I have a witness who'll say otherwise."

"She'll say what I tell her to say. Won't you, *chérie?*" Savannah didn't answer. Beaumont narrowed his eyes. "Won't you?" he said in a menacing whisper.

He raised his hand. Sean moved quickly, grabbed him and threw him against the wall.

"Don't touch her," he growled.

"She's mine. I created her and I'll do whatever I like to her."

A soft cry burst from Savannah's throat. Sean watched as she buried her face in her hands. Her hair, loose as it had been that night, tumbled around her face…but it wasn't as it had been that night. Not really. Then, it had been combed into artful disorder. Now, it hung in curls that were wild and real.

Everything about her was different from the last time. She wore no makeup, no jewels. No do-me heels and sexy dress. Instead, she had on a baggy sweatshirt, faded, loose jeans and sneakers.

She looked vulnerable. Beautiful. Sweet and innocent, the kind of woman a man would give his soul to possess.

The kind a man could take home to his mother.

Sean blinked. Beaumont chuckled. "Ahhh," he breathed.

Sean's eyes flashed to his face. Beaumont had gone from looking as if the world were about to end to smiling, if you wanted to call the smirk on his fleshy lips a smile.

"Ah, what? Did you just remember that you have enough money in your safe?"

"No, Mr. O'Connell. I just thought of what I can offer you to satisfy your demand."

"I'm not in the market for a yacht, Beaumont."

"How about a woman? Are you in the market for that?"

"No!" Savannah shook her head wildly. "Alain. You can't. I won't. I swear, if you try to do this, I'll—"

"This woman owes me five hundred thousand dollars. And you just said you came here because you want more of her. Well, you can have her," Beaumont said, jerking his chin at Savannah. "For... Let's see. A week?"

"Alain. Please, Alain..."

"Not enough? How about two weeks?" A smile crawled across his mouth. "Surely you can think of something to do with a woman like Savannah for fourteen days and nights."

Sean saw a blur of motion out of the corner of his eye, and then Savannah was on Beaumont, clawing at him while he staggered and tried to protect his face.

"I'll kill you," she panted. "I swear, I'll—"

Sean grabbed her, pulled her back against him and pinned her in place with an arm wrapped tightly around her waist. His hand lay just under her breast; he could feel her heart beating against his palm.

Once, decades before, he'd felt a heart beating that same way.

He'd been eight, maybe nine; he'd been in big trouble at home for playing hooky and had gone to a hidey-hole he knew in a lot behind the Desert Song. That day, his hiding place already had an occupant. A tiny songbird lay on its back, beak open as it panted for breath.

He knew something terrible had happened to the bird and he wanted to help it, but he couldn't. All he could do was cradle it in his hand and feel the terrified gallop of its heart.

"Well, O'Connell? Yes or no?"

To hell with that long-ago wounded bird. He had an opportunity here that could solve his problem.

"The woman," Sean said. "For two weeks."

"No," Savannah moaned, but Beaumont nodded his head and the deal was done.

CHAPTER EIGHT

SAVANNAH DIDN'T GO QUIETLY.

She shrieked, raged, yelled that she wasn't property, but Sean encircled her wrist with a hand that felt like a manacle and propelled her up the ladder to the deck.

"Move," he said through clenched teeth, "or I'll toss you over my shoulder and carry you off this damned boat."

Had she really felt her heart lift with hope when she first saw O'Connell in the doorway? She was a fool to have expected anything good from a man with his morals. So what if he'd won her that night and not taken her to bed? That wasn't enough to mark him as her savior. Whatever the reason he hadn't demanded full payment, he was going to demand it now.

He could demand what he liked, but she'd be damned if he'd get it without a fight.

Savannah slammed her elbow into his belly. He grunted at the force of the blow.

"You stupid son of a bitch," she panted. "Do you really think you can get away with this? Let go or I'll report you to the police."

"You'd have to get past your boyfriend first." Sean dragged her to where a ladder led down to the tender. "Somehow, I don't think he'd let that happen. Besides, what would you tell the cops?" She balked when they reached the ladder and he pushed her forward. "I can get fifty witnesses to tell them how you handed yourself over to me a couple of weeks ago at the casino.''

"That has nothing to do with what you're doing now."

"Sure it does. We're just picking up where we left off. Get down that ladder."

"I won't!"

Savannah jammed her feet against the teak deck coaming. Sean cursed and slung her over his shoulder, just as he'd threatened. She roared with frustration and pounded her fists against his back. The ladder swayed precariously under his feet.

"You want to go for a swim, babe? Keep that up and, so help me, I'll dump you in the drink."

She believed him. He was a man of zero principles. Maybe Alain had lied about him cheating in that card game. Maybe he hadn't. A man who'd accept a woman in payment and carry her off was capable of anything.

"Alain lied," she said desperately, as he dropped her into a seat in the tender. "He keeps a lot of money in his safe."

Sean folded his arms and spread his feet apart.

"And you'd know all about his money."

"A million, at least," she said, refusing to be drawn away from the topic. "You could tell him you changed your mind. That you want money, not—not—"

Sean smiled coldly. "But I haven't changed my mind. I have exactly what I came for."

Her face flooded with color. "Is that the kind of man you are, O'Connell? Do you buy your women?"

"You're the one who put yourself up for sale, sugar."

"That's not true! You were the one who suggested I make that wager that night."

"And you leaped at it like a dog at a bone. Besides, what would Beaumont say if I told him I was bringing you back because you were uncooperative? According to you, I came back for more of what I already got." He smiled thinly. "I don't think he'd be very happy but hey, what do I know? Maybe I don't understand the complexity of the relationship."

The threat seemed to work. He could almost see the fight going out of her. Her head drooped forward; her hair tumbled around her face. Seeing her like this, her posture one of defeat, put a hollow feeling in Sean's belly. She was a liar. A cheat. A better con artist than any he'd ever met, and that was saying a lot.

But he could make things easier. All he had to do was tell her the truth, that Beaumont had triggered an idea and it had nothing to do with sex.

"What's wrong, sugar? It's just another slice off the loaf."

Savannah's head came up. She opened her mouth, on the verge of telling him she had never slept with Alain or anyone else, but why bother? He wouldn't believe her. More to the point, why defend herself to a man like this?

He was right. She really didn't have any choice. She'd cost Alain a fortune. Worse, she'd cost him his pride. He was demanding payback and he held her sister's well-being in the palm of his hand. If she refused to do his bidding, Missy would pay for it.

"You're right," she said wearily. "What does it matter which of you I'm with? You're both snakes in the same pit."

Her words jolted Sean. It wasn't true. Beaumont had used this woman in a scheme of revenge, but he...he—

Her head was down again, her face made invisible by her hair. When she raised a hand and brushed at her eyes, he knew she was crying.

Hell. The truth was, he was going to use her, too, and he suspected that even an ethicist would have a tough time making it sound as if his using her to live a lie was better than Beaumont using her in a petty game of get-even.

But he wasn't Beaumont, damn it. Not that it mattered what she thought of him, but he wanted her to know that.

"Maybe it's true," he said gruffly. "Maybe there isn't a lot of difference between him and me—except for one thing."

Savannah looked up. He'd judged correctly. Tears glittered on her lashes and he fought the desire to take her in his arms and brush them away, until he recalled how she'd pulled that same stunt the last time.

"I don't believe in owning people, Savannah."

She gave a watery laugh. Sean stood straighter.

"You behave yourself, do as you're told, give the kind of performance I expect, and I'll pay you."

Her face turned white at the word "performance." He was about to explain what he'd meant but before he could, she drew a deep breath and expelled it. When she looked at him again, her eyes were flat.

"How much?"

Her voice was low. So low that he had to lean forward to make sure he'd heard the question. It staggered him. Was it that simple? Mention money, and she turned docile as a lamb?

It shouldn't have come as a surprise. He knew exactly what she was. The tears, tonight's sweetly girlish looks didn't mean a thing. They were window dressing laid over the skeleton of what Savannah McRae really was.

"How much?" she said again, her voice a little stronger.

Sean clenched his jaw. "Don't you want to know what you're going to be required to do first?"

Color swept into her cheeks. "I'm not stupid, O'Connell. You don't have to spell it out."

He thought of telling her she was wrong, but he'd be

damned if he was going to tell her anything more than he had to. What she did didn't matter to her. Only money was important.

Besides, she'd never believe him. What would he say? *I want you to pretend to be my fiancée?* He was having a bad enough time believing it himself. What had ever possessed him to come up with such an impossible scheme? Why hadn't he taken the time to think it over?

Then again, why would he? Life on the edge had always been his thing.

He swung away, snapped "Shove off" to the crewman. The engine started and the tender leaped forward. The roar of the motor and the slap of the sea against the hull provided enough of a sound block so the guy driving the boat wouldn't hear what he said next.

"What's the most you've ever won in a poker game?"

She gave him a chilly smile. "Women and cards. Yours is a simple world, O'Connell."

"Sleeping with Beaumont and scamming strangers," Sean said coldly. "Anybody can see that your world is far more intricate than mine."

Her eyes filled with heat. She wanted to fly at him as she had earlier; he saw it in her face. Hell, he wanted her to. Wanted to hold her against him, subdue her, kiss her until she moaned...

"Answer the question," he snapped, his anger at himself almost as great as his anger at her.

"Four hundred thousand," she said, lifting her chin in defiance. "That was my record. I'd have topped it by a hundred thou if I'd won the night I played you."

"But you didn't."

"I came close."

"Only because I let you."

"Am I supposed to apologize for that? Poker's as much a game of tactics as it is chance."

The lady gave as good as she got. That was probably her only redeeming quality.

"What you mean is, it helps to be a good actor." The wind ruffled Sean's hair. He pushed it back from his forehead. "It's why I wanted you."

Color filled her face again. Sean almost laughed.

"Forget that. I don't want you for anything kinky."

Nothing kinky, but he wanted her to act when he made love to her? She hated him. Despised him almost as much as she despised Alain.

"Five hundred thousand, Savannah. Exactly the amount I won from you." Sean smiled with his teeth. "That's what I'll pay you, if I'm satisfied with the job you do."

Her mouth fell open. For a second, she looked as if she were going to leap up and dance him in wild circles. His gut knotted with distaste. Half a million bucks could go a long way toward making a woman like this happy.

Then she seemed to get herself under control. "Those terms are acceptable."

She spoke without emotion. For the second time in minutes, he wanted to take her in his arms, not to comfort her but to shake her.

I just bought you, he wanted to snarl. *I can use you anyway I want. Doesn't that bother you?*

Evidently not.

"Done," he said, and held out his hand as the tender bumped against the dock.

O'CONNELL HERDED HER into his car. Then he took out his cell phone. She didn't pay much attention to his conversation, which seemed to consist mostly of commands.

He had a command for her, too. "Buckle up."

She'd already done that. The memory of his hand slipping across her breasts was still vivid. He'd touch her soon enough, but she wasn't going to offer up an opportunity.

Savannah shuddered. Think about something else, she told herself. Fortunately, O'Connell made it easy to do.

The man drove like a maniac.

He was in a hurry to get to his hotel. Things had not gone as he'd hoped the last time he'd brought her to his bedroom. This time would be different.

She'd given her promise.

It was too late for regrets. Agreeing to O'Connell's offer had been her only choice. Now, all she could do was hope. That he wouldn't hurt her. That he wouldn't force things on her.

She knew some of what could happen when a rich, powerful man thought he owned a woman. The men who played cards on the yacht sometimes brought women with then. She'd overhead things.

Savannah shuddered again. Two weeks, that was all. Surely, she could endure whatever he did to her for that long. He was handsome. Not that it mattered but at least she wouldn't have to gag whenever he came near her.

She knew that there were woman who'd envy her.

A woman wouldn't have to act if this man took her to bed. She'd go willingly. Eagerly. She'd sigh when he put his hands on her, moan when he teased her lips apart with his.

She shut her eyes and thought back to that first time he'd taken her to his hotel. He could have done anything he wanted. And he'd wanted, all right. There'd been no mistaking the hardness of his arousal when he'd gathered her into his arms, but she'd wept and he'd sent her away. Yes, he'd been furious and, yes, he'd humiliated her by tossing money at her feet, but he hadn't done what he'd been entitled to do.

He'd done enough, though. Touched her. Kissed her. Sometimes, in the deepest part of the night, she thought she could still feel his hands on her, his mouth…

Savannah sat up straight.

What did any of that matter? She'd made a deal with Sean O'Connell and if she kept her part of it and he kept his, she'd have the money it would take to fly to Switzerland and take Missy to a new place where she'd get the same excellent treatment. She'd cover their trail carefully so Alain could never find them.

She had to keep all that in mind. It would make what came next bearable.

The car purred as Sean downshifted. Savannah blinked and focused on the blur of palms, white sand and blue water outside the window. Had they sped past the turnoff to his hotel? Yes. Yes, they had. A town called *Bijou* lay ahead of them. It was reputed to live up to its name by being a jewel box of designer and couturier boutiques, all in keeping with Emeraude's profile as an unspoiled playground for the incredibly rich.

Why was O'Connell taking her there?

"We're going to do some shopping," he said, as if she'd spoken the question aloud.

Shopping? In *Bijou?*

"If you'd given me time to pack, you wouldn't have to buy me a toothbrush."

She tried to sound flippant. It didn't work. Her voice was scratchy and it shook. Damn it, she wasn't going to let him see her sweat. What kind of shopping did he have in mind? Leather? Teenybopper minis? A froth of lace that would turn her into an obscene version of an upstairs maid? Maybe the shops here carried such things. From what she'd observed of Alain's friends, the very rich could also be very decadent.

O'Connell slowed the car as they entered the town. Under other circumstances, she'd have been enthralled. Cobblestone streets radiated from a central fountain surrounded by lush beds of bougainvillea. Mercedes, Ferraris, Maseratis and Lamborghinis were neatly parked along the curbs.

How did they get all those cars to this dot in the ocean? Savannah thought, and almost laughed aloud at the absurdity of the question. The rich and powerful could arrange for anything. Wasn't her presence at O'Connell's side proof of that?

He pulled into a parking space, got out of the car, came around to her side. "Out," he said, pulling open the door.

She got out. It was late—almost nine—and the shops were shuttered. So much for O'Connell's shopping trip, she thought, but he took her arm and tugged her toward the nearest door.

No leather in the windows. No cheesy minis or endless yards of lace, either. There was nothing in the windows except discreet gold script that spelled out a name so well-known it seemed to ooze money.

"They're closed," she said, and came to a halt.

"They're open. I phoned when we left the harbor."

So that was what the commands had been all about. O'Connell could get a place like this to stay open for him?

"How'd you pull that off?" she said pleasantly. "Is the manager into you for a gambling debt?"

"You've got a smart mouth, McRae." Sean's hand tightened on her elbow. "Let's go."

"I don't know what you're thinking," Savannah said quickly, "but I promise you, I am not spending a penny of what you're going to pay me on anything this place sells."

He turned toward her. She saw a muscle knot in his jaw.

"Is that your deal with Beaumont? Does he give you money, then make you pay for your clothing out of it?"

Alain bought her clothes. Not jeans or shorts or the cotton tops she lived in. She ordered those online, paid for them with the small amount of money he permitted her to keep from her gambling winnings. He bought her gowns and the accessories to go with them. His taste had never been hers but lately, it made her stomach turn. He'd begun buying her things that made her feel cheap.

"You're a beautiful woman, *chérie*," he said when she protested a dress cut too low, a gown with too high a slit. "Why hide it from the world?"

But there wasn't a reason in hell to tell any of that to this man.

"My arrangements with Alain have nothing to do with you," she said coolly. "I'm talking about our deal, O'Connell."

"Relax, sugar. I have no intention of making you pay. In our little drama, wardrobe's the director's responsibility."

"Just what is our little drama? I think I'm entitled to know."

He bent his head to hers. "You're my fiancée."

"Excuse me?"

"You heard me," he said with impatience. "For the next two weeks, you're my fiancée. We're here to buy you whatever you'll need to return to the States with me and meet my family."

Savannah stared at him. So much for leather and upstairs maids. "*That's* your fantasy?"

His laugh was quick and harsh. "Believe me," he said, "it's damned near as much a surprise to me as it is to you."

He put his hand into the small of her back and opened the door. A bell tinkled discreetly somewhere in the distance as they stepped into a hushed world of ivory silk, mirrored walls and low couches. The elusive scent of expensive perfume drifted on the air.

A salesclerk, dressed in the same ivory silk that paneled the walls and covered the couches, glided toward them.

"Wait," Savannah said frantically. "What assurance do I have that you'll keep your end of our bargain?"

The cold look O'Connell gave her almost stopped her heart. He held up his hand. The clerk smiled and stayed where she was.

"The same assurance I have that you'll keep yours," he said in a low voice. "My word."

She thought about telling him his word didn't mean much, but that would have been a lie. A gambler's word was everything.

"You don't want to accept it, we can call the whole thing off. I'll take you back to the *Lorelei*. You can explain your return to Beaumont."

Savannah shook her head. "Your word is good enough."

"And yours?"

Their eyes met. He'd slipped his arm around her waist; he was holding her against him, a little smile playing on his mouth. She knew it was in preparation for the charade they were about to perform for the clerk but for a moment, oh, just for a moment, she imagined what it would be like if he were taking her to this place because she mattered to him, because he wanted to see her in silks and cashmeres, wanted to enjoy the sight of her in them in public, the excitement of stripping them from her when they were alone.

A tremor went through her, and she blanked the ridiculous images from her mind.

"My word's as good as yours, O'Connell."

"Sean."

"Does it matter?"

"Yes. My fiancée would call me by my first name."

"You want to explain what this is all about?"

His lips twisted. "In due time." His gaze dropped to her mouth. "But first—first, I think we need to formalize our arrangement."

"Formalize it?"

"Uh-huh." He looked into her eyes. What she saw in his—the heat, the hunger—made her breath catch. "Something in lieu of signing a contract in front of a notary public."

Slowly, he lowered his mouth to hers. From the corner of her eye, she saw the clerk turn discreetly away. There was no question what he was going to do. And there was time, plenty of time, to draw back or at least to turn her head to the side. Savannah did neither. She would let him kiss her. Wasn't the kiss part of what she'd agreed to?

She'd let it happen solely for that.

Still, when his mouth touched hers, she felt her knees buckle. He drew her closer, kissed her again. The blood roared in her ears and she moaned softly against his lips. Her heart began to pound. She knew that his was, too. She could feel it galloping against hers.

Sean drew back, his hands cupping her shoulders, holding her away from him. Savannah opened her eyes. His expression was shuttered and cold.

"My fiancée is ready now," he said.

The words were directed to the clerk, but they might as well have been for her. His message was clear. He could turn her on anytime he wanted. He knew it. Now, she knew it, too.

The realization made her feel cheaper than she already did.

Really, she hadn't thought that was possible.

CHAPTER NINE

THEY WERE STILL CHOOSING clothes and accessories as midnight approached.

At least, Sean was. Savannah was simply a mannequin standing before him on a little platform in front of a wall of mirrors.

At first, he didn't even bother asking her opinion. The clerk would bring out an armful of clothing and display it.

Yes, he'd say, *no, yes, maybe.*

Then the clerk would take Savannah to the fitting room where she'd put on the dress or suit or whatever Sean had chosen, slip into matching shoes the clerk seemed to whisk out of the air, and go out to the platform to await a nod of approval.

After a while, Sean began asking what she thought.

"Do you like this?" he'd say, and she'd look into the glass, at the stranger looking back, a woman with her eyes, her face, her body.

Where was the girl who'd worn clothes salvaged from thrift shop donation bins? The supposed sophisticate whose clothes were chosen by Alain? What had become of the con artist dressed in red silk?

Sean was turning her into someone she'd never been. Or maybe someone she'd always wanted to be.

Yes, she wanted to say, *oh, yes, I like it. I like it a lot.*

But she didn't because this wasn't real and he didn't actually care if she liked something or not. He was just getting tired or maybe bored. Maybe both. So she shrugged her shoulders and said yes, sure, the outfit was okay.

"We'll take it," Sean would say.

By then, the clerk had lost her laid-back façade. She looked like someone who'd won the lottery. Even her French accent started slipping, and when Sean approved a long column of white silk that had to cost the earth, moon and stars, the accent disappeared altogether in a rush of pure New York.

"Doesn't the lady look *gawjiss?*" the clerk babbled. A rush of bright pink flooded her face. "I mean—I mean, *madame* is so chic!"

Savannah laughed. It was an unlikely thing to do, considering the circumstances and her state of mind, and she buried the burst of laughter in a cough. She fooled the clerk but one look in the mirror and she knew she hadn't fooled Sean. He was grinning like the Cheshire cat. Without thinking, she grinned back.

What a great smile he had. Lazy. Open. And yes, sexy enough to make her breath catch. Had he done this before? Taken a woman on a shopping spree? Bought her things that made her feel beautiful. Looked at her as if—as if—

Savannah tore her gaze from his. What did it matter? Sean was a smart, hard-as-nails gambler. His charm, when he chose to use it, was as much a lie as the easy smile.

How could she have come so close to forgetting that?

This wasn't a shopping spree, it was a step in some complex game he'd devised. He was remaking her. Did he have a thing about only bedding women whose appearance was genteel? Maybe that was why he'd sent her packing the night he'd won her. Maybe the red dress, the heels, had backfired, turning him off as much as they'd turned him on.

A wave of exhaustion shot through her, so intense and unexpected it rocked her back on her heels. She swayed and would have fallen if Sean hadn't already been at her side, enfolding her in his arms.

"Savannah?"

He turned her to him, said her name again. She wanted to tell him to let her go but she didn't. Just for this moment, she let herself lean against him and take strength from the feel of his body.

"What's wrong?"

She licked her dry lips. "Nothing."

"Try another answer." He cupped her chin in one hand and raised her face to his. "Are you ill?"

She shook her head. "I told you, I'm okay."

"Savannah." He bent his knees and peered into her face. "Hell," he said roughly, "you're white as a sheet."

His eyes were the palest blue she'd ever seen, and they weren't cold with anger or mockery as they had been that first time in his hotel room. He had a small scar on the bridge of his nose, another that feathered out delicately from his eyebrow, and she wondered how he'd gotten them, if they'd hurt, if anyone had soothed them with a touch.

"Savannah? What's the matter?"

She shook her head. His voice was soft. For some reason, the sound of it made her throat tighten. He was right, something *was* the matter, but how could she give him an answer when she didn't know it herself?

"I'm just—I'm tired," she said, "that's all."

His eyes narrowed. She expected them to flash with those familiar angry sparks but before she could read anything in their depths, he swept her up into his arms.

"Pack up everything and send it to me at the hotel Petite Fleur first thing in the morning," he told the astonished clerk.

"Everything, *monsieur?*"

"You heard me. Toss in whatever else my—my fiancée might need. Lingerie, purses, shoes... You figure it out."

Sean let the woman dance ahead of him to open the door. He stepped out into the dark night, *bon soirs* and *mercis* flying after him like a flock of nightingales.

"Really, O'Connell," Savannah said. "I can walk."

Her breath was warm against his throat. Her hair tickled his cheek. Holding her like this, he became aware of her scent, something that reminded him of summer flowers and misting rain.

"O'Connell..."

"I'll put you down as soon as we get to the... Here we are." He let her down gently, held her close against him while he opened the door to his car. Her hair brushed lightly against his face again as he eased her inside. He shut his eyes and concentrated on the silky glide of it against his skin. She turned her face; for an instant, their lips were a sigh apart and then she jerked back and he straightened so quickly he slammed his head on the roof. "Damn," he said, hissing with pain.

Savannah made a little move, as if she were going to touch him. Obviously, he was mistaken because when she spoke, her voice was cool.

"Sorry," she said, without sounding sorry at all. "You should have let me walk."

He'd tried to do something decent and what did he get for it? A contemptuous retort and a rap on the skull. So much for being a nice guy. Still, part of him knew he was overreacting. Not that it stopped him.

"You're right," he said as he went around the car and slipped behind the wheel, "but for a couple of minutes there, you looked as if you were going to collapse." He checked for traffic, found none, and shot away from the curb. "I can't afford to let my investment get damaged."

"No. Certainly not." There was a beat of silence. "Do you think you could let me know what's going on anytime soon?"

"When I'm good and ready."

"No problem. Have it your way."

Sean glanced at her. Her hands were locked together in her lap, her profile was stony and her words had been tossed off with a lack of care, but she didn't fool him. She was nervous. Well, why wouldn't she be? Whatever he thought of her morals or her lack of them, not knowing what she was getting into had to be disturbing.

He checked the mirror and stepped down on the gas pedal. The car gave a throaty roar and sped up the narrow coast road.

"I need you to put on a performance."

"I'm not stupid, O'Connell."

"Sean," he said through his teeth.

"All those clothes... The question is, who am I performing for? What role am I expected to play? And why? Unless you're one of those men who needs a fantasy to get it on."

Her voice quavered on the last few words, but the disdain was still there. He thought about jamming on the brakes, pulling her into his arms and showing her how little he needed fantasy or anything else as a turn-on, but he wasn't stupid, either.

The unvarnished truth was, she excited him.

It was one of the reasons he'd forgotten the lateness of the hour or that he hadn't so much as bought either of them a cup of coffee. At first, he'd told himself he just wanted to get this whole thing going before he came to his senses and asked himself what, exactly, he thought he was doing.

Halfway into the fashion parade, he'd known it was because he was too busy looking at Savannah to want to do anything else.

It wasn't the clothes. She looked beautiful in everything the clerk brought out, but he'd seen a lot of beautiful women in a lot of beautiful stuff over the years. He was beyond that as a turn-on.

What he'd gotten caught up in was watching her face in the mirror, how she'd gone from wariness to acceptance to surprised joy. It made him remember the time he'd sat in on a fashion shoot of his sister, Fallon. Her expression had gone through similar changes and she'd explained that it was part of the feature they were shooting.

I'm supposed to be a plain Jane, she'd told him, *transformed into a ravishing beauty by this designer's things.*

His sister was one fine model and the camera had captured her pleasure at the transformation but then, the magazine had been paying her something like ten thousand bucks for the morning's work.

He wasn't naive. Savannah was getting paid, too. Fifty times his sister's fee, but she hadn't looked half as happy when he'd offered her the money as she had the last couple of hours, just staring into the mirror. Something was happening within her. She was coming out of her chrysalis, watching herself change, and she liked what she saw.

So did he.

Then, minutes ago, she'd giggled. Giggled, as if she and the world were both innocent. And when he smiled at her in the mirror, she'd smiled back. Really smiled, the way a woman would smile at a man who was making her happy.

Sean's mouth turned down.

Damned right, he was making her happy. He'd promised her a half-million dollar payoff and now he was buying her more clothes than she'd ever need for what would ultimately be a couple of days' charade. What she'd been looking at, in that mirror, was one extremely fortunate female.

"Well?"

He looked across the console. Savannah was looking at him, her chin up, her arms folded over her seat belt. She was waiting for an answer and no matter what he thought of her, he figured it was time she got one.

"I come from a very close-knit family."

Her lips turned up at the corners. "How nice for you."

Sean gritted his teeth. Her tone made it clear she didn't give a damn if he came from a close family or from a den of serpents, but he couldn't see any sense in giving her less of an answer than she'd need to understand the part he expected her to play.

"I have two brothers and three sisters."

She yawned. "I'm thrilled."

"Two of my sisters are married. So are my two brothers."

"Listen, O'Conn... Listen, Sean, this is all very interesting if you're into family, but I'm not. How about getting to the bottom line?"

"My mother had a stroke a couple of weeks ago."

"Oh." Savannah swung toward him. "Did she...? I'm sorry."

Maybe she was. She sounded it. Not that he gave a damn. An actress didn't have to believe in a role, she just had to play it.

"She came though it with flying colors." He grinned; he couldn't help it. Just thinking about his mother's feistiness made him smile. Mary Elizabeth would like Savannah, he thought suddenly. She'd admire her toughness. Her resiliency...and what in hell did that have to do with anything?

He frowned and cleared his throat. "But for a while there, we thought she wasn't going to make it. And afterward— afterward, I asked her what she wanted for her birthday." He gave a little laugh. "I said I'd give it to her, no matter what it was."

"That was nice."

Savannah's voice was low. He glanced at her. She sounded as if she might be smiling, but it was too dark to see her face.

"Yeah. I mean, it was supposed to be, but she caught me by surprise when she told me what it was."

She laughed, the same way she had in the dress shop. The sound was so sweet that it made him smile, too.

"Let me guess. She wanted an elephant."

"If only." Sean let out a sigh. "An elephant would have been a snap, compared to what she asked me for."

"A snap? Just a snap?"

Oh, yes. There was definitely a smile in her voice. He liked it.

"No question about it."

"I give up. What does she want for her birthday?"

Sean took a deep breath. "She wants me to get married."

"She wants you to..." She shifted toward him. "To get married?"

"I told you, an elephant would have been a snap."

Savannah stared at him. No. It couldn't be. But everything was starting to make sense. Telling her he was going to call her his fiancée in the clothing shop. All those expensive clothes. All the talk about her playing a role.

"Wait just a minute, O'Connell. Are you saying you want me to pretend that I'm—that you and I are—"

"Engaged. You got it."

She couldn't seem to take her eyes from the crazy man sitting next to her. He wanted to pass her off as his fiancée?

"Engaged?" she repeated, in a voice that seemed to climb the scale from alto to lyric soprano.

"Uh-huh. A perfect young couple, head over heels in love."

His tone mocked the words. Why did that make her feel sad?

"Come on, McRae, don't look at me as if I asked you to stand on your head while playing the piano. This isn't rocket science. People get engaged all the time. All you have to do is—"

"No."

"You've already proved what a great actress you are. The way you came on to me that night..." His voice roughened. "All an act, right?"

"Right," she said without hesitating.

"So, what's the problem? You don't have to sleep with me, if that's what's worrying you. All I require is—"

"I said, no." Savannah sat straight in her seat and stared out the windshield. Sean had just turned onto the road that led to his hotel; the entrance was not far ahead. "As in, En Oh. There's not a way in the world I'm going to do this."

"I don't want to upset you, sugar," he said in a voice that made a lie of the promise, "but you don't have a say in the matter."

She looked at him. His profile, seen in the lights of the hotel as they approached it, was stony. And, of course, he was right. She didn't have a say, not unless she could come up with half a million dollars to repay Alain...and another half million to secure Missy's future.

How could he expect such a thing of her? To pretend to be his fiancée? Pretend she loved him, wanted him, wanted to be in his arms as she had been just a little while ago?

Pain pierced her like a forsaken dream. She swung away from him as they pulled up in front of the hotel. The parking attendant and the doorman were both hurrying toward them, just as they had last time. Everything was the same, except what Sean wanted.

"People don't do things like this," she said in a low voice.

"Thanks for that bit of insight, McRae. I don't know what I'd have done without—"

The car doors swung open simultaneously. "Good evening," the attendant said. The doorman smiled at Savannah. "Ma'am," he said pleasantly, "it's nice to see you again."

Nice? She was back at the scene of the crime. What could possibly be nice about that?

She stormed past the man but she didn't get very far. Sean grabbed her arm and led her toward the steps.

"Let go," she hissed.

"So you can run? No way, sugar. You already did that once. It's old."

"I didn't run. You threw me out. Damn it, will you let go?"

"Well, I'm not throwing you out this time," he said, hustling her inside the lobby.

"Listen, you—you egocentric fraud—"

The desk clerk looked around in surprise. So did a couple who'd been talking with him. All six eyebrows reached for their hairlines.

Why not? Sean thought grimly. They probably made an interesting sight, he damned near towing Savannah toward the elevator, she trying her best to dig in her heels and halt his progress.

"Madame? Sir? May I be of service?"

It was the desk clerk, scurrying toward them, trying to smile while looking terrified.

"No," Sean snarled.

"Yes," Savannah snapped. "Find a shrink and have this man committed."

"She has an unusual sense of humor," Sean said as he

banged on the elevator call button. When the ornate glass and silver doors opened, he pulled Savannah inside the car.

"Ma'am?" the desk clerk said uneasily, and Savannah rolled her eyes.

"Oh, for God's sake," she said, "just go away!"

The doors slid shut. Sean slid his key card into the penthouse slot and the car rose. Savannah wrenched free and glared at him. "You're good at this. Kidnapping women and shoving them around."

The doors opened again. Sean caught her by the elbow, hurried her through the entry hall and into the sitting room.

"Let me be sure I've got this right," he said. "You were willing to sleep with me but when I tell you there's no sex involved, that all you have to do is pretend to be my fiancée, you go crazy."

Crazy was exactly how it sounded, but she wasn't about to admit that.

"You want me to lie."

"Oh, I see." His lips curved in a smirk. "The McRae Morality Code frowns on lies."

"Obviously, yours doesn't."

That seemed to hit the target. Sean's shoulders fell.

"You think I'm thrilled about it, you're wrong. I just don't have a choice." He went to the minibar and opened it. "Besides, what do you care? She's my mother, not yours."

"It's not right."

"You never lied to your mother?"

"I never had to. She didn't know what I did or didn't do, and..." Savannah frowned. Why tell him that? She never talked about her life, her family. It was nobody's business, certainly not O'Connell's. "Besides, you couldn't pull it off."

Sean tossed two cans of Diet Coke, a bag of chips and a couple of candy bars on a low table.

"Eat something," he commanded.

"I'm not hungry."

"Of course you're hungry. So am I, and ordering up dried-out chicken sandwiches and coffee from the bottom of the pot doesn't appeal to me."

He opened the bag of chips and held it out. The wonderful aroma of salt and fat rose to her nostrils. To her horror, her stomach did a low, long rumble.

"Not hungry, huh?" He pushed the bag at her. "Eat."

Reluctantly, she reached in and took a handful of chips. They tasted as good as they smelled, and she took another handful.

"Why can't you just tell her you shouldn't have promised such a thing in the first place?"

He sighed, sat down on the sofa and laced his hands behind his head. The movement brought his biceps into sharp delineation. It did the same for the long muscles in his thighs and when he stretched out his legs, his black T-shirt rode up an inch, revealing a hard, flat belly.

"Because I've disappointed her too many times already."

Savannah blinked. "What?"

"You asked me why I didn't just tell her that—"

"I got that." She hesitated. "But you'd disappoint her with this anyway. Eventually, you'd have to tell her the truth."

That got him to his feet. He ran his hands through his hair until it stood up in little spikes and paced from the living room to the bedroom. Savannah followed.

"Engagements fall apart all the time. She'll accept that."

"I thought you said you'd promised her you'd get married."

"Right. I did. But..." He paused, then let out a long sigh.

"You're right, I did. Okay. I'll introduce you as my wife. I'll say—I'll say we met, went crazy for each other, eloped... Now what?"

"I told you, I don't want to do it."

His smile was quick and unpleasant. "Remember what I said about not having a choice? Well, neither do you... unless you're not interested in earning that money."

"It's an impossible plan."

In his heart, he was starting to think so, too. The last thing he needed was to hear those words from her lips.

"It'll be a cinch. We'll buy a ring. Rings. Engagement, wedding bands—one for you, one for me."

"Only a man would think that's all there is to marriage!" Savannah threw out her hands. "Has it occurred to you that we don't know the first thing about each other?"

"I thought of that. It's why I need you for two weeks. It'll give us time to get acquainted, so to speak, before my mother's birthday, and...Savannah?"

She shook her head, turned her back to him, but not before he'd seen the tears in her eyes. He went to her quickly, stepped in front of her and clasped her shoulders.

"Savannah," he said softly, "what is it?"

What, indeed? He wanted her to play a game. It was a lot better than the games she'd expected he wanted, or Alain's obscene plans. Two weeks of acting and a half-million dollar payoff. How come her heart felt as if it might break?

"Listen to me," she said desperately. "What you want us to do is a mistake."

"Then you'll do it?"

Her chin came up. "You said it yourself. I don't have much choice, do I?"

Sean looked at her. Her eyes were smudged with exhaustion; the night breeze had turned her hair into a tangle of curls and her sweatshirt bore a smattering of potato chip crumbs.

She was, in other words, even more beautiful. How could a woman be a mess and still be beautiful? No way could he figure it out.

"Why don't you have a choice?" he said, after a minute.

"That's a dumb question."

"It's the first intelligent question I've asked you." His hands cupped her shoulders. "I'm not talking about our arrangement, I'm talking about your—your relationship with Beaumont." She tried to pull away; he held her fast before him. "Why do you let him run your life? Why are you with him?"

She stared at him. Could she tell him? About herself, and her childhood. About Missy. About everything?

God, was she losing her mind? This man had all but bought her. He'd *bought* her. What could she possibly tell him that would mean a damn?

"I can't—I can't explain."

"Maybe I can help. If he has something on you—"

"Has something?"

"Yeah. You know. If you've ever done something you don't want anyone to know about. Been arrested. Been charged with—"

"You think I'm a criminal?"

"No. I don't think that. I just think there must be a reason you're with a man like that."

"I'm with him," she said flatly. "That's all."

"You despise him. And he treats you as if—as if—"

"O'Connell, I'm tired. We made a deal and I'm prepared to go through with it. You want a fiancée? You'll have one."

Her voice had turned hard. So had her eyes. Who was the

real Savannah? Was she someone who didn't think it was nice to lie, or someone who'd do anything for money?

"I want a fiancée for two weeks," he said. "Then a wife for a one-time, show-stopping performance."

"A one-night wife," she said, with a bitter smile.

"Yes. Can you manage that?"

"I can manage anything for five hundred thousand dollars," Savannah pulled away from him. "Where do I sleep?"

He looked at her for a long minute. Then he smiled, though the smile never reached his eyes.

"What if I said you sleep in my bed?"

She felt her pulse quicken, but she kept her eyes locked to his. "I thought you said—"

"Maybe I changed my mind."

Again, the seconds ticked by. She couldn't read his face at all. Did he mean it? Would he demand she sleep with him? She wouldn't do it, not for all the money in the world. She wouldn't let him undress her, caress her, take her on that journey she'd never experienced. It would be terrible. It would be...

It would be ecstasy. She'd dreamed of his hands on her breasts. His mouth on her thighs. His body, pressing her down into the softness of the bed.

Savannah raised her chin. "Maybe you want too much for the money, O'Connell."

He laughed softly. "Maybe," he said, and before she could do anything to stop him, he pulled her into his arms and kissed her. It was a kiss given without mercy, hard and demanding and, heaven help her, it was everything she wanted.

She stopped thinking, stopped wondering, stopped doing anything but feeling. She wound her arms around Sean's neck and met his explosive passion, matched it, opened her mouth to the sharp nip of his teeth. He groaned, lifted her into his erection, slid his hand under her sweatshirt, under her T-shirt and cupped her breast.

"Yes," she sobbed as he bent his head and took her nipple into his mouth. A flame seemed to shoot from her breasts straight down into her belly. She dug her hands into his hair, needing his kisses against her breast, needing them on her mouth, needing him as she had never permitted herself to need anyone.

"Sean," she whispered. "Sean, please..."

"What?" His voice was thick. "Please, what? Tell me."

"I want—I want—"

All at once, he stopped. He raised his head and looked at her through cold eyes.

"I know exactly what you want," he said. "That's good, sugar. It's very good. Thanks for letting me see you'll be as terrific in this role as you were the night we met."

"No. Sean—"

"Relax." He spoke calmly, as if they hadn't just been in each other's arms. "You won't have to take your act on the road. Hell, if you can be this convincing after a couple of kisses, why would I want you to do anything more?"

Savannah's heart seemed to stop beating. She wanted to die. She wanted *him* to die. What he'd done...

"You can have the bedroom." He looked her up and down, a satisfied little smile tugging at the corners of his mouth. "Hell, McRae, nothing's too good for a performer like you."

The smile, the cutting words, brought her back to life.

"You," she sputtered, "you—you—you—"

She grabbed a vase, flung it, watched it shatter into a million pieces as it hit the door that swung shut behind him.

"I hate you," she screamed. "I hate you, Sean O'Connell!"

Savannah buried her face in her hands and sank to the floor. What a lie! She hated him, yes, but the person she hated most was herself.

CHAPTER TEN

SEAN WAS UP well before six o'clock the next morning.

He tried phoning down for coffee. Room service, it seemed, wouldn't be able to accommodate him for another half hour.

"We do have coffee at the reception desk for our early-rising guests," the clerk told him.

Grumbling, Sean headed to the lobby, poured himself a cup of the stuff from a silver pot and glugged it down.

On the way back to the elevator, he made a pit stop in the men's room. Bad idea. The face that greeted him in the mirror wasn't pretty. He needed a shave, a shower and a way to stop scowling, but everything connected to those necessities was behind his closed bedroom door.

He went back to the desk, took the silver pot and a cup, offered a terse "You don't mind, do you?" to a clerk who looked as if he'd sooner argue with one of the crocs that inhabited the island's swampy north shore, and headed back to his suite.

Half an hour later, he was going crazy. He paced, he drank coffee, he paced some more. The coffee was his second bad idea of the morning. He could damn near feel the caffeine hightailing it through his system.

As if his nerves weren't jangling enough already.

He'd had a miserable night. The living-room sofa was too short, too soft, too everything but comfortable. He'd slept in his jeans and T-shirt, and he normally slept in his skin. Not that he'd actually slept.

How could he, considering the mess he'd created? Man, he wanted out! First the stupid pledge to Mary Elizabeth, then the even stupider determination to make good on it, and now this—this thing with Savannah...

"Hell," he muttered, running his hands through his hair.

Why had he ever imagined that he could take a stranger and pass her off as his wife? That he could make a woman like Savannah seem sweet, soft and innocent?

Except, there were moments she really did seem sweet, soft and innocent. Moments like the ones last night, when he'd taken her into his arms to prove a point, when she'd trembled at his touch before losing herself in his kisses.

Sean's jaw tightened.

An act. All of it. How come he kept forgetting that her talent for make-believe was the reason he'd thought of using her in the first place? The lady was good. Really good. Anybody seeing what had happened would have thought she meant it, that she'd really wanted him.

That he'd really wanted her.

Okay. He had. Damned right, he had. Kissing her, caressing her, had nothing to do with proving things. He kept telling himself that because it made him feel like less of a sleaze.

What kind of man lusted after a woman who made her living doing God knew what for a creep like Alain Beaumont?

Sean downed the last of the coffee. It was bitter and cold, but maybe the last jolt of caffeine would kick-start his brain. He needed to begin thinking straight. Make sense of things, starting with who and what Savannah McRae really was.

That conversation he'd walked in on when he'd boarded Beaumont's yacht. The key might be there. Beaumont had been talking about some sort of deal. She'd turned it down. No. "Turned it down" was the wrong way to phrase it. She'd been frantic. Hysterical.

Terrified.

In his anger, he'd thought she and Beaumont were just arguing over money. Truth was, they'd been fighting over more than that. Beaumont wanted her to do something. She didn't want to do it. Why hadn't she just walked out on the man? Told him what he could do with his plans, whatever they were, his yacht, his wealth?

Why was she willing to stay with such a pig?

A simple question, with a simple answer. She stayed for the life and the money. What else could it be?

Sean reached for the coffee, shuddered and pushed it aside. He'd lived among the rich and famous a good part of his life, first growing up in Vegas, then as a gambler. Some were okay people. Some weren't.

And some—only a few and almost always male—were downright monsters, certain that their wealth entitled them to live by codes of their own devising. They surrounded themselves with people who accepted that conviction. He'd seen servants who might as well have been slaves, business associates who turned a blind eye to stuff that was immoral if not downright illegal, wives willing to pretend they didn't see infidelities that were right under their noses.

He'd seen the mistresses of such men tolerate treatment that made his stomach turn.

Did that explain Savannah? He'd been sure it did, except the more he saw of her, the more he had this funny feeling that he was only seeing the surface.

And how come she was in his head all the time? How come—*be honest now, O'Connell*—he'd sought her out for this bit of subterfuge?

Forget the stuff about her acting talent. She was good,

yeah, but how tough would this performance be? One night, pretending she was his wife? With a little effort, he could come up with half a dozen women who could have carried it off and who'd have found it a lark. No metaphorical arm-twisting needed.

The truth was, he wanted her playing the part, not some other woman. There was something about her that got to him and not just sexually, although yeah, she got to him that way, too.

It was why he hadn't slept last night. The intensity of the kiss had stunned him. Those things he'd said about kissing her just to see if they'd be able to make the relationship look real was bull. The truth was, he'd let go of her because the need he'd felt to take her shocked him.

He'd never felt such hunger before.

Not that he'd solved the problem by saying something he regretted and walking away. Hell, those moments he'd had her in his arms had played in his head all night, like a loop of tape. He'd tossed and turned for hours, sweaty as a schoolboy, imagining what would have happened if he hadn't come to his senses. He thought about how it would have been to undress her. Bare her to his hands and mouth. See if all of her tasted as sweet as her high, perfect breasts.

Finally, he'd leaped from the damned sofa and stalked out to the terrace. He had a bad case of ZTS, was all. Zipper Think Syndrome, the name he and his brothers had jokingly given to the way men were led around by their anatomy.

It hadn't helped.

What he needed was either a shrink or a cold shower, but both were out of the question. You didn't go to a shrink just because you wanted a woman you shouldn't want. To get to the shower, he'd have to go through his bedroom, assuming she hadn't turned the lock. Not that it mattered. He wouldn't do it.

Even the thought of it—his bedroom, his bed, Savannah lying in it asleep, warm and sweet-smelling—was a mistake.

Or maybe the mistake had been not taking what he'd wanted, what they'd both wanted, last night...

"If you want to get into your bedroom, it's all yours."

Savannah stood in the bedroom doorway wearing her jeans and sweatshirt. Idly, he wondered if she'd slept in her clothes, same as him.

From the look on her face, Sean knew they were still at war. Maybe it was time to declare a truce. How else were they going to get through the next two weeks?

"Thanks," he said, trying for a neutral tone.

"There's nothing to thank me for." She strode past him. "I'll see you around."

She'd see him around? Anger shot through him and he moved past her and blocked the door.

"What the hell does that mean?"

"It means I'm leaving. It's what I should have done last night."

"You can't leave. We have an arrangement."

"Not anymore. I thought things through, O'Connell. I can't do this."

"Maybe you didn't understand me. I said, we have a deal."

Savannah's eyes flashed. "Get out of my way."

"You owe me money. Is this how you repay your debts?"

"I don't owe you anything."

"Sure you do. Two weeks ago you laid it on the line... and lost."

Her face colored. "I tried to keep my end of that wager, O'Connell. You sent me away."

She was right, but what did being right have to do with anything? They had a deal.

"How about Beaumont?"

"What about him?" she said, but the color began draining from her cheeks.

"Give me a break, okay? I don't know exactly what I walked in on the other night, but I suspect he's not gonna be happy to see you."

Not happy to see her? The depth of Sean's understatement almost made her laugh. She still wasn't sure how she'd handle Alain; all she could hope was that he'd calmed down. Surely, he didn't really want to use her as a—a prize in a tournament.

He'd be past such craziness by now. He'd agree to let her play cards to win back the money, to let Missy stay in Switzerland, to remember that once he'd treated her with courtesy and kindness.

Right. And polar ice caps floated in the Caribbean.

"Well?" Sean folded his arms. "I don't hear you telling me Beaumont will greet you with open arms."

"That's not your problem." She jerked her chin at the door. "Please step aside."

Sean hesitated. *Stop her,* a voice inside him said. *What for?* another voice replied. So what if she left? The entire plan was a bad idea.

He shrugged and did as she'd asked. "Go on. Just be sure and tell your boyfriend he still owes me."

Savannah swung toward him, her face livid. "He's not my boyfriend."

"Whatever you say, sugar."

"He's not!"

"Yeah, whatever. Just tell him I expect my money within 24 hours, now that you've reneged on the deal he and I made."

"Damn you," she said, her voice so low he had to strain to hear it. "Damn you to hell, Sean O'Connell! Do you hear yourself? Do you hear what you're saying?'' Sean jerked back in surprise as she jabbed her finger into the center of his chest. ''The deal you and he made. The deal *you* and *Alain* made!'' Another jab, followed by a flat hand slamming against him. ''How dare you, you—you no-good son of a bitch? How dare you think you can treat me like—like a streetwalker?''

''Hey. Wait just a minute. I didn't—''

''Yeah, you did.'' She slammed him with her fist this time, and she wasn't gentle about it. ''Buying me!''

''Whoa,'' Sean said, holding up a hand. ''I did not buy you.''

''You want to get technical about it? No. You didn't. You—you made a deal with Alain.''

''No way,'' he said, with all the self-righteous indignation of a man who knows he's wrong. ''Your boyfriend—''

Without warning, her fist slammed into his belly with enough force to make the air whoosh from his lungs.

''He—is—not—my—boyfriend! He's a monster. How can you even suggest such a thing? I loathe him. Loathe him, loathe....''

Tears poured down her cheeks. Sean cursed and pulled her into his arms. She was crying as if the world were about to end and it damn neared killed him. He'd been fooling himself, trying to pretend all he wanted was to make love to her when the truth was, he wanted to protect her from whatever demons stalked her.

Gently, he lifted her face to his and kissed her. She shook her head wildly but he ignored it and kissed her again, holding her as if she were precious because she was, and he was done with trying to figure out why he should feel that way about her.

He kept kissing her, stroking his hand down her spine.

When she sighed and leaned into him, he felt as if he'd beat back those demons, at least for the moment.

The kiss deepened. Her mouth clung to his. Her hands slipped up his chest; her fingers curled in the soft cotton of his shirt and Sean knew there was no sense in kidding himself.

He'd started this to comfort Savannah but comfort was the last thought in his head right now. She tasted like honey, smelled as sweet as summer, and they fit one against the other like matching pieces of a jigsaw puzzle just begun.

His need for her was almost overpowering.

But he couldn't, wouldn't let her know that. She wasn't herself. She was in pain. In despair. She was weeping. He'd done so many wrong things since they'd met, he wasn't going to add taking advantage of her to the list.

"Sweetheart." His voice was so rough he was amazed he could talk at all. Carefully, he held her by the shoulders and took a single step back. "Savannah. Let me just…let me just—"

"Sean," she whispered and rose to him, clasping his face, bringing his mouth to hers, and he was lost.

A torrent of desire flooded his senses. He groaned and swung her into his arms, never taking his mouth from hers as he carried her into the bedroom and laid her down on the bed that was still warm from her body.

When he drew back, she gave a little cry of distress and he took her hands and pressed kisses into the palms.

"Are you sure?" he whispered.

"I've never been surer of anything in my life." Tears still glittered on her lashes, but her lips curved in a smile. "Make love to me, Sean. Please."

He undressed her slowly, kissing each bit of skin as he bared it to his mouth. Her sighs, her moans, the beat of his heart became the only sounds in the universe.

When she was naked, he spent a long moment just looking at her, the delicacy of her breasts, the gentle rounding
of her belly, the gold of her skin, but she stirred uneasily
and when his gaze moved to her face, he saw a shadow in
her eyes. Wariness. Trepidation.

Fear.

Was she afraid of what he might do to her? Had Beaumont…? No. He wasn't going to think about that son of a
bitch. Not now. Now, all that mattered was Savannah.

"Savannah," he whispered urgently, "don't be afraid. I'll
never hurt you."

She shook her head. "I'm not afraid of you. But—but
there's something I should tell you—"

"No," he said, silencing her with a kiss. What she was
going to say, that she'd been with a lot of other men, that
some of them had done things… He didn't want to hear it.
Didn't need to hear it. All he needed was this. Her mouth.
Her breasts. The way he could make her breath catch when
he licked her nipples. The way she moaned when he slid
his hands under her, lifted her to him, kissed her belly, her
thighs.

"Sean. Oh God, Sean…"

She was trembling again, but not with fear. With passion.
The intensity of her need for him filled him with joy. This
was how he wanted her. Open to him. Wanting him.

Him. Only him.

He kept his eyes on hers as parted her thighs. She
moaned; her eyes went wide as he stroked a finger over her
labia. She cried out, jolted like a filly who'd never before
carried a rider.

"Sweet," he whispered. "So sweet…"

Slowly, carefully, he opened her to him. Breathed lightly
against the waiting bud that had bloomed for him. Kissed

it. Caressed it, and suddenly she arched like a bow. Her cry soared into the heavens and she sobbed his name.

Sean pulled off his clothes and came down to her. Caught her hands, entwined his fingers with hers, watched her face, her beautiful face, as he moved between her thighs and entered her...

And discovered that his lover was a virgin.

The realization shocked him into immobility. "Savannah?"

A world of questions were in that one word. Savannah understood them all and knew she'd have to provide answers but for now, only one mattered.

"Sean." She sighed his name, lifted her head and bit lightly into his shoulder. The taste of man and musk quickened the race of her already-galloping heart. "Please. Make love to me."

Groaning with pleasure, Sean slid into her warmth and took her with him to the stars.

THEY LAY TANGLED TOGETHER, breathing raggedly, a fine film of sweat drying on their skin.

"You're a virgin," he said in wonderment.

"Not anymore," she said softly, her lips curving at the awe in his voice, at the joy in her heart, and felt his lips curve, too, against her throat.

"You should have told me."

"Oh, sure. There's always an easy way to bring something like that into the conversation."

"I'd have gone slower."

"Mmm. Slower sounds nice."

Her words were a teasing purr. Sean smiled again and bit lightly into her flesh.

"Are you all right?"

"Yes." She moved beneath him, stretching like a cat. "I'm very all right."

He lifted his head. Her face was inches from his. Her eyes glowed and her smile would definitely have tempted Da Vinci. She looked sated and happy, and his heart did a little two-step of absolute male satisfaction.

"I'm glad. Still, if I'd known…"

"Would you have believed me?"

A muscle knotted in his jaw. After a couple of seconds, he turned on his side but kept his arm tightly around her.

"No."

Savannah nodded. His honesty was one of the things she liked about Sean O'Connell. It was a rare quality.

"I'm sorry, Savannah. I know you wanted me to say I would have, but—"

She rolled toward him and put her finger across his mouth. "Don't apologize for speaking the truth. Of course you wouldn't have believed me." She traced the outline of his lips. "Why on earth would you?"

Sean sucked her finger between his teeth and bit down gently. Then he took her hand from his mouth and kissed it.

"So, he isn't—"

"No." Savannah shuddered. "God, no. He's not."

"Then, what is he to you? Your business partner?"

"Alain is…Alain *was*—" she said, hastily correcting the error "—he *was* my friend."

"Beaumont?"

She could hear the incredulity in his voice. She couldn't blame him. The man Alain had recently revealed himself to be couldn't be anyone's friend, but the Alain she knew— the one she thought she knew—was different.

"I met him a long time ago," she said, propping herself

on her elbows so she could see Sean's face. "He was—he was good to me."

"Oh, yeah. He sounded like he was being good to you the other night, all right. Almost as good as the night he sent you to seduce me."

"He didn't tell me to—to go to bed with you that night," Savannah said quickly.

"No," Sean said coldly. "He just told you to keep me so busy thinking about taking you to bed that I wouldn't concentrate on the game."

"He's changed. The Alain I knew... That Alain isn't there anymore."

The Alain she'd *thought* she knew, Sean told himself, and what did she mean, he'd been good to her? From the little he'd seen, Beaumont treated her like dirt.

"How was he good to you?"

"What?"

"You said he was good to you. I'm trying to figure out how."

There was an edge to his voice. He wanted explanations but how could she give them? She wasn't ready to talk to him about Missy or the way she and her sister had lived. Lying naked in the arms of a man she hardly knew seemed less intimate than telling him the ugly details of her life.

"He just was," she said stiffly, and started to pull away. Sean drew her close again.

"I'm sorry."

"Let me up, please."

"No." Gently, he pushed her onto her back. "I'm a fool," he said gruffly, "talking about Beaumont when we have so many other things to discuss."

He kissed her. She tried not to respond but he kissed her again and she felt her resolve slipping.

"What things?" she said softly, brushing his hair back from his forehead.

"Important things." His voice grew husky. "The way you taste." He kissed her again, gently parting her lips with his. "I love the way you taste."

She smiled. "Do you?"

"Uh-huh. Your mouth." He dipped his head, touched the tip of his tongue to the hollow in her throat. "Your throat." He dipped his head again and licked one nipple, then the other. "And your breasts. You have beautiful breasts, Savannah."

Her breath caught as his teeth closed lightly on one pink bud. "When you do that...when you do that..."

"I love the feel of your nipples on my tongue."

"Oh God. Sean..."

"What?"

He looked up. Her eyes were becoming dark; the color in her face was rising. Her skin was turning warm and fragrant and his heart was doing flip-flops in his chest. He brought his mouth to hers, whispered his desire.

"Savannah. I want to make love to you again."

She cupped his face, kissed him, openmouthed, sighed his name against his lips.

"Is it too soon? I don't want to hurt you."

"You won't. Not by making love to me. I want you to. I want—"

She cried out as he slipped his hand between her thighs.

"This?" he said thickly. "Is this what you want?"

"Yes. That. Oh, and that. And—and—"

He entered her on one long, deep thrust. She sobbed his name and wrapped her legs around his waist. He moved and the world shattered, shattered again as she took him deeper inside her. And when he threw back his head, cried out and exploded inside her, Savannah wept, not with sorrow but with joy.

Why had she thought this man was a stranger? How could he be, when she had waited a lifetime to find him?

CHAPTER ELEVEN

SAVANNAH CAME AWAKE slowly, her muscles filled with a delicious lassitude. Eyes still closed, she reached for Sean...

And found the space beside her empty. Sean was gone, and from the feel of the linens, he'd been gone for quite a while.

She sat up against the headboard, clutching the duvet to her breasts. In the air-conditioned silence of the room, she felt the sudden chill of being alone...and the foolishness of what she'd done last night.

What time was it? Ten o'clock, at least. The sun slanting in through the blinds had the feel of midmorning. Was that the reason she felt so disoriented? Or was it because she'd spent the night in bed with a man she barely knew?

Savannah closed her eyes. What on earth had she been thinking?

Quickly, she swung her feet to the floor.

Sleeping with Sean had only made things more confused. He already had a low opinion of her. What had happened surely wouldn't have made it better. Plus, he'd hired her to do a job. There was nothing personal in the make-believe story they were going to create.

By now, he was sure to have as many regrets as she did. Or—or maybe she was wrong. Maybe making love hadn't been a mistake.

"You're awake."

One look at Sean and she knew she'd had it right the first time.

He stood in the doorway, beautiful enough to make her skin prickle and removed enough to make his thoughts apparent. Arms folded, feet crossed at the ankles, his smile polite and remote, she knew immediately that he regretted what had happened.

So be it.

"Yes." She forced an answering smile as she drew the covers nearer her chin. "Sorry to have slept so late."

He shrugged. "No problem."

"You probably have a million things to do and here I am, keeping you from them."

Another shrug. "We have all day."

"Right." She hesitated. How long could you hold a smile until the muscles in your face froze? "Well, if you give me a few minutes—"

"Sure."

But he didn't move. Did he expect her to get up in front of him? Head for the bathroom, naked? It wasn't going to happen.

Enough. Savannah narrowed her eyes.

"I'd appreciate some privacy."

"Oh." He stood away from the door jamb and nodded. "I'll be in the sitting room."

"Fine. Ten minutes, I'll be out of your way."

"You're not in—"

"Oh, give me a break," she snapped, her patience gone. "Yes, I'm in your way. Yes, we're wasting time. The sooner you leave, the sooner I can get moving."

Something flickered across his face. Discomfort? Embarrassment? Whatever it was, she didn't give a damn. All she wanted was to see his back as he closed the door behind him.

"Uh, the stuff we bought... It got here a while ago."

"What? Oh. The clothes." Somehow, the thought of that stack of boxes, all of them holding things he'd purchased to turn her into someone she wasn't, made her feel angrier. "Fine. You pick out something you'd like me to wear and leave it on the chair, okay?"

"The clothes are yours, Savannah. You make the choice."

"They're not mine."

"Damn it, what is this? I come in to say good morning and next thing I know, I'm involved in an argument." His jaw shot forward. "They're yours," he said coldly. "Is that clear?"

"A lot of things are clear," she said, just as coldly. "Funny how daylight can make that happen."

"What the hell are you talking about?"

"Oh, for God's sake! Will you just get out of here?"

His mouth thinned. "Yeah. I'll do that."

The door closed with a bang. She grabbed a pillow and flung it across the room. She hadn't expected roses and champagne this morning but O'Connell could have been a little nicer. Couldn't he have pretended that last night—that last night—

Savannah shot to her feet. "To hell with you, Sean O'Connell," she muttered, hating herself for sounding as if she were going to burst into tears.

The duvet tangled around her legs as she stomped toward the bathroom and she tugged at it without mercy, which only made things worse. Words she'd learned years ago on the New Orleans streets hissed from her lips just as the door flew open.

"Damn you, Savannah McRae," Sean said, and pulled her roughly into his arms.

"Let me go. O'Connell, I swear, if you don't let me go—"

"Shut up," he commanded, tunneling his hands into her hair, holding her face to his so he could kiss her. His mouth was hot, his kisses deep and dangerous and with a little cry, she gave up fighting and kissed him back.

"I'm sorry," he whispered, his lips a breath from hers.

"So am I. I thought you regretted last night."

Sean kissed her again. "I did," he said bluntly, framing her face with his hands. "I told myself making love was a mistake. That we should have stuck to business." His eyes dropped to her parted lips, then met hers again. "It took a while before I was ready to admit the only mistake I've made since the minute I saw you was trying to pretend I didn't want you."

Savannah gave a watery smile. "Me, too," she said, and rose on her toes to press her mouth to his.

Long moments later, Sean clasped her hands, kissed them and brought them to his chest.

"I took your virginity."

"No," she said, shaking her head. "I gave it to you."

His smile was soft and sweet. "I almost went crazy sitting out there, telling myself what a bastard I was." His voice roughened. "Truth is, I'm glad you did. It means everything to me, sugar, knowing you gave me such a gift."

"Sometimes—sometimes I used to think it was the only part of me that was still worth anything, you know? That I'd done so many things over the years—"

He silenced her with another tender kiss. "I haven't been an angel, either. Besides, the one thing I'm certain of is that whatever you've done, you did because you had to."

Sighing, she let him draw her close against him, closed her eyes under the restful stroke of his hand down her spine.

"You're a good man, Sean O'Connell."

A deep laugh rumbled through his chest. "I've been called a lot of things, sweetheart, but that's a first." Gently, he pressed a kiss into her hair. "You know what else I thought about while you were sleeping?" She leaned back in his embrace and shook her head. "I thought how I could stop wasting time regretting something so wonderful, wake you with my kisses and make love to you again."

"Mmm. Sounds lovely."

"But—"

"But?"

Sean tipped her face up to his. "But," he said, smiling into her eyes, "if we don't eat some real food soon, all my get-up-and-go will have gotten-up-and-gone."

She laughed. It was, he thought, one of the loveliest sounds he'd ever heard. He touched the tip of his finger to her mouth.

"Plus, we have an appointment at noon."

"We do?"

"Uh-huh. And that means you have little more than an hour to get ready."

"I'll be quick."

His smile turned devastatingly sexy. "We can save time by showering together."

"I don't think that would work."

"No. Probably not." He stepped back. "Okay. I'll get those boxes. You take your shower."

Savannah kissed him, then started for the bathroom, but she turned back when Sean spoke.

"The thing is," he said gruffly. "The thing is, Savannah, I've been a loner all my life. It's tough, letting somebody in."

She knew it wasn't a line that would rank high in the annals of romantic declarations but it made the last of her reserve slip away. She knew what it took for him to say such a thing because it was true of her, too. It was the reason she'd panicked when she woke and he wasn't there, why she'd done everything she could to make herself believe the night had been an error.

Somehow, she kept her tears from flowing. "Yes," she whispered. "I know."

Sean's face took on a taut, hungry look. "To hell with getting things done quickly," he said, and scooped her into his arms. And, as he carried her to the bed, Savannah knew that what they'd just admitted to each other had the power to heal them both...

Or to destroy them.

THEY HAD BREAKFAST on the terrace. Afterward, Sean made a phone call. He was changing the time of their appointment, he said, but he wouldn't tell her more until they were in his car, speeding down a narrow dirt road toward the sea.

"We're meeting with a Realtor," he said casually.

Savannah stared at him. "You're buying a house?"

"Sure," he said, as if people decided to buy homes on islands in the Bahamas all the time. He flashed her a quick smile and added that he'd been thinking, on and off, about buying a place here for a while.

"Ah. So you set up this appointment a while back."

"Weeks ago."

It was a lie, though he didn't know why he was lying. He'd made the appointment this morning, even while he paced the living room and tried to figure out what in hell he was getting himself into.

But, he'd told himself, it made sense, didn't it, to own property here? He'd been investing in expensive real estate for a long time. Nobody in his family knew it—why spoil their conviction that he was as impractical as he was foot-loose?—but the fact was, he could give up gambling at the drop of a hat and still live as comfortably as any of the rest of the O'Connells.

There just wasn't any reason to give up gambling. He loved the risk, the emotional highs, had never found anything to give him that same thrill.

Until now.

That thought, unbidden, unwanted and terrifying, had almost sent him into the bedroom to wake Savannah, pay her the half-mil and tell her sorry, sweets, the deal is off.

But it was too late for that. He'd come this far; he'd see his scheme through. And yes, buying a place made sense considering one of the reasons he'd given himself two weeks with Savannah before his mother's birthday party was so they could get to know each other well enough to be convincing as lovers.

Sorry. As husband and wife.

How could they manage that in the sterile environment of a hotel? You weren't really yourself in a hotel, no matter how elegant. Maybe because it *was* so elegant. They'd get acquainted better if they were alone.

So he'd phoned the Realtor, told her exactly the kind of property he wanted and set up the appointment.

He'd felt good after that call. He'd buy a place on the beach. Hire someone to come in and pick up the place, maybe cook, but that was it. There'd be nothing to intrude on the private little world he and Savannah were about to create.

Whoa, he'd thought. What was that all about? He didn't need a private world with anybody, he only needed the right setting to make this stunt work.

He'd reached for the phone to cancel the appointment. He could buy a house anytime, and really, how much of a bother would it be to have maids or clerks or other guests around? He and Savannah could still set the groundwork for their make-believe marriage.

That was when he'd heard her stirring. He'd gone into the bedroom to be sure she understood that what had happened the previous night wouldn't happen again.

Instead, his heart had turned over at the sight of her, looking early-morning beautiful and vulnerable as she did her best, like him, to pretend the night hadn't meant a thing.

For the first time in his life, Sean had known he was tired of taking risks that put nothing but money on the line. He'd wanted to take Savannah in his arms, and he had. He'd even told her part of what he was feeling, how he'd always been a loner, but there was more. He knew that. He just didn't know, exactly, what else he wanted to say...

"Is that the house?"

Sean dragged his attention back to the road. A handsome wrought-iron fence rose ahead, a discreet For Sale sign on a stake beside it. A small TV camera, high in a tree just beyond the gate, angled toward them as he slowed the car. The gates swung open, revealing a crushed oyster-shell drive shaded by thickets of sea grape, bougainvillea and prickly-pear cactus.

The Realtor was waiting for them on the wide marble steps of an enormous, elegant house.

Sean bent his head toward Savannah's as he helped her from the car. "Do you like it?" he said softly.

She hesitated, then smiled. "It's beautiful."

Yes, he thought, it was, but it reminded him of a hotel. A hotel for two, perhaps, but a hotel just the same. He put his arm around her and when they reached the steps, he shook the Realtor's hand.

"Mr. O'Connell," the woman said pleasantly. "I'm delighted to meet you."

Sean nodded. "My pleasure." His arm tightened around Savannah. "This is Miss McRae. My fiancée."

He felt Savannah's muscles jerk, felt the sudden tension radiate through his body at his use of the word. The Realtor's smile broadened.

"How nice! And where are you folks staying right now?"

"At the *Petite Fleur*," Sean said pleasantly, "but we're hoping to move as soon as we find a house to buy." Savannah damn near jumped. He drew her closer. "Right, Savannah?"

She looked stunned but she managed a quick "yes." It troubled him that she didn't really seem all that thrilled. Should he have told her his plans ahead of time instead of keeping them as a surprise? Why had he wanted to surprise her, anyway?

Could it have been because he was still surprising himself?

"The people who built this house were very well-known on the international scene." The Realtor leaned closer. "I'm sure you'll recognize the name. They were very happy here. They did lots of entertaining. Well, you can see it's a perfect place for that. The former owners had a staff of six—"

"Six?"

"But you'd need extra help for big parties, of course."

So much for privacy but then, if Savannah liked it…

"Yeah," Sean said, "of course."

"Let me show you through the house. I'm sure you'll both love it."

Savannah didn't. Sean could tell, even though she said all the right things. He was coming to know his pretend-fiancée's expressions. Right now, she wore a smile like a mask.

What didn't she like? He had no opinion, one way or the other. Okay, maybe he did. Truth was, growing up in overblown Las Vegas, he might have preferred something smaller. Simpler. A place where he could be himself, and she could be...

His gut tightened. Savannah would only spend the next couple of weeks here. She didn't have to love the place. It just made him wonder, was all, why she didn't.

Was it because she was accustomed to the *Lorelei?* Did she want gold cupids, dark wainscoting and crimson velvet? No. He'd watched her reaction to the things the clerk showed her at the shop in *Bijou.* The simpler, the more classic, the better.

What was it, then? Was it the prospect of the two of them rattling around alone here? The house was isolated on acres of property with nothing but shore and seabirds for company. There'd be servants—that cast of six—but well-trained servants would know how to be unobtrusive.

The more he thought about it, the more likely that seemed. Why kid himself? Alone, what would they do? What would they talk about? It wasn't as if he couldn't clue her in on things that would make them seem a real couple in the comfort of the hotel.

As good as last night had been, it was only sex. Being in bed would only get them so far. There were two weeks ahead of mornings, afternoons and evenings. Two weeks of empty hours to fill.

Why had he figured they'd be better off living alone than in the hotel?

Sean interrupted the Realtor midway through a spiel about the joys of the restaurant-size kitchen range.

"Thanks," he said. "I'll be in touch."

The look on her face mirrored Savannah's. He was lying and all of them knew it.

"Of course," the woman said, sounding disappointed.

Hey, he thought coolly, she would be, losing a six-figure commission.

Savannah looked relieved.

It made him angry as hell. She should have told him she didn't want to be alone with him right away, he thought grimly as he hustled her to the car.

"If you didn't want to move out of the hotel," he growled, "you should have said so."

She shot him a surprised look. "How could I? You said you were buying a house. You never mentioned you expected us to live in it."

"Well, you can stop worrying. We won't."

"Good." Savannah folded her arms and glared straight ahead. Why was *he* so ticked off? She was the one who had the right to be angry. He'd decided to buy a house. Well, that was his affair. That he'd decided to move her into it was hers. Why hadn't he told her? To spring something like that, to let the Realtor think they were a pair of starstruck lovers... "Living together here wasn't part of our deal."

"You're right. It wasn't." The tires squealed as Sean turned onto the main road at a speed that made trees blur as they sped past them. "I had an idea we'd find it easier to get to know each other away from the hotel. It was dumb."

"You should have asked me."

"I said, it was a dumb plan."

Seconds passed. Savannah shifted in her seat. "I can see where you'd think it made sense."

He looked at her. She was sitting as stiff as a ramrod, her profile as stern as that of the sixth-grade teacher who'd sent him to the principal's office when she'd discovered him teaching a couple of his buddies how to play craps.

"Yeah?"

"Uh-huh. I mean, if we were actually engaged, we'd want to spend time alone."

Sean nodded. "That was my thinking but, like I said, it was—"

"Did you really like that house?"

Sean looked at her again. She'd turned toward him, eyes filled with defiance.

"Why?"

"For heaven's sake, O'Connell, just answer the question. Did you like it?"

"No," he said bluntly. "It was—"

"Too big."

"Well, yes."

"Too formal."

"Right again."

"If we were a couple, if we really—if we really were lovers, would we want to live in a place so huge we'd need to leave trails of bread crumbs to find each other?"

Sean grinned. "My sentiments exactly."

She nodded and looked straight ahead again. "See? If you hadn't sprung this on me, if you'd said, 'Savannah, I think we should live someplace away from the artificial climate of a hotel so we can get to know each other better, and how would you feel living in a house the size of the Taj Mahal,' we wouldn't be having this quarrel now."

She was trying her best to sound pragmatic but what she sounded was quintessentially female. Sean's grin widened.

"Is that what we're doing? Having a quarrel?"

Something in his voice made her look at him. "Aren't we?"

"Our first."

"You're kidding. We've done nothing but quarrel since we met."

"Our first as lovers," he said, pulling under a tall palm

tree on the side of the road and shutting off the engine. He undid his seat belt, leaned over and gently undid hers. "Because that's what we are," he said softly. "We're lovers, Savannah."

"You know what I meant. I meant if we were—"

Sean gathered Savannah into his arms and kissed her. She tried not to respond but his mouth was sweet and his body was warm, and it took less than a heartbeat for her to sigh and kiss him back.

"We're lovers," he said, stroking the curls back from her cheek and tucking them behind her ear. "Even the Realtor could see that."

"It was a logical conclusion, O'Connell. You introduced me as your fiancée."

"Yeah." Sean took her hand and lifted it to his lips. "Which reminds me…we have to make the trip to Bijou again."

"No way. As it is, you bought enough clothes for ten of me!"

He chuckled. "If my sisters heard you say that, they'd hustle you off to a psychiatrist."

"Oh, right. You mentioned them before. Two sisters?"

"Three, and every last one of them would—well, maybe that's an overstatement. Two of 'em, for sure, would tell you a beautiful woman can never have too many things in her closet."

That won him a little smile. "Honestly. I don't need anything. You bought me so much—"

"A ring."

Her eyes widened. "A what?"

"A ring." Sean kissed her hand again, then gently sucked the tip of her ring finger into his mouth. "Men who are engaged to be married give their fiancées engagement rings."

"Don't be silly. They don't. Not always."

"Always," he said firmly, deliberating ignoring the fact that one of his brothers hadn't married conventionally enough to have time to put a ring on his fiancée's finger. It was a reasonable demand, wasn't it? He had a mother, an entire family, to fool.

A ring. His ring, on her finger. It would only be part of the game, but...

Savannah leaned her forehead against his. "Sean. This— this is getting complicated."

"I'm just trying to make sure we seem believable."

She looked up. "Is that the reason you made love to me last night? So we'd seem—"

His kiss left her dizzy.

"You know it wasn't," he said gruffly. "I made love to you for the same reason you made love to me, because we need to be together as much as we need to breathe."

Need, Savannah thought. He'd said need. As if what they'd shared would go on. As if they had a future that stretched further ahead than two short weeks.

She sighed, closed her eyes and buried her face against his throat.

"Complicated," she whispered, with a little catch in her voice.

This time, he didn't argue. She was right but he didn't want to talk about that now or even think about it. Instead, he held her close, reveled in the feel of her in his arms, and wondered if he'd ever, in all his life, felt so complete.

"Savannah?"

"Hmm?"

"You said I should have asked you what kind of house you preferred. Well, I'm asking."

"I didn't say that. Not exactly. What I said was—"

"There's a place up the road a couple of miles. I saw the

For Sale sign and drove in for a quick look the last time I was here. I haven't seen the inside but from the outside…'' He took a breath. Why did he feel so nervous? All he was doing was describing a house. ''It's small. Well, compared to the monster we just saw, it is. Three bedrooms, maybe four.''

Savannah's smile was as bright as the sky. ''Darn,'' she said softly. ''You mean, we wouldn't need six strangers underfoot to keep things going?''

''Just you and me,'' Sean murmured, stroking the back of his hand down her cheek. ''Truth is, the house is beautiful. And it's on the beach, comes with maybe five, six acres of land you'd need a machete to get through.''

''We'd have privacy.''

Sean nodded. ''Yes. All we could ask for. There's a pool, a small garden, a conservatory like the one Cullen has at his place on Nantucket.''

''Who?''

God, there was so much she didn't know about him, so much he didn't know about her…but there was time to learn. There was plenty of time, and he was looking forward to every second.

''One of my brothers. Cull lives in Boston with his wife and baby, but he has a house on the Atlantic and this room I've always liked. Glass walls, a big telescope. He can watch the ocean, see whales and dolphins and—''

He fell silent, suddenly feeling foolish. Maybe Savannah thought whales and dolphins were kid stuff. But she smiled, and the way she smiled set his concerns to rest.

''I love to watch whales and dolphins! Whales, especially. The way they seem to dance in the sea, you know? I never get tired of seeing them, even if Alain always says I'm foolish to—to…''

Her words trailed away. For a moment, Beaumont seemed

to be in the car with them, his presence a stain on the bright
afternoon. The questions in Sean's head fought to surface,
but what mattered right now was the sudden darkness in
Savannah's eyes.

He gathered her close and kissed her until the darkness
was gone and they were alone again in their make-believe
universe.

"Beaumont's out of your life forever, sweetheart," he
said. "I promise."

Because she had already learned that Sean would never
lie to her, because the sun was shining down from a cloud-
less sky, but mostly because she was safe in her lover's
arms, Savannah did a foolish thing.

She let herself believe it.

CHAPTER TWELVE

SEAN CALLED THE REALTOR on his cell phone. Yes, she said happily, she knew the property he meant and it was still on the market.

She met them at the foot of a long, winding driveway. A couple of hours later, the deal was done.

The house was his.

Though he already owned other properties, this was the first time he'd bought one to live in, the first time he'd wanted to do that...and, most definitely, the first time he'd wanted to share his space with a woman.

The realization shook him. He reminded himself that this was all simply a logical part of a plan. Still, he felt almost unbearably happy when he saw the excitement and pleasure that glowed in Savannah's eyes as they walked through the house together the next day.

"It's beautiful," she said.

Beautiful, indeed. Sean couldn't get enough of looking at her.

The house came furnished. A good thing, because they moved in right away. Standing on the porch, Sean wondered what it would be like if this weren't make-believe. If they were really moving in together.

If the diamond ring he'd bought and slipped on her finger, and the matching wedding band he intended to surprise her with once they headed for Vegas, weren't part of a plan but marked a turning point in his life.

The thought shocked him. Horrified him. What kind of craziness was this? He wanted this woman, yes, but he'd wanted other women. This relationship only seemed special because of the circumstances.

That was all it was, he told himself, and he swung Savannah into his arms and headed for the bedroom. Laughing, she clung to his shoulders.

"What are you doing, O'Connell?"

"It's an old Irish custom," he said with a lightness he didn't feel. "We have to inaugurate the bed for good luck."

Long moments later, they lay spent in each other's arms, Sean staring up at the ceiling and knowing that it was time to stop lying to himself.

What he felt for Savannah *was* special. Two truths revealed in one day. What in hell was happening to him?

Maybe it was safer not to find out.

THE HOUSE WAS PERFECT, eight big rooms with walls of glass. Anywhere you stood, you could look at the pink sand and deep blue sea, or at the rich tangle of green that shielded the estate from the world.

The shower room in the master bath had glass walls, too. Standing inside it, warm water cascading down your body, you could turn your face up to the hot yellow sun by day, the cold white stars by night.

It was as perfect a place, Sean said huskily, to love each other as the bed.

That first night, standing in the shower, her lover's moon-washed eyes looking into hers, his hands molding her to him as he caressed her breasts, then laved them with his tongue, Savannah trembled.

"What is it, sweetheart?" Sean murmured.

She shook her head. She was happy. So happy that admitting it might be dangerous.

Sean could have told her he understood. He read what she was thinking, what she was feeling, in her eyes and knew those emotions were inside his own heart.

"Savannah," he said huskily. "Savannah, I—I—"

The words he needed were there. So close. So very close. He just couldn't find them. He only knew that whatever was happening to her was happening to him, too.

It was magic, and only a fool would try putting a name to magic.

SAVANNAH HAD NEVER LIVED with a man before.

Her years with Alain didn't count. She'd been a guest on his yacht and in his chateau, always with a room and bath of her own and no greater connection to him than to the servants who attended him.

Now, she knew she hadn't been a guest at all. She'd been a servant, a different kind of servant, but that was what she'd been. His cook prepared meals, his maid cleaned, his chauffeur drove his big black limousine...

And she was a source of amusement.

All this time she'd let herself think she was valuable to him because she played cards so well. The truth, which she'd only just started admitting to herself, was that she was good but Alain was better. Aside from that, she'd been his clever pet. A puppy taken from the streets, cleaned up, taught manners and little tricks.

He'd liked teaching her which fork to use, which wine to drink because it made him feel superior. But most of all, he'd liked watching her sit at a table filled with important men and beat them at cards because the men all thought he was the reason she was so skilled.

Now, it would give him a bigger kick to sell her to them.

Horrid as the thought was, she knew it was the truth. That was what he'd intended all along. Alain had simply used what had happened with Sean as an excuse to move up the calendar.

Was he sick? Evil? She didn't care. Fate had given her the chance to escape and she was going to take it.

It was the same fate that had given her Sean O'Connell—and would, she was certain, eventually take him from her.

Winning streaks never lasted.

The longer they lived together in the house on the beach, the more terrible that truth became.

Savannah told herself not to think about it. To enjoy these days. These nights. To be happy.

Oh, and she was happy! It didn't matter what they did. Dance in one of the island's beautiful clubs, walk the beach barefoot, dine in an elegant restaurant, have conch burgers at a little shack Sean knew near the harbor, or grill lobsters when the sun sank into the sea, whatever they did was wonderful. Her lover was wonderful. And she—she—

Savannah's thoughts skittered in panic. She what? Feelings were dangerous things. Life had taught her that early on. What she felt for Sean was affection. Gratitude. Respect. There was no sense in trying to make more of it than it was.

She did love being with him. It was safe to use the word that way. He seemed to enjoy being with her, too. True to his promise, they spent their days learning about each other. He was a meat-and-potatoes guy. She preferred salads. He liked watching documentaries on TV. She liked watching old movies. He liked chess. She'd never played the game. He taught her and after a slow start, their games often ended in stalemates.

He also adored rough-and-tumble sports. She learned that the hard way, when he swore up and down one rainy night that there was nothing on their satellite TV but football, rugby and soccer.

"Liar," she said huffily, snatching the remote from him

and clicking through the channels until she found a pair of women earnestly discussing how to get in touch with your inner self. She suffered through five minutes of it until Sean groaned and held his hands over his ears. Then she giggled, flung herself on him and said there were really better ways to get in touch with your inner self.

And he obliged. They loved and played and avoided anything serious…until one morning. They were having breakfast on the patio—mangoes from a roadside stand, croissants from a bakery in *Bijou*—when Sean suddenly asked her a question. "Tell me about yourself," he said.

The question took her by surprise. She looked up from her plate and flashed a quick smile.

"There's not much left to tell. I mean, you already know I can't cook worth a hill of beans. Remember those conch fritters?"

She grinned but he wasn't going to let her off. She knew it as soon as he took her hand, lifted it to his lips and kissed it.

"Come on, Savannah. Think of all I've told you about me these past days."

It was true. He'd regaled her with stories about his family, about growing up in a big, glitzy hotel.

"Compared to yours, my life story's dull."

"Nothing about you could be dull." Sean kissed her fingers, one by one. "I want to know everything."

She looked at him. "Do you think your family will ask you detailed questions about me?"

"My fam…" Of course. She thought he was asking because the answers would help him maintain the fiction that they were getting married. Truth was, he'd damned near forgotten that was the reason they were here. "You never know," he said, hoping he sounded sincere. "What am I gonna do when Keir asks if you got straight A's in school, or Cull wants to know if you were a Girl Scout?" He tapped the tip of her nose with his finger. "Some things are very important to the O'Connell clan."

For a second, she thought he was serious. Then he grinned, reached for her and hauled her into his lap.

"I'll bet you did get straight A's."

She had, for a while. When her mother was still alive, and even the two years in that first foster home, before the man she was supposed to call Daddy started noticing her budding breasts, and the woman she'd never been able to call Mom realized he was noticing.

"Savannah?" Sean kissed her mouth. "Hey," he said softly, "I'm only teasing. You don't have to tell me anything you don't want to tell me."

"No. You're right. You need to know more about me."

The look in her eyes made him sorry he'd raised the subject. "I don't," he said fiercely. "I'm going to be introducing you as the woman I love. Nobody's going to have the right to question either of us."

Savannah's heart skipped a beat. "As the woman you'll be pretending to love," she said carefully.

Their eyes met. "Yeah," he said, after a minute. "That's what I meant."

An honest answer from an honest man. She couldn't ask for anything more, could she? At the very least, he deserved honesty in return.

"Well," she said slowly, "I was never a Girl Scout..."

She told him everything. About her father, who'd left when she was so small she couldn't remember him. About her mother, a drug addict, and how she'd died.

She told him about her sister, cruelly disabled by an illness no one really understood, and how Missy had screamed and screamed when the authorities separated them and put

Savannah in the first of a series of foster homes and Missy in an institution.

She told him how she'd hated those homes, though she left out the uglier details, and how she'd run away from the last and worst one, how she'd found a way to snatch Missy, how they'd hitchhiked from Savannah—the city her mother had named her for—to New Orleans. How they'd survived with her earning money using skills she'd picked up and honed in one of the endless series of foster homes.

She told him all the things she'd never told anyone, and by the time she talked of Alain, how he'd rescued her and Missy, how she'd thought he was her savior, she was weeping, the sound so raw and heartbreaking, Sean cursed the fates that had kept him from finding her sooner.

"Hush," he said, as he lifted her tearstained face to his and kissed her and kissed her until the world was reduced to only the two of them. Only the two of them, because only the two of them mattered.

That was the minute when he knew that he loved her.

HE TOLD HER THAT NIGHT.

It was their last on the island. The next afternoon, they would fly to Las Vegas. He'd thought he'd tell her there. Or maybe on the plane. He'd wait a little while, until the time was right.

But walking hand in hand along the beach, under the benevolent gaze of a fat, ivory moon, he suddenly knew it would never be more right than this. He'd never felt more vulnerable in his life as he turned her toward him.

"Savannah," he said. "Savannah…"

She raised her face to his, and when he looked into her eyes, he saw something that told him everything would be all right.

"Savannah," he said softly, smiling with wonder, "you're in love with me."

She jerked under his hands. "My God, O'Connell, you have the most monumental ego—"

Sean lifted her to her toes and kissed her. "You'd better be in love with me," he whispered against her mouth, "because I love you. I adore you. You hear me, Just-Savannah? I love you with all my heart."

Time seemed to stop. Nothing moved, not the sea or the air or Savannah. Sean felt a chill in his blood. Maybe he was wrong. Maybe she didn't feel what he did. Maybe—

And then she gave a little cry and threw her arms around him.

They made love there, on the still-warm sand, and then he carried her to the house and they made love in the shower. They went to bed and slept curled together, and when they awoke before dawn, they made love again.

"I love you," Savannah whispered, looking up at him, her eyes wide with wonder as he slipped deep, deep inside her. "I love you, love you, love—"

He kissed her and they flew, together, into the blinding white heat of the universe.

CHAPTER THIRTEEN

SAVANNAH DIDN'T WANT to leave their house or their island.

That was how she'd come to think of this place where she and Sean had forged their love. They were safe here. They belonged here.

Heaven only knew what the real world had in store.

Boarding the jet for their flight to Las Vegas, her teeth were all but chattering. Sean kept his arm tightly around her and hugged her to his side.

"There's nothing to worry about. My family's going to love you."

She nodded, as if she believed him, but she didn't. Those brothers he always talked about sounded just like him. Big. Strong. Smart. They'd see right through her, know in an instant she didn't measure up to their wives who were undoubtedly women from good, solid backgrounds—backgrounds that were nothing like hers.

And his sisters... She could almost see them. Bright. Beautiful. Proper. One single, two married to men who were so powerful it made her head spin. Fallon's husband was head of an international conglomerate. Megan's was a sheikh.

A sheikh! she thought, and bit back hysterical laughter.

And then there was Sean's mother. Mary Elizabeth O'Connell-Coyle. The matriarch of the clan. Sean adored her—that was obvious. What son wouldn't adore a woman who sounded like a cross between a queen and a saint?

You couldn't leave his stepfather out of the equation. His name, Sean told her, was Daniel. He'd been a cop. Cops always made her nervous, ever since her days on the streets. They saw right through a person. It would take Dan Coyle five seconds to know what she really was, just a dirty-faced street kid who was about to pull the biggest scam of her life on some very nice people who deserved better.

She told herself it wasn't a complete scam. She wasn't Sean's wife but they were in love. They'd only be stretching the truth a little.

Who was she kidding? They'd be stretching it a lot.

The money. She had to concentrate on the money, though thinking about it was agony. She had to take it. With it, she could save her sister's life—but Sean didn't know that. She hadn't told him about Alain's threats, not just to Missy but to her. That he'd intended to use her as a prize.

She couldn't risk telling Sean. He despised Alain already. She was afraid of what he might do if he knew the true extent of Alain's villainy. Not that she gave a damn about Alain. It was Sean she was worried about.

If he went after Alain because of her, if he hurt him, got in trouble, she'd never forgive herself.

The plane was airborne. Savannah shut her eyes and told herself she had no choice. She had to do this. Had to take the money. The money. The money...

Oh God!

How could she accept money from her lover? How could she lie to his family? She couldn't, that was all. End of story. She'd find another way.

"Sean," she whispered frantically, as their plane leveled off. "I can't do this!"

Sean took her hand. "Sure you can."

"Lying to all those people...? I don't know why we ever thought it would work."

He didn't answer, not for what seemed a long time. Then he nodded. "You're right," he said calmly. "It wouldn't."

She stared at him. "Then, what are we doing? Why are we going to this party?"

"We're going because it's my mother's birthday."

"But you just said—"

"And because I made her a promise."

"O'Connell, are you crazy? Two seconds ago, you and I agreed that—"

"That lying to my family would be a mistake." Sean undid his seat belt. Slowly and deliberately, he undid hers and drew her to him. In the hushed darkness of the first-class cabin, they might as well have been alone. "So we're not going to lie." He took a deep, deep breath. "You're wearing my ring." He reached into his pocket and took out the matching wedding band. "I want you to wear this, too."

Savannah looked at the band glittering in his palm. It was beautiful but it was as meaningless as the diamond winking on her left hand. Seeing it made her want to weep.

"I won't put it on. This is wrong, Sean. Don't you feel guilty? This is your family! You love them. How could I— how could we—"

"I do love them." He put his hand under her chin and tilted her face to his. "But I love you in a way I never imagined I could love anyone." Another deep breath. Hell, it was a good thing he was sitting. He'd spent the whole day thinking about this. He knew what he wanted. Nothing would change that. Then, how come his knees were knocking together? "Savannah McRae, will you be my wife?"

She stared at him in shock. "What?"

"Marry me as soon as we get to Vegas. I don't want to wait. We've waited too long as it is." His hands tightened on her shoulders. "I adore you, Savannah. I want to spend my life with you. I'll make you happy, I swear it. Are you worried about what this will do to your sister? Don't, sweetheart. We'll bring her to live with us. Or move her where she can get the best treatment.'' His voice grew rough. ''Damn it, Just-Savannah, say something!''

Savannah's eyes filled with tears, but they were the kind he'd prayed he'd see.

''Yes,'' she said, ''oh, yes, yes—''

He didn't let her say anything more. His mouth was already on hers.

THE WEDDING CEREMONY didn't take very long, but it was perfect.

Sean bought her a dozen pink roses, held her hand tightly in his while they took their vows.

''I love you with all my heart,'' he said once they were man and wife, and Savannah smiled into his eyes and kissed him.

His family had already gathered by the time they arrived at the Desert Song Hotel. The party wasn't until the next night, but they wanted some time alone together.

They were just what Savannah had expected they'd be.

They were nothing like she'd expected they'd be.

But they definitely were stunned when Sean drew her forward and introduced her as his wife. Nobody moved, nobody said a word. Then Mary Elizabeth laughed and kissed her on both cheeks.

''My son made me a promise,'' she said, and shot a sly look at Sean. ''And he's a man who keeps his promises. Welcome, Savannah. It's lovely meeting a new O'Connell.''

They all surrounded her then. His sisters, who weren't proper or stuffy at all. His sisters-in-law, who were as down to earth as they could be. His brothers-in-law, who could have been two nice men from anywhere instead of the billionaires they were. Dan, his stepfather, hugged her and said it was remarkable how he kept gaining new daughters.

Only his brothers seemed a little reserved.

They were polite and welcomed her to the fold. But all that evening, all the next day, she caught them checking her out with quick glances. Looking at each other in a way that was disconcerting.

"Is this for real?" she heard the one named Keir mutter to the one named Cullen.

Was what for real? What did they know?

Savannah told herself it didn't matter. She had Sean. He loved her. She loved him. What could possibly hurt her now?

THE ANSWER CAME in a phone call an hour before the big party. The family, all but Mary Elizabeth, was gathered in the living room.

"We told her she has to make an entrance," Megan said. "Actually, we arranged for a big surprise."

Fallon nodded. "One of the guests is a singer Ma adores. The second she steps into the room, he's going to launch into *Happy Birth—*"

"Savannah?" Bree was coming toward them with the phone in her hand. "Sorry to interrupt, guys, but there's a call for Savannah."

"For me? Are you sure? Nobody knows I'm here."

Bree smiled and handed her the phone. "Somebody does."

Savannah put the phone to her ear. "Hello, *chérie,*" Alain said softly.

She felt the blood drain from her head. She looked around her, half-afraid he might be in the room. Sean caught her eye. *Something?* he mouthed. She forced a smile and shook her head. "Just a last minute—a last minute gift I ordered for your mother," she said, and went out on the terrace. She slid the door shut and took a deep breath. "What do you want, Alain?"

"Only what you were supposed to do a month ago, *chérie*. The public humiliation of Sean O'Connell."

She closed her eyes. "That's not going to happen."

"Ah, but it will, Savannah. And I'm indebted to you for setting things up so nicely." He chuckled. "A big family gathering, lots of important guests arriving from all parts of the globe…"

"How do you know all this?"

"I know everything, *chérie,* including the fact that you will do as you're told."

"No." Savannah clutched the terrace railing with her free hand. "Whatever you want, I won't do it. Do you understand, Alain? Everything has changed."

"Not everything," he said with a soft laugh she knew she'd never forget. There was a brief silence and then she heard a sound that almost drove her to her knees.

Her sister's incoherent weeping.

IN THE END, it was easy. When your life hung by a thread, you could do anything.

Alain told her what to do, and she did it. *And don't disconnect,* he said. *I want to hear every word.*

Savannah went back into the O'Connell apartment. It was crowding up; the first early guests had arrived. A quick look showed her that Mary Elizabeth had obeyed her daughters and hadn't yet appeared.

Savannah offered a silent prayer of thanks. Mary Elizabeth's absence was the only kindness fate would show tonight.

There was a microphone at the front of the room. For the singer, for those who wanted to offer toasts…

For what Savannah had to do next.

She went straight to it. "Everyone?" she said, and when her voice quavered, she cleared her throat and said it again. "Everyone?"

Faces turned toward her. People smiled. Surely, she was going to be the first to offer good wishes. Sean looked surprised but happy as he came through the crowd toward her.

"My wife," he said, slipping his arm around her waist. "I was going to introduce her to you all, but I guess she couldn't wait."

People laughed. Savannah swayed. "Savannah?" Sean murmured.

She stepped away from him. "My name," she said in a clear voice, "is Savannah McRae."

"It's Savannah O'Connell," Sean said, with a little smile that told her he didn't know what was happening but he'd play along.

"It's Savannah O'Connell," she said into the suddenly hushed room, "only because—because Sean O'Connell thinks that the best way to keep a promise is to lie to the people he supposedly loves."

A murmur swept the room. Jaws fell. Eyes widened. "Savannah," Sean said urgently, "don't." He reached for her but she slapped his hand away.

"A year ago, Sean O'Connell cheated at cards and walked off with a million dollars that wasn't his."

The murmur grew louder. She had to raise her voice to continue.

"I know this because—because my lover is the man he cheated. And now—and now, he's cheated again. Sean hired me to play the part of his fiancée. Of his wife. He paid me five hundred thousand dollars to—to make his mother, to make all of you think that—that he's a good and dutiful son. He isn't. He's a liar. A cheat. He's a—a—"

Sean went crazy. He caught Savannah around the waist, threw her over his shoulder and carried her from the room. It was like the night he'd carried her from the *Lorelei*.

He'd been angry at her then.

Now, he wanted to kill her.

It took all his self-control to get her out the door and drop her on her feet next to an elevator.

"Sean," she whispered, but he didn't even look at her.

"One question," he growled. "Just tell me one thing, sugar..."

Was it all a lie? That was what he wanted to ask her, but what for? He already knew the answer.

"Get the hell out of my sight," he said, "before I put my hands around your throat."

His brothers were waiting at the door. Without a word, they flanked him and headed for the fire stairs. Nobody spoke through the long descent. Nobody spoke as they headed for a corridor behind the reception desk and the office that had been Keir's when he ran the hotel.

Cullen shut the door. Keir opened a cupboard, dug around inside and took out a bottle of whiskey and some glasses. He poured; the brothers picked up the glasses and tossed down the whiskey. Sean held his glass out again and Keir refilled it.

"Well?" he finally said. "Aren't you going to tell me what a stupid son of a bitch I am?"

"You're a stupid son of a bitch," Cullen said, but without any heat.

"Yeah," Sean said roughly, and tried to swallow past the lump in his throat.

"Was she the same one?" Keir said. "The hooker you told us about?"

"Watch your mou..." Sean's shoulders drooped. He'd

told enough lies, especially to himself. "Yeah. The same one."

"And you hired her for tonight?"

"Yes. At first."

His brothers looked at each other. "What's that supposed to mean?"

"I hired her." Sean hesitated. "Then I fell in love with her. And married her. And if either of you tells me again that I'm a stupid son of a bitch—" His voice broke. He saw his brothers' horrified looks and he turned away. "Listen, I'm going to go for a walk, okay? No, you guys stay here. I want to be alone for a while."

"Sean—"

"Kid—"

The door swung open. Their stepfather looked from one brother to the other, then set his gaze on Sean.

"I got a trace on that phone call your, uh, Savannah got just before she—I got a trace."

"Pays to have an ex-cop in the family," Cullen said with a tight smile.

"It came from—"

"A yacht off an island in the Bahamas." Sean nodded. "Thanks, Dan, but I could have saved you the trouble."

"It came from the Shalimar Hotel."

Sean stared at the older man. "The Shalimar two blocks from here?"

"That's right. So I called the head of security over there, asked some questions…" Dan pulled a notepad from his pocket. "Call was placed from a suite. Number 937. Occupants are one Alain Beaumont and a young girl." He glanced at the pad again. "A Melisande McRae."

It took a second to register. "Missy?" Sean said, staring at Dan.

"Also…maybe you don't want to hear this, son, but the

front desk called me, said there was a young woman sobbing her heart out as she ran through the lobby. One of our people went out after her, got to her just before she jumped into a taxi. 'Can I do anything for you?' our guy said, and this girl—blond and blue, five-seven, maybe 110—the girl looked at him and said nobody could do anything for her, that her—this is a quote, son—that her world had just ended and—Sean? Sean, you want us to come with you?''

"Let him go alone," Keir said softly, putting a hand on Dan's arm. He waited until Sean raced from the room. Then he flashed a tight smile at his brother and his stepfather. "But I'll be damned if I can see any harm in us following him."

VEGAS WAS WHERE he'd grown up.

It was easy to get to the Shalimar, easy to go straight through the lobby to the elevators as if he were just another guest. It was even easier to find the door to suite 937, knock and say "Room Service" in a way that sounded authentic.

What wasn't easy was to keep from pounding his fist into Beaumont's face when the man opened the door.

"I didn't order room ser—" he said, but the words turned into a terrified squeal as Sean kicked the door shut, grabbed him by the throat and shoved him back inside.

"Where is she?"

Beaumont clawed at his throat. "You're choking me!"

Sean slammed him against the wall. "Where is she, you slimy son of a bitch? Tell me or so help me, I'll—"

"Sean?"

He swung around. Savannah stood in the doorway to a bedroom. Her eyes were red, her nose was running, and he knew she had never been more beautiful to him than she was at this moment. He could see a girl on the bed behind her, sleeping peacefully.

"Sean?" Savannah said again, and he flung Beaumont to the floor like the vermin he was and went to her.

"Savannah. Are you all right?"

"Yes. I'm— How did you find me?"

"Your sister. Missy. Is she all right, too?"

"She's fine. She cried when she saw me..." Savannah's voice broke. "I thought I'd lost you forever."

Sean opened his arms and she flew into them. He held her tightly against his heart.

"It's okay," he crooned. "Sweetheart, it's okay, I promise. Everything's going to be fine."

"He took Missy. He said—he said he was going to leave her at a place. A—a horrible place..."

"Hush, baby. I'm here now. I'll take care of everything."

Savannah buried her face against Sean's throat, her tears hot on his skin. From the corner of his eye, he saw Beaumont rising to his knees.

"Don't," he said softly, "not unless you want your face rearranged."

"Sean." Savannah looked up. "Sean, I love you with all my heart. I had to say those things. Beaumont—"

Sean kissed her until he felt some of the tension begin to ease from her body.

"I know you do. I should never have believed any of that stuff you said."

She gave a watery laugh. "I'm a good actress, remember? You told me that yourself."

"Please," Beaumont whimpered. "Sean. Mr. O'Connell. This is all a terrible misunderstanding."

There was a knock at the door. "Sean? Sean, you in there?"

Sean grinned, reached back and opened the door. Keir, Cullen and Dan stepped into the room. They looked at

Beaumont, cowering on the floor, then at Sean and Savannah, wrapped in each other's arms.

"Looks like you need somebody to take out the trash," Keir said.

"Please," Beaumont whispered, "gentlemen, I beg you…"

"Dan?" Sean shot Beaumont one last cold look. "Dan, your pals in law enforcement might be interested in knowing how this man took a minor from a sanitarium without the consent of her legal guardian, and what plans he had for her next."

Dan grinned. "How charming. Mr. Beaumont, I think we have several things to discuss."

Cullen looked at Sean. "You gonna be okay?"

Sean nodded. "I'll be fine."

He looked at Savannah, too. "Anything we can do to help?"

"My sister… I'd like a doctor to see her, just to make sure she's all right. And—and if you would be kind enough to find a room for her for tonight—"

"A room?" Keir snorted. "We have an entire hotel. Come to think of it, Cassie and I have a room adjoining ours that would be perfect, especially if we arrange for a nurse to keep her company. That sound okay?"

"It sounds wonderful." Savannah laughed and wiped the back of her hand across her eyes. "*You're* wonderful. All of you. How can I ever make up for tonight?"

"Just keep making the kid happy," Cullen said, smiling. "That's all we ask. Right, BB?"

Keir rolled his eyes. "You call me Big Brother again, pal, you're in trouble."

The brothers grinned, grabbed Beaumont by the arms and hauled him from the room. Dan was already on his cell phone, making arrangements with the district attorney.

"We'll send a car for you," Cullen called over his shoulder.

Once they were alone, Sean did his best to look serious. "Here's the thing," he said sternly. "You always have to tell me the truth, even if it's bad. That's what you should have done the minute that bastard phoned."

Savannah sighed. "I know. But I was afraid. I didn't know what he'd do to Missy. That was why I'd agreed to play you in the first place. Alain made threats…"

"Yeah," Sean said tightly, "well, those days are over."

"And I couldn't tell you. I was afraid you'd do something crazy and get hurt."

Sean kissed her. "The only thing that could ever hurt me," he said gruffly, "would be losing you."

Smiling, she looped her arms around his neck. "I'll never leave you, Sean O'Connell. You're stuck with me. We're married, remember?"

"Damned right we are," he said gruffly, and drew her closer. "And I've been thinking… A married man needs to settle down. Get a job—"

"A job?"

"Well, maybe not a job, exactly. Start a business. Hotels. Casinos. I'm not sure." He kissed her. "You'll have to work out the details with me."

Savannah laughed softly. "My pleasure, O'Connell."

"And I've been thinking about that ceremony we had this afternoon…"

"It was lovely," she said dreamily. "Despite Elvis."

Sean grinned. "It was, but, I don't know, maybe a once in a lifetime event should be a little more dignified."

"Dignified? You?" she said, but she smiled.

His arms tightened around her. "How would you feel if we did it all over again? The works. You in a white gown, me in a tux, my whole impossible family doing their best to drive us nuts... What do you think, Just-Savannah?''

"I think you're going to make me cry," she whispered.

"I'll never make you cry," he promised, "except with happiness."

Savannah raised her mouth to his and Sean kissed her until they were alone again in a world of their own making.

A world that would always and forever be real.

THE SICILIAN
MARRIAGE

SANDRA MARTON

CHAPTER ONE

GIANNI FIRELLI was restless.

It was six o'clock on a warm May evening and he'd been trapped at the party celebrating the birth of Stefano Lucchesi's child for what seemed forever.

The room was too crowded, the voices too loud, and if anyone stuck one more squalling baby under his nose, he was going to forget that the expected response to such an affront on a man's eardrums was a smile. Between babies-in-bellies and babies-in-blankets, there were almost enough kids here to field a football team.

It looked as if Stefano had married into a fertile clan.

As if that weren't enough, an hour ago, Tomasso Massini, one of Gianni's oldest friends, had shown up with his wife. His extremely pregnant wife.

You, too, Tommy? Gianni had thought even as he shook his hand, kissed the wife and said all the right things.

The sexy blonde with the endless legs was the only diversion Gianni had seen, but she'd turned out to be as rude as she was easy on the eyes.

Sighing, he cast a surreptitious glance at his watch. Another few minutes and he could make a polite exit. Until then, he'd smile, say the right things, and try to figure out what in God's name had impelled Stefano to give up his freedom and become not just a husband but also a daddy.

Gianni had nothing against marriage or babies. Someday, he supposed, he'd settle down, marry and have a couple of children of his own, but that was way in the future.

Not yet, though. It was much too soon.

Stefano and Tomasso seemed happy enough, but that didn't keep him from puzzling over why two sane men would give up their freedom when they were only in their thirties.

Was it something in the air?

He'd almost said that to Tomasso, but you didn't joke with a man whose wife had a belly the size of a boulder, not even if you'd known him since you were ten. He, Tommy and Stefano had grown up together on the crowded streets of Manhattan's Little Italy. Their paths didn't cross often anymore but they were there for each other when it mattered.

Obviously babies mattered.

Somebody—one of Stefano's new brothers-in-law—brushed past him, a screaming infant in his arms. A smell wafted from the child.

It wasn't baby powder.

"Sorry," the guy said, and grinned.

Gianni managed a smile in return. "No problem," he said, and headed for the terrace where he took a deep, deep breath of fresh air. Okay. He'd stay out here where he could enjoy a little quiet along with the view of Central Park forty stories below and think about whether he wanted to see Lynda tonight without having to pretend he was delighted that his two best friends had obviously lost their minds.

Maybe he should have stayed with his instincts and opted out of this party. He'd been tempted to send a gift from Tiffany's, tuck in a note explaining how sorry he was he couldn't make it in person, etc., etc., etc., but how could he not show up at this celebration for Stefano's child? He'd missed the wedding—bad weather that shut down all the airports had seen to that.

So, he was here.

The blonde with the up-to-her-ears legs was here, too.

Gianni scowled. Was he back to that? Well, there was nothing else to think about. The lady had made an impression. A negative one. And, since he hadn't come up with much else to do after he'd made the rounds, his thoughts naturally returned to her.

He'd had a toothache once. Try as he had, he couldn't keep the tip of his tongue from returning to the offending molar.

This was the same ridiculous thing.

Gianni looked into the Lucchesis' enormous living room. There she was now, talking animatedly with Tomasso's wife, Karen, as if they were old friends. She smiled, she touched Karen's arm, she even grinned.

She hadn't even managed a tilt of the lips for him.

Not that he cared. She wasn't his type at all. He preferred his women petite, dark-haired and quintessentially feminine. Lynda met those standards. She was also all curves, where the blonde was as skinny as a boy. Lynda smiled when a man smiled at her. The blonde didn't. She meted out favors with the stinginess of a miser opening his purse.

A waiter stepped out on the terrace. "Something to drink, sir?"

Gianni nodded, took a glass of red wine from the tray and raised it to his lips.

He and the blonde had arrived in the lobby at the same time. The doors of the private elevator for the penthouse were closing when he heard a voice call out.

"Hey," a woman said.

A slim hand had thrust between the doors.

Gianni hit the button that reversed the doors' direction. They opened, and he saw the blonde.

Not my type, was his first thought.

He gave her a polite smile. "Sorry. I didn't see you coming."

She gave him a long look. Her expression was one of suspicion.

"This is a private elevator," she said.

Gianni's smile tilted. "Indeed it is."

"It only goes to the penthouse."

"How convenient," he said dryly. "That happens to be where I'm going."

"Did the doorman—"

"Perhaps you'd like to see my driver's license, passport and birth certificate," he said, his smile fading. "Or perhaps I should ask to see yours."

That, at least, had put a stain of color across the arcs of her high cheekbones.

"I'm going to the Lucchesi party."

"So am I. Or, at least, I will once you step inside and the doors shut."

She entered the elevator and stood beside him, eyes straight ahead. Okay. He'd decided to give it another try.

"Are you a friend of Fallon's?"

"No," she said, without looking at him.

"Stefano's?"

"No."

"Then are you with—"

"I don't see that it's any of your affair," she said, still staring straight ahead. Then she turned toward him, her eyes cold as ice. "Besides, I'm not interested."

It was his turn to be the one whose face stung with heat.

"I assure you," he said, "I'm not—"

The elevator stopped, the doors opened. Gianni stepped out first without waiting for the woman to precede him. It was a good thing the car opened directly into Stefano's foyer. He wasn't sure what he'd have done if they'd ended up in front of an apartment door and he'd had to decide whether to ring the bell or tell her she could go straight to hell.

Pathetic, he knew. Even more pathetic that she'd reduced him to such childish musings. He'd almost told her what he was thinking but he'd spotted Stefano coming toward him and he'd smiled, only to have the blonde sweep past him, give a little squeal of delight and run straight into Stefano's arms.

"Stefano," she'd cried happily, and Gianni, mouth thinning in disgust, had let himself blend into the crowd.

Apparently the Ice Princess reserved her smile solely for a favored few.

Now, watching her, he saw her flash that smile for Stefano's wife and baby daughter as she took the child from Fallon's arms. He saw her lips purse as if she were cooing. The baby kicked its legs and the blonde not only smiled again, but she threw back her head and laughed.

It was quite a laugh. Husky. Throaty. Under the right circumstances, he suspected that laugh would be sexy as hell.

Gianni narrowed his eyes.

He could see he'd made some errors about the woman. They were unimportant, given the circumstances, but he was a man who liked to get the details straight. Her hair wasn't blond, it was half a dozen shades of palest gold. And she wasn't skinny. Slender, yes, but with rounded hips and a nicely defined backside.

And when, still laughing, she hoisted the baby high in the air, her breasts lifted and only a blind man wouldn't have noticed that they were round and full...

And not confined by a bra.

The pale green silk dress clung to her body just enough so he could see the outline of her nipples.

What were they like? Small? Large? What color would they be? Rosebud-pink, he imagined, like her mouth. Soft to the touch, silken and responsive. They'd tighten under his caress, bloom under the laving of his tongue...

Hell, what was he doing?

This was a christening, not a stag party. And wasn't it a good thing he was on the terrace so he could turn his back to the room, because his wandering thoughts were having an all-too-predictable effect on his anatomy.

Gianni concentrated on the Manhattan skyline, bathed now in the variegated orange hues of the setting sun, but thinking about the colors of things wasn't a good idea right now. It took him straight back to the blonde's breasts.

Green was a better color. The green of the boxwood, growing in some of the terrace's many planters.

The green silk of the woman's dress and the way it molded to her...

"She's beautiful, isn't she?"

Stefano had come up beside him, grinning, holding out a bottle of wine. Gianni nodded and held out his glass for a refill.

"Was it that obvious?" he said with a rueful smile.

"Are you kidding? Of course."

Gianni sighed. "Thanks a lot."

"Hey, I'm only speaking the truth."

"Easy for you to say, Lucchesi."

"Well, sure, but who wouldn't react to such beauty?"

"Let's not go overboard here," Gianni said. "She's attractive, assuming you like the type."

"Attractive?"

"Yes. You know, she's got all the right equipment in all the right places." Stefano was looking at him as if he'd lost his mind. He thought back to how the blonde had greeted his old friend, married or not. "But that doesn't make her gorgeous."

"That's a joke, right?"

"Why would I joke? I'm dead serious. Plus, she's got all the charm of a tarantula."

Stefano's expression turned grim. "You'd better be glad

you and I've been friends since P.S. 26, Firelli, or I'd pin
your ears back.''

"What wrong with you, man? You'd take me on because
I don't agree a woman's gorgeous?''

"Damned right I would. This particular woman is—this
woman is…'' Stefano's eyebrows rose again. "What
woman?''

Was this what happened to a man when he married and
had a child? Did he lose his sanity as well as his freedom?

"The blonde, of course,'' Gianni said impatiently. "The
one who greeted you with such, uh, warmth…and, by the
way, doesn't Fallon object to that kind of thing?''

Stefano's eyes widened. Then he threw back his head and
roared with laughter.

"Wonderful,'' Gianni said coldly. "I'm glad you think
this is—''

"The blonde,'' Stefano gasped. "Oh my God, the
blonde!''

"That's it.'' Gianni slapped his glass on a nearby table
and started toward the doors.

Stefano grabbed his arm. "Where are you going, you idiot?''

"Lucchesi,'' Gianni said through his teeth, "I'd hate to
wipe up the floor with you while your guests watch, but so
help me—''

"I was talking about my daughter!''

"Yes. And I told you…'' Gianni blinked. "Your daughter?'' He felt the color rise in his face. "You were talking
about—about—''

"About Cristina. Of course. And you thought I was talking about a woman.''

"Hell.'' Gianni turned away, leaned his arms on the terrace railing and stared blindly into the gathering dusk.
Things were going from bad to worse. "You're right,'' he
mumbled. "I'm an idiot.''

Stefano chuckled. "I'm happy we agree." The men fell silent for a minute. Then Stefano cleared his throat. "So, which blonde are we talking about?"

"It doesn't matter," Gianni said, waving his hand in dismissal. A couple of seconds went by. "The one who damned near threw herself into your arms when she got here."

"Not a very good description, Firelli. All women throw themselves into my arms."

Gianni chuckled. "Better not let your wife hear you say that."

"Better not let his wife hear what?" Fallon said, smiling as she joined the men. "Gianni, it's good to see you again."

Gianni smiled and kissed her cheek. "And you, Fallon. Motherhood has made you even lovelier. I wouldn't have thought that possible."

Fallon batted her lashes. "You Sicilians! You always know how to make a woman feel good."

"Some women," Stefano said. Fallon raised her eyebrows. "It seems one of our guests turned down the chance to have her name added to Gianni's little black book."

"Stefano," Gianni said warningly.

Stefano slipped his arm around his wife. "Come on, don't be shy. If you're interested in one of our guests—"

"I'm not," Gianni said quickly. "I only said—"

"Point her out," Fallon said. "I'll introduce you."

Gianni looked at Stefano, who was grinning from ear to ear. "Damn it, Lucchesi! Fallon, your husband's letting his imagination run away with him."

"I know who she is," Stefano said, as if Gianni weren't there.

"You don't," Gianni said quickly. How in hell had this gotten away from him so fast? "There must be half a dozen blondes at this party."

"But you said this one threw herself into my arms."

"And?"

"And that she was attractive." Stefano winked at his wife. "Attractive, mind you, but not beautiful."

"What," Gianni said coldly, "is your point?"

"My point," Stefano said smugly, "is that I know who she is." He paused, just long enough so that Fallon and Gianni gave him their full attention. "The lady in question is my sister-in-law."

Gianni stared at his old friend. "Your—"

"He was talking about Briana," Stefano told Fallon. "And why would a man who thinks a woman is attractive but not beautiful be fixated on her?"

"I am not fixated on her. I've never found that type of woman interest... Oh, hell. I'm killing myself here, aren't I?"

"Yes," Fallon said agreeably. She let go of her husband and linked her arm through Gianni's. "And the only way out is to let me introduce you to Bree so you can find just what, exactly, it is you never find interesting."

Stefano and Fallon were laughing, so he laughed, too, or tried to, as she all but dragged him into the crowded room. Thank God, he thought, after a quick look around. Bree or Briana, whatever her name was, was gone.

"I'd love to meet her," he said, lying through his teeth. "Too bad she seems to have left."

"She went upstairs to diaper the baby," Fallon said, heading for the curving staircase that led to the penthouse's upper level, "and I'm not going to let you back out of this."

"Fallon. Look, I'm sorry. I shouldn't have said what I said about your sister. I'm sure she's charming. Beautiful, too. And—"

"Bree," Fallon said, "there you are," and Gianni turned from his hostess and looked at the woman coming down the steps toward them.

He'd gotten it right the first time.

Briana O'Connell wasn't beautiful.

She was spectacular.

All that blond hair, tumbling over her shoulders to frame a face dominated by sea-blue eyes. That mouth, yes, rosebud-pink and just full enough to make him wonder how it would feel to sink into its soft warmth. The high breasts, slender waist, delicately rounded hips and long, hell, endless legs.

At least she wasn't trying to freeze him with a look. How could she, when she gave him a glance that lasted no more than a second?

"Bree, this is Gianni Firelli. Gianni, my baby sister, Bree."

"It's Briana," the blond vision said, and turned her attention to Fallon. "The baby fell asleep as soon as I put her in her bassinet. I left her with her nanny. Is that all right?"

"It's fine. Uh, Bree? Gianni's one of Stefano's oldest friends."

This time, Gianni got the full force of her icy gaze. "How nice for them both. If you'll excuse me…"

"Why should I excuse you?" he said, before he could stop himself. He stepped away from Fallon, moved closer to Briana and pitched his voice slow enough that only she would hear him. "Are you always so rude, or is this personal?"

Those deep blue eyes met his and suddenly he saw something in their depths, a flash of heat so intense it threatened to sear his soul.

"You flatter yourself," she whispered.

And then she was gone.

Gianni had never understood what people meant when they said their blood was boiling, but he understood it now. He stared after her, imagined the pleasure of going after her, grabbing her and shaking her until she begged for mercy…

Or of swinging her into his arms, carrying her away, taking her to a room where he could strip her of that green dress and that icy look, put his hands in her hair and kiss her until she was helpless and pleading for more...

"I'm terribly sorry, Gianni."

He blinked, focused his eyes on Fallon's face. She looked as shocked as he felt.

"Bree's not— She's not a rude person. I don't know what came over her."

Summoning a smile wasn't easy, but he managed. "It's all right."

"No, it's not. Look, let me go find her and—"

"No." His voice was sharp. Carefully he manufactured another smile and started over. "Really, Fallon, I'm not offended."

"Well, you should be. When I get her alone later—"

"Forget it. Maybe she had a difficult day."

"Bree? A difficult day?" Fallon gave a ladylike snort. "I don't know how. My sister doesn't do anything that might be considered difficult."

Except treat men as if they were contemptible, Gianni thought, but he wasn't going to say anything like that. Her sister's behavior wasn't Fallon's responsibility.

"Doesn't she have a job?"

"An endless succession of them. She's been a photographer, a travel consultant, a salesclerk, a game show research assistant..." Fallon smiled. "Our mother says she's still finding herself but to be honest, my other sister and I don't think she ever lost herself in the first place. She's just, well, flighty."

It was a nice way of saying Briana O'Connell was unreliable, not just rude and sullen. The woman wouldn't be any sane man's type, let alone his.

"Fallon," he said, taking his hostess's hands in his, "I've had a wonderful afternoon."

"You're not leaving?"

He smiled and brought her hands to his lips, pressed a light kiss to the back of each.

"I'm afraid I must. I have a dinner appointment this evening."

"Ah. Too bad. Stefano and I hoped you'd stay after the others left. He loves to talk about old times with you."

"Another time, I promise. Make my goodbyes to him, will you?"

"Yes, absolutely." Fallon linked her arm through his as they walked slowly through the foyer. "And Gianni... I'm really terribly sorry about my sister."

"No need. I've been rebuffed before."

Fallon laughed, turned to him and cupped his face in her hands.

"You're a bad liar, Gianni Firelli. We both know that there's not a woman alive who wouldn't do a maidenlike swoon if you smiled in her direction."

"From your lips to God's ear," he said lightly.

She laughed again, rose on her toes and pressed a demure kiss to his lips.

"It was good seeing you. And thank you for the beautiful gift for Cristina."

"My pleasure. *Ciao,* Fallon."

"Goodbye, Gianni."

The elevator was waiting. He stepped inside, kept smiling until the car doors closed. Then he let the scowl he'd been fighting darken his face as he took his cell phone from his pocket.

Lynda answered on the first ring. "Hello," she said in that breathless whisper that always made his muscles tighten.

Strangely enough, they didn't tighten this time.

"It's me."

"Gianni." Her whisper became a purr. "I hoped you'd call. Are you coming over?"

The elevator reached the lobby. He stepped briskly from the car, nodded to the doorman when he opened the door that led to the street.

"Let's have dinner."

"Of course, darling. Are we going out? Shall I put on something pretty... Or shall I stay as I am? I just took a bath and all I'm wearing is that pink silk robe you gave me."

Pink. Rosebud-pink, like Briana O'Connell's mouth.

"Gianni? Can you hear me?"

He cleared his throat. "I hear you, Lynda."

"What do you want to do? We could try that new restaurant everyone's talking about. You know, Green Meadows. It's supposed to be spectacular."

Green, like the dress that outlined Briana's supple body. Spectacular, like her magnificent face...

"Gianni?"

All at once, Gianni knew what he wanted to do. It had nothing to do with Briana O'Connell. Nothing at all. It was just something that had been coming for a few weeks, and it was time he dealt with it.

"Lynda?"

"Yes?"

"Don't bother making reservations. I'll be there in twenty minutes." He paused. "And get dressed," he added gently. "All right?"

He heard the swift intake of her breath. "Gianni? Is everything all right?"

"Twenty minutes," he said, and pressed the disconnect button.

An hour later, he left Lynda's apartment for the last time. She was crying and he hated knowing he'd made that happen but at the very start of their relationship they'd agreed neither of them was interested in commitment, and that when the time came to end things, they'd do it with honesty.

"I know," she'd said tearfully, when he'd reminded her of that, "but I thought things had changed."

Nothing had changed. It never did. Women always said one thing at the start of a relationship and another at its end.

Gianni sighed. Darkness had finally claimed the city and he was eager to get home, take a long shower and put the strange day behind him. He thought of hailing a cab, then decided he'd rather walk.

Tomorrow, he'd send Lynda something to cheer her. A bracelet, perhaps. Something expensive enough to assuage her tears and his guilty conscience because honesty was one thing, but dissolving a relationship with no warning was another.

The truth was, he really hadn't thought about ending things until a little while ago. He'd been satisfied enough until he'd gone to that damned party. Until he'd looked into the eyes of a woman who didn't seem to care that he existed and saw, in those eyes, something else.

That one swift, blinding flash of heat.

A sharp wind blew down 57th Street, surprisingly cold after the warmth of the day. Gianni turned up the collar of his jacket, tucked his hands deep in his pockets and picked up his pace.

CHAPTER TWO

"WHY DIDN'T YOU like him?"

Bree looked up from her salad. There it was, the question she'd been waiting for since Fallon phoned and asked her out to lunch. The only surprise was that it had taken her sister a week to make the call and almost half an hour to ask the question.

"Who?" Bree said innocently. Why give away more than was necessary?

"You know who. Gianni Firelli."

Bree popped a grape tomato into her mouth and chewed contemplatively. She had two choices. She could say "Who?" and pretend not to know what her sister was talking about, or she could tell her to mind her own business. Neither response was going to get her very far. Growing up, she'd learned what that determined tilt of her eldest sister's chin meant.

The best thing was to tackle this head-on.

"I assume," she said, putting down her fork, "we're talking about the fact that I didn't fall at the man's feet."

"Fall at his feet? A simple 'Hello, nice to meet you,' would have done it."

"I said 'hello.'"

"You know what I mean, Bree. You almost took his head off."

"I did not."

"Yes, you did. I can't believe you behaved so badly!"

Behaved so badly? Bree's chin lifted, just like Fallon's. "And *I* can't believe you still think I'm six years old."

"You were rude."

"I was honest."

"Being rude isn't being honest."

"Your opinion, not mine. Are you going to eat that last croissant?"

"No. And don't change the subject."

"I'm not changing anything. I just don't want to be badgered."

"Your manners were appalling."

"I don't know how to break this to you," Bree said sweetly, "but you're my sister, not my mother."

"And a good thing, too. If Ma's plane hadn't landed late, she'd have been at the party in time to see you in action. Can you imagine how she'd have reacted?"

"No." Bree's tone had gone from sugary to saccharine. "Why don't you tell me?"

Obviously Big Sister hadn't expected a reply to what she'd meant as a rhetorical question.

"Well, she'd have—she'd have—"

"Sent me to my room without supper? Docked my allowance?"

The sisters glared at each other. Then Fallon sighed.

"Okay, maybe I'm overreacting."

"Hallelujah," Bree said, picking up her fork again.

"But you really were abrupt."

"I wanted to be sure Mr. Firelli got the message."

"Which was?"

"That I wasn't interested."

"Gianni's a very nice guy."

"No doubt."

"And he's good-looking."

"Good-looking?" Bree shrugged, put down her fork and reached for the butter. "I suppose."

"Give me a break! You know he's good-looking."

"What I know," Bree replied, breaking off a piece of croissant and buttering it, "is that Gianni Firelli is gorgeous."

"Well, of course he is. He's…" Fallon blinked. "What did you say?"

"You heard me. He's, what, six-one? Six-two? Shoulders out to here, solid muscle straight down to his toes, black hair, green eyes, a face like a Greek god's—"

"Italian," Fallon said, staring at her.

"A minor detail. The point is, the man's incredible. An out-and-out hottie." Bree reached for her glass of white wine and smiled at the dumbstruck expression on her sister's face. "Give me a break, Fallon. I'm not dead! Did you think I hadn't noticed?"

"I don't know what I thought," Fallon said, sitting back in the booth. "Tell me more."

"What more is there? I'm sure there were a dozen women at your party who'd have happily killed for the chance to be introduced to him."

"But?"

"But, as I already told Karen—"

"Karen?" Fallon said, bewildered.

"Karen Massini. Tomasso's wife."

"Oh. Right. I keep forgetting you and she knew each other before I married Stefano."

"Only for years and years," Bree said, rolling her eyes. "We were friends in college. Close friends. Then she married Tomasso, moved to California and we lost touch, but ever since she got pregnant and they moved back to New York—"

"Yes, okay, I remember," Fallon said, impatient to return to the current topic. "So, you and Karen talked about Gianni?"

"She said she'd noticed him looking at me and... You know how these things go."

Fallon wanted to reach across the table and shake her sister. *Don't try to play matchmaker, cara,* her husband had told her at breakfast. *Gianni and Briana didn't connect. End of story.* Stefano had taken her in his arms. *Not everyone is lucky enough to fall in love at first sight.*

No. Not in love, perhaps, but something had happened between Stefano's old friend and her baby sister. Fallon was certain. Karen wasn't the only one who'd noticed the way he'd looked at Bree. And the way Bree had looked at him, even as she was giving him the brush-off.

"No," she said carefully, "I don't know how these things go. What did Karen say?"

"Oh, I don't remember, exactly." Bree patted her lips with her napkin and pushed away her plate. "Something about me taking pity on the guy and at least giving him a smile."

"You see? You were so impolite that people noticed. Poor Gianni."

"Poor Gianni," Bree said, the words coated with sarcasm, "needs your sympathy the way a bear needs a fur coat. He has a mistress."

"Oh."

"Yes. Oh. A mistress, and he was coming on to me anyway. What do you think of him now? Or didn't he bother mentioning that we'd met in the elevator and he tried a pickup line before the doors had the chance to shut?"

"Well," Fallon said, thinking back to the first time she and her husband met, "well—"

"Look, there's just something about the guy I don't like, okay? End of story."

"Bree. Honey, you've gone through how many relationships? Sooner or later, there's always something about the guy you don't like, whatever that means. Don't make a face. I know you're a big girl—"

"An adult," Bree said coolly, "but neither you nor Megan seem able to hang on to that thought."

"We just want you to be happy. To find someone to love."

"Lust isn't love."

Fallon blushed. "Sometimes it's the way love begins."

"Well, not for me." Bree's expression turned dreamy. "I'll meet the right man someday. He'll be gentle and sweet. He'll never do anything to upset me. He might not stand out in a crowd, but—"

"What about passion?"

"Sex isn't all it's cracked up to be."

"Passion isn't only about sex," Fallon said softly, "but if you think that making love isn't special, you haven't been with the right man."

"Sex Ed 101," Bree said and, just as she'd hoped, her sister laughed. Good. She really didn't want to get into this topic. "Don't worry about me, okay? And lunch is on me. No arguments."

Fallon watched Briana rummage in her handbag. "Bree?" she said, so softly that Bree looked up. "This passion thing. I know you. You're full of fire. Full of life. Why would you want to deny it?"

"Amazing," Bree replied, trying for a light tone. "Karen made the same speech. Do the two of you really think you know what's best for me?"

"I barely know Karen, but I admire her insight. Did you ever consider we might be right? Maybe you're kidding yourself. Maybe what you really want is a man who'll sweep you off your feet?"

Briana's eyes flashed. Fallon had pushed too far. It was time for the truth.

"Sweep me off my feet, huh? Like our father did to our

mother?'' She leaned forward, all attempts at good humor gone. ''I was the baby, so maybe you think I don't remember, but I do. Ma struggling to pretend it was okay with her whatever he did, smiling when she wanted to cry, never saying an unkind word to him or about him.''

''Bree—''

''Our mother turned herself into a doormat because of that 'sweeping her off her feet' crap. She lived for our father, lived *through* him, and if you think I'm going to let myself in for the same nonsense, you're crazy!''

''Is that how you think of me?'' Fallon said quietly. ''As a doormat for my husband?''

''No! I didn't mean—''

''Stefano swept me off my feet. Qasim swept Megan off hers, and one look at our sisters-in-law and I could tell it was the same for them. We're all head over heels, passionately in love with our husbands. Are we all doormats?''

''No, no, I never…'' Bree took a steadying breath. ''This is pointless,'' she said. ''I'm just not looking for passion. If it works for you, great, but I know myself. I want—''

''Something quiet.''

''Yes.''

''Something undemanding.''

''There's nothing wrong with that!''

''Something safe,'' Fallon said softly, and reached for Bree's hand. ''What are you afraid of, sis?''

''Nothing,'' Briana said quickly, and even as she said it, she knew she was lying.

She *was* afraid. Of the dreams she'd had about Gianni Firelli each night since the party. Of the way he'd made her feel. Of that one cataclysmic instant when she'd looked into his eyes and felt the earth tilt under her feet.

Of losing herself, her dreams, her hopes, her very being, in the fires of passion.

MAY BECAME JUNE, and June slipped into July.

The days were hot and muggy. New Yorkers who could afford it abandoned the city in droves. You were more likely to bump into your Fifth Avenue neighbor on the beaches in the Hamptons or on village greens in the Connecticut hills than in the city.

Gianni didn't notice the heat. He was immersed in a trial that was finally nearing its conclusion. It had been a complicated case, one that required his personal attention. He'd gone back and forth to the coast several times, even now, in the trial's final hours. Days took on a numbing similarity when you spent them on airplanes.

Invitations came in, as they always did: dinner parties at the beach, long weekends in the country. He hadn't dated anyone since the break-up with Lynda. Word had gotten out and hostesses everywhere were doing their best to inveigle him into meeting eligible women, but he wasn't in the mood. He wasn't in the mood for parties, either. Not since May. Not since Briana O'Connell had treated him with a curtness that had bordered on contempt. He needed closure.

Entering his penthouse on a Friday evening, tired after another round of flights and depositions, Gianni grimaced at that overused word. Closure was the feel-good term of the decade.

In this case, though, it was true.

He shrugged off his jacket, undid his tie and the buttons on his shirt as he made his way to the bedroom.

Lack of closure was why he couldn't get what had happened out of his mind. He was furious with himself that he hadn't told the lady what he thought of her, but how could he? He'd been a guest in Stefano's home, and she was Stefano's sister-in-law.

Gianni tossed his cuff links on the dresser, added his wallet and change, peeled down to his briefs and started for the shower before remembering the heavy vellum envelope the doorman had given him. It had been hand-delivered.

Gianni eyed the envelope narrowly. It was, surely, some kind of invitation. The delivery by messenger, the vellum stock were dead giveaways. Well, whatever he'd been invited to, he wasn't going. He wasn't in the mood for people and small talk but someone, somewhere was waiting for an answer and he believed in being polite even if...

Hell.

He tore open the envelope and felt his bad mood dissolve. Tomasso and Karen had had their baby. A girl. His smile turned into a grin. They were having a Welcome to the World party for the child. Karen's idea, without question. Gianni didn't know her well but from what he'd observed and from what Tomasso said, Karen was the antithesis of her pragmatic husband. She was day to his night, Tomasso had told him with the kind of smile that made it clear it was a winning combination.

Gianni's grin faded. Damn it, the party was tonight.

Sighing, he shut his eyes and rubbed the back of his neck. Lord, he was tired. The last thing he was in the mood for was a party, but another life had come into the world and even if he couldn't yet understand the appeal of fatherhood, he wanted to clap Tomasso on the back, kiss Karen and wish them well.

Gianni dropped the invitation on the dresser and headed for the shower.

Tonight, at least, nobody would try to play matchmaker, not with the baby the center of attention.

Better still, there wasn't a snowball's chance in hell he'd run into Briana O'Connell.

"Hallelujah," he muttered, and stepped under the spray.

So MUCH for snowballs and hell.

He ran into the Ice Princess just minutes after walking

into the party. At least, he would have if he hadn't spotted her and come to a screeching halt.

She was standing with a group of people, her back to him, but that didn't matter. The hair tumbling down her back, the endless legs, showcased by heels so spiked they should have been declared a hazard to a man's health, were dead giveaways.

All her attention was focused on a guy doing his best to make her laugh. Damned if he wasn't succeeding.

Gianni felt his muscles tense. This woman laughed easily for anybody but him.

What was she doing here? Tomasso, he thought grimly, and just then, Tomasso had the misfortune to stroll by. Gianni grabbed his shoulder and glared.

"Did you invite her?"

"Invite who?"

"Damn it, Tomasso... No. You wouldn't do that to me. It was Fallon."

"It was Fallon what?" Tomasso said, his bewilderment so genuine that Gianni knew he was blameless.

"Fallon who put Karen up to this. To inviting Briana O'Connell." Gianni jerked his head in Bree's direction. "Stefano's wife is the only one who'd—"

"Nobody put Karen up to anything. Briana is Karen's best friend."

It was Gianni's turn to look shocked. "Her best friend?"

"Well, they'd been out of touch for a few years, but yeah, best pals, way back when. They went to college together. Roomed together. They were sorority sisters. You know, the whole nine yards." Tomasso raised an eyebrow. "What's the problem?"

"Nothing," Gianni said wearily. "There's no problem."

"You sure?" Tomasso offered a friendly leer. "You and she have something going on?"

"Only if you'd describe a spider as having something

going on with a fly.'' Gianni laughed and slung his arm around the other man's shoulders. ''How about taking me to meet that new daughter of yours?''

The baby was cute, as babies went. The food was good, the ale was cold, and twenty minutes after he'd arrived, Gianni was ready to leave.

World War Three had not erupted. The Ice Princess either didn't know he was here or she knew he was here and was ignoring him. She was still chatting with the same group of people. The only thing that had changed was that now he could hear her laugh.

It was the laugh he'd heard at Stefano's. Husky. Sexy. Secretive.

It was driving him out of his mind.

How could she laugh when he was so royally ticked off? How come she didn't know he was here? She had to know. He hadn't been aware of the connection between her and Karen, but she'd certainly known he and Tomasso were friends, and—

And, he didn't have to worry about her driving him insane because he was already climbing the steps of the asylum. Why else would he stand here watching her? Why would he give a damn? Why would he feel his temper rising and his blood pressure increasing?

Okay. All right. Closure. Wasn't that what he'd wanted? He felt a muscle jump in his cheek. Closure was what he'd get, and right now.

There must have been something in his face as he strode across the room because the people she was with fell silent. Only one man was still laughing; a look from him and the laugh turned into something that sounded like a caw.

''What's the matter?'' Briana O'Connell said.

She swung around and he saw the surprise and something more flash across her face, something he would have missed if he weren't feeling it himself.

Desire, hot, raw and savage, sluiced through his blood.

"You," she said, so dramatically that he almost laughed.

"Me," he said, and reached for her arm.

"Hey." She tried to pull away. He wouldn't let her. "What do you think you're doing?"

"Yeah," the man who'd been laughing said, "what do you think you're doing?"

Gianni swung toward him. "Whatever I'm doing," he said pleasantly, "it's none of your business." The guy's face turned a sickly grey. Okay. Maybe he didn't say it pleasantly. "The lady and I have things to discuss."

He looked at Briana. Her face was as pink as the guy's was grey. He could see the pulse beating in her throat. Was she afraid of him? She ought to be. He'd had about all he was going to take.

"You're crazy. We have nothing to—"

She gasped as he slid his hand to her wrist and encircled it.

"Don't give me a hard time."

"You son of a bitch," she said, her voice trembling, but it was there again, swift as the beat of a hummingbird's wing, that flash of heat flaring in her eyes.

Gianni stepped closer.

"Your choice, princess. Are you coming with me, or do I pick you up and carry you?"

"Bree?" the guy said, and Gianni grudgingly gave him credit for having more balls than brains.

She hissed a word he hadn't thought she'd know, then slicked the tip of her tongue across her bottom lip. He felt his body tighten in response. When she tore her hand from his, he let her do it. He knew it was the small victory she needed so she could spin on one of those wicked stiletto heels and head for the front door.

He was no more than a step behind her.

Did somebody call his name? He didn't know, didn't

care, didn't think about anything but the swing of her but-
tocks, the way her short lemon-yellow skirt flared around
her thighs as she strode from the apartment.

The elevator was just outside, waiting for them as if he'd
planned it. She stepped into the car and jabbed a button. He
stepped inside and she tried to shoot past him just as the
door began to close. His vision clouded; he grabbed her arm
and spun her toward him as the doors slid shut.

"Let go of me!" She jerked under his hands, eyes hot,
breasts rising and falling with each quick breath. "What in
hell do you think you're doing?"

"What I should have done the day we met," he said, and
he hauled her against him and kissed her.

She cried out, but the sound was lost against his plun-
dering mouth. She beat her fists against his shoulders and
tried to twist her face away from his but he tunneled his
hands into her hair, angled her face to his, and kissed her
again.

"Bastard," she panted, "you no good bas—"

And then she wound her arms around his neck and
opened her mouth to his.

The first taste of her and he was lost. She fell back against
the wall of the car, her body arching against his, breasts soft
against his chest, hips lifting to the thrust of his.

"Oh God," she whispered. "Oh please…"

Gianni groaned, cupped her backside and lifted her. She
wrapped her legs around him, pressed herself against his
erection and he felt a rush of desire so primitive it was
almost his undoing.

"Tell me," he said. "Say it. Say you want me. That you
want this."

"Yes. Yes!"

He slid his hand under her skirt. Only a scrap of lace lay
between his questing fingers and her flesh. She was hot and

wet and when he felt her against his palm, he had to fight for control all over again.

He stroked her, then slid a finger inside the damp fabric that kept him from her, and she cried out, dug her fingers into his hair, kissed him with the same urgency he felt, the same blind need.

And the car rocked to a stop.

The doors opened. They must have, because the next thing he knew, he heard a startled gasp, a laugh, saw Briana's eyes open, heard her horrified cry.

Gianni didn't turn around. He reached out blindly to the control panel and hit a button. The doors shut. The elevator began to descend again.

"Briana," he said, "Bree…"

She twisted against him with the desperation of a wild creature caught in a trap and struck out with her fist. He grunted when one blow connected with his jaw.

"Damn it," he said, grabbing her hands as she slid down his body, "will you listen to me?"

The elevator reached the lobby. She shot from the car as if the demons of hell were at her heels. The surprised doorman yanked the front door wide with only seconds to spare, then stared at Gianni.

"Sir? Is everything all right?"

Gianni drew a ragged breath as he stepped from the car.

"Everything's fine," he said, and knew it was the biggest lie he'd ever told in his life.

CHAPTER THREE

AUGUST in New York always was hot, humid and altogether unbearable. The last thing any sane human being would do in such weather was stand over an ironing board, especially when the AC was gasping its death throes, but that was what Bree was doing early on the first Monday of the month.

Ironing was mindless. You could listen to the radio, hum along with an Elton John oldie and let your thoughts drift on the calm seas of boredom. That was what Bree was doing.

For instance, right now, she was thinking about whether or not to go to her brother's beach house on Nantucket Island. Cullen and Marissa had invited her up for the weekend.

"The weather's gorgeous," Marissa said when she called, "and we're going to have a barbecue. Nothing fancy. We'll just invite in some interesting neighbors."

Bree sighed as she spread a silk blouse over the ironing board. "Some interesting neighbors," in female-speak, was sure to mean "some interesting men." Her sisters and sisters-in-law, still basking in the glow of their own happiness, kept trying to fix her up with the right man. She'd already met a handsome vintner, thanks to Cassie; a suave hotelier, courtesy of Savannah; a sexy sheikh, compliments of Megan, a hotshot CEO, pointed in her direction by Fallon, and now Marissa wanted to introduce her to a Nantucket something-or-other.

One thing was certain. The O'Connell women all had

impeccable taste. The men they'd set in her path were handsome, charming and, she was sure, great catches.

It wasn't their fault that not a one was as gorgeous, as
sexy, as altogether spectacular as Gianni Firelli...and, she
was certain, not a one of them was the same kind of rotten
SOB.

Bree brought the iron down with enough force to smooth
out a wrinkle in a sheet of steel.

She'd tried to forget about him. Forget that elevator ride.
Forget that she hated herself for not having dealt with him
properly. Now, here he was, back in her head.

It was the heat. The damned heat. Bad enough it was a
million degrees outside and almost that in her apartment.
Was this a day to sweat over a hot iron in her tiny kitchen?

It was, if you were going on a job interview.

Too much heat and humidity could turn your brain to
mush. She couldn't afford that. She had a job interview in
less than an hour. Why waste time thinking about something
that was history?

Yes, she'd behaved like an idiot. Yes, the memory still
made her cringe. Yes, she wished she'd slapped Gianni Firelli's face but—

But, she hadn't.

The interview. She'd think about the interview. About
how difficult it was to get the miserable wrinkles out of this
miserable blouse because the iron was too hot and the ironing board table didn't stand straight on the worn linoleum
floor. The stupid legs wobbled...

Her legs had wobbled, when Gianni kissed her.

The faint scent of scorched silk rose from the ironing
board. Bree snatched the iron off the blouse. Too late. There
was a brown spot right on the collar the size of a quarter.

"Damn, damn, damn!"

Washable silk, the tag said. Light pressing might be required. Light? An elephant could sit on the blouse for an

hour and the wrinkles would still be there as soon as it lifted its butt. And what difference did it make? Five minutes on the street, she'd look as if she'd slept in it, anyway.

Truth was, she'd probably look that way as soon as she put it on. She was sweating. Not glowing, the way those lade-da fashion magazines said. Sweating, with a capital S.

No wonder the rent was so cheap. Well, cheap for New York City. When she'd signed the lease a few months back, she'd figured she was getting a bargain. Some bargain, she thought, as she shoved her hair back from her face.

The kitchen faucet leaked. Only one of the stove's burners worked, and there wasn't any point in talking about the air conditioner. It was supposed to cool the whole place— not much to ask, considering the size of this shoe box the landlord called an apartment.

Pitiful.

And so was she.

Bree yanked out the plug and stood the iron on its heel. That was the only way to describe a woman who was fixated on something that was weeks in the past. A man came on to you like a savage, forced his kisses on you...

Another time, another place, a woman who'd endured such indignities would have gone straight to her brothers and asked them to defend her honor. She wouldn't do that, of course—this was the twenty-first century, not the middle ages, and besides, she could handle her own affairs—but the thought of the male contingent of the O'Connell clan beating Gianni Firelli to a pulp held definite appeal.

Never mind that she'd seemed to respond to what he'd done. If she had, it was only because he'd taken her by surprise. Okay. So she hadn't handled the scene well. So what? Why keep thinking about it?

Why keep thinking about the taste of his mouth, the feel of his hand between her thighs?

Bree said a word that would have stunned her protective

brothers, crumpled the blouse into a ball and hurled it across the room.

As if she gave a pig's whistle about any of that.

The job interview. She had to concentrate on that. She needed to be at her best, look her best and how was she going to manage that with Mr. Firelli in her head and a scorch mark the size of Texas on her blouse?

The blouse was easier to handle.

She could stand the collar up. Or wear a scarf around her neck. No. The collar wasn't made to stand up. As for the scarf—Fallon would probably make a scarf look like an ascot.

She'd make it look like a noose.

Bree dumped the blouse on the bed. What to wear? She needed this job. She didn't know anything about being a gofer for a TV producer but she'd learn. She had to. What little she'd saved from her last stint as a waitress was about gone, and an hour spent yesterday with the Sunday *Times* employment section had been depressing.

The city seemed in desperate need of everything from accountants to zoologists. Unfortunately two years of college didn't qualify her for much of anything.

"You and me, kid," Sean used to say. "All the O'Connells are busy being grown-ups, except us."

Bree stepped into the shower and turned the water cold enough to raise goose bumps.

That wasn't true anymore. Sean, the untamable gambler, had been tamed. He'd sunk his winnings into ownership of an exclusive Caribbean resort while she still drifted from job to job and place to place, searching for something she'd like enough to want to do for the rest of her life.

The score, thus far, was a big, fat zero.

She shut off the shower, stepped onto the mat and wrapped herself in a bath sheet.

Who'd want to make a career demonstrating cosmetics to

bored matrons with more money than common sense? Spend a lifetime selling *prêt à porter* to spoiled rich girls? She'd have been one of those overindulged brats herself if it weren't for the fact that she flat-out refused to accept help from her family.

Financial help, anyway, and when she'd tried the other kind...well, it hadn't worked out. Waiting tables at Keir's vineyard restaurant last winter had gone well enough until she'd not-so-accidentally dumped a glass of wine on a pain-in-the-ass customer who'd complained about everything from the first course to the last.

More recently, Fallon had wangled her a stint modeling for a new diet drink photo shoot.

You probably weren't supposed to stab your index finger between your lips and make gagging noises when the guy watching from the sidelines was the client's rep. Even so, he'd hit on her. That had been even more nauseating. He was okay to look at, she supposed, but nothing compared to...

Bree frowned into the mirror. "Stop that," she said out loud, and marched to her closet.

What did TV people wear, anyway? Was the desired look funky or professional? Maybe a little of each. The navy silk suit, but with that *Bella Sicilia* T-shirt she'd picked up last time she visited Fallon and Stefano.

The doorbell rang.

Bree rolled her eyes. What now? The super had already come by to peer at her air conditioner and tell her there was nothing he could do until a new part arrived. Her usual early-morning visitor, Mrs. Schilling from across the hall, had already stopped by to update her on the alien spaceship on the roof.

Brring, brring, brring.

Time for another bulletin on the Alien Invasion.

Bree sighed, knotted the bath sheet more tightly over her

breasts and went to the door. She undid the hundred and one locks—each brother had added his own assortment—and cracked the door a couple of inches.

"Yes, Mrs. Schilling," she said, "have you heard something more from the Mart—"

The words caught in her throat. It wasn't her slightly-batty-but-sweet neighbor standing on the doormat, it was her impossibly arrogant would-be seducer, the man she'd spent the last few weeks loathing. Here he was. In the flesh. The gorgeous flesh.

What had taken him so long?

"You!" Oh God, such originality! And such a stupid thought. Bree stood straighter. "What are you doing here, Firelli?"

"I have to see you."

He wasn't much on originality, either...and why should such a hackneyed phrase make her pulse beat zoom? Definitely, the heat was frying her brain.

"A charming line," she said brightly, "but wasted on me. I am absolutely not interested in—"

"Briana. This is important. Let me in."

Like the big, bad wolf, he made the simple words sound tempting. That was the bad news. The good news was that she wasn't some silly little creature in a nursery rhyme.

"Not in a million years."

"We have to talk."

"We have nothing to talk about. And if, by some miracle we did, have you ever heard of that new invention called the telephone?"

"Damn it, this isn't a game. Let me in."

"You're right. It isn't a game." Bree started to close the door. "Go on home, Firelli. Give us both a break and just—"

"Briana." Gianni moved forward and wedged his shoul-

der in the narrow opening between the door and the jamb.
"Please."

The word, as much as that shoulder, stopped her cold.
Please? She wouldn't have thought the term was in his vo-
cabulary. At least, not when it came to women. She started
to tell him what he could do with his plea but something in
his eyes made her reconsider.

"Something's wrong," she said slowly.

He didn't answer. "Open the door, Bree."

"What is it?" A coldness began stealing over her.
"Gianni? What's the matter?"

"I've come to tell you something," he said quietly, "but
not like this. Let me in."

Her heart gave an unsteady thump. "Tell me what's going on."

Gianni ran his hand through his hair. It was already standing up in little curls, as if he'd repeated the same action
several times. Now she noticed he was wearing jeans, a
T-shirt and running shoes, and there was a shadowy bristle
on his jaw.

Gianni Firelli, unshaven and casually dressed at this hour
on a weekday morning?

"Stefano," she whispered. "And my sister…"

Her knees buckled. Gianni cursed and caught her by the
shoulders.

"No," he said sharply. "Listen to me, Bree. Your sister
and brother-in-law are fine. Your family is fine. This has
nothing to do with them."

"Then what… It's something bad, isn't it?"

She was staring at him, her eyes enormous in her suddenly pale face, and the anger he'd been riding since the
last time he saw her drained away. He had bad news for
her. Terrible news, the worst imaginable.

He had to tell her that her best friend was dead.

Gianni drew a long breath. "Bree—"

"Briana? Is it the Martians?"

He looked over his shoulder. An old woman was standing in the doorway opposite, hands clutched to her breasts.

"Have the aliens demanded our surrender?"

Any other time, he would have laughed. The woman was staring at him as if he were the devil himself, which pretty much described how he felt at the moment.

"I'm a friend of Briana's," he said gently. "Everything's fine."

The old woman looked uncertain. "Are you sure?"

"The president says we'll never surrender," he said firmly, and forced a smile to his lips.

That seemed to do it. She stepped back inside her apartment; Gianni moved forward, still holding Briana by the shoulders, and kicked the door shut.

Heat and humidity curled around him like the breath of a swamp. The room reminded him of a closet. He felt too big for it and for the emotions churning in his belly.

"Tell me," Bree said.

"Sit down first."

He knew the second she figured it out. What little color had returned to her face drained away.

"It's Karen," she whispered.

Gianni swung her into his arms. Two steps, and he was beside a tattered sofa. Carefully he lowered her to it. She scooted into the corner, watching him as if he held the secrets of the universe.

"Please. Tell me what happened. It *is* Karen, isn't it?"

A muscle tightened in Gianni's cheek. "Yes."

Tears flooded her eyes. "Oh God," she said brokenly. "Oh God!"

"And Tomasso," he said, rushing the words, knowing she had to hear it all and hear it quickly before the sledgehammer blow of pain struck him again.

"Both of them?"

"Yes."

Her head fell back, as if she'd been hit. Gianni moved closer and clasped her hands.

"I'm sorry, Briana."

"It can't be." She made a choked sound that was almost a laugh and was, he knew, the first sign of hysteria. "It isn't possible."

"I'm afraid it is."

"But how? How could—"

"They were in Sicily, visiting Tomasso's grandmother. They were driving. The roads there are narrow. Twisting. Another car—the driver was drunk. He—he—" Gianni couldn't get the words out. His throat felt as if someone were gripping it, trying to choke the air from his lungs. "It was quick," he finally said. "They didn't suffer."

Bree's eyes had become dull. Suddenly they flashed to life. "The baby?"

He nodded. At least there was some good news. "The baby is fine."

Briana began to weep, silently at first, then in great, gasping sobs that tore at his heart.

"Cara," he said thickly, and drew her into his arms.

She cried uncontrollably. He felt his eyes grow damp. He wanted to weep with her but he hadn't cried since he was five and he'd realized that if he did, his father would only beat him harder.

Instead he buried his face in her hair as he tried to figure out how to tell her the next part. Surely it would seem as impossible to her as it had to him when Tomasso's attorney phoned early this morning, first with the brutal news of Tommy's and Karen's deaths, and then with the details of their will.

"Are you sure?" he'd kept asking the man, which was incredibly stupid because he was a lawyer, too; he knew the Massini attorney couldn't have misunderstood. But the other man was patient. He read the pertinent clauses aloud. Even after that, Gianni kept saying, *yes, but are you sure?* because what he was hearing couldn't be right.

"Give me your fax number," the exasperated attorney finally said. Minutes later, Gianni had been staring at a document that would change his life.

His, and Briana's.

"When?" Bree said.

Her tears had stopped but she was still in his arms, her face hidden in the crook of his neck.

"Two days ago. Their lawyer called me this morning."

"Two days ago."

Bree shuddered against him. The room was hot, almost airless, but she was probably in shock. And she was wearing nothing but a towel.

A towel.

Gradually he became aware of the feel of her against him. The softness of her skin. The warmth of her breath. The silky strands of damp hair, tickling his nose.

"Bree."

He clasped her shoulders, tried to ease her from him, but she shook her head and burrowed closer.

"Bree," he said again, and stroked her back. Her skin was as silken as her hair, and bore the fragrance of flowers.

She was an oasis of life in a sea of death.

He understood that. Still, he despised himself as he felt his body beginning to quicken.

"Karen was my best friend," she whispered.

"As Tomasso was mine."

"We met in college, but it was as if we'd always known each other."

"Yeah." He cleared his throat. "Tommy and I were friends since we were ten."

"I just—I can't believe—"

"Neither can I."

She gave a soft sob that tore at his heart. He drew her closer and began to rock her in his arms.

"To think of them both gone…"

"Shh," he murmured, pressing a kiss to her hair. They sat in silence for a few minutes and then Briana looked up at him.

"What about—what about the funeral?"

"It's over," he said gruffly. "Tommy's grandmother made the arrangements. She's an old woman. I don't think it occurred to her that Tomasso and Karen had friends in the States who'd want to attend."

"So we—we can't even say a proper goodbye."

The pragmatist in him wanted to tell her that the Massinis wouldn't know the difference but the pain he felt, the pain he knew she felt, made him offer a different answer.

"They knew we loved them," he said quietly. "Perhaps they know it still."

Briana began to weep again. Gianni whispered to her, stroked her cheek, her hair, and suddenly she tilted her face up to his. Her eyes were enormous, as bright as stars; her mouth trembled.

"At least they had each other."

"Yes. They were lucky."

"It's terrible, to be alone."

"Terrible," he whispered back, and he would never know which of them moved first, he or Briana, but a heartbeat later his mouth was drinking from hers, her arms were wound tightly around his neck, and his mind was emptied of everything but her taste, her scent, the soft reality of her in his embrace.

He lay her back on the couch and kissed her throat, felt the leap of her pulse against his lips. Her hands were in his hair; her sighs were sweet affirmations of the power of life.

"Bree…"

She drew his head down and silenced him with another

kiss. Her lips were soft; her body was warm and alive under his hands and when she moved against him, whispered his name, Gianni was lost.

With a groan, he tore open the knotted towel. Her breasts were beautiful, rounded and small with delicate nipples the color of roses.

"How lovely you are," he whispered.

"Touch me, Gianni. Please. Please…"

Her breasts. They fit his palms as if they'd been fashioned to do exactly that. She whimpered with pleasure as he cupped them. He bent his head to her and sucked first one beaded tip and then the other into his mouth.

She sobbed his name, raised her hips in age-old invitation, asking a wordless question that could only have one answer and he gave it, spreading the towel fully so he could see all of her: the narrow waist, the rounded hips, the golden triangle between her legs.

He kissed her there, seeking the perfect pink bud nestled between her thighs with the tip of his tongue. She tasted sweeter than honey and when she arched toward him and cried out her passion, the blood roared in his ears.

"Gianni," she sobbed, "Gianni, please, please, please…"

"Yes," he said hoarsely, and in a single, swift movement he unzipped his jeans, came down to her, lifted her to him and entered her, sinking deep, deeper than he ever had before, and then she tightened around him and he stopped thinking of anything but this, this, this…

Her wild cry of fulfillment triggered his own release.

For an instant, for an eternity, the world hung suspended.

And then it was over.

Gianni's body sang while his brain recoiled at what he'd done. He rolled away, searching for the right words. Briana scrambled up against the back of the sofa, grabbed for the towel and clutched it to her.

"Oh God," she said brokenly. "Oh God…"

"Briana. I'm sorry. I didn't mean—"

"Don't say anything. Just—just go away."

Her mane of golden hair was a wild tangle that obscured her features. He wanted to pull her into his arms, smooth it back, lift her face to his and tell her he hadn't meant to take her like this, that what had happened in the elevator wasn't what he'd wanted, either.

What he wanted was to make slow, tender love with her. To kiss her mouth, then trail kisses down her throat to the hollow between her breasts until she was trembling with desire. He wanted to enter her slowly, watch her face as he did, take her with him to the heavens and hold her close as she came back to earth.

But she was glaring at him, disgust and hatred bright in her eyes. He knew that reaching for her would be a mistake. Hell, everything he'd done since they'd met had turned out to be a mistake.

"Damn it, are you deaf? Get out!"

She sounded as if he were a monster who'd attacked her. Gianni felt the first stirrings of an emotion far safer than regret.

"Look," he said carefully, "these things happen."

"These things?" she said, and the coldness in her voice was the final touch he needed.

"Sex," he said bluntly. "It's an affirmation of life. It's what people often turn to, in the face of death."

He was right. Briana knew that. She'd read books, seen films; she wasn't stupid. People had sex for reasons that had nothing to do with desire.

And that was the worst of it. That she'd done this for all the wrong reasons. Dreamed of being with this man, ugly as that was to admit, dreamed of it since the night in that elevator, and now that it had happened, it had nothing to do

with Gianni wanting her or her wanting him; it had to do
with the loss of someone who'd been like another sister.

"Briana."

She looked up. Gianni's tone was cool. He sounded like
a man about to make a speech instead of a man who'd just—
who'd just—

"We have to talk."

"You're wrong, Firelli. We don't have a thing in the
world to talk about."

Slowly he rose to his feet. Color flooded her face as he
zipped up his jeans. He didn't even have the decency to turn
away.

"Forgive me," he said in a voice that implied anything
but regret. "For a minute there, I thought the Ice Princess
had been replaced by a woman."

"I'd rather be made of ice than be a savage like you."

He reached out so quickly that she didn't have time to
get away from him, grasped her by the arms and hauled her
to her feet.

"Be careful, *cara,* or do you want me to remind you of
just how easily I can turn you from cold to hot?"

"Get—out!"

"Believe me, I'd love to. But—"

"But what? Damn it, leave right now or I swear, I'll have
you thrown out!"

A muscle jumped in his jaw. Slowly he lifted his hands
from her and took a step back.

"Tomasso and Karen left a will."

"So? I can't imagine what that has to do with me."

"Apparently Karen disagreed with my assessment of
you."

"What are you talking about?"

"She must have thought you had a heart." He paused,
and she saw the muscle in his jaw flicker again. "She and
Tommy named you guardian of their baby."

She blinked. "What?"

"They named you Lucia's guardian."

"That's impossible. Karen would have said—"

"Impossible or not, it's a fact."

Briana sank down on the couch. "But I'm not—I mean, I don't know anything about—"

"Perhaps they understood that." He folded his arms over his chest and even managed a thin smile. "You see, they didn't leave the entire job to you."

"I don't—I don't understand."

Gianni took a deep breath. "They named us both as guardians. You. And me. We're going to raise this child together."

CHAPTER FOUR

BREE STARED at Gianni. What he'd told her was impossible...but people didn't joke about death, and funerals, and certainly not about the guardianship of helpless children.

A mistake, then. Yes, of course. A mistake. She said that to Gianni. He shook his head.

"Unfortunately it isn't." He took a sheet of folded paper from his back pocket. "See for yourself."

Bree looked at the paper. She didn't want to take it from him. Maybe if she didn't, it wouldn't be real. Gianni gave her no choice. He shook it in front of her face like a matador dancing his cape before a bull.

"Read it," he said impatiently. "Then tell me if you still think it's a mistake."

It was a fax transmission, dated only a few hours ago. She clutched it with both hands and did what he'd asked, but the words made no sense. At first, she thought it was because she was still in shock from what Gianni had told her. Then she realized it was in Italian.

"I don't—it's in Italian."

Hell. Of course it was in Italian. Gianni cursed himself for being a fool, grabbed the fax and translated it in rapid English. Bree heard a numbing string of legalese, whereases and wherefores and whomsoevers tumbling after each other like drops of rain.

Evidently lawyers in Europe couldn't manage a simple sentence without enough fifty-dollar words to render it almost indecipherable any more than their counterparts in the U.S.A.

Not that it mattered.

The only important words were those that confirmed what Gianni had already told her. Karen and Tomasso had designated them as joint guardians of their baby.

"...so charging Briana Claire O'Connell and Gianni Fabrizio Firelli with the responsibility to raise our daughter, Lucia Vittoria Massini, to make all decisions for her as they see fit, until she reaches the age of majority."

Gianni looked up. Normally he hated legal jargon. Not this time. Reading the will in the impersonal language with which it had been written made him feel more comfortable.

Perhaps he could handle this better if he donned the cloak of the law.

"Questions?" he said briskly.

"The age of...?"

"Majority. The point at which a child ceases to be a minor."

"I know that," Briana said sharply. "I meant, what age is that in Italy?"

"Eighteen."

"And here?"

"The same."

"I thought girls married younger in the old country."

"They marry when they marry, and what in hell does that have to do with anything?"

"I was just thinking—you know, not about when Lucia will marry but when she'd be considered old enough to marry. Or vote. Or..." Gianni's eyebrows were aiming for the ceiling. Who could blame him? Bree waved her hand and sighed. "I guess I was trying to figure out when she'll stop being a minor."

"When we're too old to give a damn," Gianni said, stuffing the fax back in his pocket.

To his surprise, Bree laughed.

"You find this amusing?"

"No. No, of course not. It's just the way you said that…"

"Well, it's true." He sank down on the sofa next to her. "The child is only three months old."

"Four."

"Oh, well, that's a big improvement. We only have seventeen years and eight months to go."

Bree's lips twitched. Gianni glared at her and then his did, too.

"My God," he said softly. "Pity the poor kid. You and me, parents?"

"Guardians," she said quickly.

"Parents, guardians, what the hell's the difference?" His smile faded. "Listen to us, wondering how such a thing could have happened when all that really matters is that Tommy and Karen are gone." He turned toward Briana. Her smile faded, too; her blue eyes were filling with tears. "Bree. About—about what happened before…"

"Don't."

"I want you to know that I never meant to… When I took you in my arms, I only meant to comfort you."

"Yes. I know."

"I had no intention of taking advantage of you. Of the situation. It's just that—that the news about the Massinis—"

"You don't have to explain, Gianni. I understand why— why we did what we did."

Gianni nodded. "Good." He reached for her hand. "Because we're going to have to get along from now on."

"We'll get along just fine," Bree said stiffly, tugging her hand free of his, "as long as we forget about what happened."

Forget that they'd made love? That he'd heard her cry out his name as she tumbled off the edge of the world?

"Of course," he said politely.

She nodded. "Good. Because if this is going to work, you have to promise me that we'll forget this—this incident."

"I understand."

"I'm going to get dressed. Then we can decide how best to handle the situation."

Gianni smiled pleasantly. "Fine."

She walked away, head high, like a queen in full regalia instead of a woman in a towel. He had to give the lady credit. She had guts.

But he deserved some credit, too. He was getting really good at telling lies where she was concerned, first a couple of months back, when she'd run from him and he'd assured the doorman that everything was fine and now again, when he'd assured her he'd forget they'd made love.

He wouldn't forget. He was damned sure she wouldn't, either.

Not with him around to remind her.

BREE KEPT IT together until she was safely inside the bedroom but once she'd shut the door, she began to shake. Sitting down on the edge of the bed was like sitting on a raft in the middle of the ocean.

The mattress felt as if it were tilting. The room spun. She'd never fainted in her life but she didn't need a medical encyclopedia to tell her she was close to it now.

And she couldn't let that happen. If Gianni heard a thud, he'd be here in a heartbeat. The last thing she wanted was to let him see how much the entire morning had shocked her.

Or to let him see her all but naked again. God, no. Never.

What was that meditation thing she'd tried back in college? Take a deep breath. Hold it. Now blow it out. And again. Just a couple more...

The mattress stilled. The room stopped spinning, and the world went from black and white to color. Bree bowed her head. Was she losing her sanity, or was the world going crazy? A little while ago, the problem of the day had been getting a job. Now it was figuring out what it meant to be the guardian of a helpless infant...

What it meant that she'd let a man she despised make love to her.

A tremor shuddered through her. "Be honest," she whispered. She hadn't "let" Gianni make love to her, she'd begged him to do it. He was the one who'd held back; she'd initiated the kiss, all but offered herself to his caresses.

And "making love" was the wrong way to describe what had happened. They'd come together the same as they had in the elevator. Hungry. Eager. A fusion of mouths and bodies...

"Briana?"

Bree jerked her head up. She could hear Gianni's footsteps stop outside the door. Her heart leaped. Had he come for her? Was he going to take her in his arms again?

"Bree?" Transfixed, she stared at the door, waiting for the knob to turn.

"I'm going to make some coffee. Okay?"

He was asking her permission to make coffee? She bit back the swift rush of hysterical laughter struggling to surface.

"It's fine," she called. "The coffee's in the cupboard over the—"

"I already found it."

So much for asking permission. She waited until his footsteps faded away. Then she threw aside the towel and jumped into the shower again, scrubbed fiercely with a loofah though she suspected not all the scrubbing in the world would wash away the scent of Gianni's skin, the feel of his hands...

Oh, the feel of his hands...

"Stop it," she muttered, and turned her face up to the spray.

Five minutes later, dressed in the blue suit, a white blouse and sensible heels, her hair yanked back in a low ponytail, she walked briskly into the kitchen. Gianni was leaning against the counter with a mug of coffee in his hand. Another mug sat beside the coffeepot. He reached for it but she shook her head.

"I'll pour my own, thank you."

One dark eyebrow rose but he didn't say anything. A good thing, too, she thought grimly as she sipped at the hot coffee. News of the tragedy had stunned her; being named guardian had been a second shock but the shower had cleared her head. She was ready to deal with things now.

As for what had happened with Gianni—just as she'd told him, there was no point thinking about it. It was over.

What they had to do now was work out a way to supervise the baby's life, and to arrange things so that she and Gianni spent as little time as possible with each other.

She knew exactly how to accomplish that.

"All right," Gianni said, and cleared his throat. "Here's what I've been thinking..."

Bree held up her hand. "I have an appointment."

Both of his eyebrows went up this time. "Excuse me?"

"An appointment." She glanced at her watch. "Actually I *had* an appointment, but I'm going to head on uptown anyway and see if—"

"Let me get this straight. I've just told you that we have a child to raise, and you have something to do that's more important than talking about exactly how we're going to do it?"

Bree's eyes flashed. "I have a job interview to go to. A job, Firelli. You know what that is, don't you? Something people do to earn their living instead of sitting back and collecting fees from fat-cat clients.''

Gianni cocked his head. ''You have me all figured out.''

''Unfortunately for you.'' She checked the time again. ''I'll meet you at six this evening. There's a coffee shop on—''

''Is that what your brother does?''

She looked at him. ''I beg your pardon?''

''Cullen. He's a lawyer, isn't he? Does he sit back and collect fees from fat-cat clients?''

Why on earth had she said that? The truth was, she didn't even know what kind of law Gianni practiced.

''Because I don't, you know.'' He drank some coffee. ''Collect fees from fat-cats.''

''Actually I don't much care who you—''

''I'm with the Attorney General's office. I'm a federal prosecutor.''

She blinked. ''In three thousand dollar suits?''

Gianni made a deliberate show of looking down at his jeans and T-shirt.

''I don't mean now, I mean—''

''I know what you mean,'' he said, very softly. ''And I'm glad to see you haven't forgotten our last meeting, either.''

''I simply meant,'' she said, hating the rush of heat she felt rising to her face, hating even more the stupidity of the conversation she'd initiated, ''prosecutors must be doing very well these days.''

He gave a negligent shrug. ''I enjoy what I do. I don't make money at it.''

Bree fluttered her lashes. ''Ah. Another member of the silver spoon brigade.''

''Like you?'' he said, not missing a beat, enjoying the new color that was turning her lovely face pink.

He resisted the urge to say ''gotcha.'' He knew little about Briana O'Connell but looking around her cramped apartment, it was easy to see she didn't depend on a dole from her wealthy family.

It was also easy to see that she was doing everything she could to make it clear she didn't like him, including tarring him with a brush laden with stuff he didn't deserve.

He was damned if he was going to let her do it.

"Here's the bottom line," he said. "I have a lot of money, yes, but I earned every penny. I was a litigator for several years." He grinned. "Shearing those fat cats, if you'll pardon the mixed metaphor. I invested wisely, took a surprised look at my bank book one day, said what the hell and went into a field that's more satisfying." He took a last sip of the rapidly cooling coffee. "Anything else you're interested in knowing?"

"I'm not—"

"Of course you are." He turned, put down his cup and tucked his hands into his back pockets. "And I don't blame you, considering that we're going to be spending the next eighteen years together."

He'd meant it as a joke, more to see that magical rush of color to her face and maybe, just maybe, to see that icy *hauteur* slip as she turned from ice princess to a creature of fire and heat again.

But she didn't react as he'd expected. Okay. As he'd hoped. Instead she looked as if he'd just admitted he had the unfortunate habit of turning into a werewolf at the first hint of a full moon.

"I beg your pardon?"

"Eighteen years," he said calmly. Why stop now, when he was already into it? "Minus those four months, of course. Come on, princess. You remember that age of majority we talked about."

"But we won't be spending them together."

"Not entirely, no. Even real parents get a couple of weeks off every now and then."

Her jaw dropped. "What are you talking about?"

What, indeed? He'd come here with his head full of ways they could exercise the terms of Tomasso's will while maintaining distance from each other. Now he wondered how he could have thought of doing that. It would be the wrong way to honor the memory of Tommy and Karen, and completely unfair to Lucia.

Surely there was no other reason for the change in plans he was considering.

"We can discuss it later."

Bree dumped her purse on the counter and folded her arms. "We can discuss it now."

"I thought you said you had a job interview."

"I did. Hours ago. I don't think there's much point in going now." Her tone softened. "Besides, after this about— about Karen…"

"Yeah." He cleared his throat as the reality of what had brought him here hit home all over again. "I know."

"So, let's take things one step at a time. Where's the baby now? With her great-grandmother in Sicily?"

Gianni nodded. "Yes."

"She must be distraught. I mean, after what happened…"

"I agree. The lawyer said the sooner we get the baby, the better."

Bree stared at Gianni. "Get her?"

"Well, we're not going to leave her with Grandma."

"No. Of course not. It's just that…" Bree swallowed dryly. It was hard enough to think of herself as guardian for a child she barely knew but, until now, the discussion had been more or less academic. Now they were getting down to basics. "It's just that the details seem—they seem—"

"Tell me about it," Gianni said gruffly. "You know anything about kids?"

Bree thought about her newly found status as aunt. She

could change a diaper and give a bottle. Did that mean she knew about kids?

"No," she said honestly. "Do you?"

Gianni laughed. "Do I look like a man who knows about kids?"

"The happy bachelor," she said coolly. "Running from the altar as fast as his feet can carry him."

"I don't see you with a noose around your neck, either, O'Connell."

"Is that how you see marriage?"

"It's how I see long-term relationships," he said bluntly. "Someday, yeah, I suppose I'll want to have a family..."

"No need to explain. I feel that way, too. I'm not ready to settle down."

"So I gather."

"What's that supposed to mean?"

Gianni shrugged. "Stefano says you're a butterfly, flitting from place to place."

"Stefano talks too much." Bree peeled off her suit jacket. The kitchen felt like a sauna and seemed smaller than it already was. Gianni, lounging casually against the wall, damned near dominated it. She thought about continuing their conversation in the living room, but right now she wasn't sure she'd ever be able to look at the couch without blushing. "Could we talk about this somewhere else?" she said abruptly. "There's a coffee shop downstairs."

Gianni glanced at his watch and shook his head. "I'm late for a deposition. We'll meet later. Seven, at *Luna's*. Do you know it?"

"On 57th just off Madison, but—"

"We'll have a drink, then some dinner, and talk. How's that sound?"

Like a date, Bree thought. Did he think what had happened earlier would happen again?

"I can't make it," she said politely. "We can meet at five, at the coffee shop."

"You have a date?"

He said it casually, as if it meant nothing to him. So much for his thinking of tonight as a date. Now that she thought about it, why would he? What had happened this morning meant no more to him than it did to her. She'd been weak, that was all, letting a moment of grief be eased by a moment of passion. If it had seemed special it was only because of her heightened emotions. It wasn't him. Wasn't his touch, his mouth, his body...

"Briana? Do you have a date?"

She let out a suddenly shaky breath. "Yes," she said, with a polite smile. "I do."

"Break it."

His voice was soft. For a second, she thought she'd misunderstood.

"I beg your pardon?"

"I said, break your date."

His words had an edge to them now. Oh, yes. This was the Gianni Firelli she knew. Arrogant. Demanding. So full of himself he couldn't imagine a woman saying "no," and what she'd done with him this morning had only helped convince him he was right.

Time to set him straight, Bree thought, and flashed another polite smile.

"No."

His eyes narrowed. That muscle flickered in his jaw again. Slowly, deliberately, his eyes never leaving hers, he straightened and stepped away from the counter.

"Who are you seeing?"

Frasier, in reruns, but she'd never admit that. "It's none of your business."

"Wrong answer, *cara.*"

He was coming toward her, his steps slow, his expression

unreadable. Danger crackled in the air between them like heat lightning.

Bree's instinct was to turn and run but she'd grown up in desert country with mountains just on the horizon. Survival Rule One: if you suddenly found yourself confronted by a mountain lion, you didn't flee. You stood still and faced it.

Showing fear to a predator only fueled its hunger.

She held her ground until Gianni was a hand span away. Then, though she hated herself for showing weakness, she stumbled back two steps.

"You have no right—"

"We have a responsibility now, or have you decided you don't want to accept it?"

"I never said—"

"We need to make plans."

"I know that. I only meant…" Bree bit her lip. How easily he'd put her on the defensive! "Meeting at five instead of seven hardly suggests I'm unwilling to accept my responsibility."

"Our responsibility."

"For heaven's sake," she snapped, "will you stop the word games? Karen wanted me to be one of her baby's guardians, and—"

"We're co-guardians."

"More word games."

"More facts." Gianni reached out and caught one of her curls. He wound it around his finger and tugged lightly so that she had no choice but to close the distance between them. "We share Lucia's custody."

"Fine. At five this evening, we can start drawing up a plan."

"What do you know about plans?" he said, gently rubbing the soft silk of her hair between the tips of his fingers.

"Stefano says you're a gypsy. That you never stay with one thing long enough to put down roots."

"First I was a butterfly, now I'm a gypsy." Bree slapped at Gianni's hand. "Let go, please."

"Why?" He brought the strand of hair to his mouth. "I like the way your hair feels against my lips."

"Stop it. Just—just stop it, right—"

"I liked the feel of it against me when we made love."

Her heartbeat stumbled. Where was a good earthquake when you needed one? She wanted the floor to open and swallow her.

"We didn't make love. We had sex."

Gianni gave a soft laugh. "Now who's playing word games?"

"You know exactly what I mean, Firelli."

"Yes." His arms went around her and he drew her against him. She was stiff, unyielding, but the telltale race of her pulse in the hollow of her throat and the flush rising over her skin told him she was as aroused by being in his arms as he was to have her there. "In fact, I do." He bent his head, brushed his mouth gently over hers. "Next time will be different."

"There won't be a next time."

"No?"

"No."

He gave another of those soft, sexy, oh-so-self-confident laughs while she tried, unsuccessfully, to step out of his embrace.

"Eighteen years is a long time, O'Connell."

"Eighteen...?"

"Uh-huh. That's how long we're going to be involved with each other."

"We won't be involved with each other at all," Bree said with determination. She put her hands against Gianni's chest and pushed. This time, he let her go. "Sharing the responsibility for how Lucia is raised means exactly that."

Gianni folded his arms. "Exactly what?"

"You know," she said, because she wasn't about to admit that she didn't. "We'll meet periodically. Plan things."

"Things?" he repeated in a way that made her want to slug him.

"Things. Schools. Where she goes on vacation." She threw out her arms. "Things."

"Ah."

Gianni rubbed his index finger over the bridge of his nose. Briana followed the gesture. Had his nose been broken sometime in the past? A straight Roman profile, was how Fallon had described it and she'd agreed, but there was the faintest little indentation...

"...in her crib."

She blinked. "I—I'm sorry. I didn't hear what you said."

"I said, I'm sure little Lucia will be happy to hear all about schooling and holidays in her crib." His tone was so sarcastic that Bree could almost see his tongue firmly tucked in his cheek. "She's an infant, Briana. It'll be years before we have to decide on schools. We have to make some immediate decisions about her life."

He was right. Why hadn't she realized that?

"For instance, just off the top of my head, we'll need a baby nurse."

"Yes. Yes, of course we will."

Gianni nodded. "Furniture. Clothes." He gave a delicate shudder. "Diapers."

"Formula. Toys."

"All of that. But the first thing is bringing her home." Gianni paced into the living room with Bree following after him. "There's no room for a baby here," he said, looking around him.

"No," Bree said weakly, "there isn't." Things were happening too quickly. Of course, she'd be the baby's guardian. Co-guardian. But why would Gianni even think of the baby being here, with her? Was she ready for such a change in her life?

He swung around and faced her, hands on his hips, his eyebrows darkly angled slashes over his eyes.

"Besides, it wouldn't be fair to place all the day-by-day responsibility with you."

"Yes. I mean, I was thinking that, but I don't see how—"

"The apartment next to mine is for sale. The people selling it are even including the furnishings. I'll make the necessary arrangements. With luck, you can move in early next week."

"Now, wait just a minute…"

"It's seven rooms, I think. Maybe eight. I'll get hold of a contractor, have him work out a way to join the two flats."

"Join them? Damn it, listen to me!"

"And you're right about tonight. There's no need for us to meet."

Score one for the home team, Bree thought, staring at him as he paced back and forth while he planned her life, or the next eighteen years of it.

"We can discuss everything else on the plane."

"What plane?"

"The one I'm going to charter."

Well, naturally. He could afford to charter a plane, and she lived in an apartment you could fit in a flea's navel with room left over.

"We can be in Sicily by morning." He swung toward her. "You have a passport, don't you?"

"Gianni," she said carefully, "I am not moving into an apartment adjoining yours. I am not getting on a plane and flying to—"

"You said you were looking for a job."

Her head was spinning. What was happening to her life?

"Yes, but—"

"Well, now you have one. You'll handle the day-to-day custody details. I'll be there every evening, of course, and I'll hire a nurse to help you, but... What is it?" he said impatiently.

"You cannot just walk in here and—and take over my life, Firelli. Did it even occur to you to ask if I want to do this? Move out of my apartment? Live next door to you? Take care of a baby?"

He stared at her for a long moment. She waited for sarcasm or anger but he didn't show either. All he did was nod his head.

"You're right," he said quietly. "I should have asked."

"Well. Thank you. I'll have to revise my opinion of you as an arrogant, self-centered—"

"So I'm asking, Briana. Do you intend to honor our friends' dying request or not?"

Briana stiffened as she looked into his suddenly flat eyes. "That's cruel. You're trying to reduce this to one issue but it's a lot more complex than that."

"Answer the question, please. Will you do what Karen and Tomasso wished, and stay and see this through?"

God, how she wanted to hit him! "I told you, it isn't that simple!"

Gianni grasped her shoulders and lifted her to her toes. "No speeches, damn it! Answer the question. Will you do it or not?"

She could feel the hate inside her, coiled like a venomous snake. Hate for him, for how he was taking control of her.

"Yes," she hissed. "You know I'll do it. But I'll hate every minute I'm forced to spend in your company. Just remember—"

His mouth came down on hers, hard and hot and demanding. Bree tried to twist away but he clasped her face, tunneled his hands into her hair, held her while he took what he wanted until, at last, she gave a little cry and parted her lips to his.

His kiss softened, became a low-burning flame that she knew could become a blazing fire in a heartbeat. Stop, she told herself, stop, but that fire was what she wanted. How could she deny it, with his mouth on hers? Bree rose to Gianni, drank him in, lost herself in his kiss.

When he finally lifted his head, she was trembling.

"I'll be back at seven," he said. "Be ready for me."

Then, damn him to hell, he turned on his heel and swaggered out the door.

CHAPTER FIVE

BREE SPENT A WHILE fuming but it didn't last long.

She hated to admit it, but Gianni was right. Lucia was what mattered. Nothing else. She had no choice. Of course she'd be the baby's guardian. She'd loved Karen. Karen wanted her to raise her daughter.

How could she possibly turn away from that?

She just wished Karen had discussed this with her, she thought as she yanked clothing from her closet and tossed it into the suitcase on her bed. Of course she'd have said yes, but then the responsibility wouldn't have come as such a shock. Surely asking someone to raise your child was one of the most important things parents could do. Shouldn't Karen have mentioned it? Shouldn't Tomasso?

Maybe not. The Massinis were young. Life stretched ahead of them. Accidents happened to other people.

Bree dug a wadded-up tissue from her pocket, dabbed at her eyes and determinedly blew her nose.

Now that she thought about it, maybe Karen had intended to tell her she wanted her to be Lucia's guardian. They'd chatted on the phone just a couple of weeks ago. *Tommy and I are planning a trip,* Karen had told her. *Let's have lunch when we get back, okay? You and I haven't had the chance for a good, long talk in ages.*

For all she knew, the baby's guardianship would have been the subject of that talk.

Bree plucked a dress from its hanger, folded it and added it to the things in the suitcase.

Not that it mattered now. Karen and her husband were gone, and she was their baby's guardian. She, and Gianni. Whose idea had that been? Karen's? Tomasso's? Just thinking about that little scene before he'd left enraged her. Him standing there, cool as a cucumber, laying out the life he'd planned for her as if he owned her.

She'd tried telling herself that he couldn't be all bad if Karen had named him as co-guardian but that logic didn't help.

Maybe Tomasso had insisted. *He's my oldest friend,* he might have said. *I want him named along with Briana.*

No. Bree sighed and sank down on the bed next to her suitcase. Karen wouldn't have given in to pressure any more than Tomasso would have entrusted his beloved daughter to someone just because he was an old pal. Gianni was an attorney. Maybe they'd named him not just because he was Tomasso's oldest friend but because of his knowledge of the law.

So, why had they named her? What could they have seen in her? Karen and she were close, and Karen had no family to turn to, but how could she have chosen Bree to raise her little girl when she knew Bree's faults so well?

They'd roomed together at college, met for lunches and dinners ever since. Karen knew, maybe better than anyone, that Bree had yet to find what she wanted to do with her life. Karen knew she was irresponsible, bouncing from job to job and city to city. She knew Bree had never committed to anything.

Or to anyone.

Was that someone you'd pick to be your daughter's guardian? Unless…

A couple of months ago, she and Karen had gone to a lecture together. Actually it was ballyhooed as a Life Energy Event. Bree smiled, closed her eyes and drifted back to the afternoon and Karen's phone call.

"Did you ever hear of James LaRue?" she'd asked.

Bree had laughed. "The only people who've never heard of James LaRue are living on an icefloe in the Arctic."

"Well, Tommy's all set to baby-sit and I have two tickets to LaRue's sold-out, razzle-dazzle, opening night performance at Madison Square Garden. Wanna go?"

As a columnist for a Greenwich Village newspaper, Karen got tickets to lots of things.

"I don't know if I can sit through an hour of motivational mumbo-jumbo," Bree answered, and Karen laughed.

"Two hours," she'd said gaily, "but if it's really awful, we'll leave. Come on. It'll be fun."

So they'd gone. And "fun" didn't even come close. The right word, they'd decided ten minutes into LaRue's act, was bizarre.

What's your Life Energy Score? the guru shouted at his audience.

Five, the audience members yelled back. Or eight or three or any number between one and ten.

"It's ten if you have things like a career goal, if you're dedicated to a cause, if you're in a serious relationship, stuff like that," Karen explained, leaning close and raising her voice so Bree could hear her over the enthusiastic roar of the crowd.

Bree rolled her eyes and asked what happened if your answer was minus four? They grinned at that but when LaRue solemnly announced he was going to come into the audience so people could share their Life Energy stories with him, Karen rolled her eyes, mouthed "Enough," and pointed at the exit.

Talking, giggling, they'd ended up at a hole in the wall joint in Little Italy for pizza and *vino.* Bree, licking cheese off her fingertips, swore it was the best pizza she'd ever had.

"Tommy found it," Karen said. "It's just one of the

bonuses a good little girl from Iowa gets when she marries a Sicilian.''

Bree had laughed. So had Karen. Then, suddenly, she'd reached for Bree's hand and squeezed it.

"Oh, Bree," she'd said softly, "I'm so happy."

Bree had smiled. "Who could have guessed?"

"You know how we used to say we couldn't understand wanting to share your life with a man?"

"Wanting to let him take it over, you mean," Bree had answered, her smile fading. "Are you telling me you've changed your mind? That you think letting that happen is a good thing?"

"I'm telling you that we were wrong. Tommy and I share our lives. It's what I want for you, honey. It's what you deserve."

Bree had thought of a dozen answers, but how could you give any of them to your best friend when she'd all but admitted she'd given up her independence and truly believed doing it had made her happy?

Instead she'd gone for the light approach.

"Aha," she'd said, "I get it. You figure if I get into a committed relationship, I'll stop getting minuses from LaRue the Guru."

She'd laughed. Karen hadn't.

"If they gave points for kindness, generosity and goodness of heart," she'd said fervently, "you'd score a perfect 10."

Briana rose to her feet and pushed down the lid of her suitcase. Was that the night Karen had decided on her? Were her supposed traits—kindness, generosity and goodness of heart—the things she'd looked for when she'd entrusted Lucia to her care?

The suitcase lid fell into place and she shut the lock with a snap.

The only thing she could do now was hope that those

qualities were all she'd need to assume her new responsibility—and make certain that the imperious Mr. Firelli understood that they were in this as equals.

If he thought he was in charge, he was in for a very big surprise.

AT SEVEN, the surprise turned out to be Briana's.

Gianni had said that was when he'd pick her up.

"Be ready for me," he'd said, an overbearing statement with just enough sexual overtone to have put her senses on alert. When the doorbell rang, she was primed for anything...

Anything but the middle-aged man in neatly pressed khakis and pale blue shirt who greeted her with a polite smile.

"Evening, Miss O'Connell. I'm Charles. Mr. Firelli's driver."

Why be surprised? Gianni would have a driver and a big, expensive car to match. Charles took her suitcase and she followed him downstairs to a big, expensive Mercedes.

It made her smile.

"Has something amused you?" Gianni asked as she got into the back seat.

"Nothing," she said, and folded her hands in her lap.

He was so terribly predictable. The car. The way he was dressed—gone were the jeans and T-shirt. He was dressed like a banker in a pale grey suit, white shirt and dark red tie. Even the portable computer, open in his lap, suited the picture of a wealthy, important man doing his best to appear wealthy and important.

He was also gorgeous enough to make her mouth water, but what did that have to do with anything?

"I'm glad to see you're prompt."

Gorgeous, and as egotistical as a Caesar. She wasn't foolish enough to take the remark as a compliment.

"Meaning, you thought I wouldn't be."

"It's too soon to know what I think. Despite what has happened, we don't know each other very well."

The words were as frank as they were true, delivered with all the emotion of a man commenting on the weather, but she thought she saw something flicker in that distant gaze of his that made her skin heat.

"I don't intend to discuss this morning."

"I was referring to our conversation."

He hadn't been. She was sure of it, just as she was sure he was trying to rile her. What could she say in reply that wouldn't sound defensive? She wouldn't rise to the bait.

"So was I," she said coolly. "We got off on the wrong foot. We're in this thing together, like it or not, and we'll need to set some conditions."

"For instance."

"For instance, from now on, you're not going to make decisions without consulting me."

His brows rose. "Have I done that?"

"We're flying to Sicily tonight, in your chartered plane. When we get back, I'm moving into an apartment you've selected. I'm going to care for Lucia with the help of a nurse you'll hire." Bree bared her teeth in a smile. "Have I left anything out?"

To her surprise, Gianni laughed. "Not that I can think of."

"Well, it has to stop. I don't like being told what to do."

"Because?"

He asked the question so politely that at first she thought he was serious. Damn, he *was* serious. *Karen, how could you have done this to me?*

"Because I can think for myself, Firelli, hard as it may be to believe."

"Most of my relationships have been with women who like to be taken care of," he said bluntly.

"Well, I don't need to be taken care of," Bree said coldly. "And this isn't a relationship, not the way you mean. We hold a joint responsibility together. That means we make decisions together."

"I don't like decisions made by committee. It's one of the reasons I didn't join a large legal firm."

"I didn't ask what you liked, I told you how it's going to be. We're in this together, like it or not. We're going to have to make whatever adjustments it takes to make this arrangement succeed."

Gianni closed his computer, folded his arms and gave Briana a hard look. She, like him, had dressed for the seriousness of the occasion: white suit, hosiery, white shoes, the kind he'd heard women refer to as sling-back sandals. She looked responsible, reliable—and good enough to eat. Like a vanilla ice cream, one he'd start licking at the top and slowly work his way down, down, down...

Damn it!

He'd spent the afternoon telling himself what happened this morning had gotten his desire for her out of his system.

What a hell of a lie. If anything, he wanted her more than ever.

He knew her taste. Her scent. The little sounds she made when he caressed her. He knew the shape of her breasts, the softness of her thighs...and he was turning himself on just imagining what it would be like to take her again, slowly this time, slowly enough to savor each moment as he brought her to the edge, as she trembled beneath him.

"Did you hear what I said?"

She was looking at him with defiance etched into her face, all but daring him to argue. He supposed she was right. They'd have to work together as equals if this arrangement had a chance of working out, but what he'd told her was true. He liked taking the commanding position in a relationship; the women he'd been involved with were content with it, too. He knew it was an old-fashioned concept but it suited him to play the more assertive role. He'd been born in Sicily and raised in an American neighborhood that had its roots deep in the soil of an ancient culture.

His eyes narrowed as he remembered Briana in his arms a few hours ago. She hadn't demanded equality then; she'd been eager to let him master her. To lead her in a dance as old, as powerful, as time.

He could make her bend to him again. He had only to reach for her, pull her into his arms. She'd protest but when he kissed her she'd moan, wind her arms around him, open her mouth to the thrust of his tongue...

Gianni cleared his throat and forced the images from his mind. The child. Tomasso's daughter. That was all that mattered.

"I heard you," he said calmly. "And you're right." The shock in her eyes almost made him laugh. "I shouldn't have made decisions without consulting you."

"No. No, you shouldn't."

"So, which of the arrangements would you like to change?" He cocked his head and took pleasure in watching her struggle to regain the high ground. She had courage. Courage, and beauty enough to stagger a man. It was an interesting combination.

"Perhaps you'd prefer to wait a few days to go to Sicily?"

"Of course not. I only meant—"

"Or maybe you'd rather we flew a commercial jet."

"Don't be ridiculous! You know I wasn't referring to—"

"Is it our new living arrangements that distress you? Would you rather I took an apartment in your building?"

Bree snorted. Gianni looked interested. "Something else you've found amusing?"

"You? Living where I live? That would never happen."

"And the reason is...?"

"It's old, it's dirty, it's cramped. The street is noisy and not particularly safe…"

She blushed. He offered a thin smile. "Sounds like the perfect place to raise a child, doesn't it?"

"All right. You've made your point. But—"

"But, in the future, we should discuss our options when we make decisions that affect us." Us? *Us?* What kind of word was that? "Decisions we make that affect Lucia. That's one of the advantages of living in adjoining apartments. We can talk about things in the morning, over breakfast. Or at night, over dinner…"

He broke off in mid-sentence. What in hell was he talking about? She was thinking the same thing; he could see it in her face. He was painting a picture of domesticity, and domesticity had nothing to do with this. Theirs was a legal arrangement, nothing more. They'd live near each other for expediency but that was hardly the same as living together.

"Let me clarify that," he said. "We'll agree on, let's say, one morning meeting and one evening meeting a week so we can talk over problems, make plans, whatever. How does that sound?"

As if he were making decisions again. Still, the idea made sense.

"Fine."

Gianni nodded. "When we get back to New York, I'll phone an agency about a baby nurse."

"A nanny."

"Right. I'll interview several candidates, narrow the field down to two, and you can… What?"

"*I'll* phone an agency," she said. "*I'll* interview several candidates. *I'll* narrow the field down to two, and then you can interview them and choose one."

Bree waited for his reaction. So much for the idea of shared responsibility. His eyes had grown dark; she figured an explosion was likely, which was why she was stunned when he drew a deep breath, then exhaled.

"All right."

Oh, but he wasn't happy. She could tell by the way he snapped open his computer and glared at it, by the way he never spoke another word except for telling her to fasten her seat belt after they'd boarded the plane.

Five hours later, they touched down at Palermo. He got behind the wheel of a shining black Ferrari that had been waiting at the terminal; she got in beside him.

No driver, she was thinking, when he turned to her and spoke for the first time in all those hours, issuing the same order as the one he'd issued on the plane.

She let him get as far as the word "Fasten."

"Amazing as it may seem," she said sweetly, "I do not need a man to tell me when to buckle my seat belt."

"What you mean is," he said, "you don't need a man for anything."

"Now you've got the—"

She gave a startled cry as he pulled her into his arms and crushed her mouth under his. She struggled but he was relentless, lost in her honeyed taste, in the feel of her. She bit him; he ignored the swift, sharp pain, went on kissing her until she moaned and wound her arms around his neck, just as he'd let himself imagine, her hands in his hair, her body arched against his so that their heartbeats became one.

Letting go of her was the hardest thing he'd ever done. She fell back in her seat, eyes wide with shock. He wanted to tell her he was as stunned as she was, that whatever was happening here was beyond his comprehension, too, but instinct warned him that the best thing he could do right now was say nothing that didn't have to be said.

"Buckle that damned belt," he growled, and gunned the engine to life.

Tomasso, he thought as they sped away, *Tomasso, old friend, what the hell have you gotten me into?*

CHAPTER SIX

RAIN PUDDLES DOTTED the slick coastal road that led toward the Madonie Mountains. A low fog rose from the dark pavement and was pierced by the Ferrari's headlights.

Briana stared straight ahead, her hands tightly folded in her lap.

Gianni hadn't spoken since he'd kissed her, then growled his last order. She'd been too angry to say a word. Angry at him for kissing her, angry at herself for ultimately kissing him back.

And for remembering what it had been like to lie in his arms this morning.

Making love with him had been damned near accidental. Making love? What they'd done had been too quick, too frenzied, too wild to be called that, but oh, it had been incredible. Her skin still tingled where Gianni had touched it. Her mouth still felt the heat of his kisses. She could still hear her own little cries, his groan when he'd thrown back his head and come deep inside her.

She stole a surreptitious glance at the man beside her. He was driving too fast, taking the curves hard, jamming his foot to the floor on the straight-aways, but she'd be damned if she'd ask him to slow down. He'd interpret it as a sign of weakness and she couldn't afford to let that happen. He'd run roughshod over her too many times as it was, especially with that last kiss. Kissing her, forcing her to accept his kiss, was some kind of perversely macho exercise of power...

Forget it. She wasn't going there again.

Bree lay her head back against the seat.

What could Karen and Tomasso have been thinking, to put two such different people into a situation like this?

Not that she gave a damn what Gianni was feeling, but he had to be as upset as she was. Like her, he had to be looking ahead and seeing how impossible this arrangement was going to be. Being a guardian to a baby, having your co-guardian living next door, could only be a nightmare for both of them.

She'd cramp his style.

He'd cramp hers.

Suppose she wanted to bring a man home some night? She could see herself slipping the key in the lock, shutting the door after the man as he laughed softly and tucked her into the curve of his arm. She'd turn her face up for a kiss...

A kiss that would be nothing like Gianni's. It wouldn't be mind-numbing. Dominating. Powerful enough to turn her bones to liquid.

No. But it would be pleasant enough.

And that's all that would happen. A kiss, maybe two. What more would she do, knowing Gianni was right next door? That he might have a woman with him.

Stop it, she told herself fiercely, just stop it!

X-rated images weren't her style. For God's sake, being a mother wasn't her style, either. From waiting tables to motherhood or the next best thing to it, in the blink of an eye. It sounded like the title of a bad autobiography, but that was exactly what had happened to her.

She could learn to handle that, but she wasn't about to let Gianni create a plan for her life that would put him in her face, watching everything she did, telling her what to do and when to do it.

No way.

Headlights appeared in the darkness. A truck whooshed

past. Bree's hair, already tangled by the breeze, blew into her face and she swept it back behind her ears.

He was right about some things. Her apartment, for instance. Truth was, she wouldn't want to raise a child there but it was a quantum leap from admitting that to agreeing to live under his thumb.

Karen and Tomasso must have had some overall idea of how they'd want Lucia raised. It made sense that they'd wanted her to handle their little girl's day-to-day life while Gianni dealt with the legal and financial issues.

She and he didn't have to live under the same roof to accomplish that.

She'd move, but she'd choose where. Nobody was going to make that decision for her, and she'd tell him that when they reached their destination, which had to be soon.

What was the name of that town where they were supposed to make the turn-off?

"Cefalù."

Bree swung toward Gianni. Had she spoken aloud?

"We just passed a sign that said Cefalù but I didn't see how far it is. Did you?"

How could she read a sign when she was trying to figure out what had happened to her life?

"It's night," Bree said sharply. "You're driving like a madman. If you want me to read signs, slow down."

"I like driving fast."

Even in the shielding darkness, she could see the purposeful angle of his jaw and that little muscle ticking just above it, a dead giveaway that he was angry. What did he have to be angry about? She was the one on the losing end of this relationship.

"'I like driving fast,'" she mimicked. "Such a mature response."

"I know this road. I've driven it before."

She looked at him again. "You didn't tell me you'd met Tomasso's grandmother. What's she like?"

"I haven't met her but from what Tommy said, her spine is made of cast-iron and she has ice-water in her veins."

"But he loved her. Otherwise, why would he have come all this distance to let her see the baby?"

"Duty. Honor. Idiocy." Gianni shrugged. "The rules of *la famiglia* run deep in Italian families. Tommy didn't like the woman. He just wanted to do the right thing."

"The right thing," Bree said softly. "And now, he and Karen—"

"They're gone. What matters is their daughter. It's up to me to honor their wishes."

"You mean, it's up to us," Bree said coldly. She shifted in her seat, folded her arms and stared straight ahead. "How quickly you forget that the will said Gianni Firelli *and* Briana O'Connell."

"All right. It's up to us."

The truth was, he suspected Tomasso's grandmother wasn't going to see things that way. He had the feeling he was going to have to do some fancy maneuvering in the next couple of hours. He knew enough about Sicily, Sicilians and their sometimes outmoded codes of honor to be wary, but why tell that to Bree now?

He checked his mirrors, pulled into the next lane and raced past the car ahead of them.

"Tommy's lawyer warned me that *Signora* Massini may try to stop us."

"Stop us from what? From taking the baby? Why didn't you tell me?"

"There's nothing to tell you until we see if that's the case." He checked his mirrors again and moved into the right lane. "I did some research on our situation this afternoon." He glanced at the clock. "Yesterday afternoon," he said with a little laugh. "Hell, I can't remember the last time I slept."

Neither could Bree, but she didn't care about that now.

"And?" she said impatiently. "You did some research, and what? Don't tell me that this old woman Tommy hated is going to demand she raise his daughter!"

Gianni glanced at Bree. Her hair was tangled by the wind and she raised her hands to it and pushed it away from her face, eyes glittering in a way that told him she wasn't going to tolerate an answer she thought wrong.

So much passion. So much emotion. Things were simpler when you lived by the law but he had to admit, there was something about the way this woman embraced life that fascinated him.

There was no middle ground with her, no holding back.

There'd been no holding back this morning, when she'd begged him to take her. When she'd opened her mouth to his kisses, opened her thighs to his touch, wrapped those long legs around his waist...

His hands tightened on the steering wheel.

Forget that. They were involved enough, thanks to the terms of Tomasso's will. Eighteen years of dealing with each other stretched ahead of them. Eighteen years? He knew of marriages that didn't last that long! The only way to survive the relationship was to keep it impersonal. No connections, except as they affected Lucia.

Briana had her life. He had his—but only a fool would try and pretend things wouldn't change. How would he bring women home, with Briana a thin wall away? Not that he brought women home often...

Okay. Not that he ever brought them home. It was easier to spend the night at a woman's apartment. That way, he could get up and leave. After the proper length of time, of course.

Did Briana bring home her lovers? Was that what she

figured on doing, once they were living next door to each other? Gianni's jaw tightened. It wouldn't happen. No men. Not in her bed. No men, period. No affairs. No—

"What's the matter with you, Firelli?"

He blinked, looked at Bree, let out his breath. "Sorry. I was, uh, I was thinking about—about Tommy's grandmother."

"Well, so am I. That's why I just asked if she can break the terms of the will."

"Legally? No. No, she can't."

"Well, then—"

"But if she can find a way to delay things, she might."

"And? What do we do then?"

"We come up with something to convince her she'll be fighting a losing battle."

"Such as?"

"I won't know," he said honestly, "until if and when she makes a move."

Bree sank back in her seat. "And all this time," she said, half to herself, "I've been picturing this wizened little old lady, wearing black from head to toe, sitting outside a cottage on a cobblestone road in a two thousand year old village, just waiting for us to arrive."

Gianni grinned. "You've seen one *Godfather* movie too many, *cara*, though I admit, parts of *la Sicilia* meet that description."

"Not the part I've seen. Stefano's castle," she added, when Gianni looked at her. "Have you been there?"

"I've seen photos." He checked his mirrors again, pulled into the next lane and passed a slower-moving vehicle. "I don't expect the Massini place to be a castle but I think you can give up the idea of it being a simple cottage in a little village."

"Only in *The Godfather,* huh?"

"In real life, too, depending on where you're born, and

whether you're rich or poor. My great-grandfather came from a village not far from here. It's why I know this road.''

''You still have family here?''

He shook his head. ''No. But I've been back a few times. I wanted to see where I came from.''

''And?''

''And,'' he said, giving her a quick smile, ''the town that might have been the setting for a couple of those movies.''

''Should I be addressing you as Don Firelli?'' Bree said lightly.

''If my great-grandfather had had his way, you'd probably be doing exactly that,'' Gianni said, with no trace of humor. ''We're coming up on another sign. I'll slow down. See if you can read it this time.''

He eased his foot off the accelerator. Bree all but pressed her nose to the glass. The sign still flashed past—he must have dropped all the way to eighty or ninety miles an hour, she thought, rolling her eyes—but she was able to decipher it.

''It says we're twenty kilometers from Cefalù.''

''Good. There should be one more sign for the town before we reach our turn-off. Keep your eyes peeled.''

''Were you serious about your grandfather?''

''Great-grandfather. Very serious.''

''He was in the Mafia?''

''He was a *bandito*. There's some question whether he was also *Mafioso*.'' He grinned. ''But he was a man of high moral principle. At least, that's the family lore.''

No wonder Gianni had such an imperious attitude. It was in his DNA.

''We just passed another sign. Was it for Cefalù?''

Was it? She hadn't noticed. She was too caught up in imagining Gianni as a bandit. Gorgeous. A little dangerous. Sexy.

She sat up straight. ''You're going too fast again,'' she

said irritably. Who cared if he was descended from *banditos,* gorgeous or not? "How can I read anything, especially in a language I don't speak?"

"You don't have to speak Italian to read a sign." He glanced at the speedometer. "And I'm not going too fast."

"I'm sure that'll be a great comfort to Karen's little girl if we end up as roadkill."

Gianni shot her a narrow-eyed look. The lady had a way with a phrase.

Still, she was right. The Ferrari was a thoroughbred, begging to run, but the baby, their responsibility to her, was all that mattered. He let a few seconds pass to show Briana who was boss. Then he eased his foot off the accelerator.

"You're right. Lucia's welfare is what's important." He glanced at her. "What do you know about babies?"

"Not much."

"But you're—"

"A woman?"

Gianni almost laughed at the dangerous edge in her voice. "You're an aunt. That puts you one-up on me."

Bree sighed and sat back in her seat. "You can put what I know in a thimble and have room left over. Babies cry. They smile. They eat. They sleep. Mostly, they pee and poop. Why Mr. Firelli, sir, was that a shudder?"

"We'll need things."

"Things?"

"A crib."

"A car seat."

"A car seat," Gianni said, and craned his neck to look into the almost non-existent rear compartment of the Ferrari.

"There are laws back home about car seats, but I was thinking about the flight. I can hold her while we drive to Palermo, if you promise to drive slowly—assuming you even know how to drive slowly—but we should buy a car seat to put her in on the plane."

"Of course," Gianni said.

What he meant was, what in hell was happening to his life? Bree knew that because she was thinking the same thing.

"I suppose," he said, "we should discuss how to deal with Tomasso's grandmother."

"Discuss it?" Bree thrust a hand into her hair and tried to tuck it behind her ear. "You mean, you're not going to come up with an offer she can't refuse?"

"Very funny. You want to do comedy or talk about what to do when we reach *Signora* Massini's house?"

She sighed, put her hand to her temple and rubbed it. The long flight, the longer day, had left her with a headache.

"Talk," she said wearily. "What else do you know about the *signora?*"

Gianni shook his head. "Not much. Just what I've told you."

"So, the reason Tommy and Karen didn't name her as their baby's guardian was that Tommy didn't like her?"

"That, and the fact that Lucia is an American citizen. They'd have wanted her raised in her own country."

"Well, I can't see how the *signora* could disagree with that."

Gianni looked at Bree. "In a logical world, she wouldn't. Unfortunately, it isn't a logical world."

"It would be, if you ran it."

"What's that supposed to mean?"

"Oh, you know. Everything would be done just so. A schedule for this, another for that."

"There's nothing wrong with order."

"There's nothing wrong with spontaneity."

"Is that why you can't hold down a job?"

"Is that why you want to run my life?"

They looked at each other. Then Gianni laughed. "Oil and water," he said. "You and me. I don't know what

Karen and Tomasso were thinking when they chose us as guardians.'' He stepped on the gas and shot past another vehicle. "I think our best approach to Grandma is going to be a cautious one. Let her set the pace until we know what's in her head.''

"Won't she come right out and tell us?"

"This is Sicily, Briana. Old customs still prevail.''

If *The Godfather* theme floated through her head one more time, Bree figured she was going to owe royalties to the guy who'd written it.

"Are we back to little old ladies in black?"

"We're back to facts. Fact one, Tommy didn't like her. That's saying a lot. He was the kind of guy who loved everybody. Fact two. Tommy's attorney has already given us fair warning.''

"Which you only just decided to share with me.''

"Fact three,'' Gianni said, ignoring the taunt, "it'll be best if you follow my lead.''

"Fact four,'' she replied, glaring at him as she tucked back a strand of hair, "have you forgotten our agreement? We make decisions together.''

"Damn it, woman, must we fight every step? I'm only suggesting we stick to the old adage. When in Rome…''

"You mean, when in Sicily, men are men and women are good for only one thing.''

He wanted to tell her she was good for lots of things. She was smart, she had a glib tongue—he was even starting to enjoy their arguments—but that, definitely, she had a special talent for that one thing…

But he wasn't stupid.

"Look,'' he said patiently, "there are things we can say to soften her up. For instance, we can tell her we'll bring Lucia to Sicily for summer visits.''

That sounded reasonable. "Fine.''

"We'll assure the *signora* that Lucia will learn her native language."

"Okay."

"And that you're going to learn it, too."

Bree looked at Gianni. "Gee," she said sweetly, "isn't this nice? You've already started following our new policy."

"My primary concern is that she might grab on to the fact that we're not married."

"Married?" She sat up straight and glared at him. "We're not even friends!"

"We were more than friends this morning."

It wasn't what he'd intended to say, but, damn it, did she have to keep putting her hands to her hair? Each time she did, her breasts lifted. Each time she moved in her seat, she came within an inch of brushing against his hand as he shifted. And what was that scent she was wearing? Jasmine? Tea Rose? Lily of the Valley?

"That," she said stiffly, "was an accident. I've forgotten all about it."

"The hell you have," he said gruffly.

"God, what an ego! I'm amazed there's room in this car for me."

The tires squealed as Gianni suddenly pulled to the side of the road and turned to her.

"You haven't forgotten this morning any more than I have," he said as he put the car in neutral and undid his seat belt.

Bree stared at him in alarm. "What do you think you're...? Gianni!" She slapped at his hands but he was quick. A second later, her belt was open and he was gathering her in his arms. "Damn it," she sputtered, "are you crazy? We don't have time—"

"We do," he said softly, his smile tilting. "We have all the time in the world for this."

And he kissed her.

It wasn't the way he'd kissed her before. If it had been, she knew she'd have fought, but this kiss was slow. Devastatingly slow. It was the way a man kisses a woman when he wants to seduce her. When he wants to excite her. When he wants her to know nothing is as important as this moment, this kiss.

Bree melted.

"Kiss me back," Gianni whispered against her mouth and she did, clasping his face, parting her lips, sucking on his tongue when he slid it between her teeth. He cupped her breast. His fingers brushed the nipple and she gasped, arched against him, felt the electricity streak from her breast to her belly to the place between her thighs that was already turning warm and wet. For him. Only for him.

She'd never felt this. Never wanted this. Never needed, needed, needed—

The headlights of an oncoming car caught them like a spotlight. Bree cried out and tore her mouth from Gianni's. He cupped her head, brought her face to the hollow of his throat but she pushed her hands against his chest and struggled until he let go of her.

"Briana," he said. "Briana…"

She shook her head. "Don't."

"Don't?" His voice roughened. He caught her by the shoulders, brought his face level with hers. "It's too late to play games, *cara*. I want you. You want me. We're adults. Why lie to ourselves and to each other?"

"Oh God," she whispered brokenly. "I don't know what's happening…"

"If it's any comfort," he said, with a harsh laugh, "neither do I." He pressed his lips to her temple. "I'm not going to apologize. I wanted to kiss you more than I've ever wanted anything in this world."

Bree reached out her hand as if to touch him, then pulled it back.

"We're complicating things," she whispered.

"Do you really think pretending we don't want to make love is going to uncomplicate them?"

"If—if we get involved, Gianni—if we do, what happens when we—when we end the relationship? We'll still have to deal with each other, because of Lucia."

He knew she was right. No matter what you said at the start of an affair, a man and a woman couldn't go from being lovers to being friends.

Yes. She was right. But what did that matter, when he wanted her so badly he ached? When he knew it was the same for her?

"Nobody can see the future, Bree."

"No. But we'd be fools not to try."

A muscle knotted in his jaw. He thought about taking her in his arms, kissing her until she stopped thinking. Putting his mouth on her breasts, sucking the nipples until she cried out with pleasure. Slipping his hand between her thighs, under her panties, stroking her until she came apart in his arms, until she begged him to unzip his trousers, lift her into his lap so she could lower herself on him, impale herself on him, take him deep, deep, deep...

Damn it, he was driving himself crazy!

Gianni sat back, fastened his seat belt and put the Ferrari in gear.

"Buckle up," he said sharply.

She did. He checked for traffic, pulled onto the road and wished to hell he could grab Tomasso by the collar and shake him.

Hey, paisano, he'd say, *look what you've done! There I was, leading a perfectly normal life and then...*

And then?

Then, he'd met Briana. And she'd turned his world upside down.

CHAPTER SEVEN

THEY MISSED the turn-off twice before they doubled back and found it.

It wasn't a road at all but an old cart track that wound up the side of the mountain. In minutes, they were deep within an overgrown forest, tree branches whipping past only inches away.

Gianni put up the convertible top.

"Lovely road," Bree said lightly.

"Just great," he said through his teeth. He cursed at a particularly deep rut, shifted gears and slowed the car's speed until they were almost crawling.

"Maybe we ended up taking the wrong turn-off after all," Bree said, clutching the dashboard for leverage.

"The only other one we found was a dead end, remember? Besides, there's no going back. There's nowhere to turn around."

"Why would anybody want to live on a road like this?"

"To keep visitors out."

"How nice. Thank you for that encouraging thought, *Signore* Firelli."

Gianni flashed her a smile. "My pleasure, Miss O'Connell."

Bree grabbed for the door handle as the car lurched over another series of bumps.

"Seriously, if this road, or whatever you want to call it, is a measure of *Signora* Massini's hospitality, it's just one more reason to dislike her."

"Let's try to reserve judgment, okay?"

"That doesn't sound very lawyerly to me."

"Just goes to prove you don't know much about lawyers."

"One of my brothers is a lawyer. He never reserves judgment. Cullen always knows what's right and wrong." Bree looked at Gianni. "Sound familiar?" she said with saccharine charm.

"This is a different situation," Gianni said. He didn't really believe it, but he figured it wouldn't hurt to start with an open mind. "Maybe Tomasso's attorney got the wrong vibes. Maybe Tomasso had some personal thing that made him dislike the old lady. Maybe—"

"Maybe that's the house."

Gianni stuck his head out the window to get a better view. "Oh, damn," he said softly.

Damn, indeed. The house, outlined against the rapidly lightening sky, was still a distance away but even from here, Bree could see that it was enormous.

"You said it wouldn't be a castle."

"And I was wrong. It looks like something relocated from Transylvania."

"Want to change your upbeat take on what kind of friendly reception is waiting for us?"

Bree's tone was casual but Gianni wasn't buying it. He reached for her hand and enfolded it in his.

"Scared?" he said softly.

"No." She hesitated. "Terrified."

"Don't be." He brought her hand to his lips. "The law is on our side, remember?"

"Do you expect anybody who lives in a place like this to worry about the law?"

Gianni grinned. "*Signora* Massini is hardly the bride of Dracula."

"Maybe not, but if I see bats flying around the front door, I'm going to scream."

"*Cara*. The *signora* is only human."

"Right. But it's—it's like a one-two punch, you know? Meeting her. And meeting Lucia." Bree turned to him. "I think that's what really has me worried. Meeting our— our— What do you call a child when you're her guardian?"

"You call her a tremendous responsibility. And, to be honest, I'm as wary of what comes next as you are."

"I can't imagine you afraid of anything."

"Not of the *signora*. No matter what trouble she gives us, assuming she gives us any, we can handle her. But the baby... That's another story. What I told you before is true. I don't know a thing about children."

"We'll be okay as long as we don't let her figure that out."

"Tomasso's grandmother?"

"The baby." Bree smiled. "Cassie—my brother Keir's wife—Cassie said that was the way she got through giving their baby the first bath. She said she was terrified, but everything was okay because the baby didn't know it."

"Sounds like good advice for dealing with Lucia as well as the *signora*."

"You're pretty smart when you want to be, Firelli."

"Mark this day down," Gianni said solemnly. "Briana O'Connell gives Gianni Firelli a compliment."

"Just don't let it go to your head."

"It won't." He sighed, let go of her hand and shifted gears as they emerged from the trees into the clearing. "That might be the last compliment you ever give me, *cara*, considering that I don't have a clue as to what we're walking into."

"Why does that sound so ominous?" Bree said, trying for a light touch and failing miserably.

He pulled the car over. "By now, Tomasso's grandmother has had time to think things over."

"Is that good or bad?"

Gianni shrugged. "Damned if I know. I suppose she could welcome us warmly. It's a long shot, but it's possible."

"So is snow in August."

"If she does, we'll stay for a few hours, get some sleep, give her a chance to say her goodbyes to the baby and then head for the airport."

"And if she's not glad to see us? What do we do then?"

He gave a long sigh. "I'm not sure. Postponing the inevitable might be a mistake."

"Meaning, we should take Lucia and leave right away."

"Yes—assuming that's a viable possibility."

"Why wouldn't it be? The will—"

"We don't want to make it look as if we're kidnapping the baby."

"We wouldn't be. The will—"

"We're in Sicily, not the United States. I told you, the customs—"

"Are different," Bree said impatiently. "I heard you. Still, the law is the law."

"Amazing," Gianni said wryly. "Here I am, a realist, trying to make you, an idealist, understand that there are times the law isn't all that matters."

"Is that what you think I am? An idealist?"

"I think you're a dreamer, *cara.*" He lifted her hand to his mouth. "That you've spent your life searching for something you still haven't found." His eyes met hers. "Am I right?"

Bree stared at him. What were they talking about? Not Tomasso's grandmother. Not the baby. Then, what? Was Gianni thinking about what had happened a little while ago? Had she given it all away then? Did he know that nothing in her life had prepared her for what he made her feel when she was in his arms? That each time she looked at him, she wanted—she wanted—

Light poured into the car, blinding them. Bree screamed; Gianni said something quick and harsh in Italian and flung his door open. There were sounds of scuffling.

The light went out.

When her eyes finally adjusted to the greyness of the emerging dawn light, Bree saw Gianni struggling with a monster at least ten feet tall. She sprang from the car, grabbed a rock and raised it as high as she could.

"Stop it," she yelled, and swung with all her might. The monster staggered and dropped at her feet.

Bree hardly glanced at him. Instead she threw herself into Gianni's arms.

"Gianni? Gianni, are you all right?"

"I'm fine."

"Let me see." She ran her fingers over his face, checking for cuts. "I was so scared! I thought you—I thought it—"

Gianni caught her hands and pressed a quick kiss to them.

"I'm fine, *cara.*" He knelt down beside the man, picked up the flashlight he'd dropped and switched it on. "Let's see if we can say the same for our friend."

"He was trying to hurt you."

"No," Gianni said gently, "he was talking to me."

"But—but I saw his hands and arms going in all directions."

"There's an old joke among my people," Gianni said dryly. "Tie up our hands and we'd be tongue-tied." He turned his attention to the huddled form on the ground. *"Siete tutto il di destra?"*

Bree stared at the monster, who no longer appeared to be ten feet tall. Nowhere even close to that. The reality of what had happened, what she'd done, hit home. "Oh God," she said shakily. "Is he—did I—?"

The man on the ground groaned and felt his head.

"Signore?"

Gianni nodded. *"Si. Chi sono voi?"*

"Sono il maggiordomo di Signora Massini." He groaned again and touched his fingers to his head. *"Che cosa è accaduto? Che cosa lo ha colpito?"*

This time, it was Gianni who groaned.

"What did he say? Who is he?"

He ignored her and rattled off what she knew were more questions. The fallen monster answered. Gianni nodded. Then he looked at Bree.

"Take his other arm. Help me get him to his feet."

Bree squatted beside the man and put a hand under his elbow. *"Grazie,"* he said in a shaky voice. No, she thought, worrying her lip with her teeth as they stood him erect. Not ten feet. Not eight. Five, maybe. Only maybe.

"Do you speak English?" Gianni said.

"Si, signore. Uno piccolo. A little."

"I'm going to put you in my car and drive you to the house. All right?"

"Yes. *Grazie.* Thank you." The man put his hand to his head again. "What hit me?"

Bree opened her mouth. Gianni shook his head as he carefully handed him into the car.

"I'm not sure. A tree branch, perhaps. This area, where the road comes out of the woods... It needs attention."

"Si. I will speak with the gardener."

"You do that," Gianni said, and shut the door.

"Gianni? What's going on?"

Gianni sighed. He looked up to the pale cream of the morning sky and thought about how simple and predictable his life had been until yesterday.

"They saw our headlights from the house. When the lights stopped moving, the *signora* decided either we'd broken down or we were the press, trying to sneak in."

"The press? But why would the press—"

"I don't know. I suppose the accident made the local papers. The *signora* is something of an important figure, or so it would seem."

"So—so who's this man?"

Gianni's mouth thinned. "He's the butler."

"The—"

"The butler. You bashed the butler in the head."

Bree slapped her hand against her heart. "Ohmygod!"

"Indeed," Gianni said dryly.

"But I thought—I thought he was trying to—to hurt you…"

Her eyes were enormous, her hair was wild and she was trembling. Gianni felt his throat constrict. He wanted to tell Briana something but he wasn't sure what it was. Instead he whispered her name and pulled her into his arms.

"Thank you," he said gruffly.

"For what?" She gave a shaky laugh. "I thought I was taking out the Frankenstein monster. Instead I creamed the *signora's* butler. That's a heck of a way to start our visit, don't you think?"

"Well, it was impressive." He smiled, then pressed a kiss in her hair and held her at arm's length. "She'll never know."

"You think?"

"I know," he said firmly. "A tree branch. That's what did it."

Bree sighed. "Okay."

"You swing a mean rock, *cara.*"

She grinned. "I grew up with three brothers. We played baseball a lot."

He smiled back and brushed her hair from her eyes. "Baseball, huh?"

"Sure. Keir taught me."

"Did he teach you to take on monsters, too?"

"Cullen taught me that," she said, laughing softly.

"What about driving shift cars? Any of your brothers give you those lessons?"

"Of course," she said primly. "Sean."

"Remind me to thank them when I meet them."

"Will you?" Bree said, her smile tilting. "Meet my brothers, I mean?"

Of course he would. Years of dealing with each other stretched ahead of them. In all that time, they'd be bound to step into each other's lives.

But that wasn't what she was thinking. Neither was he. She was thinking of the feeling growing between them, one that seemed to have a power all its own.

A muscle knotted in Gianni's cheek. "Of course," he said softly. "I'll have to tell them how brave their sister is."

"And stupid. I can't believe I attacked the butler."

"For what it's worth, I attacked him, too."

"You didn't conk him in the head."

Gianni laughed. "No. I didn't." He tilted Bree's chin up. "You were brave, *cara*. Now, I'm going to ask you to be brave again."

"How?"

"By meeting Tomasso's grandmother alone."

Bree blinked. "What?"

"The Ferrari won't hold all of us, and I'm not about to let you walk all the distance through this meadow alone."

"Don't be silly. What could possibly hurt me?"

"Wild boars," he said, with no smile at all. "Wild dogs. You can find both in these mountains. You'll drive, Briana. I'll walk."

"But—but—"

"Just don't get into conversation with the *signora* until I get there. I'll only be a few minutes behind you." Gianni's hands slipped to her shoulders. "Stick to the basics. Intro-

duce yourself. Tell her you're pleased to meet her. Tell her
I'll be right along.''

"Tell her I beaned the butler and oh, by the way, I've
come to take her great-grandchild.''

"A tree branch beaned the butler,'' he said evenly. "And
you've come to do the bidding of the last will and testament
of our friends. But there'll be no need to tell her that. All
you have to do is be polite and mark time until I arrive.''

"You mean, you want me to do the old Sicilian female
thing. Listen, nod my head and smile.''

"You couldn't do the old Sicilian female thing, such as
it is, if your life depended on it.''

Bree sighed. "I know. I just don't…'' She cast a glance
over her shoulder. The huge grey stone house, looming cold
and desolate on a hill, was fully visible now. "Ugh. I can
see why Tomasso didn't want his baby raised here.''

"And we've yet to meet the *signora*,'' Gianni said
grimly.

"You said it wouldn't be a castle, and it isn't.'' She gave
a nervous laugh. "Did I say I was worried about bats? Vam-
pires might be the real bet.''

Gianni cupped her face, bent to her and brushed his
mouth lightly over hers.

"Get going,'' he whispered. "Just remember, if things
get tough, all you have to do is get the lady into the noonday
sun and we'll be fine.''

Bree smiled, as he'd hoped she would.

"See you in five, Firelli,'' she said airily.

Then she got into the Ferrari, ground the gears hard
enough to turn Gianni's face white, patted the arm of the
man seated beside her and drove off, while Gianni trudged
after the car.

It didn't pay to listen to the sounds the clutch made.

It didn't pay to wonder what *Signora* Massini would think
when she saw her wounded butler. He was pretty sure she

wouldn't buy the tree branch story, but would she figure out that Bree had tried to brain the man?

A smile curved his mouth.

His Briana was quite a woman. Strong. Resilient. And, at the same time, soft. Sweet. Vulnerable. Yes, indeed, his Briana...

Gianni blinked.

His Briana? What kind of thinking was that? He liked her. Liked her a lot, which was saying quite a bit when you considered he'd thought her the curse of all womanhood only a day ago, but she wasn't his. There wasn't a woman on the planet he'd ever thought of as "his" and there wouldn't be, not for years and years and years.

This was sex. Okay. Sex and like. Liking. Whatever in hell the word was, Gianni thought irritably as he plodded toward the house. He could want Bree and like her at the same time, couldn't he? So what if what he felt for her was different?

Not that he'd ever gone to bed with a woman he didn't like. The truth was, he had to like a woman before he wanted her. Well, no. Bree was the exception to that. What he'd felt for her initially hadn't been anything positive...

But he'd wanted her anyway.

"Hell," Gianni muttered.

Okay. It was time to take a step back. Return, as it were, to logic. Get the baby. Go home to the States. Get Briana and the child settled in next door, hire a nanny, organize things so they ran smoothly and then slip back into his own life...

"...wouldn't feel the way he did! You are an impossible—"

The breeze swept the rest of the words away, but it didn't matter. Gianni knew the voice was Bree's.

He stopped in his tracks.

"No," he said under his breath, "please, no."

The house was only a few yards away. He winced at the sight of the Ferrari parked, more or less, with its front tires drunkenly perched on the base of a set of wide flagstone steps.

The butler, poor man, was nowhere in sight.

Two women held center stage. One was a tall, imposing figure leaning on a silver cane.

The other was Briana. And from the way she was gesturing as her hair swirled around her face, he knew damned well she'd forgotten everything he'd told her.

CHAPTER EIGHT

GIANNI TOOK a deep breath, forced a smile to his lips and bounded up the steps.

"Briana," he said cheerfully. "You made excellent time." She swung around and glared at him. He returned a warning look, then smiled again as he extended his hand to the *signora,* who pointedly ignored it. "*Signora* Massini. *Buon giorno. Com'è sta? Mi dispiace sono in ritardo, mai—*"

"What are you telling her?" Bree demanded.

It wasn't easy, but Gianni kept his smile. "Calm down," he said through his teeth.

"I asked you a question. What did you just say?"

Gianni flashed another smile at the stiff-faced *signora.* "*Signora. Uno momento, per favore.*" His smile vanished as he grabbed Bree's wrist and pulled her aside. "I said hello, for God's sake. Hello, how are you, I'm sorry I'm late."

"You're sorry *we're* late," Bree snapped, "or has that 'we make decisions together' thing already gone by the wayside?"

"Bree. Take it easy. I don't know what's happening here, but—"

"What is happening," the *signora* said, her voice icy enough to put a layer of frost on the rapidly lightening day, "is that your companion chooses not to understand what she's been told."

"You mean, you speak English?" Bree said hotly. She

swung toward Gianni. "She pretended she couldn't. Only one sentence. That's all she kept repeating. 'You are not welcome here.' That was what she said, over and over and—"

"It was all it is necessary to say. Unfortunately your companion refuses to believe it."

Gianni could feel his smile slipping. He hadn't expected a warm welcome but he certainly hadn't anticipated being turned away at the door. And then there was the intonation Tomasso's grandmother had twice put on the word "companion…"

"We've come a long way, *signora*. Surely this isn't an example of Sicilian hospitality."

"I am not Sicilian, *Signore* Firelli, as you can surely discern from my speech. I am Roman, brought to this godforsaken island by my late husband."

"Not Sicilian," Bree snorted. "She's lived here for, what, a hundred years?"

"Bree," Gianni said tightly, "let me handle this."

"I am sorry you've made a long trip for nothing, *signore*."

"Does she call coming for Karen's and Tommy's baby 'nothing?'"

"Bree, damn it, will you keep quiet?"

"If you choose not to teach this girl her place, I shall."

That did it. Gianni gave up the smile and any attempt at cordiality. "This is Briana O'Connell. She was Karen's closest friend and, as you well know, she is now Lucia's guardian."

"She has been given that title, yes. As have you."

"Right. And unless you want to face us in court, I suggest you step aside and let us in."

The *signora* smiled. "An empty threat, *signore*. This is Sicily. Things move slowly here." She took a step back.

"If we ever do meet in court, it won't be for years and years. Now you will excuse me. I have things to do."

"Tomasso's attorney has friends in high places," Gianni said. It wasn't really a lie. Every lawyer had, or thought he had, friends in high places, but this woman didn't have to know that. "And I have contacts, too. Contacts in the press." That, at least, was true. He was a Federal prosecutor. He'd handled cases that dripped with notoriety. He'd never given so much as a nod to any of the dozens of reporters who'd begged for exclusives but if he had to, he would now. "I wonder what those who live on what you refer to as this godforsaken island would say about a wealthy woman who believes she's above the law."

"Oh, she's wealthy, all right," Bree said. "Look at this house. This—this Frankenstein's castle where she thinks she has a chance in hell of raising our baby—"

Our baby. The words made Gianni's heart stop. He looked at the fire in Bree's eyes, grasped her hand and wound his fingers through hers.

"Your choice, *signora*. We do this the easy way—or we do it in public."

There was a beat of silence. Then the *signora* rapped her cane sharply on the fieldstone. The butler Bree had slugged appeared behind her. He looked fine, Gianni saw with relief, if you didn't pay attention to the lump on his head.

"Bartolemo. Get their luggage. Put it in the blue bedroom."

"Thank you," Gianni said politely.

"For what?" The *signora's* smile was sly. "For agreeing to speak with you?" She paused. "Or for putting you in one bedroom? Your lack of morality is not my affair, *Signore* Firelli, not unless it impacts my great-granddaughter. I promise you, I will not let that happen."

And that, Gianni thought as they followed her into the

cavernous foyer, that was the situation they faced, neatly packaged in the proverbial nutshell.

THE BLUE ROOM was enormous, with furniture to suit. The ceiling was at least twelve feet high and decorated with cherubs and harps. Silk draperies hung against the windows and enclosed the four-poster bed. It was a room filled with what were surely priceless antiques and centuries of history.

Bree hated it on sight.

"It's got all the vitality of a corpse," she said, as soon as Bartolemo bowed himself into the hall and shut the door. "This whole house is like a graveyard."

"I'd say it was more like a museum," Gianni said, yanking off his jacket and tossing it on a chair, "but I won't argue with your definition."

"And that woman. Who does she think she is?"

Gianni, who'd taken in stories about what peasants could expect from Italian aristocracy with his mother's milk, laughed.

"She knows who she is, *cara. Signora* Emma Olivia Gracia Massini."

"You know what I mean."

"I know exactly what you mean," he said, flinging his necktie after the jacket. "Trouble is, she's probably right. She's a powerful woman."

Bree looked at him. "Are you telling me she can win? That she can keep the baby, despite the terms of the will?"

"She can delay things interminably, if she chooses."

"But you faced her down. You got us through the door."

Gianni sat down on the bed. The endless hours, the upheaval in his life, were suddenly catching up with him.

"I threatened her with publicity. It's the last thing members of *la famiglia* want."

Bree's eyes widened. "*Signora* Massini is—"

"Her husband was. I knew I'd heard the name before,

but when I saw this house, when she said her husband had brought her here from Rome…'' He plumped the pillows behind him, yawned and sat back. ''Publicity's our ace in the hole, *cara*.''

''I thought the law was our ace in the hole.''

''Yes, but she's right about how long it would take for this to wind through the courts.''

''What about all those contacts Tommy's attorney has?''

Gianni sighed. ''Who knows? At this point, I'm only sure of two things. The *signora* wants to avoid publicity—and she doesn't want her great-granddaughter raised by a pair of immoral Americans.''

He could almost see Briana bristle. ''Speak for yourself, Firelli. I am not immoral.''

''You're not married.''

''Neither are you.''

''We're going to be Lucia's guardians but we're male and female.''

''A brilliant observation.''

''And we're not married to each other.'' Gianni's eyes met hers; a slow, sexy smile tilted across his mouth. ''Who knows where that might lead?''

Bree felt her cheeks heat but she kept her gaze steady on his. ''It won't lead us anywhere. Not again. I told you, things are complicated enough without—''

''I know. I agree. I'll find a solution, but first I need some sleep.''

She seemed to notice the one enormous bed for the very first time. ''Why did she put us in here?'' she said crossly. ''When she said the blue suite, I thought it meant we'd have two bedrooms.''

''It's her way of telling us she knows we're lovers.''

''But we're not.''

''What a short memory you have, *cara*.''

Bree slapped her hands on her hips. ''We are not lovers,''

she said firmly. "I'm going to go downstairs, find the *signora* and tell her—"

"We'll tell her something, but not now." Gianni yawned. "We have to get some sleep or the *signora* will dance rings around us."

He was right. Bree could feel exhaustion seeping through her bones. "All right. I'll take a nap in that chair."

"Don't be ridiculous." He patted the bed. "Lie down here."

"In the same bed as you?" She folded her arms. "No way."

"The bed is the size of a football field. You take one side. I'll take the other. You won't even know we're sharing it."

"No."

"Oh, for God's sake!" He was off the bed and beside her before she could react. She squealed as he lifted her in his arms, carried her to the bed and dumped her on it. "Close your eyes," he said sternly. "Go to sleep." He grabbed her when she tried to get up. "You're staying put, O'Connell."

"I'm not the least bit tired."

"You're out on your feet." Gianni stretched out beside her. "Close your eyes. Go to sleep. I don't want you going near the *signora* again without me."

"I don't take orders from you. How come you keep forgetting that?"

"I'm Sicilian. I know the customs here."

"I'm an intelligent woman. I can figure them out."

"Oh, yeah," he said sarcastically, "I could tell that after watching how well you handled *la signora.*"

Bree glared at the ceiling. "She's an awful person."

"She's the person we have to deal with."

"I want to see the baby."

"Me, too." Well, that was a lie. Why would he want to

see the baby when he was terrified of even touching it? Something so small. So fragile. So dependent. So determined to change his life for years and years to come. "But we need some sleep first."

"I want to see her now."

Bree started to move. Gianni turned on his side, wrapped an arm around her waist and pulled her back against him.

"Get over here."

"Let go!"

"Damn it, do not fight me on this!"

"You said you'd take one side of the bed and I'd take the other. You said—"

"Shut up, *cara*."

"I am not tired!"

"Yeah, well, I am."

There was a brief silence. "My clothes will get wrinkled."

Tired as he was, he almost laughed. "The last resort of a desperate woman," he said. "Put your head on the pillow. Go to sleep."

"You can force me to lie here, but you can't force me to sleep."

"No," he said wearily, "I can't. Just keep this in mind. I'm a light sleeper. You try to get away, I'll know it."

"Bastard," she huffed.

Gianni, the light sleeper, answered with a snore.

Bree lay stiff under the weight of his encircling arm. They were tucked against each other like a pair of spoons.

She ground her teeth together.

All those promises about decisions and the minute they were confronted by the *signora*, they flew out the window.

He was right when he'd said he liked taking care of women. And she was almost ready to admit—never to him, of course—that she could see why women liked having him take care of them. Being in his arms, his body hard and warm against hers, his breath soft in her hair, she couldn't think of a place she'd rather be.

Still, she wouldn't sleep. Never. Not like this. Not like...

Bree's lashes brushed her cheeks. Seconds later, safe in Gianni's embrace, she was asleep.

LONG SHADOWS slanted across the bed.

Gianni opened his eyes. Late afternoon? Had he really slept that long? He yawned, stretched...and felt the warmth of a woman's body pressed tightly against his.

Bree.

She was sound asleep but sometime during their nap, she'd turned toward him. Now she lay in his arms, her head nestled against his shoulder, one hand on his chest, one leg flung across his. She'd wrapped herself around him despite all those protests about sharing the bed.

She felt soft, smelled sweet, looked young and trusting and more beautiful than any woman he'd ever known.

Gianni felt his heart turn over.

Gently he shifted his weight until she lay even closer in his arms. She sighed, and the whisper was like a caress against his throat.

She was more than beautiful.

He smiled. He knew she wouldn't think so. Her hair was what women called a mess. He thought sleep-tousled curls were sexy. There was a dark smudge of mascara below one eye and her lipstick, pale to begin with, had completely worn off.

Gianni's arms tightened around her.

She was a tough woman, his Briana. At least, that was what she wanted the world to think. He knew differently. She had a softness, a delicacy that left her vulnerable. She needed someone to protect her. To keep the world at bay. To hold her and comfort her.

She needed—she needed...

"Mmm."

Bree's eyelids fluttered. She sighed again, stretched against him as delicately as a cat. Her body curved against his, her breasts warm against his chest, her hips arching into him.

She was going to be upset when she came fully awake and realized she was lying in his arms, that they were sharing the same space, that her mouth was close enough for him to kiss.

Her eyes opened. Confusion clouded the deep blue irises. "Gianni?" she murmured, and he did what any man would do in that situation.

He kissed her.

She stiffened. She was going to push him away and, damn it, she had every right. He'd promised not to touch her, agreed that this—this attraction, whatever you wanted to call it, could only complicate a situation that was already impossible.

But then she made a little humming sound, curled her arms around his neck and her mouth, her sweet-as-honey mouth, opened to his.

Gianni groaned and deepened the kiss.

Her body arched against his. Her hand cupped his jaw.

"Briana," he whispered, and kissed her throat.

"Yes," she said, "yes. Oh, yes."

He rolled her onto her back, kissed her throat again. Her blouse was in the way; he tried to undo the top button but his hands were shaking and finally he growled with frustration, grasped the silk lapels and tore it open.

She wore a white cotton bra. He'd been with women who bought their lingerie with sex on their minds. This was the least erotic thing he'd ever seen, yet it turned his already-hard erection to steel. The swell of her breasts above the bra was a line so delicately feminine he felt his throat constrict.

He bent his head, kissed that curve, kissed one breast, then the other. Bree sobbed his name, buried her hands in his hair and brought his mouth to hers.

He lingered over the kiss.

Alone in the universe, there was time to do what he had not done yesterday morning.

Time to savor the sweetness of her mouth.

The silk of her skin.

The taste of her nipples on his tongue.

When she whispered his name, there was time to let the music of it echo inside him.

And when she touched him, God, when she touched him, moving her hands over his face, his shoulders; slipping them under his shirt so he felt their heat against his bare skin...

Gianni gritted his teeth.

He wanted this to last forever.

"Slowly," he said, when her hand dropped lower. "Slowly," he groaned when she cupped his erection and sent him too close to the edge. It killed him to clasp her hand and lift it from him but he did it, brought it to his mouth, sucked her fingers, pressed an open-mouthed kiss to the center of her palm even though he longed to tear off the rest of her clothes.

He wouldn't.

It had all gone too quickly that first time. This time would be slow. It would be for her.

It would be because he had never wanted a woman as he wanted Briana.

He bent to her, kissed her mouth, her throat, put his lips to her breast and nipped the beaded flesh outlined beneath the soft white cotton. She moaned and he kissed her again so that her sweet, hot little cries became part of him. He sat her up, undid the clasp of her bra. She caught it as it fell away from her and he shook his head, caught her wrists, bared her breasts to his eyes.

Ah, dear God, her breasts. Her beautiful, beautiful breasts. They were small, high, the color of cream, the crests budded flowers of deepest rose. He cupped them, kissed them, swept his thumbs across the tips.

Her eyes darkened.

"Do you like the feel of my hands on you?" he said. "Tell me. Tell me what you like."

"That," she said as he ran his fingers over her nipples again. "Oh, that. That…"

He sucked one nipple into his mouth and then the other, and she cried out in passion. Gianni licked her, teased her with his tongue. Then he brought his lips to hers and kissed her while he caressed her.

When she was sobbing in his arms, he lay her back against the pillows.

"Briana," he whispered, "Briana…"

There was more to say, but he didn't have the words. Controlling himself took all his strength.

"Touch me," she whispered, and he came close to forgetting all his good intentions.

He pushed up her skirt, slipped his hand between her thighs. Her panties were already wet; he bit back a groan as he fought the desire to unzip his trousers and bury himself deep inside her.

This was for her. All for her.

He pulled her panties down and watched her face as he stroked her. Her eyes blurred but they stayed on his.

"Gianni," she sobbed. "Gianni…"

Gently he parted the delicate female flesh. Sought the bud within. Found it, caressed it and with a soft cry, she came apart in his arms. He drew her tightly against him, running his hand down her back, stroking her face, dropping soft kisses on her hair, rocking her against him until she stopped trembling and her breathing steadied.

Then he cupped her face and lifted it to him.

Her skin was flushed, her lips parted. She looked like a woman who had been well-loved and his heart flooded with some new, unknown emotion.

"Are you all right, *cara?*" he whispered.

She nodded and slicked the tip of her tongue across her bottom lip. "I'm sorry," she whispered. "Gianni, I'm so—"

He stopped her words with a kiss.

"It's what I wanted," he said softly. "I wanted to see you come for me."

"But—but what about you? That wasn't—it couldn't have been enough."

He shook his head and silenced her with another kiss.

"It was everything," he said gruffly.

The damnedest thing was, it was true. His heart still pounded, his body still ached with need, but nothing he'd ever done with a woman before this had ever left him with such a profound feeling of completion.

She smiled and burrowed closer.

Seconds later, he felt her relax. Her breathing slowed. She was asleep.

Her head was on his shoulder. He could feel the muscle starting to complain but an aching muscle was a small price to pay for what had just happened.

For what was happening, though he'd be damned if he knew what it was.

Bree murmured something. It sounded like his name. Gianni hoped it was.

He drew her even closer.

Lying here was a mistake. It was time to get up, take a shower, find the kitchen in this drafty old pile of stone and get a cup of coffee. *Espresso,* the more super-charged the better. He had to think about what to do next, how to get the baby away from the *signora* without ending up mired in legal quicksand.

Back home, stuff like this could drag on forever. From what he knew of the law here, forever might be just the beginning.

He'd only delayed things by threatening publicity. The *signora,* he was sure, would figure a way around that soon enough.

Her threat about morality was the problem.

Unless things had changed in these little hill towns, the idea that a baby of Sicilian descent was going to be raised by a man and women who weren't married would be anathema.

If she played it right, the *signora* could come out of this a local saint, intent on maintaining the moral code.

Gianni sighed.

Nothing was clear yet. He was still too wiped out to think straight.

Gently, he kissed Bree's mouth. Then he drifted off to sleep.

WHAT WOKE HIM this time wasn't the softness of Bree in his arms.

It was a blast of light.

He opened his eyes, cursed softly and screwed them shut again.

"Hey," he said, struggling up against the pillows, "turn that thing off."

"Get up, Firelli."

Cautiously he opened his eyes again. Briana was standing at the foot of the bed. She'd showered—her hair was damp and curling on her shoulders—and changed her clothes.

She'd changed her mood, too, judging by her unsmiling face.

He swung his legs to the floor and ran his hands through his hair. "What's the matter?"

"Oh, nothing. Nothing except the fact that we've wasted the entire day, thanks to you."

"Bree. Wait a minute…"

"And we've done exactly what that old witch wanted us to do, also thanks to you."

Gianni's head came up. "Huh?"

"She put us in this room to drive home a point. You said so yourself."

Had he said that? His head was fuzzy. When was the last time they'd eaten? Better still, when was the last time he'd had a jolt of caffeine? Damned if he didn't need one now to clear his brain.

"Cara," he said carefully, "I'm not following you. What point?"

"That we're—we're lovers."

Color rose in her face. Seeing it made him shake his head.

"We *are* lovers. Besides, what does that have to do with anything?"

"We are not lovers. We're—we're two people who took a complicated situation and made it worse after we agreed we wouldn't."

"Briana." He got to his feet and walked toward her. "Listen to me. Just because we made love—"

"I don't want to talk about this now. I want to see Lucia."

"And we will. But your attitude—"

"I don't have an attitude, Firelli."

And pigs could fly. "Bree," he said, striving to stay calm, *"cara…"*

"Will you stop calling me that?" she said, slapping his hands away as he reached for her. "Just get yourself ready so we can go find the *signora.*"

Gianni's eyes narrowed. "I don't know what's going on in your head, Briana, but I don't like it."

"That really breaks my heart."

"This discussion isn't over."

"I'll give you ten minutes. Then I'll go looking for the *signora* on my own."

"Do that," he said softly, "and I promise, you'll regret it."

Briana's chin lifted. "That's right. Go into macho mode. When in Sicily—"

"Watch what you say to me."

"Why? Will you beat me if I don't?"

A thin smile spread across his mouth. "I've got a much better way of bringing you to heel than that," he said, pulling her against him and crushing her mouth beneath his.

Bree wanted to sink into the kiss, wind her arms around his neck and lean into his warm, strong body.

Except, that would be playing right into his hands. It was what men like this expected of women. It was how they controlled them.

She slammed her hands on his arms, twisted her mouth away from his. "Stop it! Are you crazy? I just told you, that's over."

He looked into her eyes. "Is it?"

Gianni turned his back, strolled into the bathroom and shut the door. When she heard the shower come on, she sank back against the wall.

What had happened before wasn't only his fault. She had to admit that to herself, if not to him. But it wouldn't happen again.

Waking that second time, wrapped in Gianni's arms, remembering what she'd felt when he made love to her, the incandescent joy, the soaring wonder...

Terrifying. All of it.

That she, who knew better, would forget everything she knew about that kind of passion, was unbelievable. That she'd lose all sense of self was incredible. That she'd let a man gain such control over her was unbearable.

Her head drooped.

She had not signed on for any of this. Gianni was going to have to understand that. No way could they be Lucia's guardians until they sorted things out. They were not lovers. They would not be lovers. She would not let herself feel— let herself feel—

Someone knocked at the door.

Bree stood away from the wall, ran her fingers through her hair, touched her lips.

"Yes?"

A woman answered in what sounded like a babble of Sicilian. Bree only understood one word. *Bambino.*

It was enough.

She took a deep breath, opened the door and a woman in a white uniform handed her the tiny bundle that would forever change her life.

CHAPTER NINE

THE BABY was gorgeous.

She was also adorable, perfect, scrumptious and undoubtedly a genius, even at this tender age.

Bree, smitten by emotions new to her, could tell all that on sight.

By the time she'd followed the nurse down the stairs to a sitting room the size of a small theater, every fear she'd harbored about handling Lucia had been swept aside.

The baby lay in her arms as if she belonged there, gazed up at her face and instantly took control of Briana's heart.

The responsibility was still awesome, maybe even more so now that the moment of assuming it had actually arrived, but all her instincts told her she was more than capable of dealing with her new role.

As for the changes this would make in her life... They didn't matter. Whatever it took to raise this child, she would do. Gladly. Nothing she'd ever taken on had come close to seeming so right.

"We're going to get along just fine," she told the baby.

Lucia gurgled.

"I don't know a lot about babies but then, babies don't know a lot about grown-ups. We'll learn together."

Lucia regarded her solemnly, her chocolate-brown eyes wide and unblinking. Then she smiled and reached out a tiny hand to swat at Bree's chin.

Bree laughed, clasped the hand and gave a smacking kiss to each little finger.

"You're a sweetheart!" She looked at the nurse. "Lucia is—she is *mucho bella.*"

She'd probably gotten her languages confused but it didn't matter. The nurse, who'd been watching the proceedings with hawk-like intensity, visibly relaxed.

"Si, signorina. È un bambino meraviglioso."

"Gemma is right. Lucia is a wonderful child."

Bree swung around. *Signora* Massini stood in the doorway, unsmiling, every hair in place, as formidable in appearance as she'd been that morning. She'd changed from her suit to a long black gown. Did the lady dress for dinner all the time, or was this another attempt at intimidation?

The answer came quickly enough. The *signora* did a slow visual appraisal, taking in Bree's damp, untamed curls, her linen trousers, T-shirt and sandals with a smile that could only be called condescending.

"It's in her genes. Some things apparently skip a generation, but good breeding will always win out."

To hell with you, Bree thought, and looked her straight in the eye.

"Yes. It does. After all, her mother and father were remarkable people."

The *signora's* mouth twisted. "My grandson was remarkable only in his selfish determination to live a life he preferred, and his wife was a nobody." The cane tapped lightly against the hardwood floor as she came toward Bree. "This child will not be like either of them."

"This child," Bree said coolly, "will be the person she chooses to be."

"An unfortunate American attitude."

"An exemplary *modern* attitude. And I suggest you keep your thoughts about Tommy and Karen to yourself, *Signora* Massini. I don't want to hear them."

"You won't have to, Miss O'Connell. You've had this time with Lucia before dinner and, if you wish, you may see her again before you leave in the morning.'' She smiled thinly. ''I can keep my opinions to myself for that long.''

The baby cooed happily. How was she to know the course of her life was being decided? Bree smiled down at the child, then brought her to her shoulder.

''We're not leaving without Lucia.''

''And I am not giving her up.''

''You don't have a choice. The will—''

''The will is a piece of paper. Attorneys are paid well to turn pieces of paper into confetti.''

''They're paid even better to enforce the wishes of the people who wrote them.''

Gianni smiled politely as he walked into the room. He'd lingered outside the door long enough to know that Bree was revving into full battle mode. That was the last thing he wanted.

The only way to win here was to outplay the *signora,* and a verbal battle wasn't going to do it.

''*Cara,*'' he said, smiling at Bree. ''Where did you go? I finished my shower and found our room empty.''

Bree flushed. Was he crazy, talking so easily about their relationship?

''I wanted to see Lucia,'' she said stiffly.

''And here she is.'' Gianni looked at the baby. Big eyes, tiny nose, small mouth. That about exhausted all he knew of children this young. Bree was looking at him expectantly. Was he supposed to say something to this football-sized bundle? ''Cute,'' he said gamely.

''She's adorable,'' Bree said, and gave the bundle the kind of smile she'd never yet given him.

''She is healthy,'' the *signora* said. ''Her nurse takes excellent care of her.''

Gianni held out his finger. The baby grabbed it, dragged it to her mouth and chomped down.

''She doesn't have any teeth!''

"She's too young to have teeth. See? She's smiling."
Briana smiled, too. "She likes you."

"At this age, a child has no likes or dislikes," *Signora*
Massini said coolly. "Not as we know them. Infants react
to stimuli. Heat, cold, hunger, whatever. Just now, Lucia
may have gas. To attribute complex emotions to babies is
ludicrous."

Bree stared at the woman. "Do you honestly believe
that?"

"It's scientific fact."

"No wonder Tommy didn't want you raising his child!"

"Briana," Gianni said quickly. "Why don't you let me
hold Lucia for a while?"

"With that sort of attitude," Bree said, ignoring him, "I
don't even know if we'll let Lucia visit you every summer."

"There will be no need for visits," the older woman
snapped. "Lucia will live here, with me."

Bree swung toward Gianni. "When are you going to tell
her she's out of line!"

"How about letting me hold the baby?" he said.

It wasn't what he'd intended to say and it sure as hell
wasn't what he wanted to do. The pale pink bundle scared
the bejeezus out of him. The kid was all big eyes and jerky
arm motion...and, oh man, was that a trickle of drool coming from one side of its mouth?

But he had to do something to keep Bree from going to
war. Bad enough she'd come down here alone, to face the
signora. Face her? Hell, she was baiting her and that was
the last thing that would be effective in dealing with a
woman who thought she owned the planet.

The only possible diversion was the baby.

"May I?" he said again, and held out his arms.

Bree looked at him warily. Didn't he look as if he knew
what he was doing? Gianni curved his lips in a smile.

"Hey, pussycat," he said.

That did it. Bree handed the kid over.

He took the transfer carefully, one hand on the baby's bottom, one curving around her back. She weighed more than he'd figured. More than a football, anyway.

"Support her head," Bree cautioned, and he nodded as if he'd known that all along while he adjusted his grip and cupped his hand over the baby's neck and the back of its head.

Not it. Her. This was a her.

A very small her.

She was also warm and sweet-smelling, though he couldn't quite place the scent.

"Baby powder," Bree said softly, and he realized he must have spoken aloud. "And you don't have to hold her like that."

"Like how?"

"Like she's made of glass. She won't break."

No? The kid looked as if she might, but people had been having and handling babies for thousands of years. Maybe they weren't as fragile as they seemed. Carefully he relaxed his grip and drew the bundle closer to his chest.

"Da," the baby said, and grinned.

"Look, she's smiling at you again."

"That is not a smile. It is gas."

Gas? Hell, no. The kid was definitely smiling.

"She has yet to smile at anyone. I assure you, what you see is not a smile."

Yes, indeed. It was a smile, no matter what the old witch said. Lucia was flashing him a wide, toothless grin.

"The child has never seen you before. Why would she smile?"

"Perhaps," he said pleasantly, "she recognizes the people who are going to raise her."

So much for not baiting the dragon but, hell, he wasn't going to let her get away with that. The baby was smiling, and if she'd never yet done such a thing before, one look at this house and this old woman and he understood the reason.

Signora Massini eyed him coldly. "This is a pointless argument. Give her back to her nurse, *Signore* Firelli. It is bedtime."

"Let me say goodnight," Bree said, and reached for the baby.

"Sure," he said softly, and put Lucia in her arms.

He watched as she bent her face to the child's. She was crooning something to her and the baby made a little gurgling sound of pleasure as she patted Bree's cheek.

Amazing.

They'd talked about this moment, about what it would be like when this baby, this bolt of lightning from out of a serene blue sky, finally came into their lives.

What did either of them know about babies? He'd expected to feel fear. Okay, terror the first time he held Lucia and he had. Briana had expressed the same doubts but watching her now, laughing as the baby tugged on her nose, he suddenly knew how right this was.

Karen and Tomasso had chosen well. Bree would make a wonderful guardian.

She'd make a wonderful mother.

He could almost see her holding another baby while a slightly older Lucia clung contentedly to his hand, except the new baby would have Bree's golden curls, her blue eyes...

Or they might be green, like his.

Gianni took a hurried step back.

"Briana," he said, "give the baby to her nurse."

"In a minute."

"Now."

She looked at him, her eyes narrowing in a way he knew was dangerous, and he forced a quick smile.

"We have important business to discuss with *Signora* Massini." He took a deep breath, told himself to slow down. "And, to tell the truth, I don't remember the last time we ate." He turned to the *signora* with a polite smile. "You are inviting us to dinner, aren't you?"

"Dinner tonight. Breakfast tomorrow." Tomasso's grandmother tapped her cane against the floor. "After that, *signore,* I am afraid we must part."

THE DINING ROOM made the sitting room seem cramped.

Twenty-four ladder-back chairs were lined up at a table that stretched through a room hung with tapestries. A fire blazed on a hearth Bree suspected might be big enough to hold her entire apartment. She'd thought the fire just another bit of pretension until they'd been seated and goose bumps rose on her arms.

It was summer outside. In here, it was winter.

Why not? she thought, desultorily shifting bits of cake from one part of her plate to another with her fork. This was another world, never mind another weather system.

The three of them were seated at one end of the table, the *signora* at the head, she and Gianni on either side. They'd eaten their meal in silence, all five courses, from tasteless consommé to tasteless dessert. No. Not true. Nobody had eaten. Instead they'd gone through the motions.

There'd been no conversation. She'd started to talk about the baby, and Gianni had tapped her foot with his. A while later, she'd opened her mouth again and before she'd gotten two words out, he'd tapped her foot again, harder this time, hard enough so she'd glared at him across the polished mahogany.

Now, her eyes flashed.

When I'm good and ready, his flashed back.

Oh, yes, they were handling this together, all right. She was furious at herself for deferring to Gianni but there was the one slim chance he was right, that he understood the medieval customs of this place and she didn't.

A silent maid tiptoed in and took away their dessert plates, then tiptoed back with a coffee service. The *signora* poured tiny cups of *espresso,* complete with tiny curls of lemon peel.

"Thank you," Bree said stiffly when the *signora* held out her coffee.

She took a sip. Thank God, this part of the meal was edible. And thank God the endless meal was coming to an end. If Gianni didn't say something soon—

"This is excellent *espresso,*" he said politely.

The *signora* inclined her head.

"And an excellent meal."

Another inclination of that elegant head.

"But it's time to discuss our situation."

The *signora* looked at him across her tiny cup. "We've already done that. I have no intention of accepting my grandson's will as legitimate."

"On what grounds will you contest it?"

She shrugged. "That is not my decision, it is my attorney's. There are several, ranging from the undue influence of Tomasso's wife—"

"What are you talking about?" Bree said hotly. "Karen would never— Ouch!"

It hadn't been a tap on the foot this time but a swift kick in the ankle.

"If your attorney is reputable," Gianni said, "and I am sure that he is, he'll tell you that proving undue influence will involve a lengthy and expensive court battle."

"Perhaps." The *signora* lifted her cup to her lips. "Neither is a problem, *signore.* Expense will not be an issue, and the time remaining to me will be sufficient for my needs."

"You mean," Gianni said, "you know you're going to lose and you only want to delay things as long as possible."

The old woman gave him a little smile.

Gianni pushed his coffee aside. "*Signora.* We have no wish to deny you contact with Lucia. We'll be happy to bring her to see you often."

"That's an interesting but useless offer. It does not address the problem of raising Lucia. Even if Tomasso were still alive, such visits would be pleasant but not meaningful. For one thing, occasional visits have little impact on a child's development. For another, involvement with children is a joy for some women. It never was for me. I had a son because it was expected of me, not because of any deep maternal yearnings."

"My God," Bree said. "Gianni? Did you hear that?"

"Then why would you even want to be involved in raising a child again?" Gianni said, ignoring Briana.

"Nurses, nannies, governesses… They are the ones who will be involved. I need simply to pay their salaries."

"Then," Gianni said, struggling to keep his temper, "putting all those things aside, do you really want to spend the next months, even years, in courtrooms?"

"Gianni," Bree said, "you can't let her—"

"All that time," he said tightly, "all that publicity. Will it be good for the Massini name, do you think?"

The *signora's* lips thinned. "You threatened me with that earlier, *Signore* Firelli, and I admit it does not please me, but my grandson left me no choice."

"No choice than to spend a fortune in legal fees, drag your name and the child's through the tabloids and, in the end, lose?" Gianni sat forward. "You *will* lose. You must know that. Have you discussed this with your attorney? I'm sure he'll tell you the same thing, *signora.* A last will and testament is a binding document, especially when it concerns the welfare of a child. Courts always prefer to follow the wishes of the parents."

Did he see the cup tremble, ever so slightly, in the *signora's* hand?

"Do you want your great-grandchild to grow up as an item in the tabloid press? Tomasso and Karen wanted us to raise Lucia, to give her the love and care they would have given her, not to see the Massini name and their daughter's life chronicled in sleaze sheets around the world."

Oh, yes. The cup was definitely trembling. The *signora* knew she was heading for thin ice.

"You make an excellent case, *signore*. Unfortunately you've left something out."

"And that is?"

The thin lips curled with contempt.

"Morality. Propriety. Decency." She put the cup on the saucer with enough force to make it shudder. "I am aware such things have little bearing in today's world, but they are important in mine."

Bree rolled her eyes. "Lovely. She's prepared to ignore Tommy's and Karen's wishes, to let the baby be fodder for the tabloids, and she has the nerve to talk about—"

"Bree." Gianni smiled, though smiling was the last thing he felt like doing. They were close to settling this; instinct, honed by years in the courtroom, told him so, but Briana could ruin it if she let anger get the best of her.

He pushed back his chair and walked around the table to where she sat.

"Bree," he said, his voice soft but his hands hard as he laid them on her shoulders, "Let *Signora* Massini speak."

"You have been blunt, *Signore* Firelli. I shall be blunt, as well. You are correct. My actions will do little but delay things."

"Then why—"

Gianni pressed down on Bree's shoulders. She huffed but fell silent.

"My attorney and his firm are clever. They will, as you

said, see to it that determining guardianship of Lucia will take years. Many years." The thin mouth curved again, this time in a self-satisfied smile. "By the time you gain full legal possession of her, she will be old enough to have been taught a proper moral code. She will not be affected by living in a house with a man and woman who have chosen to live together in sin."

The *signora's* voice had risen on the final words so that they seemed to hang in the silence of the huge room.

Then Briana laughed.

"Are you serious?" She peered up at Gianni, standing motionless and stone-faced behind her. "Is she serious? She's going to keep that little girl here because she thinks you and I are sleeping together and she doesn't approve?"

"She is serious," Gianni said softly.

Signora Massini plucked her cane from where it hung on the arm of her chair and stamped it against the marble floor. As if by magic, the butler hurried into the room.

"Indeed, I am quite serious. And now, if you will excuse me, it is getting late. Bartolemo, help me to my—"

Gianni cleared his throat. *"Signora."*

Tomasso's grandmother gave a put-upon sigh. "What is it now? You have nothing to say that I wish to hear."

"On the contrary," Gianni said quietly. His hands cupped Bree's shoulders. She looked up, saw a glitter in his eyes that made her belly knot. "We could have saved ourselves this entire discussion, *signora*." He took a deep breath. "You see, just this afternoon, Miss O'Connell did me the honor of agreeing to become my wife."

CHAPTER TEN

SOMEHOW, Bree got through the next few minutes without saying a word.

Somehow?

She gave an unladylike snort as Gianni propelled her through the door into their bedroom.

The combination of his hands digging into her shoulders and her shock at what he'd said had proven to be an effective gag, but the second the door shut behind them, she jerked away from him and exploded.

"Are you crazy? Telling that woman I'd agreed to...that I'd said I would..." She flung her arms wide. "I can't even say it! My God, Firelli, what came over you?"

"Calm down."

"Calm down? Calm down?" Bree's voice rose to new heights as she kicked off one shoe and watched with satisfaction as it bounced off the wall. "Do you think she's stupid? Do you think she'll really fall for that? Do you think—"

"Damn it," Gianni growled, "lower your voice! She'll hear you."

"She'll hear me?" Bree repeated incredulously. "You think she won't see through that incredible lie?"

"Did you hear her response, or were you too busy working up to hysteria?"

"I heard it, all right. She said she was surprised. That her attorney had told her we hardly knew each other."

"And I said her attorney was wrong. That your brother-in-law, Tomasso and I had been friends when we were kids, and that you and I have been seeing each other for a long time.''

''And you think she bought that?''

''It doesn't matter a damn if she did or if she didn't. The last thing she said is what counts.''

Bree gave a snort even less ladylike than the first.

''You mean, that she's delighted to know Lucia will be raised in a moral household? That now she can be assured the baby's upbringing will not sully the Massini name?''

''Exactly.'' Gianni stalked to the window, turned and stalked back again. ''That's all that matters to her.''

''Big surprise.'' Bree sent her second shoe flying. ''But there's one little problem, Firelli. We are *not* getting married. It doesn't matter if she hears me now or not. She'll figure it out soon enough. And here I always thought a person needed a functioning brain to get through law school. Boy, was I wrong!''

Gianni glared at Briana. Wonderful. Dinner with the Wicked Witch and now a crazy woman for dessert. Hadn't he spotted a drinks tray somewhere in this room? The damned place was so big you needed a road map.

Yes. There it was, on the sideboard. Two decanters and a couple of glasses. He had no idea what the decanters held. One liquid was amber, one was a pale gold.

He didn't care.

What he needed was a drink. The sharp burn of alcohol to clear his head and then maybe, just maybe, he could get back the clarity of that one moment when telling the *signora* that he and Bree were getting married had seemed the solution to their problem.

How could he have imagined that?

Bree was still raving, pacing back and forth, throwing up her hands, telling him that he'd succeeded in making things more complicated.

"It's your specialty," she said. "Complicating things."

Was she referring to his ploy to get the baby, or to what had happened a few hours before, in this bed? Gianni opened one of the decanters, poured an inch of its contents into a heavy crystal glass and tossed it back.

Scotch. Good scotch that went down like warm velvet. He poured another.

Yes. She had to be talking about that. About him making love to her. Why go back to that? It was over. It hadn't meant a thing. He couldn't even remember what it had been like, tasting her mouth. Her breasts. Feeling her nipples on his tongue, her heat burning against his hand. Hearing her soft cries, watching her beautiful face as she came for him. For him. Only for...

Jesus.

He slammed down the glass. He needed a clear head, not another shot of whisky.

"Enough," he said.

"I haven't even gotten started! How could you? What were you thinking? Why on earth would you say—"

"Enough," he roared, and slammed his fist down on the sideboard. The tray jumped. So did Bree, he noted with grim satisfaction. "Sit down and listen."

"Listen to what? I can't think of anything you could say that would—"

"Let me talk."

"I already did that, and where did it get us?" Bree blew a curl off her forehead and folded her arms. "In a mess," she said, answering her own question, "that's where."

"Telling the *signora* we were getting married was—it was expedient."

"You mean, it was dumb."

"If you'd stop raving and start thinking, you'd see it."

"What I saw was her face. She may have sounded as if she bought the story but one look said otherwise."

"I admit, she looked...skeptical."

"Skeptical?" Bree barked out a laugh. "That's a nice way of putting it."

Gianni felt a muscle knot in his jaw. She was right. *Signora* Massini had looked as if she'd just watched a magician try to convince an audience he was going to conjure a rabbit from a hat when they could already see its ears peeking above the crown.

"Then we'll just have to make her believe it," he said, folding his arms. "Or don't you want us to raise Lucia?"

"The law is on our side. You told me that a dozen times."

"It is." He paused. "But the *signora's* right. The law can move slowly."

"Tomasso and Karen left a will."

"For God's sake," he snapped, "use your head! She laid it out for us. For starters, we're on her turf."

"So? The will—"

"Bree, damn it, keep quiet for once and pay attention!" Gianni ran a hand through his hair, paced away from her, then paced back. Bree was right. He *had* told her the law was with them—and then he'd come face to face with the *signora*. Trying to explain his grandmother, Tomasso had once called her the original immovable object.

Tommy, Gianni thought with a sigh, *paisano, you were right.*

"Well, we have a couple of choices," he said, tucking his hands in his pockets. "One, we kidnap Lucia."

"That's fine with me."

"And we get stopped in Palermo—assuming we get that far—and spend the next hundred years in jail."

"Don't yell, okay? I just have to point out that the will is legal."

"Kidnapping isn't."

Much as she hated to admit it, he had a point. Bree sighed

and rubbed her forehead, where a permanent ache seemed to have taken up residence.

"You said we had a couple of options."

"We can dig in our heels for a legal battle. I'll contact some people I know, ask them to recommend someone here, the lawyers will meet, face off..." Gianni shook his head. "And maybe, with luck, Lucia will come to live with us by the time she's ready to start school."

"Are you serious?"

"They can stall us with endless delaying tactics. That's a given in any court system. And we're dealing with a powerful woman. Who knows how many buttons she can push?"

"What about our consulate? Won't it help us?"

"Help us do what? Intervene in what's basically a custody fight?" Gianni shook his head. "The government's not going to get involved in this, Bree."

Bree stared at him. "Do you mean—she'll win?"

Gianni squatted in front of her. "She can only win if we give up, and we aren't going to do that. Tomasso asked this one last thing of me. I will honor his wish."

Bree's eyes searched Gianni's. That last statement had calmed her. She knew he meant it. She'd learned a lot about this man in an amazingly short period of time. He was, absolutely, a man of his word.

"And I'll honor Karen's," she said quietly.

"Then we're agreed. We have to do whatever it takes."

"And you really think going through the courts might take months?"

"Years," he said bluntly.

He took her hands in his. Her skin was cold; the fire had gone out of her eyes and been replaced by despair. He wanted to tug her into his arms, kiss her until her skin took on heat and color, until her eyes glittered with life, but that would only complicate things.

"Oh, God." She put her hand to her mouth. "Then, that beautiful little girl might end up in this awful place for a long time!"

His hands tightened on hers. "She might—but we're not going to let that happen."

Bree swallowed hard. "You think—you honestly think— *Signora* Massini will back off if she thinks we're getting married?"

"Yes."

"Gianni. You saw the expression on her face. She didn't believe you."

He knew she was right. He could still see the look the old woman had given him, hear the cynicism in her voice when she said, "Really. How nice for you both." What sense was there in denying it?

"Okay." He gave a rueful smile. "Maybe not."

Bree touched her hand to his cheek. "You're a good man, Gianni Firelli," she said softly. "Coming up with such an idea, even if it isn't going to work."

Gianni caught her hand again and held it in both of his. "It can work, *cara.*"

"How? Tomasso's grandmother is a lot of things but she isn't stupid. What are we going to do, huh? Promise to send her an invitation to the wedding? She'll never release the baby on those terms."

"You're right, she won't." He lifted her hand to his lips, spread her fingers and pressed a kiss to her palm. "Still, there's a way."

"What way?"

"You won't like it."

"Is it legal?"

He nodded.

"That's good."

"Better still, it's guaranteed to work."

"If it works and it's legal, what won't I like?" She smiled. "Come on, tell me."

His eyes caught hers. In the sudden silence, Bree could hear the thunder of her heart.

"We get married," Gianni said.

AN HOUR LATER, they were seated facing each other on opposite sides of the bed. Bree was still shaking her head and saying no, no, they couldn't.

They could, Gianni insisted, of course they could. This was nothing more than a gambit in a chess game where the queen was an intractable old woman.

"I am not going to marry you," Bree said. "The *signora* will know it's only so we can get Lucia from her."

"She won't. I'll talk to her, explain that we'd decided, on our way here, that we wanted to make our relationship legal—"

"We don't have a relationship!"

"—and that we intended to keep that decision private," Gianni continued, as if she hadn't spoken, "but that we changed our minds when we realized her concerns are about Lucia."

"She has no concerns about Lucia," Bree said hotly. "Her only 'concerns' are for herself."

"I know that. You know that. But there's no reason we can't let her think we see her point."

Bree shook her head. "She won't believe you."

Gianni gritted his teeth. "Why are you so damned stubborn? All right. Let's try it your way. Suppose she doesn't believe me. So what?"

"What do you mean, so what? If she realizes we're only getting married to placate her, she'll—she'll—"

"She'll what? Tell us the marriage isn't to her liking? Listen to me, Bree. People everywhere marry for all kinds of reasons. In a place like this, an old-world culture, it's even more true. Marriages in these hill towns are often based on things that have nothing to do with love.''

Nothing to do with love.

Bree knew he was right. People did marry for reasons that had nothing to do with love, and love would surely have no bearing on this marriage—assuming she were foolish enough to agree to it. Then, why did his blunt words hurt so much?

"Bree. You know I'm right. Men and women marry for money. For property. For the good of their families. That we would marry for the benefit of a child would be a positive thing in the *signora's* eyes."

"But not in mine. I've always thought—I'd imagined marrying a man I felt—I felt something for."

Gianni reached for her hands. "You felt something this afternoon," he said, his eyes on hers.

Color rushed to her face. "That was sex."

"Sex is a part of marriage. An important part."

"No." Bree tore her hands from his and got to her feet. "I can't do it."

"Can't, or won't?" His voice hardened as he rose from the bed. "There's a difference."

"Gianni, try to understand. This is—it's wrong."

"Indeed," he said with sudden coldness. "And letting this woman, the last person in the world Tomasso and Karen would have chosen to be Lucia's guardian, letting her raise their daughter is right?"

"Of course it isn't! But—"

Bree's words stumbled to a halt. But what? Tomasso's grandmother had made it clear her only concern was for propriety. One lie, and propriety was no longer a problem.

The baby would be theirs.

Gianni must have read something in her face. He came to her and clasped her shoulders. His touch was light, his voice a whisper.

"We have no choice, Bree. We have to do this for Tomasso. For Karen. For the baby."

She looked up at him. "If—if we did this, how soon would we—"

"As soon as Italian law permits. With luck, you'd be my wife before the week ends."

His wife. She would be Gianni's wife. Bree began to tremble. "I don't—I can't imagine—I just can't—"

"I can," he said, and kissed her.

The kiss was soft as a butterfly's wing, only the brush of his mouth on hers. Bree made a little sound and leaned toward him; Gianni groaned, his arms swept around her and gathered her, hard, against him.

And she was lost.

She was a creature born on the sigh of the wind and Gianni was her world, her safe haven, he was—he was—

With a soft cry of alarm, she tore free of his embrace. "Don't," she whispered. "I can't think when you—when you—"

"Don't think," he said fiercely. "Just say yes."

Funny, but she'd seen a hundred movies with scenes like this. The man and woman standing close together, he gazing down at her, asking her the question she'd been longing to hear…

Except, this wasn't a movie.

Briana felt a sudden ache in her heart. She was close to weeping and couldn't imagine the reason. Gianni's question was all business.

Her answer would be the same.

"If I agree," she said, "it will only be on certain conditions."

"Name them."

"It won't be a real marriage."

A tight smile tilted across his mouth. "You're the one who keeps reminding me that the *signora* isn't a stupid woman. Have you changed your mind, *cara?* Do you suddenly think we've only to go away for a day, come back and tell her we're now husband and wife and she'll fall for it?''

"No." Bree took a shuddering breath. "No," she said carefully, "I know she'd never buy a story like that."

"Then, what are you suggesting?"

Another deep breath. Suddenly she couldn't seem to get enough air into her lungs.

"We marry, as you suggested. We take the baby. We go back to the States—and we get a divorce."

His eyes went flat. "I see."

"It's the only way to handle this," she said quickly. "The marriage will satisfy the *signora.*"

"And the divorce will satisfy you."

"You, too." Her throat felt parched and she swallowed convulsively. "I mean—I mean, you don't want to marry me any more than I want to marry you. Right?"

The muscle in his cheek knotted and unknotted. "Absolutely right."

"You said this was an old-world culture. Well, what we need is an old-world marriage of convenience."

"And a quick dissolution of it."

"Exactly. That suits you, doesn't it?"

There was a long silence. Then he shrugged. "Why not?"

"Good." Bree ran the tip of her tongue over her bottom lip. "There's just one other thing…"

A tight smile lifted one corner of his mouth. "What more could there be, *cara,* after we've said 'yes' to a quick marriage and a quicker divorce?"

"Another condition."

"What?"

She hesitated. Gianni could see her working up to something and he knew, instinctively, he wouldn't like it but then, he hadn't liked the initial condition either, and wasn't that crazy? If she hadn't suggested the divorce, he would have.

This marriage was about expediency. It had to do with honoring Tomasso's memory and nothing else.

"What other condition?"

"This will be a marriage in name only."

"A marriage in…" His eyes narrowed. "What in hell is that supposed to mean?"

Bree could feel her pulse beating high and fast in her throat.

"We're not going to do—what we did this afternoon." Gianni arched one eyebrow and she felt her face heating. "Don't look at me as if you don't remember."

"Believe me, *cara*, I remember exactly what we did this afternoon. And the reason is…?"

"It's wrong."

His eyes darkened. "We're both adults. We're attracted to each other. Why should making love be wrong?"

"Because it is. Because it complicates things. I told you that before."

"When you said that, we were unsure of what lay ahead. Now we know. We've seen the baby and why Tomasso's grandmother objects to giving her to us." Gianni took a step closer and cupped her face. "We've even figured out how to make that objection go away. How can we complicate this by making love?"

"We're Lucia's guardians, Gianni. That responsibility will be with us for a very long time. It's like a—a partnership."

"So?"

"So, would you sleep with your business partner?"

"If you'd seen any of the partners in the law firm I belonged to, *cara*, you wouldn't ask that question."

"I'm not going to debate this. Those are my terms. No sex."

Gianni frowned. Damned if she wasn't right. You didn't sleep with business associates, not if you wanted to be able to continue the business relationship after you grew tired of each other—and you always grew tired of each other. That was the way it was with men and women.

But they'd already violated that policy. They'd made love and, damn it, he wanted more of her. She wanted more of him, too. He knew it. The way she'd moaned in his arms today, the way she'd trembled. The scent of her, the silkiness of her skin...

"No sex," she said, her voice trembling just a little. She cleared her throat. "We won't sleep together, Gianni. If you want me to say yes to this marriage, you'll say yes to that."

His eyes weren't just dark, they were storm clouds.

"Let me get this straight. I give you my name. In return, I get an empty bed and a fast divorce. Have I got that right?"

"Oh, that's charming. You're going to *give* me your name?" Bree tossed her head. Why had she been so nervous a minute ago? How could she have forgotten this man's impossible ego? "Get this straight, *signore*. The only thing you're *giving* me is a temporary marriage I don't want."

"Stop wagging your finger at me."

"We're doing this for our friends. For their daughter. Not so you can have me in your bed."

"I told you to stop shaking your finger at me, Briana."

"And I'm telling you, take it or leave it. We do this my way, or... What are you doing? Let go of me, damn it! Firelli. Firelli—"

His arms folded around her and his mouth took hers in a long, almost savage kiss. Bree fought. Bree struggled. And then she let it happen, let the taste of him flood through her, let the feel of him heat her blood. She whispered his name, wound her arms around his neck as he slid his hands down her back, cupped her bottom and lifted her into him until their bodies were melded together.

His hand came up, cupped her breast. She groaned into his mouth as his fingers played over her nipple, as he slid his hand under her skirt, caressed her thigh, moved closer and closer to her feminine core...

And then he thrust her from him.

"The first rule of negotiation," he said curtly. "Don't demand terms you're not prepared to follow."

Bree launched herself at him. "Bastard," she hissed. "No good, slimy, good-for-nothing—"

Her hand flew toward his face. Gianni caught it and forced her arm behind her back.

"Watch what you say to me, *cara*. Watch what you do. Deep down, I'm still Sicilian. I don't take insults lightly."

He let her go and she fell back against the wall, hot with rage, shaking with it...

Stuck with it.

There wasn't a thing she could do that would make her feel better. She couldn't hit him, couldn't storm out of the room, couldn't even tell him to take his sorry self and sleep elsewhere because he'd beaten her to it.

As she watched, he flung a pillow and blanket on the chair that stood farthest from the bed.

"The bed is yours," he growled. "And if you say one more word to me tonight, I promise, you'll regret it."

"What I regret," Bree shrieked, "is that I ever had the misfortune to meet you!"

But she didn't say it until after he'd gone into the bathroom and slammed the door.

GIANNI GLOWERED at his reflection in the mirror.

He looked like a man who wanted to wander into a bar, pick a fight with the meanest looking SOB in the place and work off his frustrations with his fists. If he'd been anywhere but here, in the forgotten middle of nowhere, that was exactly what he'd have done.

Grumbling under his breath, he turned on the cold water and splashed some over his face.

He could get into the Ferrari and drive for a while. The *signora* would probably hear him leave the house but what did that matter? The walls of this old crypt were God only knew how many feet thick. Still, the way he and Bree had been going at it, the old witch had surely heard them by now.

The real problem with taking the car was that Bree would undoubtedly lock him out. He'd have to kick the door in when he got back, which wasn't a bad idea because then he'd swing her into his arms, carry her to that damned bed, kiss her mercilessly until she—until she—

Gianni groaned, grasped the edge of the sink and closed his eyes.

He wasn't a man who started fights with strangers. He wouldn't force himself on a woman…except, damn it, that was the whole point.

That was why he was so furious.

They both knew he wouldn't have to force himself on Briana.

She'd come to him willingly. Eagerly. She'd open her mouth for the touch of his tongue, part her thighs so he could lie between them. And when he entered her, he'd do it slowly. So slowly. Moving inside her. Feeling the kiss of her wet heat.

Gianni stared into the mirror again. The man that looked back might have been a stranger.

Complications? He wanted to laugh. That was too simple a word. He was in over his head, joined to a spitfire first by the guardianship of a child and soon by the bonds of matrimony.

So she wouldn't sleep with him. So what? He wasn't an

animal in rut. They'd have to suffer through a sham of a marriage for, what? A week? They'd marry, fly home, and married life would be history.

Just thinking about how simple it was made him feel better.

The water was still running. He ducked his head under it until his teeth chattered. Now, he could go back into that room and behave like a civilized man. He'd even apologize to Briana for losing his temper.

Except, she was asleep.

Gianni shut off the light, fought his way into a chair that wouldn't have held a poodle, let alone a man, and managed to get a couple of hours of sleep.

He woke just after dawn, body aching as if he'd been drawn on a rack, but still with that good feeling of being in control of his emotions. He went downstairs, found the kitchen and the coffee, then closeted himself in the library for a two-hour session on his cell phone.

Now he'd wait for Bree to wake up. Then he'd tell her what he'd arranged, apologize for going crazy last night, assure her he had no problem at all with her no-sex condition.

Gianni opened the door and slipped into the bedroom.

She was lying on her side. Like him, she'd slept in her clothes. Her hair was spread over the pillow; her lips were rosy and slightly parted. Her skirt was rucked up to her thighs.

She had such long legs. He could remember the feel of them, locked around his waist. So what? He was still in control, still going to make that apology.

"Bree," he said softly, and when she opened her eyes and looked at him, he told her that they'd be married by nightfall.

Her pupils dilated with shock. "By nightfall?"

"Yes." He was pleased with how calm he sounded. "The sooner the better. I had to pull some strings, but it's all set."

She sat up against the pillows, lifted her arms and pushed her hair back from her face. His gaze fell to her breasts. He could still remember their taste. The taste of her mouth.

"Married. You. And me."

"Yes. And there's something else, something I should have said last night."

The words *I'm sorry* were on the tip of his tongue. God, she was so beautiful. So much a woman.

"What should you have said?"

Still calm, still in control, he said he'd been thinking about that second condition.

"And?" she said, her eyes locked to his.

Gianni took a breath. "And," he heard himself say, "I'll be patient. I'll wait until you come to your senses, *cara*." His voice roughened. "And when you do, I'll take you into my bed."

CHAPTER ELEVEN

ONE NIGHT on Italian soil and Gianni Firelli had turned into an arrogant, dyed-in-the-wool Sicilian. Fortunately he was so smugly, disgustingly self-centered that it was almost painfully easy to outthink him.

She'd been so angry when he'd delivered what amounted to a challenge that she hadn't been able to think straight. Hours went by before she calmed down enough to realize how to handle his statement.

She'd simply ignore it.

He knew she wouldn't turn her back on the baby. She'd go through with the marriage. After that, Gianni could wait for her to go to his bed until the cows came home.

She didn't even bother responding. Instead she stalked past him, head high, went into the bathroom and slammed the door even harder than he had the prior night.

He was gone when she came back into the bedroom and she managed to avoid him all morning, but at noon she walked into the library without realizing he was there, talking on his cell phone. She turned on her heel and walked straight out again, but not before overhearing part of a conversation.

"Yes," she heard him say, "that's right. The flight is scheduled for eight this evening."

He was arranging their trip home. They wouldn't have to wait to start divorce proceedings. Goodbye, Italy. Hello, America. Soon, she could tell her husband-of-convenience to go to hell.

What a lovely moment that would be!

That thought kept her smiling during the long day. So did the baby, who loved having her belly kissed. Then Gianni came into the garden where she sat on the grass with Lucia in her lap and announced that she had an hour left.

She knew what he meant. An hour until she became his wife. She felt a rush of panic but she'd sooner have died than let him know it.

"An hour until what?" she said sweetly, and then she rounded her eyes. "Oh, of course. Until we get married. Sorry. I almost forgot."

He didn't smile back. He looked hard and grim and altogether forbidding. He also looked as beautiful as she'd ever seen him, in a dark suit and white silk T-shirt, his hair damp from the shower and curling lightly as it fell over his forehead.

Legions of women would have given their souls for this moment, but she wasn't one of them. She wasn't a fool. She knew what he wanted of her—not just sex but the passion that would turn her pathetic and defenseless, that would leave her heartbroken when this joke of a marriage ended.

"I'll be ready," she said in a cool voice. "Don't worry about it."

He did smile, then, in a way that made her breath catch. "I'm not worrying about a thing, *cara,*" he said softly.

As he strolled away, she handed the baby to the nurse and concentrated on the fact that they'd be on that plane before the ink was dry on their marriage license.

THEY WERE MARRIED at Trapani, in a wedding hall set aside for civil ceremonies. She'd expected a dank town office manned by a bored clerk but the hall was handsome and the mayor was charming. He took her hand and kissed it and spoke to her in Italian. The translator, a legal requirement for non-Italian couples entering into marriage, beamed and told her the mayor thought she was the most beautiful bride he'd ever seen and that he wished her much happiness.

Caught off-guard, Bree felt the prick of tears. The mayor undoubtedly told all the brides they were beautiful. It was what he'd said about happiness that got to her. A woman should be happy on her wedding day. She should be happy, assuming she wanted a wedding day in the first place.

Bree had never given it much thought. If she had, she surely wouldn't have dreamed of marrying a man like the one standing next to her. None of this was real, of course, but if it were, if Gianni loved her, he'd want more than her love in return. He'd want everything. Her heart, her mind, her very essence.

Nobody was ever going to lay that kind of claim to her.

The ceremony was mercifully brief. When it was over, the *signora* shook hands with Gianni and even with her. The nurse wiped away her tears and offered a quick kiss on the cheek. The baby, lying in the nurse's arms, gurgled happily and waved her arms.

"I am pleased," the *signora* said.

The queen had given her blessing. It was the final stamp of approval. Bree felt a little of the tension drain away. She shot a surreptitious glance at her watch and felt even better.

In a little more than two hours, they'd be on that plane heading for the States. She decided to help move things along.

"Gianni," she purred, leaning delicately into him, "don't you think we ought to get started?"

He looked down at her as if she'd just performed some fabulous trick. "I know you want us to be alone, *cara*," he purred back, "but surely we can spare a few moments to chat with our guests."

Guests? The *signora* and the nurse were their witnesses, but Bree went along with the game. She slid her arm through his. Why not torture him, if only a little?

"I'm sure *Signora* Massini will understand, darling. You can always phone her from the plane."

Gianni smiled, and something in the smile made the hair rise on the back of her neck.

"What plane, *darling?*" he said.

"Why—why, the one that leaves Palermo at eight. The one going to New York."

"Ah. *That* plane." Gianni slipped his arm around her waist and drew her close against him. "Unfortunately it will take off without us."

Bree stared at him. "But I heard you. In the library. You were making reservations…"

"I was canceling the arrangements I'd made for a charter flight home." He smiled, but the smile never reached his eyes. "The *signora* suggested we not leave quite yet."

"The *signora* suggested?" Bree tried to pull away but Gianni's arm only tightened around her. "And, just like that, you gave in? You didn't think about asking me what I wanted to do?"

"We can think of these next few weeks as a honeymoon," he said easily.

She knew he was talking that way for the *signora's* sake but she didn't care. If anything, it only made her angrier. Did he really think this mockery of a marriage gave him the right to make unilateral decisions?

"I want to go home, Firelli. Now."

"You will do as you're told, Briana," he said without any semblance of a smile.

Bree blinked her eyes. The mayor, the translator, the *signora* and yes, even the nurse were all watching the little scene with interest but not with concern.

She was in a foreign country, without funds, without friends. She didn't even speak the language. For the first time, Briana realized how truly alone she was.

AN HOUR LATER, after Gianni had checked them into a suite in a hotel overlooking the sea, she turned on him in barely contained fury.

"You had the entire day to tell me about this," she said through her teeth.

Gianni sighed. They were standing on their terrace. He could imagine other couples on other terraces in this hotel that he'd been assured was the most romantic in all of Sicily, their arms around each other as they watched the sun kiss the bosom of the sea.

Why he'd thought he needed a romantic hotel was beyond him. This had never been anything but a sham marriage and now, to top things off, he had to listen to his pretend-bride rant and rage. He kept reminding himself that she was upset because they wouldn't be leaving Sicily just yet.

But, damn it, she didn't have to sound as if she'd just been sentenced to life in prison with a barbarian for a cellmate.

"I told you," he said grimly, "the *signora* sprang the news on me late this afternoon."

"That she wouldn't give us the baby until she was convinced we were really married."

"Yes."

"Of course we're married! What did she think that wedding was?"

"A trick. She saw right through us."

"I said she would, didn't I?"

Gianni narrowed his eyes. "If you're going to play the blame game, get your facts straight. What you said was that she'd see through our claim that we intended to get married."

"Your claim, Firelli. Not mine."

He thought about responding to that, then decided against it. Quarrelling with Briana was like playing a frenzied tennis match. Rally followed rally.

"She's agreed that she'll give the baby up at the end of the month."

"The end of...? That's three weeks away! What are we supposed to do in all that time?"

"I've rented a house."

Bree slapped her hands on her hips. "Does it ever occur to you to consult me on anything?"

"There wasn't time."

"No. I can see that. There wasn't time for anything except trying to force me into getting into bed with you!"

He moved fast, so fast that she stumbled and fell back against the wall. Gianni caught her wrist.

"At last," he growled as he towered over her, "something we can agree on. Wanting you in that bed was dead wrong."

"I'm glad to hear you ad—"

"I don't know what in hell I was thinking. A man wants a woman in his bed, not a shrew." He dropped her wrist and stepped back. "Don't wait up," he said coldly. "I won't be back until late."

Bree glared after him as he strode from the terrace. "My door will be locked. You just remember that!"

Gianni grabbed his jacket and slung it over his shoulder. "At least there's a couch in this damned place. I won't have to break my back in a chair made for dwarfs tonight."

"Did you hear me, Firelli? I said—"

He spun toward her, his hand on the doorknob. "I heard you," he said quietly. "Believe me, O'Connell, you don't have to worry. I have no intention of violating your precious 'condition' for marriage."

The door slammed shut after him. Bree stared at it and then, for no accountable reason, her eyes filled with tears.

"I'm delighted to hear it," she whispered. "Except— except my name isn't O'Connell anymore."

Then she leaned on the railing and wept.

THE NIGHT WAS THICK and black.

No moon. No stars. Not even a lamp to pierce the darkness of the hotel's parking lot. Stepping out of the Ferrari was like stepping into a pool of inky silence.

Gianni slipped into the hotel, walked through the vast lobby and nodded at the night clerk who looked surprised to see him. It was a good bet that this wasn't the kind of place where guests wandered around alone in the middle of the night.

The elevator took him to the top floor. Gianni went down the dimly lit hall to the suite, inserted his room key into the door and eased it open. The sitting room was pitch-black. He shut the door, then paused to let his eyes adjust to the dark.

The first thing he saw was the open bedroom door. His heart thudded. Bree would only have left it that way for a reason. She'd come to her senses. She was waiting for him, in the bed that should have been theirs...

Hell.

No way would that happen. He'd been lucky she wasn't waiting in the sitting room with a heavy object in her hand. A rock, maybe, he thought, and had to smile at the memory.

His smile faded. She'd only have left that door open for one reason. She'd left him. Called for a taxi, a private car... The point was, she was gone.

He tossed his jacket aside, hurried into the bedroom and switched on the light.

He was right. She was gone. The bed hadn't even been touched... But her suitcase, standing next to his near the closet, was still there.

His gut twisted into a knot. "Bree?" He went to the bathroom, opened the door...

Empty.

"Bree," he said again, "Briana?"

The terrace was empty, too. His gaze was drawn to the railing, to the sea beating far below.

No. God, no...

"Gianni?"

He swung toward the sitting room. The spill of light from the bedroom lent soft illumination to the couch and to the woman huddled on it.

"Bree."

He went to her quickly, angry words building in his throat, but when he saw her, he knew his anger was only a cover for a relief so profound it stunned him.

His wife was sitting in a corner of the couch. She wore one of the heavy silk robes provided by the hotel and her hair hung over her shoulders in a wild golden cloud. Her eyes, when she raised them to his, were swollen and red.

Possibilities danced through his head accompanied by a rage so profound he thought he might explode. Someone had broken in. Someone had hurt her.

Hurt his Briana.

Gianni squatted in front of her and took her icy hands in his.

"What happened?"

She looked down and shook her head.

"Damn it, tell me what happened! Did someone hurt you?"

Another shake of the head. He felt some of the weight lift from his heart.

"*Cara,*" he said more gently, "talk to me. Tell me why you're crying."

"I don't know," she whispered. "I don't know why I'm crying."

Bree knew it sounded stupid but that was the truth. Gianni had been gone for hours; she'd wept for almost all that time and she didn't know the reason.

Maybe it was because she'd thought about how crazy he

could be, driving the Ferrari, and pictured him dead on the road. Maybe it was because she'd imagined him sitting in a bar, smiling at a woman who was happy to smile back.

Or maybe it was because this was her wedding night, real or not, and because she'd spent every minute since they'd agreed to the ceremony lying to him and to herself, pretending she didn't want him to take her in his arms, to kiss her, to whisper to her and, yes, make love to her.

Gianni stroked the riot of curls back from her cheeks.

"Briana," he murmured, "*cara, mi dispiace.* I'm sorry."

She shook her head. "You have nothing to be sorry for. You were right. We had to go through with the wedding, and we have to stay on long enough to convince the *signora* this marriage is real."

"But I should have consulted you first. You were right, each time. I'm just not—I'm not used to sharing decisions." He cleared his throat. "And I should never have expected anything from you."

"Expected…" Smudges of color rose in her face. "Sex, you mean."

"Making love. That was what I wanted, Bree. For us to lie in each other's arms and finally make love." He cupped her face, his fingers weaving into her hair. "I would never expect you to humble yourself to me, *cara.* Despite my stupid words, you must know that."

Bree offered a wobbly smile. "I know."

"No matter how badly a man wants a woman, she must want him, too."

Another shaky smile. "Do you know, the longer we stay in Sicily, the more you sound like a Sicilian?"

He laughed softly. "That sound you hear isn't the sea, *cara,* it's a collective sigh of approval from all my ancestors."

There was a silence. Then she drew a deep breath. "If we're dealing in truths…"

"Yes?"

"Then—then, here's mine." Bree raised her head until their eyes met. "I wanted you as much as you wanted me." She paused. "I still do."

He felt his blood leap. "Are you sure?"

"Yes. Oh, yes, yes, yes—"

Gianni took her mouth in a long, deep kiss. She moaned softly as his tongue swept over hers. When she did, he rose to his feet, taking her with him. He could feel the heat, the softness of her body through the robe, and he gathered her close and kissed her again.

She sighed, rose to him, clasped his face between her hands and he felt his swiftly hardening arousal turn to stone.

Quickly his mouth hot on hers, he carried her into the bedroom. The lamp he'd lit when he was trying to find her cast a soft glow on the bed. He set her down beside it and kissed her eyes, her mouth, her throat. Her head fell back; her lashes drooped languorously to her cheeks and he felt her start to tremble.

"Gianni…"

"Yes, sweetheart. Yes, *cara.*" He took her hand, kissed it, then pressed it against his erection. "It's the same for me."

It was. God, it was. His body was on fire.

Slowly he told himself, *slowly.* In so many ways, this would be their very first time together.

He undid her sash, eased the robe back on her shoulders. She caught it as it began to slip away but he captured her hands, brought them to her sides and let the garment become a lake of silk at her feet.

She wore a bra and panties beneath it, but not the plain white cotton he remembered from the last time. This bra was sheer black silk; the thong that covered her mons was sheer black, too, and he felt a moment of crazed jealousy that it cupped her so intimately.

Slowly he bent his head to her breasts, kissed the barely contained flesh. "God, you're so beautiful," he whispered, and caught first one silk-covered nipple and then the other between his teeth.

Bree's cry rose into the night. He looked up, saw the expression on her face, the joy, the hunger, and he groaned and knew it was going to be difficult to keep himself under control. He wanted to tear off that thong, bury himself inside her...

No. Not yet. Not until he'd explored her.

He reached behind her, undid the bra, let it tumble to her feet. Her breasts were perfect, and waiting for the touch of his hands. His mouth. He cupped them, watched her face as he rolled the nipples between his fingers, savored the swift, telltale hiss of her breath and the way she sobbed his name.

Gianni ran his hand down her back, cupped her backside. His fingers drifted across her hip, beneath the thong. He could feel her heat. Her wetness.

He bent and eased the thong down her legs, steadied her with one hand while she stepped out of the wisp of silk. He lifted her foot to his mouth, kissed the arch. Then he stood up and cupped her shoulders. She made a woman's automatic gesture of modesty and he shook his head, took her hands again and kissed the palms.

"I want to see you, *cara,*" he said hoarsely.

He took a step back and swept his eyes over her. She was exquisite. Perfect. Her face. Her breasts. The slender waist and curved hips, the long, elegant legs...

And she belonged to him.

To him, only to him. And, heaven help him, he had to have her now or lose what little remained of his sanity.

Gianni stripped off his clothes, took his bride in his arms and drew her down to the bed. At the first touch of his skin against hers, she arched against him and sighed his name. He took her mouth hungrily, nipped her throat, and suddenly he felt her hand on him. Holding him. Caressing him, her palm like velvet, her fingertips like silk along his swollen length.

"Bree," he said, "*cara*, be careful…"

"I don't want to be careful," she whispered.

The words inflamed him almost as much as her touch. He paused just long enough to reach back and dig into his trouser pocket for a small packet, tear it open with his teeth and slide the condom on.

Then he parted her thighs.

"Now," she said, "Gianni, please, please, please…"

Her words ended on a sob as he entered her. She was hot. Wet. Tight. So tight.

"Bree," he said, and caught her hands. "Briana."

She moved beneath him. Whispered his name. She moaned as he slid back, almost withdrawing from her, then thrust forward again.

He bent to her, inhaled the scent of vanilla and woman, kissed her mouth, her throat, her closed eyelids.

"Yes," she said, "Gianni, yes," and he groaned and thrust again, harder and harder while she wrapped her legs around him, and when she cried out and shuddered, Gianni threw his head back and let it happen, let the years of searching, of needing, of wanting something he'd never known fall away from him in a heart-stopping, explosive rush.

THEY FELL ASLEEP in each other's arms.

An hour later, an eternity later, they awoke and made love again. Before dawn, they stirred one last time. Gianni kissed his way down Bree's body, gently parted her thighs and tasted her sweetness with his tongue. She buried her hands in his hair, sobbed his name and when he sensed she was on the brink of that precipice that leads to the stars, he rose up, took her mouth with his, sank into her and they came together in a blur of heat and sighs.

Sometime during what little remained of the night, Gianni turned off the lamp and drew the blankets over them.

They slept on, entwined, until a knock at the door awakened them. "Who could that be?" Bree whispered.

"I'll take care of it." Gianni gave her a sweet, slow kiss. "First, though, good morning, *cara.*"

Whoever was at the door knocked again.

Bree smiled against his lips. "Don't answer," she said softly. "Whoever it is will go away."

Gianni grinned. "They'd better not. That's our breakfast and I can tell you right now, *signora,* I have one huge appetite."

She laughed softly. "You convinced me, *signore.* Get the door."

"Only if you promise not to move."

"I promise," she said, with such promptness that he knew she was lying. Smiling, he kissed the tip of her nose.

"You move from this bed, you'll have to pay the penalty."

"Mmm," she said, so sexily that Gianni almost decided answering the door wasn't worth it. But her stomach chose that moment to give an unladylike growl and he chuckled, pulled on his trousers and went to admit the waiter.

Bree sprang from the bed, pulled on the robe and dashed into the bathroom. She used the toilet, brushed her teeth, ran her hands through her tangled hair and took a look in the mirror.

It was supposed to be a quick look, but how could it be when the woman smiling back at her was a stranger? Her eyes shone. Her skin glowed. Her mouth was pink and gently swollen but most of all, most of all, that woman in the mirror looked happy.

She looked ecstatic. She looked, she felt, like a woman who was in—who was in—

"Aha," Gianni said, wrapping his arms around her. "Thought you'd get away from me, did you?"

She turned in his embrace. Even the sound of his voice made her feel happy. An emotion far stronger, far more dangerous than desire quickened her heartbeat.

"Bree? What is it?"

She shook her head. For a minute, speech was impossible.

His smile faded. "Tell me what's wrong." He stroked the curls back from her temple. "Are you sorry about last night?"

"No. Oh, no. It was—it was wonderful."

Gianni's eyes darkened. "Yes," he said softly, parting the robe, cupping her breasts and teasing the tips with light brushes of his fingers, "yes, it was." Bree whispered his name, her voice breaking as she did, and he lifted her onto the edge of the vanity and stepped between her thighs. "*You* were wonderful," he said, and kissed her.

"Gianni?" Bree took a breath. "I want you to know I've never... What happened last night was..."

"For me, too," he said gruffly.

"I loved last night. Everything we did. I love—I love—"

She fell silent, stunned at what she'd almost said.

Gianni ran his hand down her belly. "What do you love, *cara?* Tell me."

Bree looked into his eyes. They were so green. So deep. If she weren't careful, she could fall into their depths and lose herself forever.

"Making love," she said quickly, "with you."

He nodded. She loved making love with him. That was good. It was what he'd wanted to hear. It was all he wanted to hear...

Wasn't it?

Wasn't it? he thought again, and because he suddenly felt as if he were balanced on a tightrope over the Grand Canyon, he blanked his mind by taking his wife in his arms and losing himself deep inside her.

CHAPTER TWELVE

THE HOUSE Gianni had rented was perfect.

It sat on a cliff overlooking the sea, bathed in sunlight and surrounded by flowers. An infinity pool in the lush gardens behind it seemed to meet the horizon and drop off the edge of the earth.

Gianni watched Briana as they walked through the bright, airy rooms. He'd made the rental arrangements sight unseen. The realtor had assured him the house was handsome and that had seemed enough.

Now, he wanted it to be beautiful for his wife's sake.

"What do you think?" he finally said, doing his best to sound casual.

Bree smiled at him. "It's beautiful."

He hadn't realized he'd been holding his breath until she said exactly what he'd been hoping to hear.

"Good." He gave a little laugh. "Terrific," he said, and slipped his arms around her.

"What about you? Do you like it, too?"

"If you're happy, I'm happy, *cara*," he said softly and as he kissed her, he knew he'd never said anything more true.

HAPPY?

After three more weeks, Bree knew there had to be a better word to describe what she felt. She was filled with joy. With ecstasy. She'd stepped into a new world. Who'd have dreamed it was what she'd wanted, what she'd searched for, all her life?

Sitting in the garden behind the house, watching Gianni play with the baby, her heart felt full to overflowing. She had a child she loved and a man she adored...

And a marriage that was a lie.

What had become of her uncomplicated life?

Marriage, love, babies...all those things had been for other women, not her. At least, this kind of love hadn't been for her. She'd told Fallon the truth all those weeks ago. The man for her would be easygoing. Uncomplicated.

Safe.

No ups, no downs. Their relationship would be predictable, a ship sailing a steady course on a smooth sea.

Then Gianni stormed into her life. There was nothing safe about him.

He was demanding. He had a temper. He made decisions without consulting her and when they made love, he wouldn't let her stay on the shore, where it was safe. He carried her out on the waves with him, took her up and up and up...

Briana's chest tightened.

She loved him so much that sometimes, after they made love, she wept. Who'd have dreamed you could love a man so fiercely that being with him could make you weep?

She never let him know any of that, of course. He was a good, caring man and he wanted her in his bed. He'd been honest about that from the beginning, even while she'd lied to him, to herself, about wanting him.

There'd been times since then when she'd thought—when she'd hoped—what he felt for her was more than desire. The way he talked to her. The looks he gave her. The easy touch of his hand over her hair as he walked by.

Surely all those things meant something.

Bree smiled as she watched him pretend to eat the baby's tiny toes.

The other night, at dinner, she'd looked up and found him watching her with something in his eyes that made her heart stop. *Ask him,* she'd thought. *Ask him what he feels for you.*

She hadn't. How could she? She'd always thought of herself as a courageous woman but it would take more than guts to ask such a question. What if you got the wrong answer?

She couldn't risk it. She'd lost her heart, but not her mind.

Still, she'd come awfully close last night. After they'd made love, while he was kissing her, he'd tasted her tears.

"Cara?" he'd said, "what is it? Why are you crying?"

I'm crying because I love you and I don't want to lose you, she'd almost said. The admission had been a whisper away but just then Lucia began to cry. It was time for her bottle and it was Gemma's day off.

Bree had leaped from the bed like a woman with a reprieve in sight. Gianni had caught hold of her hand.

"You stay here," he'd said. "I'll take care of the baby."

"No," she'd said brightly, "that's okay. I'm already up."

She'd heated a bottle of formula, gone to the nursery, taken the baby in her arms and sat in a rocker, feeding her, crooning to her, wishing she'd been brave enough to tell Gianni the truth and glad she hadn't.

They had an arrangement, and he had not suggested changing it. One more week and they'd return to New York. She and Gianni would go through with a civilized divorce. She'd go back to being Briana O'Connell. He'd go back to being a bachelor. They'd live next door to each other, raise Lucia together, and she'd pretend she didn't care what happened on the other side of the wall that separated them any more than he did.

"Hey."

Bree looked up as Gianni sat down in the grass beside her, the baby in the curve of his arm. It was a hot day and he was wearing his swim trunks and nothing else. Lucia, wearing a diaper decorated with teddy bears, grinned tooth-lessly at the man she obviously adored.

You and me, kid, Bree thought, and her throat tightened.

"You okay?" Gianni said softly.

"Fine. Just enjoying the sun."

"Mmm." He leaned over and kissed her shoulder. "You taste delicious."

"Suntan lotion," she said, smiling. "How's Lucia doing? Does she need a diaper change?"

"I already did it."

His tone was smug. She could hardly blame him. Chang-ing a diaper—a full diaper—had been a challenge. The first time she'd presented him with the job he'd stepped back in horror.

"Me?" he'd said.

"You," she'd replied. "We share everything, remem-ber?"

"Yeah. Sure. But—" He'd wrinkled his elegant Roman nose. "*Cara.* The baby—the baby—"

"Smells," Bree had said blithely. "That's why her diaper needs changing."

To his credit, he'd done it. Oh, he'd gone a little pale but so had she the first couple of times. Truth was, she knew almost as little about babies as he did. Aunts gave bottles, changed wet diapers, not stinky ones and, in general, stood on the sidelines and made cheerful noises.

Being a mother was different.

No. She was a guardian. Not Lucia's mother. Not Gianni's wife. Not the woman he—

"There's that look again. Such deep thoughts, Briana."

Bree gathered her scattered thoughts. His smile was in-imate; she felt her toes curl. Was there a more beautiful sight in the world than a gorgeous man holding a gorgeous baby?

"Not deep at all," she said lightly. "I was just wondering what we should have for lunch."

Gianni's smile tilted. His eyes got the dark, dangerous glint that made her breasts tingle.

"I know exactly what we should have," he said softly. "Come inside with me, *cara*."

"The baby…"

"It's her nap time." He got to his feet and held out his hand. "Come with me."

Briana let him lead her into the coolness of the house. He'd developed a way of giving orders that made them sound like wishes instead of commands, though she'd have followed his husky invitation to bed any time.

She drew the blinds in their bedroom while he took Lucia to the nursery, but she didn't undress. He liked to take off her clothes and she loved to have him do it. He came to her and took her in his arms. In the hushed afternoon darkness, he took her with him to a world she'd never imagined existed.

He might not love her, but he cared for her. No man could be this tender with a woman without caring.

I love you, she thought as he held her against him, *Gianni, I love you so much…*

Briana closed her eyes and tumbled into sleep.

SHE WAS ASLEEP.

Gianni touched his lips to Briana's hair. How he loved the smell of her. The taste. The feel of her in his arms.

The simple truth was, he loved her. If he didn't tell her soon, he was going to go crazy. He just had to find the right moment.

Be honest, Firelli.

There'd been a few right moments but he was a coward

What if she looked at him after he'd opened his soul and said she didn't feel the same way?

Being so cautious was a new experience. All his life, he'd gone after what he wanted without hesitation. A scholarship to a university, when the other kids he knew—except for Tomasso and Stefano—were satisfied with high school diplomas. A degree in law, when most people in the old neighborhood thought their law was the only kind that mattered. A partnership in a firm where everybody's name but his was followed by Roman numerals, and then the move to the Federal Prosecutor's office when his law partners said he was insane to give up what he had.

Until now, he'd set his eye on the prize and gone after it.

This was different.

His ego had been on the line those other times. Now, it was something much more vulnerable.

His heart.

These had been the best three weeks of his life. Soon, they'd fly back to New York. He didn't want to; he'd thought about staying here longer but there was an important case waiting for him and he was obligated to try it.

He'd always been good about meeting obligations. He'd lost his father when he was nine; his mother, accustomed to an old-world role in her marriage, had been lost. Before long, he'd been making grown-up decisions. How to stretch the pitifully small social security payments to meet their bills. Who to pay first each month, the grocer, the butcher or the landlord?

At the beginning, he'd resented being the one in charge. After a while, it became second nature. He'd never realized that taking charge could also mean taking over...

Until Briana came along.

She sighed in her sleep and flung her arm across his chest. He drew her closer.

He'd denied her accusations at first but, deep down, he knew she was right. He didn't ask anyone's opinion, ever, he just made a decision and went with it.

That was okay when you were trying to fill your *papa's* shoes. Being hesitant, especially in the old neighborhood, would have been a sign of weakness. It was okay when you were a hotshot lawyer dealing with difficult clients, better than okay when you were taking down the sleaze of the earth in a federal courtroom.

But it made for problems when you fell in love with a tough-minded, independent woman.

That worried him, too. Not about spending his life with a woman who stood up to him. Hell, no. One thing he'd learned these three weeks was that a woman like that was just what he needed.

What troubled him was what Briana might think about him. What if she thought he was still too overbearing? What if he said, *Cara, I adore you and I won't divorce you,* and she said...

Whoa. He'd have to be careful. Forget, *I won't divorce you.* The way to say it was, *I don't want to divorce you.* Otherwise, they'd be right back where they'd started, glaring at each other, him telling her he didn't have to consult her on everything, her telling him he damned well had to.

He didn't want to risk losing her over words carelessly spoken.

Briana stirred in his arms. Her eyes opened and she smiled at him. "Did I fall asleep?"

Gianni nodded. "Yes. Right here, in my arms where you belong."

She got a strange look on her face. "Is that what you think? That I belong in your arms?"

Damn it, he'd done it again. Said something because he loved her that she'd probably heard as proof of his arrogance.

"*Cara.* I only meant—"

"I know what you meant."

He thought he'd ruined things with a misspoken phrase but she slipped on top of him, brought her open mouth to his, and they lost themselves in each other's arms.

THE DAYS SPED BY until there was only one night left.

Gemma had gone; they were alone in the house. Gianni, Briana, the baby—and a growing tension.

The atmosphere had taken a dark turn. Bree was edgy. So was Gianni. He knew the reason for his mood. He still hadn't found the right time, the right way to tell her he loved her.

As for Bree...he couldn't come up with a reason to explain her edginess. Last night, after dinner, he'd looked up and found her staring at him with something he couldn't read in her face.

"What's the matter, *cara?*" he'd said.

The muscles in her throat had constricted, as if she were swallowing hard.

"Nothing," she'd finally answered.

He'd known damned well she was lying but before he could pursue the topic, the baby started to wail.

Lucia, normally the most sunny of babies, had become fretful. They took her to a doctor who diagnosed an ear infection and assured them it was nothing to worry about. An antibiotic helped but she still woke up crying. They took turns walking the floor with her; when they weren't doing that, they were worrying. All in all, it made for little opportunity to have what Gianni had begun thinking of as A Serious Discussion.

This last night, he was a wreck. The baby, thank God, was fully recovered. He decided it was now or never. He had to tell his wife that he loved her and wanted her to stay married to him.

Gianni figured they'd go out for dinner. Maybe there'd be fewer distractions. They'd have to take the baby but he knew of a café in town with outdoor tables. There, over coffee, he could look into Briana's eyes and put the rest of his life in her hands.

But Bree didn't want to go out. She wanted to eat in. "I'll cook," she said. "After all, this is our last meal."

It was a portentous phrase. They looked at each other, both of them trying to smile.

"In this house, you mean," he said.

"Or anywhere, considering my talent in the kitchen."

He knew she was trying to diffuse the tension but why say something like that? Was she glad the month was at an end? Was she looking forward to going home, picking up the strands of her life, ending their marriage?

There was no point in negative thoughts. And perhaps staying home was a good idea. This way, they'd be alone. He'd wait until the baby was asleep. Then he'd take his wife in his arms or maybe go down on one knee, and tell her what was in his heart.

Sure, they were already married but this would be a real proposal. A declaration of love that would last forever…and he'd go crazy, if he had to wait until later.

Why not do it now?

"Briana," he said. "We have to talk."

He must have sounded urgent because she swung toward him, a strange expression on her face.

"About what?" she said, in such a choked voice he was suddenly afraid she knew what he was going to say and didn't want to hear it.

"*Cara.*" He held out his hand. "Come sit down. I want to tell—"

His cell phone rang. He almost groaned but he answered it, listened, then rolled his eyes. *La signora* was the last person he wanted to talk to right now.

She'd become an almost constant visitor this past week. She said she wanted to see the baby but she hardly looked at Lucia. Instead, each time she stopped by, her black eyes followed Briana's and Gianni's every move.

"*Signora.* Let me call you back…"

The *signora* interrupted him. Gianni sighed, listened…and smiled.

"What?" Bree mouthed, but he shook his head.

"Of course," he said. "Good. Very good. I appreciate it. I know, yes. You're trying to make things simpler. Thank you, *signora.* I'll be in touch. Right. Goodbye."

"What's she done that made life simpler?" Bree asked.

Gianni wanted to tell her but he had something else to tell her first.

"Later, *cara.*"

"Now, Gianni. She said something that made you look like the cat that ate the canary."

"She did, but I want it to be a surprise." A surprise worthy of champagne and caviar. "Bree? Are you sure you don't want to go out for dinner?"

Didn't he want to spend their last evening alone in the house that almost felt like home?

"If you want to go out," she said stiffly, "we can."

"No. Staying home is fine. Staying in, that is. I mean, this isn't really our home. Our house. I mean—"

"I know what you mean," she said, and turned away from him.

He looked at her rigid back. He wanted to go to her and take her in his arms, tell her he was nervous as hell because he was going to ask her to stay married to him, that the *signora* had given him news that would be icing on the cake, but it was better to wait. Just a little longer. The baby would be asleep, they'd be alone…

Gianni cleared his throat and lifted Lucia from her baby

seat. "I'll put the baby to bed. You pour us some wine, okay?"

"Okay."

Bree waited until he'd left the kitchen. Then she sank down at the counter because she really wasn't sure her legs would hold her anymore.

She was a wreck. It was now or never time.

Somewhere between waking in Gianni's arms this morning and bathing Lucia this evening, she'd made a huge decision. She'd decided to tell him how she felt.

Well, not all of it. She'd say she was willing to stay married a little longer, if he wanted. If he said yes, that was exactly what he wanted, if his smile was loving, if he kissed her as tenderly as he had when he'd woken her in *Signora* Massini's blue bedroom, maybe she'd screw up the rest of her courage and admit she'd fallen in love with him.

But something had just happened. That call from the *signora*... What was that all about? A surprise, Gianni said, but only children believed that all surprises were good.

Should she change her plans?

No. No, she wouldn't. She was a gambler's daughter and for the first time in her life, she felt like gambling. Nothing ventured, nothing gained. Wasn't that what people said?

Briana took a deep breath and began taking things out of the refrigerator. A perfect dinner, an excellent wine and then—

And then, she'd do it.

NOTHING VENTURED, nothing gained...and nothing according to plan.

She set the table on the terrace. Halfway through their proscuitto and melon, a black cloud appeared from out of nowhere, stalled directly above them and drenched the terrace in rain.

Bree shrieked. Gianni laughed. They grabbed the wine,

the plates, the silverware and ran inside. At least the sudden downpour broke the silence that had settled over them.

"Are you soaked, *cara?* Do you want to change?"

Change? And delay things even more? "I'm fine."

"Good. I'll set the dining room table."

Bree brought in the chicken and mushrooms she'd made a hundred times before. Her "company for dinner" dish had never failed but it had, tonight. The chicken was rubbery, the mushrooms were soggy, and the winey sauce she'd spooned over the pasta tasted like burned vinegar.

"It's delicious," Gianni said bravely.

"It's awful," Bree said, and put down her fork. Nothing was going right. Talk about portents... "Gianni," she said, and at that same moment he said, "Briana."

Their eyes met. He put his fork on his plate and balled his hands into fists on the white linen table cloth, that muscle ticking in his jaw.

Bree's heart fell. He looked like a man about to have a root canal.

"You first," she said.

"No. You go ahead."

"I'd rather wait for you."

He nodded. He cleared his throat. He pushed back his chair, started to get to his feet, changed his mind and sat back again, hands still knotted, that little muscle ticking away like a metronome.

"Damn," he muttered. "Briana."

"Yes?"

"I have—I have something I've wanted to tell you for days."

Tic, tic, tic. "Go on."

"Let me tell you about *Signora* Massini's call first." That was the simpler part of what he wanted to tell her. Go for the easy stuff first. "It seems she's been thinking about Lucia's future. She's offered to sign papers that will eliminate the possibility of her making any future attempts to claim Lucia."

It was wonderful news, but not what Bree had been hoping to hear.

"She also pointed out that our thirty days are up." He gave a strained smile. "I assured her we were aware of that."

Another little slide of the heart. Bree nodded. She didn't trust her voice.

"Her offer simplifies things considerably." He paused. "It means Lucia can really be ours."

"I don't understand. She *is* ours."

"Well, yes." He hesitated. "But there could have been difficulties because of our divorce."

There was no place left for Bree's heart to slide, now that it was at her feet.

"Our divorce," she repeated.

"Exactly." Gianni leaned toward her and took her hand. "I wasn't sure how a court would rule if we had to petition for Lucia's custody after we dissolved our marriage."

"Dissolved our marriage," she said, like a well-trained parrot.

Gianni swallowed hard. This wasn't going well. Talking to a jury was turning out to be easier than baring your heart to the woman you loved. And why was she looking at him like that? He couldn't tell if she was angry or sad or happy and God, he wanted her to be happy.

"All I could come up with was that we'd have to stay married a little longer, and that wasn't what we'd agreed to do."

"No," Bree said calmly, "it wasn't."

"Now the question is moot. The *signora's* not going to stand in our way." Gianni took a breath. Ready or not, it was truth time. "No legal battles ahead, *cara*. No need for me to ask you to prolong our arrangement. We can go home and simply be together.''

"Sleep together, you mean."

Gianni looked blank. "Well, of course. But—"

"No."

"Excuse me?"

She pulled her hand from his. "I said, we're not going to go home to this—this happy little fiction you've created."

"Briana, listen to me—"

"I did listen." Bree shoved back her chair and rose to her feet. "You're right. The good news is that we won't have to prolong our arrangement."

"No. We won't, *cara,* because—"

"Do not call me that again!"

Gianni shot to his feet. What in hell was happening? He'd told his wife that Lucia could be theirs, that they could adopt her and be her real parents. Now, he'd told her he didn't want a divorce. And she was looking at him as if she wanted to kill him.

"What's wrong with you?" He could feel his temper rising and he fought to keep it under control. "Don't you want Lucia? Don't you want to be with me?"

"I want Lucia. I do *not* want to 'be' with you."

His eyes narrowed. "But I thought—all these weeks, the times we made love—"

"I know what you thought. Our arrangement would end. Sleeping together wouldn't."

"Will you forget the damned arrangement?"

"Stop shouting."

"I am not shouting," he yelled, and slammed his fist on the table. "I'm talking sense, which is more than you're doing."

"I am talking sense, *signore.* You just don't like what I'm saying."

"What the hell are you so angry about?"

"The fact that you can ask me that means there's no point trying to explain it to you."

Gianni laughed wildly, stabbed his hands into his hair and looked up.

"She's crazy," he told the ceiling. "Absolutely insane!"

"You mean, I *was* crazy. I'm perfectly sane now."

"Damn it to hell," he roared.

Lucia began to wail.

"Now see what you've done," Bree said. "You woke the baby."

"Bree." Gianni took a deep breath. She didn't want to stay married to him. She didn't love him. No. He couldn't, he wouldn't believe it. "Briana," he said carefully, "we have to talk."

"We just did. It's over."

"Damn it to hell, Bree..."

"You already said that."

"Briana," he said, his voice rough with warning, "I forbid you to do this!"

Bree laughed. Laughed, damn it!

"You never did get it, Firelli," she said. "I don't take orders."

She strode past him and while he was still trying to decide what in hell had just happened, he heard the nursery door slam shut and the lock click home.

CHAPTER THIRTEEN

GIANNI DIDN'T even come after her.

Bree heard the front door slam, then the roar of the Ferrari as he tore down the driveway.

Good. Fine. If she moved quickly enough, she'd never have to see him again until after the divorce, and then only when it involved Lucia.

The baby was still sobbing. Bree lifted her from the crib and cradled her against her breast.

"Don't cry, sweetheart," she crooned. "Everything's going to be fine."

The baby's sobs became whimpers. Bree kissed her forehead, held her a little longer, then lay her gently in the crib.

"You and I are going on a trip," she whispered. "Won't that be fun?"

Lucia gave a last, ragged sob before her lashes drooped to her plump cheeks. Bree bent over the crib and kissed her. Then she made her way to the master suite.

The suite she'd shared with Gianni.

The rumpled bed where Gianni had carried her, lazy as a cat from an afternoon spent in the sun, seemed to take up half a wall.

"You need a nap, *cara,*" he'd said, but what he'd done to her on the silky sheets had nothing to do with napping. He'd kissed her, touched her, brought her to climax after climax…

The calculating, self-serving, autocratic son of a bitch!

She'd *never* loved him. Not for a moment. It had been

lust. Her brothers called it Zipper-Think Syndrome and believed it was their own private joke.

Bree pulled open the closet door.

Wrong. She'd known about their guys-are-all-the-same comedy routine for years. The only surprise was finding out the hard way that being led around by your hormones wasn't something that only happened to men.

She swung her suitcase onto the bed, yanked open a dresser drawer so hard it almost fell to the floor.

Fallon had accused her of never having experienced real passion. Well, she thought grimly, she had now—and to hell with it. And as if that weren't bad enough, she'd turned out to be such a damned goody-goody that she'd had to kid herself into thinking what she'd felt for Gianni was love.

How could she have been so stupid?

Love was a lie perpetuated on women by men determined to turn them into androids.

Bree tossed her clothes into the suitcase. Not everything. She'd brought only enough for a weekend and when Gianni the Emperor decided they'd have to stay longer, he'd taken the baby and her on a whirlwind shopping trip. She'd bought half a dozen things for herself but the next day, the store had delivered boxes filled with virtually everything she'd tried on or even looked at.

"I didn't buy these things," she'd said.

The emperor had smiled. "I did, *cara.* It was my pleasure."

Damned right, his pleasure. This entire month had been about him and his pleasure. For all she knew, he'd hatched this thirty day scheme for his pleasure.

"You can take these things and stuff them," Bree told the room as she marched back and forth between the closet, the dresser and her suitcase. "I don't want them any more than I want you."

A shrink would probably tell her that her reactions were

understandable. She'd lived a lifetime in a month. Karen's death, the news about the baby, Gianni shouldering his way into her world and dragging her off to a place time had forgotten, all of it capped by a phony marriage...

At least one good thing had come out of it.

Lucia.

Bree sank down on the edge of the bed. All those years, drifting from job to job and place to place, searching for something without knowing what she'd been searching for and now here it was, sweetly wrapped in pink.

Who'd have believed she'd find so much joy in being Mom to this little girl? She wasn't; not really. She knew that, but for a while it had seemed as if she was.

They'd been a family. She, the baby, Gianni.

Tears stung her eyes, though she couldn't imagine why. She'd always known her arrangement with Gianni wasn't going to be permanent, and if she'd clung to the desperate hope he'd want to change that, whose fault was it but her own?

What she felt for Lucia was the only kind of love that had meaning.

Bree drew a shuddering breath. What now? A minute ago, she'd been filled with energy. Now, she wanted only to curl into a ball and sleep. No. She wouldn't do that. The thought of sleeping under the same roof as Gianni tonight made her shudder. Getting on the plane with him tomorrow, following docilely as he took her to the apartment he'd decided she and Lucia would share, would be even worse.

She wasn't his property. He couldn't tell her what to do...

And she didn't have to live next door and watch him go on with his life as if this month had never happened.

What she'd told him was true. They didn't have to live side by side. They didn't even have to live in the same state. Divorced couples—those who'd really been married— shared custody of children with one parent on one coast, one on the other. Why should sharing guardianship be any different?

Why hadn't she thought of that right away?

Bree hissed a word that hadn't passed her lips since the days her brothers used to waylay their sisters and dump them, fully dressed, into the pool at the Desert Song.

It was time to reclaim her life.

Okay. She needed a plan, and fast. Getting out of here before Gianni returned was number one. She knew she'd never be able to control her temper, and she didn't want to give him anything, not even a show of fury.

He wasn't worth it.

Leaving was easy enough. Pack some stuff for the baby— she damned well wasn't leaving Lucia behind—call a taxi, tell the cabbie to take her...

Where?

The easy choice was her sister's home on the other side of this same island. She'd made a point of not getting in touch with Fallon. How could she have explained a marriage that wasn't a marriage? She could do it now, she supposed...

No. That wouldn't work. The last place to escape Gianni was in the home of his best friend.

Bree chewed on her lip.

She could go back to New York, hole up in her apartment...and find Gianni on her doorstep, demanding compliance with the plan he'd laid out for her life.

Boston, then. To Cullen. Forget that. Cullen and his wife had a brand new baby. So did Keir and Cassie. Sean was still on his honeymoon, and Megan was off on a diplomatic trip with her husband.

Too bad. Meg, of all of them, would have understood. She'd also married for expediency. But it wasn't the same at all. It turned out that Meg and Qasim had loved each other from the beginning. It had just taken them a while to acknowledge it.

Gianni had never loved her. Never. And she—she—

Bree swallowed hard. She had never loved him, either.

She needed a safe harbor. A place where nobody would hand her over to Gianni before she was ready to deal with him. Once they were divorced, she'd meet with him and work out details as they concerned Lucia.

There was only one place to go. Las Vegas. Vegas was the capital of quick marriages and almost-as-quick divorces. It was also her home, at least, it had been for most of her life.

There was only one drawback. Its name was Mary Elizabeth O'Connell-Coyle. Facing her mother, explaining the situation, wouldn't be fun, but one look at Lucia and Mary Elizabeth would melt.

And keeping Gianni away would be easy. All she'd have to do was tell her stepfather she didn't want Gianni to come near her and that would be that.

Just let *Signore* Firelli try and blow past the Desert Song's security team.

Decision made, Bree moved quickly. Her suitcase was packed. Now, she filled a diaper bag with stuff for the baby, phoned the airport and called for a taxi. The only thing left to do was write a note for Gianni. For all she knew, he'd be just as happy to come back and find her gone but he'd surely worry about Lucia.

Bree grabbed a pen and a piece of paper.

Lucia is with me, she scrawled. *I'll contact you as soon as I've finalized my plans.*

She read the note aloud. Good. It was direct and definite, the way she should have been from the start. She propped the note on a table in the hall, just as a car pulled up in the driveway. Her heart leaped. Was it Gianni? Had he come back to tell her—to tell her—

A horn beeped. Bree let out a breath she didn't know she'd been holding. It was the cab; no Ferrari would ever make such a pathetic sound.

She opened the door. *"Uno momento,"* she yelled.

Then she scooped up the baby and everything else, and closed the door on what surely had been four weeks of madness.

BREE PHONED her mother from the airport.

"Hi," she said brightly. "You guys in the mood for a visit?"

"Oh, sweetheart, that would be lovely. When?"

Bree hesitated. "How about right now?"

"You mean, you're here? In Las Vegas?"

"Yes. Is that okay? If you and Dan are busy…"

"Briana, what a thing to say. We'd love to see you. This is a wonderful surprise."

"Actually—actually, I have another surprise, Ma." Bree hesitated. She wanted to be careful with this. Her mother had recovered from a stroke only a few months ago. A surprise, even one that was smiling and making tiny bubbles through a rosebud mouth, might need delicate handling. "I, ah, I have someone with me."

As soon as she'd spoken, she knew she'd phrased it badly. She could almost see Mary happily leaping to the wrong conclusion.

"I'm delighted to hear it! What's his name?"

Here we go, Bree thought, and took a steadying breath. "It's not a 'he,' Mother, it's a baby."

There was an almost endless pause. "Excuse me?"

Bree closed her eyes. She was exhausted—she'd had to change planes twice—and hungry and depressed, though she couldn't figure out why. She'd survived the Month From Hell. What was there to be depressed about?

"A baby," she said wearily. "Ma? It's probably easier if I explain everything when I see you."

"Just tell me one thing, Bree. Is this child yours?"

"Yes. No." Bree sighed. "She's mine, legally. Did I give birth to her? No."

"Ah. In that case," Mary said, sounding a little disappointed, "I suppose there really isn't a man in your life."

"Not anymore," Bree said, and hung up the phone.

THEY WERE WAITING for her at the hotel entrance. Her mother, looking healthy and beautiful; her stepfather, his face creased in a puzzled but welcoming smile. Mary hugged Bree, looked at Lucia, and sighed with delight.

"Oh my, aren't you precious? What's your name, sweetie?"

"Her name is Lucia. Do you remember my friend, Karen? She came here with me for spring break our second year in college?"

"Yes, of course."

"Karen and her husband were in a terrible accident. They—they didn't survive it. It turned out they'd named me Lucia's guardian."

Amazing, how easily the story could be told, if she just left out the part about Gianni. That could come later.

Mary's smile softened. "How sad," she said gently. Her eyes met Briana's. "Karen made a good choice, naming you to care for her daughter."

Bree blinked. She'd always assumed her mother saw her as a gypsy. "Do you think so?"

"Of course, darling. You have the biggest heart in the world." Smiling again, Mary held out her arms. "Hello, Lucy. You come right here, to Grandma."

"But she's not—"

She's not actually my daughter, Bree started to say, but

the truth was, Lucia—Lucy, as Mary had already dubbed her—was her child, in her heart.

Gianni treated her as if she were his child, too. If only she and Gianni…if only their marriage…

"Bree?" Mary's smile faded. She handed the baby to Dan and moved toward Briana. "Darling girl, what's the matter?"

Bree shook her head. She'd never been much for unloading her troubles on Mary. Her mother had always been busy juggling enough problems of her own.

"Sweetheart," Mary said softly, "please, what is it? You look as if your heart is breaking."

A cry burst from Briana's throat. "It is," she sobbed, and flew into her mother's arms.

BREE SAT on a high-backed stool at the kitchen counter, hands wrapped around a mug of tea.

Mary had been wonderful. No questions, no lectures. She'd simply herded them all up to the penthouse, tucked Lucia into a crib magically produced by Housekeeping, sent Dan off on an errand, then put the tea to brew.

"Herbal," she said, "to relax you."

Now she was bustling about the kitchen. Mary had a housekeeper and cook; she'd had people to "do" for her for years but that never kept her from doing lots of things herself.

"But why, Ma?" Bree remembered asking once, when her mother was hurrying to get dinner on the table.

"Because it makes me happy," Mary had replied.

Because it's what Pa expects, Bree had thought. Watching her mother now, she wondered if she'd been wrong. Ruarch was long gone, but her mother still loved to fuss. She'd made the tea and cinnamon toast because she knew it had been one of Briana's childhood favorites. Now she was peeling potatoes, then carrots, pausing to check on whatever it was in the oven that smelled so heavenly.

"Roast beef," Mary said, and Bree realized she'd asked about it out loud. "It's Dan's favorite."

Bree took a sip of tea. "Pa's was meatloaf."

Mary smiled. "You remember that, hmm?"

"How could I forget? You made it once a week."

"Well, of course. I made it because your father loved it, the same as I made chocolate chip cookies for you, vanilla pudding for Sean... It's a joy, doing things for people you love."

Bree put down her mug. "Is that the reason you never said anything whenever Pa uprooted you and dragged you off to some new place?"

She hadn't expected to ask the question. Now that she had, though, she was glad it was out. Her mother's hands stilled for a second. Then she smiled and went on working.

"He didn't drag me, Briana. Where did you get that idea?"

"Oh, I could tell. You'd get that look on your face. That 'not again' look."

"Not again?" Mary shook her head. "If that's what you thought, you were wrong. I admit, it wasn't easy, starting over each time." She wiped her hands on a towel, poured herself some tea and smiled across the counter at Briana. "But I understood that your father needed to keep searching for his dream."

"I see."

"No," Mary said gently, "you don't. Go on, Bree. Say what's on your mind."

Bree looked up. The question, so long unasked, came easily to her lips. "What about your dream, Ma? Didn't that count for anything?"

"Your father was my dream, Briana. And before you tell

me what you've longed to tell me for years, that I let him run my life—"

"I never said—"

"You didn't have to, darling. You were as transparent as glass." Mary reached for her daughter's hand. "He was my dream, and I was his."

"I'm not saying he didn't love you."

"You'd better not," Mary said, smiling, but with a steel undertone in her voice. "Your father was a gambler. So was I. I gave up a staid, stultifying life for one that was unpredictable and always exciting. I followed the man I loved." She leaned closer. "Your father would come home and say, 'Mary, darlin', I've heard of a wondrous new opportunity.' And I'd say, 'You tell me about it, Ruarch, while I start packing.' If you think that's a weakness, Briana, to love someone enough to be willing to walk beside him no matter where the path leads, then you've yet to fall in love. Truly, passionately in love."

Fallon had told her the same thing weeks ago. Were her mother and sister right? Had she seen her passion for Gianni as a weakness?

What she'd felt for him had terrified her.

"Bree? Honey, you *have* fallen in love, haven't you? I can see it in your eyes."

Tears suddenly streaked Briana's face. "It's too late," she said in a broken whisper. "Besides, it doesn't matter. He was my dream, but I wasn't his."

"Oh, sweetheart." Mary dug in her pocket and took out a tissue. "Dry your eyes, blow your nose, and tell me everything."

Bree started at the beginning and left nothing out, spared herself nothing, not even how much she loved Gianni. How she longed for him to return that love, to adore her as she adored him, to cherish as real the vows they'd taken at their wedding.

"I want to be with him for the rest of my life, but he doesn't want that." She looked at her mother, her eyes still wet with tears but shining with defiance. "I won't be someone he can discard when he tires of me."

"Are you certain that's how he feels, Briana? Have you talked to him?"

"He told me," Bree said, her voice breaking. "He said we didn't have to worry about legal battles with Lucia's great-grandmother anymore. He said our marriage—our make-believe marriage—wasn't a problem. He wants the divorce we agreed upon the day we married." She swallowed dryly. "And I'm going to give it to him. Then I'll move a million miles away, far enough so I never have to see him again except where it concerns Lucia, and—"

"And exactly how do you propose to do all that," a furious male voice demanded, "when I will not permit it?"

Briana's eyes widened. Her mother looked past her, the expression on her face changing from concern to curiosity.

"Answer me, Briana. How will you divorce me without my permission?"

Bree stood up, took a long breath and turned around. Gianni stood in the breakfast room, arms folded, legs apart, his face drawn into a scowl. He was a study in rage.

Her heart—her foolish, foolish heart—rose. Then she remembered that he was a man who wanted to control a woman. Who wanted her body, not her love. And she knew she would not, must not, let him see how much he had hurt her.

Bree lifted her chin. "What are you doing here, Gianni? I told you I'd contact you."

"Once your plans were final," he said coldly. "Yes. I found that a particularly charming line for a wife to leave in a note to her husband."

"I am your wife only for the moment."

"You are my wife for as long as I say you are." Gianni's

gaze shifted to Mary Elizabeth. "You must be my wife's mother."

"For the last time, Firelli, I am not your—"

"I am," Mary said politely, holding out her hand. "How, um, nice to meet you, Mister Firelli." She shot a look at Bree. "My daughter's told me a great deal about you."

Gianni grinned. "Lies, all of it," he said, taking Mary's hand and bringing it to his lips. "I'm delighted to meet you, Mrs. Coyle, despite the circumstances."

"Mary, please."

"What is this?" Bree said hotly. "My mother's happy to meet you, you're happy to meet her? And how'd you get up here, anyway? Security doesn't let anyone on this floor without permission."

His smile fled, as did his charm. "We can discuss that later. For now, get your things. And the baby. You're coming with me."

"She's not going anywhere she doesn't want to go," Dan said, stepping out from behind Gianni. "Bree. Honey, this man says he's your husband." His eyes narrowed on Gianni. "But I'll throw him out myself, if that's what you want."

"Don't try it," Gianni said softly. "You're Briana's stepfather and I'd like to start on the right footing but this is between my wife and me."

"Stop saying that," Bree snapped. "I am *not* your wife."

"I have a marriage certificate that says you are."

"It's a piece of paper."

"An official piece of paper. Get your things, Briana. I'm tired, I'm hungry, I'm mad as hell and I refuse to waste time discussing something that's already been decided."

Bree stared at him. He *was* tired; there were dark shadows under his eyes and stubble on his determined jaw. She wanted to go to him and kiss the shadows away.

Was she crazy? Who gave a damn if he had shadows under his eyes? He could have craters, for all she cared.

And why was she thinking of him as her husband? He wouldn't be, not in a couple of weeks.

"There's nothing to discuss."

Gianni looked at his watch. "I'll give you five minutes. Then I'm taking Lucia under one arm, you under the other, and leaving."

"Oh, please! That Sicilian routine won't work here."

He took a step toward her, his eyes hot on hers. "Did you really think you could run away from me, *cara?* Did you think I wouldn't come after you?"

"Don't '*cara*' me, either. What's the matter, *signore?* Did I dent your ego? Is it always you who does the leaving?"

"What the hell are you talking about?"

"Give me a break, Firelli. You know damned well what I'm talking about. You're the man. You do the leaving, not me."

Gianni folded his arms. He had to do something with them, otherwise he knew he'd reach for Briana, grab her by the shoulders, shake her until she admitted she loved him and wanted him because, damn it, she *had* to feel the way he felt or he'd go crazy.

"You can't leave me," he said smugly. "You can't divorce me, not without my approval."

"Welcome to the real world, *signore.*" Bree folded her arms, too, in unconscious imitation. "This is the good old U.S. of A., not *la Sicilia.* I can and will divorce you, and you can't stop me."

"But I can, *cara,*" he said softly, a thin smile curving his lips. "Our marriage was performed in Italy."

"So?"

"So," he said, the lie as sweet and simple as sugar on his tongue, "it can only be dissolved there."

Bree jerked back. "What?"

"I said—"

"I heard what you said. I don't believe you. You were the one who said I could go to Mexico or the Caribbean for a divorce, remember?"

He remembered, all right. What a stupid thing to have told her, but he'd said it before he'd been willing to admit he was head over heels in love with this stubborn, impossible, headstrong, magnificent woman.

"I was wrong."

"Ha! The great emperor, wrong?" Bree tossed her head. "Impossible."

"There won't be a divorce, *cara*," he said softly. "You and our baby are coming home with me."

Our baby. The words were so right. If only he meant them.

"No," Bree said, and hated herself for the little tremor in her voice. "I'm not going with you, Gianni. I don't want to live the way you've planned." She felt the sting of tears again. *God,* she thought, *God, please, don't let me cry.* "I know you'll be a good guardian for Lucia. I didn't mean it when I said I'd move a million miles away, but I won't live next door to you. I won't sleep with you—"

"You won't live next door," Gianni said softly, "you'll live with me, and you'll sleep with me, make love with me, because you're my wife, my heart, and I'm not giving you up, Briana. Not ever."

Silence filled the kitchen. Then Mary cleared her throat. "Dan? Now might be the perfect time for me to show you that area in the casino that needs re-decorating."

"Now?" Dan said incredulously. "Right now?"

"Right now," Mary said firmly, slipping past Briana, pausing just long enough to kiss her cheek and whisper something in her ear. "Good luck, Mr. Firelli," she said softly.

"It's Gianni," he said, his eyes never leaving Bree's.

Mary smiled. "Indeed. Relatives should never stand on formality."

"Relatives?" Briana said. "Relatives? Mother, for heaven's sake…"

She was talking to the air. Her mother had taken her stepfather's arm and tugged him from the room. In the distance, a door slammed.

Briana and Gianni were alone.

Gianni came closer. Bree stepped back but there was no place to go; the counter was behind her. Her husband was in front of her. But he wasn't her husband. He didn't want to be her husband.

"You can't divorce me, *cara,*" he said softly.

"Of course I can." Bree meant to sound determined; instead, she sounded heartbroken. She couldn't let him see that she was weak. She couldn't! "That was our arrangement, remember?"

His gaze was like a caress on her lips. "I remember everything," he whispered, framing her face with his hands. "Everything," he said, and brushed his mouth over hers.

"Gianni. Don't."

"Why not? You're mine. If I want to kiss you, I can."

"I am *not* yours. I'm not anyone's. I'm—"

"You're right. You belong to yourself, Briana—and I love you all the more for it."

He drew her to him. She was stiff. Unyielding, but as his arms closed around her, a little sigh whispered from her lips.

"Cara." He put his hand under her chin. "Look at me. Yes. Like that. With your heart, your soul in your eyes." Gianni smiled. "You said you wanted a divorce and I believed you, but I was a fool. A woman who trembles in a man's arms, who gives everything she is to him, is not a woman who wants to leave a man."

"No! I don't know why you'd think—"

He brushed his lips over hers again, his mouth lingering,

warm and sweet against hers. Bree fought against it but it happened anyway, her lips softening, clinging to his, her hands lifting to his chest.

"I love you, Bree. And you love me."

"No! I don't love you, Gianni. I don't know why you'd think—"

He kissed her again and she trembled. "You always talked about complications, but nothing could have been more complicated than what happened the night I finally worked up enough courage to tell you I wanted us to have a real marriage."

"What?"

"I made a mess of it, Bree. It took me hours to realize how badly I'd screwed up." He framed her face with his hands. "I wanted to make it perfect, *cara.* Telling you how much I loved you. Telling you that the *signora* had agreed to let us adopt our little girl—"

Bree's eyes widened. "Oh, Gianni," she whispered. "Did she really say that?"

He nodded. "And you told me that you couldn't wait to leave me."

"No. Oh, no. I never said—"

"You didn't, *cara.* I realized it after I calmed down." Gianni drew her close and kissed her again, a long, tender kiss that threatened to melt her bones. "You misunderstood me, and your pride made you answer the only way you could." Smiling, he ran his thumb over her bottom lip. "You were wonderful. Tough. Brave... But you damned near broke my heart."

Briana looped her arms around her husband's neck.

"I thought loving you was a weakness," she said softly. "But I was wrong. Loving you is my strength, Gianni. It's what I was meant for. It's—"

"Everything *cara.* I know, because it's like that for me, too."

They smiled into each other's eyes, a man and woman who'd spent their lives looking for each other. Then the soft sounds of a baby waking up drifted into the room.

"Lucia?" Gianni said.

"My mother calls her Lucy."

Gianni grinned. "Sounds like a good American name to me."

One more sweet, deep kiss. Then Gianni slipped his arm around his wife and they went to claim their daughter.

DOWNSTAIRS, in his office, Dan Coyle looked at his wife and tried to figure out what was going on.

"I don't follow any of this, Duchess," he said. "Our Bree comes home with a child that isn't hers, tells you she's married to a man she wants to divorce, he turns up and you abandon her?" He shook his head. "It's beyond me to understand, but I suppose you know what you're doing."

Mary Elizabeth O'Connell-Coyle patted her husband's hand.

"What I'm doing, my love, is planning a wedding. I'm sure Briana and Gianni will want a real one, now that everything's settled."

"What's settled?" Dan asked in bewilderment.

"Why, everything," Mary replied gently. "We have each other, and all six of my children are happily wed. What more could a woman ask?"

Dan smiled, leaned in and kissed her.

"What more could anyone ask," he said softly, "than to find love?"

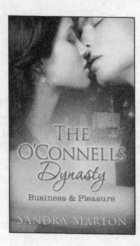
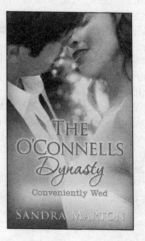

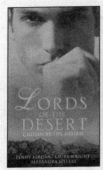 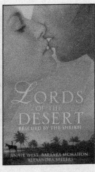 

millsandboon.co.uk Community

Join Us!

The Community is the perfect place to meet and chat to kindred spirits who love books and reading as much as you do, but it's also the place to:

- Get the inside scoop from authors about their latest books
- Learn how to write a romance book with advice from our editors
- Help us to continue publishing the best in women's fiction
- Share your thoughts on the books we publish
- Befriend other users

Forums: Interact with each other as well as authors, editors and a whole host of other users worldwide.

Blogs: Every registered community member has their own blog to tell the world what they're up to and what's on their mind.

Book Challenge: We're aiming to read 5,000 books and have joined forces with The Reading Agency in our inaugural Book Challenge.

Profile Page: Showcase yourself and keep a record of your recent community activity.

Social Networking: We've added buttons at the end of every post to share via digg, Facebook, Google, Yahoo, technorati and de.licio.us.

www.millsandboon.co.uk

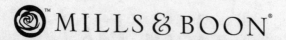